GHOST FORCE

Also available by Patrick Robinson

Fiction
Hunter Killer
Scimitar SL-2
Barracuda 945
Nimitz Class
Kilo Class
H.M.S. Unseen
Seawolf
The Shark Mutiny

Non-fiction
Classic Lines
Decade of Champions
The Golden Post
Born to Win
True Blue
One Hundred Days
Horsetrader

GHOST FORCE

Patrick Robinson

WILLIAM HEINEMANN : LONDON

Published in the United Kingdom by William Heinemann in 2006

1 3 5 7 9 10 8 6 4 2

First published in the United Kingdom in 2005 by William Heinemann

William Heinemann
The Random House Group Limited
20 Vauxhall Bridge Road, London SW1V 2SA

Random House Australia (Pty) Limited
20 Alfred Street, Milsons Point, Sydney,
New South Wales 2061, Australia

Random House New Zealand Limited
18 Poland Road, Glenfield
Auckland 10, New Zealand

Random House (Pty) Limited
Isle of Houghton, Corner of Boundary Road and Carse O'Gowrie,
Houghton 2198, South Africa

The Random House Group Limited Reg. No. 954009

www.randomhouse.co.uk

A CIP catalogue record for this book is available from the British Library

Papers used by Random House are natural, recyclable products
made from wood grown in sustainable forests. The manufacturing processes
conform to the environmental regulations of the country of origin

ISBN 9780434013135 (from Jan 2007)
ISBN 0434013137

Typeset by SX Composing DTP, Rayleigh, Essex
Printed and bound in Great Britain by
Clays Ltd, St Ives Plc

AUTHOR'S NOTE

For this, my ninth 'technothriller', set in the future and sailing perilously close to the wind, I needed to be more careful with my sources than usual.

For reasons which I hope will be obvious to the reader, I would not wish to implicate any senior officers of the armed forces on either side of the Atlantic in the many politically lethal issues explored in these pages.

So I decided to accept no direct advice or instruction from anyone. Rather, I would base the story on the strongly held views voiced to me by so many commissioned officers over several years.

This book involves a new journey to the cold South Atlantic, and the ever-vexed questions surrounding the ownership of the remote Falkland Islands. I have inevitably drawn on the mountain of information that I received from the British Task Force Commander of the 1982 war, Admiral Sir John 'Sandy' Woodward, whose autobiography I helped to write fourteen years ago.

This time, however, I did not go to him with every twist and turn in the road. Nor did I drive him mad for detailed explanations of the mass of high-tech naval data of which he is a world-acknowledged master and commander and where I remain, as ever, the layman.

I ploughed a lonely furrow, distilling many highly controversial opinions into my own story. I hope its covert message will be appreciated by serving and, indeed, retired officers. With perhaps a chilling lesson for the kind of politician that we all despise.

Any mistakes and wayward opinions, whether technical, tactical, or strategic, are mine alone. And nothing should be laid at the door of any senior armed-forces officer, still serving or not, whose acquaintance or friendship I have long valued.

This applies to perhaps a dozen people, but especially to Admiral Woodward who, on this occasion at least, remains shining-white innocent of any involvement with my occasionally acid-dipped pen.

– *Patrick Robinson, 2005.*

CAST OF PRINCIPAL CHARACTERS

United States Senior Command
Paul Bedford (President of the United States)
Admiral Arnold Morgan (Private Adviser to the President)
Admiral George Morris (Director, National Security Agency)
Lt. Commander Jimmy Ramshawe (Personal assistant to Director, NSA)
Admiral John Bergstrom (SPECWARCOM)

Central Intelligence Agency
Agent Leonid Suchov (Deputy Chief, Russian Desk)

United States Navy SEALs
Commander Rick Hunter (Assault–Team Leader)
Lt. Commander Dallas MacPherson (2I/C. Explosives)
Chief Petty Officer Mike Hook (explosives)
Petty Officer First Class Don Smith
Petty Officer First Class Brian Harrison
Seaman Ed Segal (helmsman)
Seaman Ron Wallace (helmsman)
Chief Petty Officer Bob Bland (military breaking and entering)

United States Navy
Captain Hugh Fraser (CO USS *Toledo*, SEAL-team insert submarine commander)
Lt. Commander Alan Ross (*Vigilantes* combat pilot)

United Kingdom (Political)
The Prime Minister of Great Britain

Peter Caulfield (Minister of Defence)
Roger Eltringham (Foreign Secretary)
Commander Alan Knell (Conservative Member of Parliament, Portsmouth)
Robert Macmillan (Conservative MP)
Derek Blenkinsop (Labour MP, East Lancashire)
Richard Cawley (Conservative MP, Barrow-in-Furness)
Sir Patrick Jardine (Ambassador to the United States)

United Kingdom (Armed Forces)
General Sir Robin Brenchley (Chief of Defence Staff)
Admiral Sir Rodney Jeffries (First Sea Lord)
Admiral Mark Palmer (C-in-C Fleet)
Admiral Alan Holbrook (Task Force Commander)
Captain David Reader (CO HMS *Ark Royal*)
Major Bobby Court (Company Commander, Mount Pleasant)
Captain Peter Merrill (Commander Immediate Response Platoon, Falkland Islands)
Sgt Biff Wakefield (RAF Rapier Missiles, Mount Pleasant)
Brigadier Viv Brogden RM (Commander Landing Forces, Falkland Islands)
Lt. Commander Malcolm Farley (CO Royal Navy Garrison, Mare Harbour)
Captain Mike Fawkes (CO HMS *Kent*)
Captain Colin Ashby (CO HMS *St Albans)*
Commander Keith Kemsley (CO HMS *Iron Duke*)
Captain Rowdy Yates (CO HMS *Daring*)
Commander Norman Hall (CO HMS *Dauntless*)
Captain Colin Day (CO HMS *Gloucester*)
Captain Simon Compton (CO HM Submarine *Astute*)

United Kingdom 22 SAS
Lt. Colonel Mike Weston (Commanding Officer, Hereford HQ)
Captain Douglas Jarvis (Team Leader, Fanning Head Assault)
Combat Troopers: Syd Ferry (communications); Peter Wiggins (sniper); Joe Pearson; Bob Goddard; Trevor Fermer; Jake Posgate; Dai Llewellyn
Lt. Jim Perry (Team Leader SBS, Lafonia)

Russian Senior Command
The President of the Russian Federation

Valery Kravchenko (Prime Minister)
Oleg Nalyotov (Foreign Minister)
Gregor Komoyedov (Minister for Foreign Trade)
Boris Patrushov (Head of FSB – secret police)
Oleg Kuts (Energy Minister)
Admiral Vitaly Rankov (C-in-C Fleet, Deputy Defence Minister)

Russian Navy
Captain Gregor Vanislav (CO *Viper 157*)

Siberian Political and Oil Executive
Mikhail Masorin (*deceased*) (Chief Minister, Urals Federal District)
Roman Rekuts (new leader, Urals Federal District)
Jaan Valuev (President, OJSC Surgutneftgas Oil Corporation)
Sergei Pobozhiy (Chairman, Sibneft Oil Corporation)
Boris Nuriyev (First VP Finance, Lukoil Corporation)
Anton Katsuba (Oil Operations Chief, West Siberia)

Argentine Senior Command
The President of the Republic
Admiral Horacio Aguardo (Defence Minister)
Dr Carlos Montero (Minister of Industry and Mining)

Argentine Armed Forces
Admiral Oscar Moreno (C-in-C Fleet)
General Eduardo Kampf (Commander 5-Corps)
Major Pablo Barry (Commander Marine Assault, Falkland Islands)
Lt. Commander Ricardo Testa (Head of Security, Rio Grande Air Base)

Principal Wives
Diana Jarvis (Mrs Rick Hunter)
Mrs Kathy Morgan

UK Prime Minister's Principal Guests
Honeyford Jones (pop singer)
Freddie Leeson (soccer player), Madelle Leeson (former nightclub employee)
Darien Farr (film star), wife Loretta (former TV weathergirl)
Freddy Ivanov Windsor (restaurateur)

PROLOGUE

As a general rule, Admiral Arnold Morgan did not do state banquets. He put them in the same category as diplomatic luncheons, congressional dinners, state fairs, and yard sales – all of which required him to spend time talking to God knows how many people with whom he had absolutely nothing in common.

Forced to choose, he would even have preferred to spend an hour with the political editor of CBS Television or the *Washington Post*, either of whom he could cheerfully have throttled several times a year.

It was thus a matter of some interest this evening to witness him making his way down the great central staircase of the White House, right behind the President and his guests of honour. The admiral descended in company with the exquisitely beautiful Mrs Kathy Morgan, whose perfectly cut dark-green silk gown made the Russian president's wife look like a middle-line admin clerk from the KGB. (Close. She had been a researcher there.)

Arnold Morgan himself wore the dark-blue dress uniform of a US Navy rear-admiral, complete with the twin-dolphin insignia of the US Submarine Service. As ever – shoulders back, jaw jutting, steel-grey hair trimmed short – he looked like a CO striding towards his ops room.

Which was near to the mark. In his long years in service as the President's National Security Adviser, he reckoned that the White House *was* his ops room. He always called it 'the factory', and he had conducted global operations against enemies of the United

I

States with an unprecedentedly free hand. Of course, he had kept the President posted concerning his activities. Mostly.

And now, with the small exclusive reception for the Russians concluded in the upstairs private rooms, Arnold and Kathy stood aside at the foot of the stairs, alongside the Russian Ambassador and a dozen other dignitaries, while the two presidents and their wives formed a short receiving line.

This was deliberate, because the Russians always brought with them a vast entourage of state officials, diplomats, politicians, military top brass, and, as ever, undercover agents – spies – badly disguised as cultural attachés. It was, frankly, like seeing a prizefighter's attendant goons and bodyguards dancing a minuet.

But here they all were. The men who ran Russia, being formally entertained by President Paul Bedford and the First Lady, the former Maggie Lomax, a svelte blonde Virginian horsewoman, fearless to hounds but nerve-racked by this formal jamboree in support of US–Russian relations.

As far as President Bedford had been concerned, the presence of Arnold Morgan had been nothing short of compulsory. Although the telephone conversation between the two men had been more like a verbal gunfight.

'Arnie, I just got your note declining the Russian banquet invite – Jesus, you can't do this to me!'

'I thought I just had.'

'Arnie, this is not optional. This is a Presidential command.'

'Bullshit. I'm retired. I don't do state banquets. I'm a naval officer, not a diplomat.'

'I know what you are. But this thing is really important. They're bringing all the big hitters from Moscow, civilian and military. Not to mention their oil industry.'

'What the hell's that got to do with me?'

'Nothing. 'Cept I want you there. Right next to me, keeping me posted. There's not one person in Washington knows the Russians better than you. You gotta be there. White tie and tails.'

'I *never* wear white tie and tails.'

'OK. OK. You can come in a tuxedo.'

'Since I don't much want to look like a head waiter, or a goddamned violinist, I won't be wearing that, either.'

'OK. OK,' said the President again, sensing victory. 'You can come in full-dress Navy uniform. Matter of fact, I don't care if you turn up in jockstrap and spurs as long as you get here.'

Arnold Morgan chuckled. But suddenly an edge crept back into his voice. 'What topics concern you most?'

'The rise of the Russian navy, for a start. The rebuilding of their submarine fleet in particular. And their export of submarines all over the world.'

'How about their oil industry?'

'Well, that new deep-water tanker terminal in Murmansk cannot fail to be an issue,' replied the President. 'We're hoping that they'll ship two million barrels a day from there direct to the USA in the next few years.'

'And I guess you know the Russian president already has terrible goddamned problems transporting crude oil from the West Siberian Basin to Murmansk . . .' Arnold was thoughtful. He added slowly '. . . And you know how important that export trade is to them.'

'And to us,' said President Bedford.

'Gives us a little distance with the towelheads, right?'

'That's why you gotta be at the banquet, Arnie. Starting with the private reception. Don't be late.'

'Silver-tongued bastard,' grunted Admiral Morgan. 'All right, all right. We'll be there. Good morning, Mr President.'

Paul Bedford, who was well accustomed to the admiral's excruciating habit of slamming down the phone without even bothering to say goodbye, considered this a very definite victory.

'Heh, heh, heh,' he chortled in the deserted Oval Office. 'That little bit of intrigue on a global scale. That'll get the ole buzzard every time. But I'm sure glad he's coming.'

Thus it was that Arnold and Kathy Morgan were now in attendance at the state banquet for the Russians, gazing amiably at the long line of guests entering the White House.

So many old friends and colleagues. It was like a fraternity reunion. Here was the Commander of the US Navy SEALs, Admiral John Bergstrom and his *soignée* new wife Louisa-May, from Oxford, Mississippi; Harcourt Travis, the former Republican Secretary of State with his wife Sue; Admiral Scott Dunsmore, former CNO of the US Navy with his elegant wife Grace. The reigning Chairman of the Joint Chiefs, General Tim Scannell, was with his wife Beth.

Arnold shook hands with the Director of the National Security Agency, Admiral George Morris, and he greeted the new Vice-President of the United States, the former Democratic Senator from Georgia, Bradford Harding and his wife Paige.

The Israeli Ambassador General David Gavron was there with his wife Becky, plus, of course, the silver-haired Russian Ambassador to Washington, Tomas Yezhel, and the various ambassadors from the United Kingdom, Canada and Australia.

Arnold did not instantly recognise all the top brass of the Russian contingent. But he could see the former Chairman of the Joint Chiefs, General Josh Paul, talking with the Russian Foreign Minister, Oleg Nalyotov.

He vaguely knew the Chief of the Russian Naval Staff, a grim-looking ex-Typhoon Class submarine Commanding Officer, Admiral Victor Kouts.

But Admiral Morgan's craggy face lit up when he spotted the towering figure of his old sparring partner, the Russian admiral Vitaly Rankov, now C-in-C Fleet and Deputy Defence Minister.

'Arnold!' boomed the giant ex-Soviet international oarsman. 'I had no idea you'd be here. They told me you'd retired.'

Admiral Morgan grinned and held out his hand. 'Hi, Vitaly – they put you in charge of that junkyard navy of yours yet? I heard they had.'

'They did. Right now, admiral, you're talking to the Deputy Defence Minister of Russia.'

'Guess that'll suit you,' replied the American. 'Should provide ample scope for your natural flair for lies, evasions and half-truths . . .'

The enormous Russian threw back his head and roared with laughter. 'Now you be kind, Arnold,' he said in his deep rumbling baritone voice. 'Otherwise I may not introduce you to this very beautiful lady standing at my side.'

A tall, striking, dark-haired girl around half the Russian's age smiled shyly and held out her hand in friendship.

'This is Olga,' said Admiral Rankov. 'We were married last spring.'

Admiral Morgan took her hand and asked if she spoke any English since his own Russian was a little rusty. She shook her head, smiling, and Morgan turned back to Vitaly and shook his head sadly. 'Too good for you, old buddy. A lot too good.'

Again the huge Russian admiral laughed joyfully, and he repeated the words he had used so often in his many dealings with the old Lion of the West Wing.

'You are a terrible man, Arnold Morgan. A truly terrible man.' Then he spoke in rapid Russian to Mrs Olga Rankov who also burst out laughing.

'I understand we are sitting together,' said Arnold. 'And I don't believe you have actually met my wife Kathy.'

The Russian admiral smiled and accepted Kathy's outstretched hand. 'We have of course spoken many times on the telephone,' he said. 'But believe me, I never thought he'd persuade you to marry him.' And, with a compliment and a gesture more appropriate to a St Petersburg palace than a naval dockyard, Vitaly added with a short bow and a flourish, 'The legend of your great beauty precedes you, Mrs Morgan. I knew what to expect.'

'Jesus, they've even taught him social graces,' chuckled Arnold, carelessly ignoring the fact he was a bit short in that department himself. 'Vitaly, old pal, seems we both got lucky in the past year. Not too bad for a couple of old Cold Warriors.'

By now the guests were almost through the receiving line and had moved to the sides of the room, leaving a wide entryway to the State Dining Room. Within a few moments, President and Maggie Bedford came through, escorting the Russian president and his wife to their dinner places, with all of the guests falling in – *line astern*, as Arnold somewhat jauntily told Vitaly.

The President took his place next to the former KGB researcher directly beneath the Lincoln portrait. Maggie Bedford showed the boss of all the Russians to his place next to her at the same table, and everyone remained standing until the hostess was seated.

The banquet, on the orders of Paul Bedford, was strictly American. 'No caviar, or any of that restaurant nonsense,' he had told the butler. 'We start with Chesapeake oysters, we dine on New York sirloin steak, with Idaho potatoes, and we wrap it up with apple pie and American ice cream. There'll be two or three Wisconsin cheeses for anyone who wants them. California wines from the Napa Valley.'

'Sir,' the butler ventured, 'Not everyone likes oysters . . .'

'Tough,' replied the President. 'Russians love 'em. I've had 'em in Moscow and St Petersburg. Anyone who can't eat 'em can have an extra shot of apple pie if they need it.'

'Very well, sir,' replied the butler, suspecting, from vast experience, that Arnold Morgan himself must have been in the shadows advising Paul Bedford. The tone, the curtness, the certainty.

As it happened, there had indeed been one short conversation when the Oval Office had called Chevy Chase to check in on the menu content. 'Give 'em American food,' Arnold had advised.

'Strictly American. Big A–A–A. The food this nation eats. We don't need to pretend sophistication to anyone, right?'

'Right.'

And now, with the apple pie just arriving, the Strolling Strings, a well-known group of US Army violinists, began to play at the rear section of the room. Their short concert clearly followed a similar brief, comprising all-American numbers, such as 'Over there!', 'True Love' (from *High Society*), a selection from *Oklahoma*, 'Take me Out to the Ball Game' . . . and concluding with 'God Bless America'.

Finally the President rose and made a short speech extolling the virtues of the Russian president and the new and close trade links developing between the nations.

The chief guest of honour then stood and echoed many of the President's statements before concluding with a formal toast 'to the United States of America'.

At this point the entire room stood up and proceeded towards the door which led out to the Blue Room where coffee would be served, followed by entertainment in the East Room, and then dancing to the band of the United States Marines in the White House foyer.

The crowd was steadily moving towards the doors, when one guest suddenly stopped. Mikhail Masorin, the senior minister from the vast plains of Siberia, which occupy one-twelfth of the land mass of the entire Earth, had suddenly pitched forward and landed flat on his face. He collapsed right in front of Arnold, Vitaly, Olga and Kathy, and the huge Russian admiral had actually leaned forward to try and break his fall. But he was a fraction of a second too late. Masorin was on the floor, twisted on his back now, his face puce in colour, gasping for breath, both hands clutched to his throat as he frantically worked his jaws, fear and agony etched on his face.

Someone shouted, *'Doctor! Right now!'*

Women gasped. Men came forward to see if they could help – mostly Americans, Arnold Morgan noticed. Casting around for someone who would be able to do something, Morgan realised quickly that Masorin was very nearly beyond help. He was desperately trying to breathe but his face showed a slight blue tinge now.

By now two or three people were shouting, *'Heart attack! Come on, guys, let the doctor through . . .'*

Within a few minutes two doctors were in attendance. One of

them filled a syringe and unleashed a potent dose of something into Masorin's upper arm, but they could only bear witness to the death throes of the Siberian head honcho.

In seconds, he was gone, dead even before the Navy stretcher-bearers could get to him. Dead, right there, on the floor of the State Dining Room in front of his own president and the leader of the United States.

President Bedford forced himself to shake off the shock and fired a series of quiet orders into the small knot of people around Masorin. Luckily, only those few in the immediate vicinity realised that one of the Russian guests had actually died and the body was carried away before the other dignitaries were fully aware of what had happened.

Arnold Morgan and Paul Bedford watched the crowd warily, but the rest of the evening passed uneventfully and shortly before 11 p.m. the White House Press Office felt obliged to put out a general press release that the Chief Minister for the Urals Federal District, Mr Mikhail Masorin, had suffered a heart attack at the conclusion of a state banquet, and had been found to be dead on arrival at the United States Naval Hospital in Bethesda, Maryland.

Admiral Morgan and Kathy made their farewells a little after midnight.

'Terrible about that poor Russian, wasn't it?' said Kathy, as they headed north-west to Chevy Chase. 'He was at the next table to us, couldn't have been more than fifty years old. Must have been a very bad heart attack . . .'

Her husband hadn't said much for the remainder of the night. Now he turned away from the window he'd been staring out of. 'Bullshit,' he said succinctly.

'I'm sorry?' said Kathy, slightly perplexed.

'Bullshit,' confirmed the Admiral. 'That was no heart attack. He was writhing around on the floor, opening and shutting his mouth like a goddamned goldfish.'

'I know he was, darling. But the doctor *said* it was a heart attack. I heard him.'

'What the hell does he know?'

'Oh, I am so sorry. It entirely slipped my memory I was escorting the eminent cardiovascular surgeon and universal authority Arnold Morgan.'

Arnold looked up, grinning now at his increasingly sassy wife. 'Kathy,' he said. Then, more seriously, 'Whatever killed Masorin somehow shut down his lungs instantly. The guy suffocated, fighting for air, which you probably noticed was plentiful in the State Dining Room. Heart attacks don't do that.'

'Oh,' said Kathy. 'Well, what does?'

'A bullet, correctly aimed. A thrust from a combat knife, correctly delivered. Certain kinds of poison.'

'But there was no blood anywhere. And anyway, why should the CIA or the FBI or whatever want to get rid of an important guest at a White House banquet?'

'I have no idea, my darling,' said Arnold. 'But I believe someone did. And I'll be mildly surprised if we don't find out before too long that Mikhail Masorin was murdered last night. Right here in Washington DC.'

CHAPTER ONE

0830 Wednesday 15 September 2010

Lt. Commander Jimmy Ramshawe, assistant to the Director of the National Security Agency in Fort Meade, Maryland had his feet and his antennae up. Lounging back in his swivel chair, shoes on the desk, he was staring at an item on the front page of the *Washington Post*.

TOP RUSSIAN OFFICIAL
DROPS DEAD IN WHITE HOUSE
Siberian political chief
suffers fatal heart attack

'Poor bastard,' muttered the American-born but Australian-sounding Intelligence officer. 'That's a hell of a way to go – in the middle of the bloody State Dining Room, right in front of two presidents. Still, by the look of this, he didn't have time to be embarrassed.'

He read on, skimming through the brief biography. The forty-nine-year-old Mikhail Masorin had been a tough, uncompromising Siberian boss, someone who stood up for his people and their shattered communist dream. Here was a man who had brought real hope to this 4,350-mile-long land mass of bleak and terrible beauty, of snowfields and seven time zones.

Of the three Siberian 'kingdoms' which make up this huge area, the two others being the Siberian Federal District between the

Yenisei River and the Lena River, and the Russian Far East, the Urals Federal district was easily the most important. Here was where most of the oilfields were located. Beneath the desolate plains of Western Siberia, the freezing place which locals claimed to be 'forgotten by the Creator', lay the largest oilfields on earth.

One of the reasons why Mikhail was adored in Siberia was because he was a politician who wasn't afraid to speak brass tacks, frequently reminding his Russian rulers that the oil upon which the entire national economy was built was Siberian and that it was the natural property of the Siberian people. He wanted more money for it from the central government. Not for himself, but for his people.

And now Mikhail was gone, and Jimmy Ramshawe's hackles rose a lot higher than his shoes on the desk. 'Strewth,' he said quietly, taking a swig of his hot black coffee. 'Wouldn't be surprised if a bloody lot of people were glad he died. And none of 'em Siberian.'

It was at times like this that Lt. Commander Ramshawe's famously reliable instincts sprang to the fore. Suspicion, mistrust, misgivings and downright disbelief, as well as a few harsh lessons taught to him by the Big Man fought their way to the front of his mind: *whenever a major politician with a lot of enemies dies, check it out . . . never trust a goddamned Russian – and never believe that anything is beyond them, because it's not . . . the KGB lives, trust me.*

'Wouldn't be the biggest shock in the world if the old bastard calls on this one,' he said, refilling his coffee cup. And he was right about that.

Three minutes later his private line rang. Jimmy always thought there was an irritable, impatient note in its modern ring-tone when the Big Man was on the line. And he was right about that, too.

'Jimmy, you read the *Washington Post* yet? Front page, the dead Siberian?' Arnold Morgan's tone echoed that of the telephone.

'Yessir.'

'Well, first of all, you can forget all about that heart-attack crap.'

'Sir?'

'And stop calling me 'sir'. I'm retired.'

'Could've fooled me, sir.'

Arnold Morgan chuckled. For the past few years he had treated Jimmy Ramshawe almost like a son, not simply because the young Aussie-American was the best Intelligence officer he had ever met, but also because he both knew and liked his father, an ex-Australian Navy admiral and currently a high-ranking airline official in New York.

Jimmy was engaged to the surf goddess Jane Peacock, student daughter of the Australian Ambassador to Washington, and Arnold was very fond of both families. But in Jimmy he had a soulmate, a younger man whose creed was suspicion, thoroughness and a tireless determination to investigate, someone always prepared to play a hunch, and with a total devotion to the United States, the country where Jimmy had been brought up.

He might have been engaged to a goddess, but Jimmy Ramshawe believed Arnold Morgan was God. Several years ago Admiral Morgan had been Director of the National Security Agency, and ever since had continued to consider himself in overall command of the place.

This system suited everyone, not least Admiral George Morris, the ex-Carrier Battle Group commander and current NSA Director, extremely well, because there was no better advice than that of Admiral Morgan.

When Admiral Morgan called the NSA, Fort Meade trembled. His growl echoed through Crypto City – as the Military Intelligence hub was called. And, essentially, that was the way Arnold liked it.

'Jimmy, I was at the banquet, standing only about ten feet from the Siberian when he hit the deck. He went down like he'd been shot, which he plainly hadn't. But I watched him die, rolling back and forth, fighting for breath, just like his lungs had quit on him. Wasn't like any heart attack I ever saw . . .'

'How many you seen?'

'Shut up, Jimmy. You sound like Kathy. And listen . . . I want you very quietly to find out where the goddamned body is, where it's going, and whether there's going to be an autopsy.'

'Then what?'

'Never mind "then what?" Just take step one, and call me back.' Slam. Phone down.

'Glad to see the old bastard's mellowing,' muttered Jimmy. 'Still, Kathy says that's how he's talked to at least two Presidents. So I guess I can't complain.'

He picked up his other phone and asked the operator to connect him to Bill Fogarty down at FBI headquarters. Three minutes later the top Washington field agent was on the case, and twenty minutes after that Bill was back with news of the fate of the corpse of Mikhail Masorin.

'Jimmy, I walked into a goddamned hornets' nest. Seems the

Russians want to take the body directly back to Moscow tomorrow afternoon. But the Navy is not having it. Masorin is officially in their care while the body's in the USA. He died on American soil, and they're insisting the formalities are carried out here, including, if necessary, an autopsy.'

'What do the Russians think about that?'

'Not a whole hell of a lot,' said Bill Fogarty. 'They are saying Masorin was an official guest of the President in the United States, and they should be afforded the diplomatic courtesy of treating his death as though it had happened in their own embassy where he was staying.'

'Will they get their way?'

'I don't think so. Under the law, a foreign national who dies in the USA is subject to the lawful procedures of the United States. If something has happened to a high-ranking Russian official, it is within the rights of the United States to demand the most exhaustive inquiries into the causes of death until we are satisfied that every avenue has been explored. Even then, the body is released only on our say-so. And they still have the body at the hospital at Bethesda.'

Jimmy paused for a moment, thinking. Then he said, 'Bill, I'm gonna make one phone call. And I have a hunch it's going to end all speculation. After all, anyone who was in the White House at that time must be a suspect if there is a question of foul play. And that must include the President and all his agents and officials. That body's not going anywhere for a while, except the city morgue.'

Thanking Bill Fogarty, Lt. Commander Ramshawe immediately called the Naval Hospital. The conversation took two full minutes. The body of Siberia's Number One political commissar would be leaving for the morgue inside the hour and an autopsy would be carried out this afternoon. The Russians were, apparently, not pleased.

Jimmy hit the buttons for the Chevy Chase link.

'Morgan – speak.'

'Sir, the body of Mr Masorin will be at the city morgue in a couple of hours. The Russians are trying to kick up a fuss and get permission to remove it back to Moscow. But that's obviously not going to happen.'

'Doesn't surprise me any, Jimmy. Tell the pathologist we're looking for poison of some kind. I'm damn sure it wasn't a heart attack.'

'You think one of our guys got rid of him?'

'Well, that's what it looks like. But you never know with the Russians. A short, sharp murder in the White House gives 'em marvellous cover. Because then they can feign outrage at this disgraceful breach in American security, while they make their getaway, home to that God-awful country of theirs.'

'You mean they might have killed their own man?' Jimmy was taken aback but not really surprised. And Morgan apparently felt the same.

'It's happened before, both during and after the old Soviet era. But let's not get excited. We'll wait till we hear the autopsy report. Then we'll take a very careful look . . . Hey, well done, kid – but I gotta go. I'd better talk to the Chief.'

1600: same day

Lt. Commander Ramshawe's veteran black Jaguar pulled into the parking lot behind the city morgue and headed straight into one of the VIP reserved spaces. This was an old ruse taught him long ago by Admiral Morgan: *no one, ever, wants to tangle with a high-ranking officer from the NSA. Park wherever the hell you like. Anyone doesn't like it, tell 'em to call me.*

Inside the building, the area where the autopsy had been conducted was busy, despite the fact the FBI had denied the Russians entry. There were two US Navy guards on the door and three White House agents milled around in the corridor. The coroner, Dr Louis Merloni, was there, with the Chief Medical Officer from Bethesda in attendance. The autopsy had been carried out by the resident clinical pathologist, Dr Larry Madeiros. No details of the examination had yet been released.

Jimmy showed his NSA pass to the guards and was admitted immediately. Once inside he said firmly, 'Dr Madeiros?'

The pathologist walked over and held out his hand.

'Lt. Commander Ramshawe, NSA,' said Jimmy. 'I would like to talk to you for a few minutes in private.'

They walked across the wide examination room to an adjoining office, and almost before they'd had time to sit down Jimmy Ramshawe said, 'OK, Doc, gimme the cause of death.'

'Mikhail Masorin died of asphyxiation, sir.'

'You mean some bastard throttled him?'

'No, I don't mean that. I mean he was given a substance, a poison of some type, which caused the transmission of nerve impulses from

13

the brain to the muscles to be seriously impaired. In the end to the point of limpness. When this process hits the chest muscles, breathing stops.'

'Jesus Christ. You don't think he was poisoned by something in his food?'

'No. I found a very fine puncture mark on the back of his neck, right side. I think we shall find he was injected with the poison through that hole.'

'Do we know what the poison was yet?' Jimmy wanted to make sure he got every detail for Arnold Morgan.

'No idea. All the bodily fluids are still in the lab. That's blood-cell counts, as well as bone marrow, liquids from the liver and kidneys, and all other biochemical substances found in the body. It'll take a while, but I'm pretty sure we're going to find something very foreign deep inside that corpse.'

'The bloody corpse itself is very foreign,' said Jimmy cheerfully. 'That makes the poison *amazingly* foreign.'

'Unless it was American,' replied the doctor, archly.

'Well, yes, I suppose so,' said Jimmy. 'When will you know?'

'You can call me on my cellphone at ten o'clock tonight. I'll let you know in confidence what we've found. Thereafter the report will be issued first thing tomorrow morning to the hospital and to the medical officer of record in Bethesda, and then to the FBI and the White House agents.

2200: same day
Australian Embassy, Washington DC

Jimmy excused himself from the Australian Ambassador's dinner table and walked into the next room where he punched in Dr Larry Madeiros's number on his cellphone.

'Hello, sir. It was curare, and quite a sizeable shot of it. A most deadly poison originating from South America.'

'Kew-rar-ee,' said Jimmy. 'What the hell is it?'

'Well, curare is a generic name for many different poisons made from the bark and roots of forest vines,' said the doctor. 'The main one's called Pareira, and the lab technicians here think that's the one. Five hundred micrograms of that stuff will cause death in a few minutes. And Mr Masorin had more than that. It's a classic poison and it seems it's a favourite of the professional assassin.'

'Steady, Doc, old mate. This was a White House state banquet. There weren't any professional assassins walking around there.'

'As you wish,' said Doctor Madeiros stiffly. 'But that is very much the history of this particular poison.'

'Well, thanks anyway, Doc. You've been a big help.'

Jimmy clicked off and instantly dialled Admiral Morgan's number.

'You were dead right, sir. Someone hit Masorin with a lethal shot of poison injected into his neck. More than 500 micrograms, according to the pathologist . . .'

'Know what it was?'

'Yup. Curare, a type called Pareira.'

'Wait a minute, Jimmy. I got a book of poisons here. I was waiting for your call. Lemme check this out – yeah, right, curare, a known poison since the sixteenth century, a gummy substance used to tip hunting arrowheads by Indian tribes up the Amazon river in South America.'

Jimmy could hear Morgan flipping pages so he said quickly, 'Sir, I'll alert Admiral Morris to what's going on. And then I guess we'll let the rest of the investigation take its course. It's not really our business any more, is it? Civilian matter now, right?'

'Exactly so, Jimmy. But I'm sure as hell glad we know what's going on. Murder.'

For the US government, it wasn't quite so easy to get rid of the case. From an official point of view, inquests, coroners' statements and autopsies were a pain in the rear end, especially as they were always public and had to be entered in the public record. Thus it was that on the morning of Thursday 16 September, the FBI announced to the world that the death of the Siberian Chief Minister, Mikhail Masorin, was indeed suspicious.

Traces of the lethal poison curare had been found in the body, and the investigators were now treating the case as a murder inquiry.

MURDER IN THE WHITE HOUSE, bellowed the *New York Post*. SIBERIA BOSS ASSASSINATED, thundered the *Washington Post*. All of it on the front page, in specially reserved end-of-the-world typeface.

And while the maelstrom of a media frenzy swirled around the Russian visitors, the President's Aeroflot state airliner took off for Moscow from Andrews Air Base on Thursday evening. The body of Mikhail Masorin was not on board.

For some reason best known to neurotic news editors, the US media, including the 24-hour news channels, leaped to the conclusion that an American had been responsible for the Siberian's death. Perhaps it was just too far-fetched that the Russians would choose the White House as a theatre in which to assassinate one of their own.

And the American media, to a man, jumped on the story of an American-based terrorist, possibly a Chechen rebel in disguise, firing some kind of poison dart into Masorin's neck so that he had subsequently died while dining with the President of the United States and 150 of his friends.

The media grilled the FBI, grilled the Washington Police Department, grilled the White House press office. It took three entire days before it dawned on them all that no one had the slightest idea who had really killed Masorin, and that there had been no Chechen rebels at the state banquet.

Busy concocting stories of their own, none of them realised the massive rift that had opened up between the presidents of the United States and Russia. The Russian leader had almost begged Paul Bedford to allow him to take the body home to Moscow, only to have his pleas rejected again and again.

It seemed that the Russians could not understand that the boss of the United States could not just do anything he pleased. The key point of a Western democracy – that when it came to the absolute crunch the law of the land, correctly administered, remained sacrosanct – still eluded them.

Masorin's body was going nowhere until the investigation was complete. Someone had plainly murdered him. Possibly inside the White House. And until that someone was identified, the corpse was staying put in the home of the brave.

Jimmy Ramshawe was thoughtful. He sat in his colossally untidy office, surrounded by mounds of paper. Although each pile was neatly stacked there were so many of them that they crowded out his desk, clogged his computer table, and turned the carpeted floor into a death trap.

One thought was uppermost in his mind: *the Big Man thinks the bloody Russkis killed Masorin in the White House because no one would ever dream they would pull off something quite like that.*

Jimmy knew the Russian president would shortly be landing in Moscow and that his public-relations machine would be full of venom. All aimed at the leaky, decadent security arrangements in the United States . . . *which has somehow caused the death of our beloved brother – sorry, comrade – Mikhail Masorin.*

'And a right crock of shit *that* is,' Jimmy muttered with all the natural-born charm of an Aussie swagman. 'I'm with the Big Man on this one. And I consider it's in the interests of the United States of America to find out what the hell's going on – I'd better go and see the boss.'

Admiral George Morris, a portly ex-Naval Battle Group commander with the appearance of a lovesick teddy bear and a spine of steel, listened attentively.

He betrayed scarcely a flicker of surprise when Jimmy delivered his punchline: 'Sir, I think Admiral Morgan believes the Russians bumped old Mikhail off, right there in the bloody State Dining Room.'

'Yes, he does,' replied Admiral Morris. 'So do I. Want some hot coffee?'

Jimmy blinked. 'Yes to the coffee, sir. But how do you know?'

'Arnold just told me, 'bout fifteen minutes ago.'

'Strewth.'

'Jimmy, Admiral Morgan knows more about the Russian mindset than any man I ever met. And I've known him for over thirty years, most of them as a pretty close friend. And there is one view of his which ought never to be discounted.'

'What's that, sir?'

'That even after President Reagan forced them to take down the Berlin Wall; even after he made them dismantle the old Soviet Union a coupla years after he'd gone, in 1991, all those old instincts for brutal central control remained as strong as ever. And it's going to take decades to get rid of them. Barbarous actions, poisoning and assassinations, all aimed at crushing dissent, stamping out free expression. Remember Stalin himself who said very simply, "If you have a man who represents a problem, get rid of the man. Then there's no problem." Both Arnie and I believe Mikhail Masorin was just such a problem. The fact that his territory held most of Russia's oil and that he controlled it closely. Perhaps he threatened to secede from Russian rule and take his oil with him?'

Jimmy mulled this over. 'Well, not any more he wouldn't,' he then said. 'And no bloody error.'

Morris fiddled with the coffee pot. 'Arnold and I would like you to continue your investigations on a full-time basis for the next couple of weeks. We really ought to find out what the hell's going on.'

'Christ, sir. Mind if I have some of that coffee now? That's a bloody lot to digest.'

Admiral Morris smiled and poured Jimmy a cup. 'Take a look at some of the really suspicious deaths which have taken place in the past, say, forty years. And you might start with Georgi Markov.'

'Who?' Jimmy asked from behind the rim of his mug.

'An expert on Soviet affairs who worked with the BBC in London – a good journalist with excellent contacts behind the Iron Curtain. He wrote some hair-raising stuff about the Soviets and the KGB and I believe he was a good friend of Alexander Solzhenitsyn. A real thorn in Russia's side . . .'

'Ah, righto, sir. I'll get right on it.'

Lt. Commander Ramshawe retreated to his lair and logged on to the internet. It took him ten minutes to find a reference: *Georgi Markov, Bulgarian dissident working for the BBC . . . assassinated in London, 1977 . . . later discovered to have been jabbed by a pellet weapon disguised as an umbrella, firing a tiny platinum sphere containing a deadly poison, almost certainly curare.*

Subsequent revelations by the former KGB colonel and renowned pro-Western double agent Oleg Gordievsky indicated that Markov had probably been assassinated by a KGB freelancer. And, what was more, that the assassination had been carried out with the approval of the head of the KGB, Yuri Andropov, later the General Secretary of the Communist Party of the Soviet Union.

'Strewth,' said Jimmy Ramshawe for the second time in half an hour. 'One bloody surprise after another.'

He trawled through all manner of disappearances – of politicians, of dissidents and of anyone else deemed to be whatever the Russian was for 'pain in the ass'. Finally he alighted on the big one, the one that had for ever blighted the name of the Russian leadership. And the plan hadn't even worked.

Viktor Yushchenko, the opposition leader in the infamous Ukraine election of 2004, a hugely popular pro-European politician, was spectacularly poisoned just before the election but didn't die.

His face, hideously pock-marked and disfigured, was shown to the entire world just a few weeks after he had looked perfectly normal. The murder attempt had taken place at a political dinner with Ukraine security services, and the doctors who subsequently treated Yushchenko in Vienna claimed to have found over-whelming evidence of poisoning by dioxin.

It was more than obvious that his stance as a pro-European, pro-democracy candidate posed a serious threat to the Kremlin, with its love of state control. Here was a man, and here was a problem. And Josef Stalin himself had instructed them how to be rid of it.

Jimmy Ramshawe was gratified to note that Viktor Yushchenko eventually became President of the Ukraine, and that his health had slowly returned to normal. But his ordeal was a timely reminder that the vicious, old KGB methods of elimination were alive and well in modern Russia. Not just alive, and not just well, but ruthlessly woven into the fabric of Russian politics, where they'd been since the 1920s when the KGB's predecessors first built their laboratories to develop special poisons to use against dissidents. Modern ideas of political freedom and human rights had never taken root in Russia, and probably never would.

At least, that was the view of Admiral Arnold Morgan and his colleague Admiral George Morris. 'And who the bloody hell am I to argue with those two?' muttered Jimmy. 'They got me. The ole Ruskies most definitely took a pop at Mikhail and this time they didn't fuck it up.'

By now, Admiral Morris had left for a meeting at the Pentagon. Jimmy elected to spend the rest of the afternoon trying to find out just what Masorin had done: it had to be something so bad the heavies from Moscow had decided to take him out, right after dinner in the White House, damn nearly in full view of the entire world.

Jimmy Ramshawe picked up his telephone and asked to be put through to CIA headquarters in Langley, Virginia.

'Hi, Mary. Is Lenny in this afternoon?'

'He sure is, sir. You want to speak with him?'

'Would you just ask him if I can come and see him, right now?'

'Hold a moment . . . yes, that will be fine. Mr Suchov said the usual place, say forty-five minutes?'

'Perfect, Mary. Tell him I'll be there.'

Six minutes later Lt. Commander Ramshawe's black Jaguar was ripping down the Spellman Parkway heading south. He cut onto the Beltway at Exit 22 and aimed the car west, anti-clockwise, and stayed right on the great highway which ringed Washington DC until it crossed the Potomac River at the American Legion Memorial Bridge.

Seventeen miles along the Beltway had taken him fifteen minutes. Now he picked up the Georgetown Pike for two miles, straight through the CIA headquarters main gate where a young field officer from the Russian desk met him and accompanied him to the parking area near the auditorium.

Jimmy thanked him and walked through to the CIA's tranquil memorial garden, pausing briefly to gaze at the simple message carved into fieldstone at the edge of the pond – *In remembrance of those whose unheralded efforts served a grateful nation.*

Like most senior Intelligence officers, a place in Jimmy's soul was touched by those words – and visions instantly stood before him: of grim, dark streets in Moscow or the old East Berlin or Bucharest, of men working for the United States, alone, in the most terrible danger, stalked by the stony-faced agents of the KGB. Always the KGB, with their hired assassins, knives and garrottes.

'I hope the nation bloody well *is* grateful, that's all,' he said, as he walked through spots of bright sunlight towards the blue-painted seat by the pond where he always met Leonid Suchov, one of the most brilliant double agents the West had ever had.

He smiled when he thought of Lenny. A stocky little bear of a man, who walked lightly on the balls of his feet, hardly ever stopped smiling, and who could slide a knife between your ribs as soon as look at you. Which was the principal reason why he was still alive and not buried somewhere in the bowels of the Lubyanka.

Lenny was Romanian by birth, and had lost both his parents, schoolteachers in Bucharest, when he was twelve. Typecast as dissidents, they had been grabbed by KGB thugs and were never seen again. Lenny, however, growing up with a profound hatred of the Communist Party, Moscow, the Iron Curtain and everything to do with that monstrous regime, still had places to go.

Lenny was a champion wrestler. Never quite good enough to win an Olympic medal himself, he became a world-class coach and had been one of the team that had helped steer the great Vasile Andrei to the Graeco-Roman heavyweight gold medal for Romania at the Los Angeles Games in 1984.

For aficionados the name Andrei still brought curt, knowing nods of respect. In each of his four bouts in LA the mighty Romanian had defeated his opponent in less than four and a half minutes, an almost unprecedented feat of strength and skill.

And Lenny was right there, heading up the coaching squad. The only difference being that, while the rest of the team went home to Romania, Lenny Suchov was spirited out of the Olympic Village and then flown in a United States Navy helicopter to Vandenberg Air Force Base north of Santa Barbara, and thence to Washington.

His disappearance had been a huge embarrassment to the Romanian Olympic authorities – and equally humiliating to staff members of the KGB who had recruited Leonid Suchov many years before as a full-fledged spy with orders to pass on information directly from any Western city in which the Romanian wrestling team competed.

They didn't know that the jolly little wrestling giant with a handshake like the grip of a mechanical digger had been working diligently on behalf of the CIA for twenty years. During this time his eminence in Romanian and Soviet sports circles had afforded him privileges at the tables of the most powerful Communist Party officials behind the Iron Curtain.

He had inflicted untold damage on all the Eastern European secret police services, exposing their agents, networks, radio bands, codes, addresses and phone numbers to the CIA field chiefs. He had been directly responsible for at least fifty assassinations conducted by the CIA in those brutal days of the Cold War.

And with each victim Lenny drank a silent toast to Emile and Anna Suchov, his long-lost parents. And no one ever suspected him. As a matter of fact, neither the Soviets nor the Romanians realised what he'd been doing for the past two decades, even after he had defected in Los Angeles.

They actually issued a statement confirming that Leonid Suchov had left the Romanian Olympic organisation in order to marry an American and become private coach with one of the major American universities. They expressed their gratitude for all that he had done and wished him well for the future.

Meanwhile, back at CIA headquarters the beloved wrestling coach from Bucharest was installed as deputy head of the Russian desk, at one of the biggest salaries ever paid to a former agent.

And here he was at last, thought Jimmy Ramshawe as he saw Lenny moving swiftly around the pond, light on his feet, a big smile of greeting across his swarthy features.

Christ, he still walks like a poofter, thought Jimmy. *But I'd bloody hate to remind him.*

'Jimmy Ramshawe! Where you been?' Lenny's smile lit up the entire memorial garden.

'Stuck at that factory in Maryland,' Jimmy replied. 'Trying to earn an honest living.'

'There's no honesty in our line of business,' said the Romanian. 'You know that. I know that. We just gotta stay cheerful, hah?'

Jimmy grinned and shook the Romanian's hand. Lenny looked at him sideways. 'Now, is this about Mikhail Masorin?'

'How the hell do you know?' Jimmy was stunned.

'Jimmy – this is my business. You didn't believe that heart attack nonsense, did you?'

'Well,' Jimmy admitted grudgingly, 'only because Admiral Morgan told me he didn't believe it either.'

'Phew! That Admiral Morgan. He's something, right? Doesn't miss a trick.'

'Really, Lenny, I've come to ask if you have any idea why they wanted him dead?'

'To be honest, Jimmy, I'm surprised he lived so long.'

Jimmy made a noise of surprise.

'Well, he was one of the most dangerous men in the entire country,' Lenny said, looking around, more from habit than anything else. 'A perceived enemy of the state, a threat to the Moscow government.'

'You mean some kind of traitor?'

'No. More a patriot . . . come on, let's walk for a while. I don't like static conversations. Someone might be listening.'

Both men stood up and walked slowly to the edge of the pond. Lenny said: 'Jimmy, do you have any idea how important the oil industry is to Russia? Russia holds the world's largest natural gas reserves, and it's the second-largest oil exporter on Earth. Only Saudi Arabia can pump more crude onto the world market. The World Bank thinks Russia's oil and gas sector accounts for twenty-five per cent of its GDP while employing only one per cent of the population. Russia has proven oil reserves of more than sixty billion barrels. That's three million barrels a day for sixty years.'

'Beautiful. But what's that got to do with poor old Mikhail being hit by a poisoned dart from a bloody blowpipe?'

'Everything. Because darn near every barrel of that oil is in Siberia. And Masorin was effectively the boss of the western end of Siberia where nearly all of it is and every oil company and fellow politician looked up to him like he was a god.' Lenny plucked a couple of leaves from an overhanging branch, crushing them with sudden fury, then tossed them into the water.

'It's well known that he was sick to death of the enormous taxation levied by Moscow on what he called *his* people's oil. And he was sick of the price-gouging, the way Moscow wants all the oil cheap, cheaper and cheapest. Russia has been living in fear that a man like him will one day rise up and take it all away. The country would collapse economically. And remember, Siberia has another ready market right on their doorstep: China. And Beijing will pay much more generously for the product. Moscow faces ruin if these Siberian bosses, both oil and political, cannot be brought into line.'

Lenny's gaze followed the leaf ball, slowly sinking into oblivion below the murky surface of the pond.

'Lenny, those are what you might call bloody high stakes.'

'Jimmy, those are the highest stakes on this planet. And I'm assuming you understand the pipeline problems?'

'Not really, but I guess they have a pretty damn big one pumping all that oil over the land mass.'

'It's a truly colossal system, Jim. The biggest in the world. The Southern Druzhba – that's the export line west of Moscow – runs oil right across the Ukraine, north into Prague, and south-west across Hungary and Croatia to the Adriatic oil port of Omišalj. The same system branches to Odessa on the Black Sea and to the Caspian.

'There is a branch further north – the Baltic Pipeline System (BPS) running oil to the ports of Butinge and the new tanker terminal at Primorsk on the Gulf of Finland. Siberian oil flows everywhere, across Estonia, Latvia and Lithuania.

'And the new northern pipeline all the way to the new terminal at Murmansk up on the Barents Sea is one of the engineering marvels of the modern world. Right out of the West Siberian Basin, it's over 1,200 miles long and it passes through terrible country – mountains, marshes and ice fields.'

'And then some bloody upstart threatens to turn off the tap, right?'

'You always had a way with words, young Ramshawe,' Lenny grinned. 'But you're right. Some bastard suddenly threatened to turn the tap off. Masorin might not have been absolutely serious, but Moscow has no sense of humour at the best of times.'

'And didn't I read somewhere about a row over the Far Eastern pipeline?'

'You sure did. The key to that is the Siberian city of Angarsk – that's a place near Lake Baikal to the north of Mongolia. It used to be the end of the oil pipeline, but then they extended it, right around the lake for 2,500 miles to the Siberian port of Nakhodka on the Sea of Japan, and a new market, OK?'

'Got it,' said Jimmy. 'More big profits for Moscow, right?'

'Right. But – somewhat sneakily – the East Siberian government moved ahead with a new 1,500-mile pipeline directly into the inland Chinese oil city of Daqing. The Chinese built and paid for a huge length of it, and the Siberians pretended it was all part of the general expansion of the Russian oil industry. But if push came to shove, we know who would control and service that particular stretch of pipeline.

'The fact is the Siberians now have a direct line into one of China's comparatively rare, but extremely well-organised oil complexes, with excellent pipelines to transport the product everywhere. And China will take damn nearly all the oil it can get its hands on. And they'll pay the price. That scares Moscow.'

Lt. Commander Ramshawe was thoughtful. 'I suppose,' he said slowly, 'it's kind of a natural marriage. China's got a zillion people and hardly any resources, Siberia's got a zillion resources and no people.'

'Precisely so,' replied Lenny Suchov. 'And no one knows quite what would happen if the Siberians declared autonomy from Moscow, and elected to go their own way under the brilliant but now dead Mikhail Masorin. Russia would be virtually powerless. You can't fight a modern war in a place that big. And anyway, Russia does not have the resources for that kind of operation.

'Siberia could shut down the oil for a while, and get along just fine. Moscow, and Russia with it, would perish. You still wonder why Mr Masorin is no longer alive?'

Both men gazed across the pond for a minute. Finally, Jimmy broke the silence.

'And what will happen now?'

'Who knows? But I imagine there is seething anger in Siberia. They will have guessed what happened to their leader, and I imagine they will begin to level huge demands at Moscow. Always with the unspoken threat: *Whose oil is it anyway?*

'Jesus. Moscow will not love that,' said Jimmy, unnecessarily.

'No, they most certainly will not.'

The two men continued their slow walk around the memorial garden, silent again. Eventually Lenny said, 'Have you finished with me? We just took delivery of some surveillance film from the White House. There was a camera on during that dinner and we might just see who delivered the fatal attack on Masorin.'

'Probably just one of their goons,' said Jimmy. 'And it's dollars to doughnuts he's safely tucked up in bed in Moscow by now.'

'I agree. But we may recognise him. Or *I* may. And we'll slip his name into one of our little black books, hah?'

'Yeah, I guess so. Thanks for the geopolitical lesson, Lenny. It's bloody unbelievable how much trouble the oil industry causes, eh?'

'Especially since it's mostly owned by despots, hooligans and villains . . .'

Jimmy chuckled. Ahead, he saw his field-officer guide from the Russian desk appear, ready to walk him back to the parking lot.

'Bye, Lenny – stay in touch.'

And Jimmy watched the double agent from Bucharest walk away, on little spring-heeled steps, still smiling as he made his way back into one of the most secretive buildings on Earth.

0800 (local time) Monday 20 September
Western Siberia

Winter had arrived early on the great marshy plains above the oilfields. And the road up to Noyabrsk was already becoming treacherous. Two hours out of the industrial oil town of Surgut, heading north, a mere 400 miles south of the Arctic Circle, the huge articulated truck from the OJSC oil giant had its windshield wipers flailing against the vicious snow flurries which would soon turn the ice-bound landscape milk white.

Temperatures had plummeted during the night and the great wheels of the truck thundered over ice crystals already forming on the highway. In the passenger seat, Jaan Valuev, President of the OJSC Surgutneftgas Corporation, sat grimly staring into the desolate emptiness ahead, clutching his arctic mittens.

Jaan was a Siberian by birth, a billionaire by way of hard, relentless work. He hailed from Surgut, back south on the banks of the Ob, the fourth-largest river in the world. His mission today was secret, and he travelled in the truck to preserve his anonymity. Out here, in the purpose-built dormitory towns which surrounded the oil rigs, the icicles had ears and the clapboard walls had eyes.

Jaan Valuev wanted no one to know of his presence in Noyabrsk. So far, except for Boris and Sergei, only the driver knew he was on his way. And the big truck kept going, fast, the speedometer hovering at 120 k.p.h., great tracks of pine and birch forest occasionally flashing past, but mostly just bleak white flatland, bereft of human life, the icy wilderness of the West Siberian Basin.

They came rolling into Noyabrsk shortly before nine a.m. The

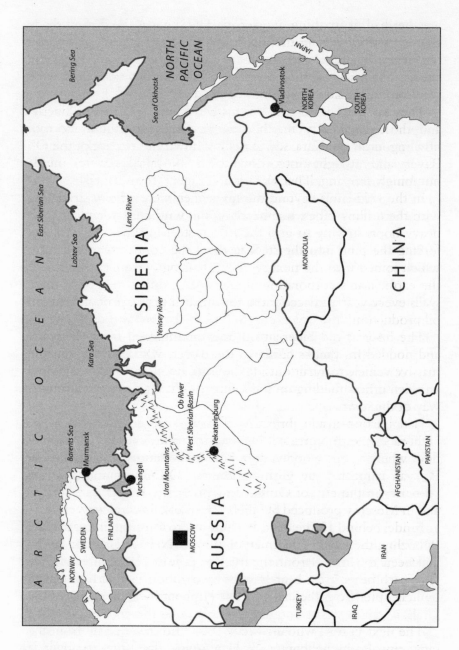

Russia, showing the dividing line of the Ural mountains. To the east lie the vast plains of Siberia, all the way to the Pacific Ocean.

weather had, if anything, worsened. The sky was the darkest shade of grey, with lowering thunderheads. The temperature was minus ten degrees Celsius, and malicious snow flurries sliced down the streets. The locals call them *bozyomkas* and, as *bozyomkas* went, these were on the far side of venomous.

They say there is no cold on this Earth quite like that of Siberia, and those gusts, fifty m.p.h. straight off the northern ice cap, howling in off the Kara Sea, shrieking down the estuary of the Ob River and straight into downtown Noyabrsk, were mind-numbingly freezing. That was cold.

In the wild lands beyond the town men were already struggling with the drilling pipes, manhandling the writhing hydraulics, their heavy boots striving to grip the frozen steel of the screw-drill rig, forcing the pipe into the steel teeth of the connector mechanism which joined it to the next segment, lancing two miles down into the earth. Jaan's corporation alone, OJSC, drilled ninety of these wells every year and accounted for thirteen per cent of all Russian oil production.

The 52-year-old Siberian oil boss disembarked from the truck and nodded his thanks curtly to the driver, who had brought the massive vehicle to a halt outside the main doorway of a three-storey wooden office building on a side street right off the main through-way of the town.

Jaan hurried inside, brushing the snow off his fur coat as he entered the warm corridor. He walked briskly upstairs to the first floor where a large wooden door bore the lettering SIBNEFT – the Russian name for the gigantic Siberian Oil Corporation, whose refineries in the city of Omsk, down near the Kazakhstan border, and in Moscow produced 500,000 barrels of oil products every day.

Inside, behind a large desk, in front of a roaring log fire, sat Sergei Pobozhiy, the fabled Chairman of Sibneft. Neither Jaan nor Sergei had been to this oil-frontier town for at least two years and they gave each other great bear-hugs of recognition. Sergei had arrived by helicopter from the city of Yekaterinburg in the foothills of the Urals.

The next visitor, who arrived at 9.30, had travelled up from the same city also by helicopter. Boris Nuriyev, first Vice-President of Finance at the colossal restructured Lukoil Corporation, was a stranger to Jaan and Sergei, but all three of them were Siberian-born, and all three of them had been close friends with the late Mikhail Masorin. This time they shook hands formally and sat down, drinking black coffee while they awaited the arrival of the fourth and final member of the meeting.

He came through the door at 9.40, direct from the rough little Noyabrsk airport. His private corporate jet had landed directly into the teeth of the wind and had almost been blown off the runway. The government car which picked him up was a black Mercedes limousine, with chains already fitted to the tyres. A gift from the Chinese government.

Roman Rekuts, a big man, well over six foot, three inches, gave no bear hugs, mainly because he might have crushed the spines of the other three men. But each of them shook hands warmly with the last arrival, welcoming the new head of the Urals Federal District, the man who had replaced Mikhail Masorin. A Siberian-born politician, Rekuts had served under Masorin for four years.

Sergei Pobozhiy motioned for Roman Rekuts to remove his coat and to sit in the big chair behind the desk. The Sibneft boss poured fresh cups of coffee for them all, and suggested that the new Urals minister begin proceedings. Nothing written down, just an informal chat between four of the most influential men in Siberia.

'Well,' Rekuts began, 'we are unanimous that Moscow agents assassinated Mikhail Masorin. The American newspapers confirm the findings of the autopsy, and the coroner in Washington is expected to deliver a verdict that Masorin was murdered by a person or persons unknown.

'I imagine that the Russian security contingent which travelled to the United States with the Russian president will maintain the Americans must have done it. Of course, no one is going to believe that – or, at least, the Americans won't.

'Gentlemen, we are discussing here a matter of approach. What is it we want?' Rekuts paused briefly, looking at each of them in turn. 'We want revenge, and we want money. The export taxes on Siberian oil, levied by Moscow are very high and we do not get even a reasonable share of it.

'It would obviously suit us much better if the oil corporations – your good selves that is – paid a higher tariff to Siberia, and made the central government both pay a higher price for domestic oil and then share some of their huge export-tax revenues with the country of origin. That's us.'

'Of course, we are not really a country,' said Boris thoughtfully. 'We are, and always have been, a part of Russia.'

'A situation which could probably be changed,' said Sergei. 'Let's face it, Siberia really is a separate entity. The Urals form a great natural barrier between us and European Russia. We're talking a 1,200-mile range of mountains stretching north–south all the way from the Arctic Circle to Kazakhstan. That's a barrier, a true break point. Enough to discourage anyone from using force against us.'

'True enough,' Jaan agreed. 'And the Russian government knows it has no possibility of suppressing us by force. Even the mighty army of Nazi Germany never penetrated the Urals. We're safe from invasion, and the Chinese love us, so we don't have that much to fear. If we demand financial justice, Moscow will have little choice but to give it to us.'

Sergei, who, with Masorin gone, was probably the most militant of them, spoke again. 'We could just round up the other two Siberian regions and inform Moscow that we plan to secede from the Russian Federation. Just like the smaller countries did from the Soviet Union.

'We would continue with trade agreements, much like the present status quo. But in the absence of cooperation from Moscow, and due to their participation in the murder of the leader of the Urals Federal District, we would state that we intend from now on to call the shots financially, control our own oil, and increase our trade with China.'

'To which they would say, "No. Out of the question",' said Roman, mildly.

'Then we issue our first veiled threat that there may be some interruption in production,' replied Sergei.

The room fell silent. The snow squalls lashed against the double-glazed windows, and the wind howled.

'You hear that weather out there?' said Sergei. 'That is our greatest strength. Because you have to be Siberian to work out here, to cope with the terrible conditions. I know we ship in labour for the rigs from Belarus and other cold climates. But the bedrock of our workforce is Siberian. Without native labour the entire oil industry would collapse. No one else is tough enough to stand the harsh environment.'

'Gentlemen, how serious are you about a declaration of independence?' Roman was pensive.

'Not very, I don't think,' said Boris. 'But I think we all believe the threat would send a lightning bolt through the Russian government that would quickly bring about an agreement that the Siberian regions deserve more from the treasure which lies under their own lands. It's really the only recompense the people have.'

'The expressed intention of opening up increased trade with China would frighten them,' said Jaan. 'We already have shortages and bottlenecks on the pipelines. If Moscow thought we intended to ship more and more oil down the new pipeline to China I think they'd be very nervous. Especially if we were getting a much better price for it.'

'And of course we ought not to forget the new tanker terminal in Murmansk,' added Boris. 'Right now we're shipping 1.5 million barrels of Siberian crude a day directly from the Barents Sea to the east coast of the United States. Moscow would hate to jeopardise that.'

'Any shortages up there would infuriate them. But they already know the danger. And they know the sympathies of the big oil corporations are very much in favour of the Siberians. Especially as so many of us *are* Siberians. The truth is, Siberia not only owns the oil, Siberia also controls it.'

Outside the ice storm continued to blow from the north. Sergei stood up and placed another couple of logs on the fire, saying quietly as he did so, 'Moscow is 1,500 miles from us. So if we decide to increase our production to China, there's nothing they can do about it. Except negotiate – on our terms. And the murder of Masorin has not helped their cause, either in this room or out there among the people.'

'Gentlemen, I think this calls for a summit meeting, sometime in the next ten days. Is that likely to be possible?' Roman was getting down to brass tacks.

'Yes. I think we could manage that,' replied Sergei. 'Say three top oil executives – ourselves – and perhaps three more, plus four or five major Siberian politicians, Roman and the other two regional leaders plus two energy ministers from the Urals Federal District and maybe the other Mikhail, the one from the Far East.'

'Place?' said Roman.

'Well, it can't be out here,' stated Boris. 'We'll be lucky to keep this little gathering under wraps, even if we get out the moment the weather slows down. I'd suggest Yekaterinburg, because it's bigger, more anonymous, and we can arrive from several different directions. It doesn't matter if any individual one of us is recognised, so long as no one knows we're meeting together.'

'It's important we show Moscow a united front which truly represents the will not only of the Siberian oil industry but of the Siberian people,' said Roman. 'They can't assassinate us all, can they?'

'I suppose not,' muttered Sergei.

Lenny Suchov was on the secure line from CIA headquarters. Lt. Commander Ramshawe took the call.

'You heard the verdict, Jimmy? It's all over the papers this morning.'

'Sure did. Murder by persons unknown.'

Lenny went on, hardly listening. 'We got a picture of the guy who probably shot the curare into Masorin's neck. Only from the back. But he's a big guy, and he's leaning over talking. We've checked every inch of the surveillance film. No one else got that close all evening, at least not while Masorin was dining.' He sounded excited, but then added more soberly: 'The FBI are making formal inquiries at the Russian embassy, showing them our film, but the guy is back in Russia. And word is the White House does not want this to go much further. We got major oil trade agreements with Moscow, and the new export route from Murmansk is working well and profitably for everyone. Guess the President doesn't want to piss 'em off any more than we already have.'

'That'd be right,' said Jimmy. 'Anyway, in the end, it's nothing to do with us, really. It's a Russian murder and a Russian matter . . . Anything else?'

Lenny took a breath, then said quietly, 'One of our guys in the Siberian oilfields thinks something is brewing up there, politically.'

'Yeah?'

'Apparently, earlier today—'

'You can't get much bloody earlier . . .'

Lenny chuckled. 'Pay attention, young Ramshawe,' he said. 'Otherwise I'll have you assassinated. As I was saying, one of our guys was out at the little airport in Noyabrsk when a private jet landed, bearing none other than Roman Rekuts – that's the new political chief who's replaced Masorin as boss of the Urals Federal District.

'Anyway, our man tracked him into the town and saw him go into the Sibneft offices where he stayed for three hours. Our guy sat in his car, just up the street, in a snowstorm, and saw Jaan Valuev leave the same building – he's the billionaire who runs OJSC, one of the biggest oil companies in Russia. Our man did not see anyone else leave, and he waited until dark at four p.m. But Valuev was picked up by an articulated truck, right across the street.'

'Is all that significant?' asked Jimmy.

'Well, they were in these small Sibneft site offices. You know, that's the enormous Siberian Oil Corporation. We got the biggest man in the business, Jaan Valuev, sneaking in and out of articulated trucks, and the political boss of Western Siberia showing up for just three or four hours. Sounds like a serious powwow to me.'

'You think it has something to do with Masorin's murder?'

'I've no doubt they mentioned it. But the Siberian oil establishment is restless at the moment. They're sick of Moscow, dying to trade more with China, and when two or three very big cheeses start meeting in secret, in the wilds of the western Siberian plains, it's good to know.'

'I guess it is,' said Jimmy. 'And I'm going to record all of this in my files. Although I'm not quite sure whether it'll ever see the light of day again.'

'If Russia suddenly attacks its Siberian colonies and causes a world war, you'll be glad I called you, hah? Glad to know Lenny was still steering you straight!'

'I'm always glad of that, old mate,' replied Jimmy. 'Dad's coming down to Washington for a couple of weeks soon – will you have dinner with us?'

'That would be very nice. Goodbye now – how you say? – "old mate".'

1530 Monday 27 September
Eastern foothills of the Ural Mountains

The city of Yekaterinburg lies 1,130 miles east of Moscow. It is a city of a million souls, a light, airy modern place with wide avenues, parks and gardens. Many of its historic public buildings are constructed in the same fawn-and-white stucco as those in faraway St Petersburg.

Some of the more elegant architecture of the old city, dating back to the 1720s, has been preserved; not, however, the Ipatyev house which stood on a piece of land opposite the cream-and-turquoise tower of the Old Ascension Church. The house was long gone, bulldozed on the orders of Leonid Brezhnev. Today there is just a stark white memorial cross among a stand of trees.

It marks the spot where, on 16 April 1918, Tsar Nicholas II, his wife, son and daughters were slaughtered in the basement of the merchant Ipatyev's residence, gunned down, bayonetted and bludgeoned by the secret police squad which had been guarding them on behalf of the Bolsheviks.

The name Yekaterinburg will always stand as a symbol of those brutal murders. As if to make sure that no one ever forgets, a statue stands there, right in the middle of Central Avenue, the former Lenin Street, of Yakov Sverdlov, the organiser of the killings.

Not a hundred feet from the statue, in another basement, the lowest floor of an office building owned by Sibneft, one of the most secret meetings ever to be held in Yekaterinburg was taking place. Certainly it was one of the most clandestine gatherings in the city since the days leading up to the death of Tsar Nicholas and his family.

At the head of a long polished oak table sat the towering figure of Roman Rekuts. At the far end sat Sergei Pobozhiy, Chairman of Sibneft, flanked by his two co-conspirators, the billionaire Jaan Valuev from OJSC Surgutneftgas and the powerful Lukoil Financial Vice-President, Boris Nuriyev.

The First Minister of the Central Siberian Federal District was there, together with the new Chief Executive of the Russian Far East who had brought his Energy Minister, Mikhail Pavlov.

Roman Rekuts had brought his new deputy with him, and Sergei Pobozhiy was accompanied by his West Siberian Chief of Operations, the grizzled, beefy ex-drillmaster on the exploration rigs, Anton Katsuba.

Every one of the nine men in the room was Siberian-born. And not one of them failed to be attracted by the prospect of a clean break with Moscow. Of forming a new Republic of Siberia, a free and independent state with its own flag and currency. Yekaterinburg already had its own flag, a white, green and black tricolour, and there was even talk of a Urals franc.

But the meeting was collectively certain of one sacrosanct rule: they must keep their close ties to Moscow in the oil business while retaining the freedom to trade with their anxious, more affluent industrial neighbours to the south and east, in the People's Republic of China.

There had been instant camaraderie in the boardroom since the meeting began, as men with similar stated aims excitedly pointed out the advantages of such freedom to the energy corporations and to the people of Siberia alike. They had begun at three p.m. and intended to proceed until dinner, which would be taken at the big table, before finishing their communiqué to Moscow.

But the meeting ended early. Just after 4.30 p.m. the double

33

doors of the boardroom were booted open and an armed Soviet-style guard in a military uniform bearing no insignia crashed through the door, aimed his Kalashnikov assault rifle and opened fire. Three bullets punched in a dead straight line into Roman Rekuts's forehead.

In a split second a lot more guards were in the room. They cut down Sergei Pobozhiy with a hail of bullets to the neck and chest, and they blew away Jaan Valuev in the same way.

Boris Nuriyev stood up and held his hands out in front of him, futilely trying to block the fusillade of bullets in the fleeting miniseconds before he too was gunned down. He fell forward, his blood pooling onto the rough draft of the demands that he and his colleagues had been going to present to Moscow.

Anton Katsuba, who'd been seated at the centre of the table opposite the boardroom doors, had slipped down out of sight. But the big man made a stupendous comeback, rising up from under the seats like a rogue elephant and clamping a mighty hand around the windpipe of one of the attackers.

By now he was the only one of the nine conspirators left alive. In the moment of stunned confusion he grabbed the guard's rifle and opened fire, killing two of the soldiers and wounding three more before he was cut down in a hail of bullets from the remaining six. Just minutes earlier the room had had an atmosphere of excitement, energy and optimism. Now it resembled a slaughterhouse, the carpet awash with blood, the walls splattered with gore and riddled with bullet holes. It was a grotesque scene, all too reminiscent of the events of 16 April 1918 that had taken place in the old Ipatyev basement not so far away.

One difference was that these modern soldiers of the Russian Federation would have no need for the bayonets that had been used to finish off the Tsar and his family. There was no need to plunge cold steel into the bodies of the oilmen and the Siberian politicians as the guards had done to finish Nicholas, and the Empress Alexandra, the little boy Alexi, and the Grand Duchesses Marie and Olga, and Tatiana and Anastasia.

The ripping slugs of modern AK-47s were a lot more efficient than the bullets of the old service revolvers of the early twentieth-century. Not one of the original nine men who had assembled in this room was now breathing.

Elsewhere pandemonium reigned. The Russian army, which had roared into Central Avenue from the nearby headquarters, had sealed off the entire thoroughfare. Outside the building there were three large army trucks and one military ambulance.

Stretcher parties were running in through the main doors. Everyone working in the building remained at their desks. Armed guards were posted at every door. Huge green screens were erected to shield the main entrance from the public's gaze, and they also concealed the rear of the trucks. Soldiers with body bags were sprinting down the stairs to the basement. More servicemen with ladders, paintbrushes and rollers, cans of paint and containers of ammonia, were descending the steps in single file.

Everything from the room was being removed: eleven dead bodies, three wounded guards, the big table, carpets, chairs, papers. Everything. Behind the screen outside the door the army trucks were being loaded, their engines revving.

The first of them, the one containing all the bodies, was under way less than twenty minutes after the opening burst of fire had cut down Roman Rekuts. It swung out of Central Avenue heading north, directly towards the Arctic tundra north-east of the Ural Mountains on the estuary of the Ob River.

The truck containing the bloodstained carpets and furniture was next, roaring up the snowy street and, like its predecessor, heading north. The ambulance was next, then the final truck, carrying the screens and with a dozen infantrymen in the back to assist with the burning and general destruction of the evidence when they finally reached their destination in the small hours of the morning.

The Russian military had shown itself at its most thorough. No one would ever know the fate of the nine men who had sought freedom for their homeland of Siberia to trade its oil without the heavy yoke of the Russian government around its necks.

Perhaps even more sinister, no one would ever know how Moscow had found out the meeting was taking place. But, as they say in the Siberian oil industry, even the icicles have ears and the wooden walls have eyes.

Midday (local time) Tuesday 28 September
Private residence of the Russian president, Moscow

There were just three visitors this morning: the Commander-in-Chief of the Russian army, east of the Urals; the head of the FSB, who was rapidly developing a reputation similar to that of his many KGB predecessors; and the Russian Energy Minister, Oleg Kuts.

'Anyone heard anything?' asked the Russian president.

'Not a word, sir. It seems no one knew who was in the meeting, no one knew what had happened, no one saw the clean-up, and no one's heard a word since. So far, that is.'

'Good,' said the president. 'Very good. Please congratulate your commander on a very skilful job, very well executed.'

'I'll make a point of it,' said the Russian general, kicking the heels of his jackboots together to make an exaggerated sharp crack.

'No word from inside the oil industry, I trust?'

'Nothing, sir,' replied Oleg Kuts. 'But that's understandable, since it seems no one has any idea who was in that room. I don't suppose anyone will realise they're missing for another twenty-four hours at least.'

The Russian leader turned to the sallow-faced head of the FSB. 'Your men found out anything?'

'Not really, sir. Except that at least six of the men in the basement travelled to Yekaterinburg by completely different routes. None of them travelled together, and they used private planes, helicopters and cars, and two of them at least finished the journey on the trans-Siberian railway, one from the east, one from the west.'

'A very secret meeting, eh?'

'Yes, sir. Highly classified.'

'We were certainly on the right lines, then?'

'Most definitely, sir.'

'But in my view this all leads to one inevitable conclusion, gentlemen: we can't go on doing this sort of thing. And I truly do not know how long we can keep the lid on Siberia. In the end they are going to try again, because the temptation of riches from China is simply too great.'

The Russian president looked at his men, his eyes thoughtful, speculative.

'We need to home in on at least one major foreign oil supplier who is not in Siberia. We cannot have all our eggs in that one huge basket.'

'I know, sir. But these days, anyone who has any oil whatsoever is desperate to hang on to it and reap the rewards themselves. No one will share their resources.'

The Russian president smiled thinly. 'We may have to use our powers of persuasion. Minister, you should conduct an immediate study and find a new supplier with substantial reserves, who might be – shall we say – vulnerable . . .'

CHAPTER TWO

J aan Valuev, had for the past six years led something of a double life. As the hard-driving boss of OJSC he was the very picture of a New Russian industrialist, a suave, well-tailored chief executive, presiding over the fortunes of an oil giant with an income of more than $6 billion a year, annual growth of seventeen per cent, and 100,000 employees.

His wife had died four years previously, and at the age of fifty-two Jaan still lived in the grand mansion on the edge of the city of Surgut where they had brought up their two children. Both boys were now studying engineering at the Urals State Technical University in Yekaterinburg, alma mater of Russia's first President, Boris Yeltsin, and his long-suffering wife Naya.

This university was the largest east of the Ural Mountains and had once boasted twelve graduates on the Central Committee of the Communist Party. Jaan Valuev was its biggest private benefactor, and unlike all the other Russian oil chiefs he also heavily supported social programmes in his home town of Surgut. Generally speaking, Jaan Valuev had been a pillar of Siberian society.

But there was another side to him. Instead of the traditional lavish dacha on one of the more scenic coastlines of the Black Sea, Jaan preferred western Europe. He owned a spectacular beachfront estate two miles east of the Marbella Club in Andalusia, southern Spain, and kept a permanent $300-a-night suite at the superb Hotel Colon on Cathedral Avenue in the heart of Barcelona.

He owned an opulent white-fronted Georgian house in The Boltons, off London's pricey Brompton Road, and a twenty-acre country estate in the hills above the Thameside village of Pangbourne in Berkshire. He had found his way into this glorious English countryside through his great friend, the urbane multi-millionaire publisher, hotelier and soccer fanatic John Madejski, chairman of Reading Football Club and owner of the towering modern stadium on the borders of the M4 motorway.

It was this love of soccer that had brought the two men together. In 2009, upstart little Reading had fought its way to the English Premier League and had ended up playing mighty Barcelona in front of 60,000 people in the European Champions League at the Noucamp Stadium in Spain's second city.

And who should emerge that day, almost shyly, as the great new power in the Barcelona club? The billionaire behind some of the biggest player-transfer deals in the history of Spanish football – Jaan Valuev. Barcelona beat Reading 4–1, but the Siberian entrepreneur and the English tycoon became instant pals, and Jaan bought a house just two miles from the imposing Madejski estate in Berkshire.

By 2010, Jaan Valuev was chairman of Barcelona FC. And tonight, Tuesday, 28 September, Barcelona were in London for the European Champions League game against England's greatest football club: Arsenal, founded in 1823 and the by-word for excellence and sportsmanship in a sometimes tarnished world game. Barcelona versus The Gunners in the ultra-modern new Emirates Stadium in the heart of North London, a game to be savoured by aficionados. And 60,000 fans, 8,000 of them from Spain, were already making their way across London by taxi, bus and subway to watch this clash of titans, the champions of the Spanish League against the champions of England's Premiership.

Inside the marble halls of the Emirates Stadium arrangements had been made for a sumptuous VIP dinner at 8.45 p.m. immediately after the game. The Arsenal chairman would host it and among his guests would be the Barcelona chairman and his buddy John Madejski – who was rumoured to be preparing a sensational bid to buy Arsenal Football Club in partnership with Jaan Valuev.

But these awesome financial shenanigans were all taken in good heart, and the game was under way right on time with the stadium packed. There was only one blot on the big-game landscape: the conspicuous absence of Jaan Valuev, whose body was in a mass grave deep in the icy wastes of the arctic tundra in Northern Siberia.

The seat next to John Madejski was empty. It was still empty when Barcelona scored, and when the teams came in for half-time. The Barcelona deputy chairman, Andre de Stefano, was absolutely mystified.

'I have an e-mail from his secretary, dated yesterday. He was flying in today directly from Yekaterinburg in a private jet owned by Emirates Airlines. I have the flight arrival time but the airline guys say he never boarded the plane.'

'Well, where the hell is he?' asked the Reading chairman.

'Tell you the truth, we thought *you'd* probably know.'

'I haven't spoken to him since Sunday when he said he'd see me here for a glass of wine before the kick-off.'

'So unlike him,' said Andre, 'to have informed no one he wasn't coming. Something must have happened.'

'Well, it's close to midnight in his part of Russia,' replied John Madejski. 'His office is shut, and I tried his mobile twenty minutes ago and it was switched off – so perhaps he had to fly somewhere else first and will get here for the second half. That's a huge business he runs.'

'I still think it's totally unlike him to vanish without informing anyone. But . . . maybe a girl friend?' chuckled De Stefano.

'What! Instead of watching the game against Arsenal? No chance,' replied Madejski.

And so the second half kicked off without Jaan Valuev. Arsenal scored three times to thunderous roars which could have been heard in Piccadilly Circus six Underground stops away.

The game ended and the dinner began, with places rearranged to close the gap left by the absent Siberian soccer chief.

At the end of the evening, as John Madejski slipped out of the stadium where his chauffeur Terry had the big blue Rolls-Bentley waiting, a reporter from the London *Daily Telegraph* approached the Reading chairman for a quote about the game. But what he really wanted was a quote about the rumoured bid to buy Arsenal.

John Madejski would usually have been far too wily to fall for that. But he was worried about Jaan and replied somewhat abstractedly. 'It was a wonderful game,' he said, 'played with great spirit. We saw four superb goals and Arsenal deserved their victory.' Lost in thought, he added more to himself than to the reporter, 'To tell you the truth, it was a little disappointing for me, because Mr Valuev was unable to get here. I'm mystified as to why he would miss this important event. He would have loved it, even though his beloved Barcelona lost.'

The football writer couldn't believe his luck that the normally taciturn Madejski had let this nugget of information slip, especially on the heels of all the rumours about the acquisition of AFC. The info was too late for tonight's report. That was already filed. But tomorrow's follow-up to the biggest game of the season would carry the headline and sub-head:

SIBERIAN OIL BILLIONAIRE
MISSES BARCELONA'S BIG ONE
Mystery of Jaan Valuev's
Arsenal No-Show

The report that followed argued that Jaan had missed the game because of the protracted speculation that he and John Madejski might be scheming to buy Arsenal Football Club.

The report quoted Madejski as saying, 'Rubbish.' And the Barcelona club as saying they were not privy to all of their chairman's travel arrangements. No, they had not heard from him since the defeat in North London.

Yes, they were quite certain he would be back in the directors' box for the game against Spanish rivals Real Madrid at the Bernabeu Stadium in the Spanish capital a week from Saturday.

1100 Friday 1 October
National Security Agency, Fort Meade, Maryland

Lt. Commander Jimmy Ramshawe was in heaven. Or as near to heaven as an organisational hell such as his own office permitted. A colleague from the National Surveillance Office just returned from Europe had dropped him off a pristine copy of yesterday's London *Daily Telegraph*.

This was a fairly regular occurrence up here on the eighth floor behind the massive one-way glass walls of the OPS-2B Building. Lt. Commander Ramshawe's voracious appetite for top foreign newspapers was well known.

Leaning back in his swivel chair, feet on the desk, he sipped a cup of fresh coffee, before reaching for his newspaper and turning to his favourite pages. Not much going on in London today, though, and he flicked through the newspaper until he finally landed on the sports pages.

And there one word jumped straight out at him. *SIBERIAN.*

Right in the headline. If the word had been set in smaller type he'd almost certainly have missed it.

But there was no missing this. *SIBERIAN OIL BILLIONAIRE.*

'Hello,' said Jimmy. 'One of the late Mr Masorin's mates. What's he done to get himself in with the bloody football players?'

One minute later: 'Christ, the bugger's vanished. Those Siberians aren't having much luck lately.'

He perused the article once more, then picked up his phone and called Lenny Suchov. Just a hunch.

'Lenny, you seen anything about this Siberian oil guy who's gone missing?'

'Funny you should mention that. We just got a highly-classified report in from our man up in Noyabrsk pointing out the Chairman of Sibneft – that's the Siberian Oil Corporation – has vanished, not been seen for two or three days.

'Our guys think he may have been snatched by agents of Moscow and put in the slammer just like they did to poor old Mikhail Khodorkovsky, the biggest Yukos oil shareholder, six years ago. But how the hell did you find out about it?'

'I've just read it in the London *Daily Telegraph*.'

'Impossible. This has only just broken. It's not even in the Russian newspapers yet.'

'Maybe not, but the old Siberian was supposed to be at a football game a coupla nights ago in London and he never showed.'

'A what!'

'A football game. He's the chairman of Barcelona.'

'What the hell are you talking about? The missing Siberian is called Sergei Pobozhiy. And he's supposed to be at Sibneft's northern site office near the oilfield in the West Siberian basin. Not at a football game.'

Jimmy grappled with the London broadsheet. 'Different guy. My man's called Jaan Valuev. He's the boss of some Russian oil company but it doesn't say here which one. Anyway, it *does* say he's vanished.'

'Christ, Jimmy, that's two missing and one dead in the last couple of weeks, all major Siberians. What's going on?'

'Beats the hell outta me, old mate.'

'OK, I'll get another couple of field agents on this. Tell you what. I'll keep you posted. But this isn't anything military, or to do with national security. Give me a call in an hour, and I'll tell you where we stand.'

The president of Russia, a big bear of a man with ruddy cheeks and a loud voice and a former deputy head of the Soviet secret police, missed the old sledgehammer rule of the authoritarian central government more than most.

He rubbed along adequately with both houses of the Russian parliament – the Duma – but as the elected head of state he had enormously broad powers, including the appointment of his deputy, the prime minister, and all government ministers.

Some presidents of the Russian Federation were more approachable than others. This one was very remote, yearning in his heart for the old days of the Politburo and the huge brutal power of the Soviet machine which could deal with any 'trouble' instantly and ruthlessly. This president was not really a committee man.

If anyone had found out what had been perpetrated at the oil summit in Siberia he might very well have faced a career-ending onslaught in the Duma. But this president held power, like so many of his recent predecessors, with an iron grip. The Duma found out only what he wanted them to know.

Russia was ruled from this grand suite of offices where the president now sat, sipping coffee at the head of a highly polished table. With him were four men, gathered in the domed rotunda on the second floor of the Senate building, the ultimate seat of Russian power, situated on the east side of the Kremlin.

The great yellow and white triangular, eighteenth-century neoclassical edifice, stood east of Peter the Great's arsenal building, alongside the old 1930s Supreme Soviet and behind the ramparts flanking the Senate Tower. Like the current Russian president, Vladimir Ilyich Lenin had both lived and worked in the Senate building, a historical fact very much appreciated by the reigning president. Even better did the leader in 2010 like the fact that this rotunda had hosted the Red Army Supreme Command under Stalin.

The Russian president sat back in his chair, feeling – as he always did in the rotunda – a vast sense of confidence, impregnability, and destiny. The men who depended entirely upon him for their exalted positions and grandiose lifestyles would hang upon his every word.

The president smiled at those whose undying trust he enjoyed. There was Prime Minister Valery Kravchenko, who like himself was a native of St Petersburg. Also present were the current head of the FSB, Boris Patrushov, the Energy Minister, Oleg Kuts, and the Minister for Foreign Affairs, Oleg Nalyotov, strutting around in his vast authority, pompously occupying the office once held by the great Andrei Gromyko.

The last man at the table, placed to the right of Nalyotov, was Gregor Komoyedov, the former Moscow oil executive who now had taken over the critically important Ministry for Foreign Trade. Above them all fluttered the white, blue and red horizontal tricolour of the Russian Federation, high atop the flagstaff at the pinnacle of the rotunda.

Twelve hundred metres to the south, the Moscow River flowed icily eastwards, lazily as Russian history. And beyond the great Senate Tower, in Red Square, a thousand tourists stared up and over the Kremlin ramparts, most of them gazing at the towering gilded dome of Ivan the Great's Bell Tower, still the tallest structure in the Kremlin, and once the tallest building in Moscow. From the wide windows of the rotunda the Russian president and his colleagues could see the riotous colours, the greens, the yellows and the blood-red livery of St Basil's Cathedral with its twisting domes jutting skywards to the south of Red Square.

'Gentlemen,' said the president. 'First of all, I think we owe a vote of thanks to Boris Patrushov, to the brilliant way in which he first located and then dealt with that treasonous and seditious conference which took place in Yekaterinburg. I think our shared role model, the late First Secretary, Leonid Brezhnev, would have been very proud.'

The head of the FSB looked down modestly at his notes and said quietly, 'Thank you, comrade. But I should say that our success was due entirely to the very alert observation of our little mole in the office of the chairman of the Siberian Oil Corporation. The rest was routine for me. That conference represented a threat to the Russian people. A threat to the bedrock of our economy. It had to be extinguished.

'We have probably suppressed it for maybe five or six years. But we have not killed it. Not that we could ever kill it. The will of the Siberians to profit and prosper from the oil and gas which lies beneath their godforsaken frozen soil will surely assert itself again.

'But first I would like to deal with more immediate matters. The – er – termination of the careers of the treacherous men who gathered in Yekaterinburg on Monday. Plainly they will be missed. Probably already have been—'

Foreign Minister Nalyotov intervened. 'With respect, comrade, the Western press has already picked up a lead on the disappearance of Jaan Valuev, the Surgutneftgas President . . . apparently failed to turn up at some soccer game . . . caused questions in sports circles . . . now we have formal inquiries from the foreign media asking if he's been found.'

The president nodded, very seriously. 'Anything else?' he asked.

'Well, they also seem to think Sergei Pobozhiy, the Chairman of Sibneft, has mysteriously vanished. I think Gregor Komoyedov might have some information.' He looked over at the Energy Minister who said, 'Very little, I am afraid. But I understand there have been some serious inquiries inside the corporation as to his whereabouts. The chairman does not often go missing and I did hear they were talking to his wife. That'll be public knowledge in twenty-four hours.'

'Plainly,' said the president, 'we must move on this. I think the best course of action would be an accident in a military aircraft deep in the tundra. We need not give details, as the mission was highly classified. But I have drafted a press release, which should be issued directly from the military.' He opened a slim file and read out the first few paragraphs of a neatly typed document.

'With deep regret we announce the loss of a Russian Air Force jet which disappeared over the Arctic tundra somewhere north of the Siberian oilfields earlier this week. Unfortunately, the aircraft was known to have been transporting several important personnel from the Russian national oil and gas industry, as well as several senior Siberian politicians. Severe weather conditions have made the search for bodies almost impossible.

'Their ultimate destination was Murmansk where an international conference at the new tanker terminals was to have been held. Air Force helicopters are currently in the search area but no wreckage has yet been found, and we have no information on the cause of the crash. Because of the classified nature of the mission the Air Force will not be releasing the names of any of their own personnel.

'Families of the deceased executives and politicians are currently being informed. The government and the military authorities are treating the incident as an accident which occurred in flight, though there will of course be a thorough investigation into the possible reasons why the jet went down.'

'Excellent,' said Boris Patrushov, the relief of a man who had just ordered and masterminded the cold-blooded murders of several innocent Russian civilians clear in his tone of voice. 'It'll take a few days and a few awkward questions. But we'll alert the military media authorities on the procedures we expect them to adopt.

'And we'll make it known that the government would prefer this very sad incident to be treated with care and sensitivity. Sensationalising the death of such men would incur the anger of the authorities. It might also be a good idea to bestow some kind of decorations – medals – on these men who died in the service of their country.'

'Very good idea,' said the president. 'Perhaps the Cross of the Russian Federation for the civilians, and regular combat medals for the pilots.'

'Perfect,' replied Patrushov. 'And of course in the end we'll blame the appalling weather and the impossibility of landing the aircraft after an instrument failure, and an apparent problem with the hydraulics.'

'Yes, I think that will see our little problem off very nicely,' said Prime Minister Kravchenko. 'Very nicely indeed.'

'Meanwhile,' continued the president, 'I think we should discuss the heart of the problem.'

'Which is?' asked Kravchenko.

The president looked grave. He glanced around the small group of men. 'What would become of Mother Russia if ever the Siberians were to succeed in going their own way? They certainly would not be the first of our satellites to do so. But they would be, by a long way, the most dangerous.

'And if they demanded or took far greater licence in deciding the destination of their own oil and gas – well, that could prove nearly fatal for us. Because they would almost certainly turn to China, and a close, cosy relationship between those two, right down at the arse end of the fucking Asian continent would not be great . . .'

'Neither financially, geographically nor diplomatically,' mused Kravchenko. 'World sympathy would immediately swing to Siberia, the poor freezing underclass of the old Soviet Union, never had anything, never been fairly treated by Moscow, struggled with the world's cruellest climate for centuries and now the bullies of the Kremlin want to suppress them yet again—'

'Yes,' the president interrupted. 'I think that was quite sufficiently graphic. And I think I speak for everyone when I say we might, one day, simply lose control of that Siberian oil. We won't be ruined, there'll still be riches and rewards for the Russian government. But it won't be like now. The goose's golden eggs will become a bit more . . . well, brassy.'

The Russian president stood up and pressed a bell for the Senate butler to come through and bring them coffee and sweet pastries. In front of a gigantic portrait of the elderly Catherine the Great accompanied by her brown and white whippet, he exchanged a few words with the man, specifying the precise texture of the thick dark coffee he required and the consistency of the pastries.

Then, almost seamlessly, he picked up where he had left off, proceeding to outline a plan of such terrifying wickedness and treachery that each of the four officials who were listening were stunned into silence.

'We are going to need a new supply of oil,' he said. 'From somewhere in the world where there are ample reserves – billions of barrels of crude – which we can seize. I know it's not going to be easy, and that anyone who has it wants to keep it. But there is a new and very serious player in the game – China. And within a few short years they are going to want every last barrel they can lay their hands on.'

He hesitated for a moment as the door opened again and the butler came in with their coffee. The servant nodded respectfully and set the large silver tray down on an antique sideboard before shuffling back out.

Turning to Energy Minister Kuts, the president said, 'Oleg, read to them those stats you gave me yesterday, will you? I think everyone will be interested, and I would like my memory to be refreshed.'

'Certainly,' replied Kuts, shuffling his files. 'I should perhaps begin by stating that more than fifty-six million cars, vans and sport-utility vehicles are rolling down China's highways at this very moment. That and their other industrial demands account for probably sixteen per cent of the world's energy consumption – second only to the US which gobbles up twenty-four per cent.

'By 2020 it is estimated that China will be very close to that twenty-four per cent – probably using eleven million barrels a day, plus 3.6 trillion cubic feet of natural gas. And that's likely to put their backs to the wall.

'Hardly a day passes without some kind of power outage in China, especially in the winter, when their ageing pipelines occasionally fail. Their electricity grid grows more decrepit every year. Domestic oil output is rapidly declining in the big north-eastern fields around Daqing, and their reserves in far western China mostly lie beneath the high, dry deserts – which means their best shot at claiming those reserves, deep beneath the surface, is going to be very, very expensive.

'That's why, even as we speak, China is out there scouring the globe for new opportunities in oil exploration. They will naturally try to push their way into neighbouring Siberia with promises of a huge Chinese market for local oil. In the meantime, they will be trying hard, financing and trading, to open up oil-exploration fields in Australia, Indonesia, Iran, Kazakhstan, Nigeria, Papua New Guinea and the Sudan.

'Gentlemen, China calls it *supply security*, and the name of that game is diversification. They're in it up to their elbows and we're lagging far behind. We're too dependent on Siberia. We must raise our sights. And I think you will find that our most esteemed leader has some very advanced views on that.

'Yesterday I briefed him as well as I could on the global situation. Who has new oil? Where are the big new fields? Is anyone vulnerable to persuasion? If not, how *can* we persuade them? During the next few minutes, gentlemen, you will hear why our president may one day be talked of in the same breath as Brezhnev, Gorbachev and Yeltsin. The great visionaries of our time.'

The president smiled. 'Thank you for those generous words, Oleg. Let me outline the very obvious difficulties that face us in many of the world's oil-rich countries. Take the Middle East . . . well, we may make some headway there but it would be mostly in Iran. The rest of the Gulf, the principal Arab producers, are always in the hands of the Americans.

'The Saudis, the Emirates, Iraq, Kuwait, Bahrain and Qatar are all controlled by the USA – particularly after the presidency of George W. Bush. None of them move without an OK from the White House.

'Indonesia was once up for grabs. But the Americans are strong there now and the Chinese are getting close. The Brits are running out of North Sea oil altogether. Europe is devoid of all energy resources except coal. The USA will never relinquish any of the oil from the Alaskan fields, and Mexico and Venezuela prefer to deal with Washington. Thanks again to President Bush.'

The Russian president rearranged his papers. 'Which brings us to two of the biggest oil strikes of this century so far – the one on South Georgia, which lies way down in the South Atlantic, uncomfortably close to the Antarctic Circle, and those two huge new oilfields on the Falkland Islands.'

'The Falkland Islands?' exclaimed Oleg Nalyotov. 'That's more hopeless than all the other places put together. It's a British colony which twenty-eight years ago was the scene of one of the most vicious little three-month wars in modern history.

'If you remember, the Argentine military seized it, claimed it and occupied it. And before you could say *niet* the Royal Navy assembled a battle fleet, charged down the Atlantic and did what they said they'd do.

'The Brits blew the invaders off those islands, quite literally, with artillery, guided missiles and bombs. They landed a force of ten thousand and some terrible British admiral sent a big Argentine cruiser, the *General Belgrano*, to the bottom of the Atlantic and drowned more than three hundred sailors.

'My general advice would be not to fool with the Brits. They get very touchy. And I happen to know it's Exxon and British Petroleum who are going to develop those oilfields. That's a US/UK alliance. We should be wary of those two multinationals as well, especially when there's a lot of money involved.'

The president looked up and nodded. 'My dear Oleg,' he said patiently, his earlier warmth cooling a little. 'You do not think for one moment I intend to become involved in a fight with either Britain or them, do you? Frankly, I'd rather fight the Siberians – or the Chinese, for that matter.

'But there is one rather hot-headed little nation which might very easily be persuaded to do our dirty work for us. It's called Argentina, and they are not afraid of anyone when it comes to those islands. The *Malvinas*, they believe, belong to them. The very word *Malvinas* drives them mad.

'Grown Argentine men, military officers, beat their breasts and start raving about how proud they would be if their own sons fought and died for the islands. One of the Argentine admirals in the last conflict stated he would die a happy man if the blood of his son, killed in combat, was to seep into the soil of the *Malvinas*. There is no reason in that country, just passion – *VIVA LAS MALVINAS!* and all that nonsense.

'Their claim is essentially ludicrous, utterly dismissed by London. But with a little clandestine help from us, they might just be persuaded to go at it again. You know, capture the islands, which are scarcely defended, seize the oil, expel the oilmen from

Exxon and Shell. And allow us the rights – in return for a generous royalty.

'We then put in two big Russian oil companies, build them a tanker complex, and sit back and take our cut, in the form of taxes on the oil exported to the Gulf Coast of the United States. Works for everyone, correct?'

'Sir, it is my duty to warn you that the Americans would be absolutely furious and might use military force against the islands,' Krachenko said respectfully but with a note of urgency in his voice.

'I don't think so,' the President retorted. 'The Americans might be furious, but in the end they would do a deal. The Brits, however, would not. They'd attack the islands, just as they did in 1982. But this time they would most certainly lose. And there would be absolutely nothing they could do about it. Everyone involved in our military knows it. Great Britain's Labour governments have weakened their war-fighting capability to a truly stupendous degree.

'They do not have the troops: they have ruthlessly abolished some of their best regiments, merging them, closing them. They have cut back their navy, selling many ships and scrapping others. They've reduced their air combat force to virtually nothing. The Brits would be a pushover.

'The Argentines would crush them. Especially with a little help from us. If I was the British Defence Minister I would not even think about trying to recapture the Falkland Islands, should Argentina decide to claim them.'

The Russian press release was issued by the Russian Air Force in Moscow at midnight. Scarcely changed from the precise wording typed out by the Russian president that morning, it reached the international wire agencies shortly before one a.m. on Saturday.

It was still Friday afternoon in Washington, though. A few papers picked up the item, although most had much more on their minds than an obscure military air crash in Northern Siberia, in which a few oil execs might have perished.

Over on the eighth floor of the National Security Agency, on the other hand, Lt. Commander Jimmy Ramshawe took one glance at the release from Moscow and damn nearly rammed the ceiling with the top of his head as he jumped directly upwards out of his office chair.

'*HOLY SHIT!*' he breathed. And the words on the sheet of copy paper jumped straight out at him . . . *Siberia . . . oil . . . death . . . air crash . . . no trace . . . no details . . . WHOA!*

Having almost walked into the wall with excitement, he reeled around and hit the phone buttons to reach the former assassin in the CIA, Lenny Suchov.

Lenny had clearly been expecting his call. 'I know, I know, Jimmy, I just got it. How *about* that? Something's going on here. I am certain of that.'

'I agree, Lenny. But I'm not sure where to start. I suppose I could get US Air Force Intelligence to find out precisely which aircraft from which base somehow took off and never returned. I could have someone get inside the rescue operation and find out how many Russian aircraft are on the case . . .'

'Jimmy, I think that might prove a waste of time. The Russians would not have bothered to sabotage a damned expensive military aircraft and murder two or three of their own air force officers. It's completely out of character. No, young Jimmy. This aircraft crap is a cover-up. And quite a noisy one. They'll be aware that within a few days there'll be people all over the place trying to solve what the stupid newspapers will call *The Mystery of the Missing Russian Jet* – and they'll have to offer a measure of cooperation.'

'Jesus. This is like listening to Sherlock Holmes. You're more bloody devious than the Russians . . .'

'That, Lt. Commander Ramshawe, is what I believe your government pays me to be.'

Jimmy chuckled. 'Well, former genius of the Black Sea wrestlers, what the hell do we do now?'

'You sit tight. I'm going to get some field agents on the case, simply to find out who died in Siberia. I'm looking for names. The whole list of who's suddenly gone missing. Then we can sit down and try to fit the pieces together. Jimmy, this may actually have much more to do with your area of operations than we think.'

'Sit tight? I'm not sitting bloody tight. I'm phoning the Big Man, right after I contact Admiral Morris.'

Jimmy said goodbye to the spymaster from Langley and punched in an e-mail message for Admiral Morris, his boss, to contact him from the West Coast where he was attending a conference with the FBI in San Diego. He informed the admiral that something had come up concerning the White House murder, and he was proposing to have a chat with Arnold Morgan.

Jimmy then called Admiral Morgan and quickly realised he had done so at a bad time.

'Christ, Ramshawe. It's nearly four bells – I *never* take phone calls on the last dogwatch. I'm trying to get ready for the evening.'

'Sorry, sir. But something's come up you'll want to know about—'

'How the hell do you know what I want to know about . . .?'

'Well, sir, I think—'

'Think, think, think. The whole damned world's thinking, mostly crap. I'm not interested in what you think. Call me with facts, fine. Not goddamned thoughts, hear me?'

'These *are* bloody facts, Admiral, otherwise I wouldn't have called . . .'

'That's entirely different,' the Admiral harrumphed. 'But I'm still busy. Can these facts wait, or is the entire goddamned planet on the brink of war?'

'Not long, sir. This is important.'

'All right, all right. Now listen. In precisely two hours I have to meet Mrs Kathy Morgan in *Le Bec Fin,* one wildly expensive restaurant in the heart of Georgetown on one of the most expensive streets in the free world . . . I suppose you wanna come?'

'Jeez, Admiral. That would be great.' But Jimmy added, after a sudden memory of the Admiral's excellent taste in French wine, 'So long as I don't have to pay.'

And then, realising this might be a good moment to push his luck to the absolute brink, asked, 'Can Jane come?' He knew that Kathy adored his fiancée, but was nonetheless aware that Arnold's answer might not be orthodox. Arnold's answers usually weren't.

'Can Jane come?' he rasped. 'Oh sure, why not check whether there's any other members of her family at a loose end tonight – few cousins, aunts, maybe a coupla neighbours? How about your mom and dad, could they make it down from New York in time? Got any visiting uncles from the goddamned outback, might fancy a bowl of kangaroo soup at a high-class establishment at about twenty-five bucks a spoonful – bring the whole goddamned lot if you like. I'll remortgage the house.'

At the other end of the phone Jimmy was laughing. 'Actually, I meant just Jane, sir,' he said eventually.

''Course she can come,' grunted the Admiral. 'Eight bells. *Le Bec Fin.* And don't be late. My best to your dad.' Bang. Down phone.

Jimmy called Jane at the embassy and told her he'd pick her up at 7.45. Then he spoke to Admiral Morris who was very thoughtful about the Russian press release and what Lenny Suchov had said. 'Good plan to run it past Arnie . . . I'm sorry I can't join you.'

Jimmy resisted the temptation to inform his boss that the merest suggestion of another guest at the table might have sent Arnold into a paroxysm of mock indignation. Instead he just said, 'I'll give him your best, sir. And it sure will be interesting to hear what he thinks about the old Russkis.'

'Jimmy,' said Admiral Morris, 'we know what he thinks about the Russkis. But this press release from their air force will get his attention.'

'It better,' replied his assistant. 'Otherwise I might find myself with the biggest dinner check I ever saw.'

Eight bells. Le Bec Fin
Georgetown, Washington DC

It was raining steadily when Jimmy Ramshawe's black Jaguar came whipping through the puddles and pulled up right outside the entrance to the restaurant. A doorman immediately stepped out with an umbrella and motioned for Jane to jump out.

Then, somewhat surprisingly, he motioned for Jimmy also to disembark. 'Admiral's orders, sir – we're to park the car for you . . . you *are* Lt. Commander Ramshawe, aren't you?'

'That's me, old mate.'

'Yes, I thought so. The Admiral said when some kind of a black English racing car comes speeding up the goddamned road, let the beautiful blonde in the passenger seat out first, then bring the Australian driver in, and park the car.'

'Sounds just like him.'

'Yessir. Remie will take care of you right inside the door.'

The maître d' steered them to the back of the restaurant where Admiral Morgan and Kathy were quietly sipping glasses of a superb 2001 Meursault, which had set the Admiral back almost $100.00. The bottle of white burgundy was in an ice bucket set in a raised stand on the floor at the end of the table.

'Hi, kids,' said Arnold, standing to greet first Jane, then Jimmy, while Kathy got to her feet as well and hugged Jane.

The waiter had already placed two extra wine glasses on the table, and the Admiral dipped into the bucket and pulled out the bottle, splashing it out generously. Never occurred to him that either of his guests could possibly want anything else. And he was dead right about that.

'That, Admiral, is outstanding,' said Jimmy.

'And your new information better be of the same quality,' Arnold grinned. 'Delicate, yet with a powerful core, with deep promise of greater things to come . . .'

'Would you ever listen to his rubbish?' said Kathy, her natural Irish intonations bubbling to the fore. 'He's got more blarney than my grandma, and she lived there, a mile from the castle!'

'Now, Kathryn,' said the Admiral, 'I want you and Jane to have a nice little chat while I listen to the considered Intelligence of young James. That's why he's here.'

The Lt. Commander said nothing. He just produced the copy of the press release from Moscow and handed it to Arnold Morgan.

The Admiral read carefully, his eyebrows slowly raising. 'Holy Mary, Mother of God,' he breathed. 'Those bastards have knocked down a planeload of Siberian oil chiefs – two weeks after murdering another one in the White House.'

'Not quite,' said Jimmy. 'No plane.'

'Huh?' said the Admiral, looking, for once, baffled.

And Jimmy recounted the thoughts of the retired assassin, Lenny Suchov.

Without hesitation, Arnold Morgan said, 'He's absolutely correct. They'd never destroy a perfectly sound military aircraft when they could achieve the same ends with a handful of carbine bullets. Plus, the non-existent air crash makes a perfect cover story – which no one will ever crack. Because it never happened.'

'Right up there in the tundra,' said Jimmy. 'Inside the Arctic Circle, Northern Siberia, where the ground is always frozen, and where a blizzard could cover all traces of any air crash in a couple of hours. It would never be seen again.'

'Do we expect the CIA to come up with an accurate list of the big-deal oil execs who have apparently perished?'

'That's in motion. Lenny Suchov's on the case. He thinks there's one or two very important Siberian politicians involved. And he's absolutely sure the Russian government had 'em all shot.'

'The question is, why?' said Arnold. 'What has the Siberian oil industry done to deserve all this?'

'Who knows? But Lenny thinks it's a problem that occasionally comes to the surface. A kind of undercurrent in Siberia, a belief that the local population does not get a fair share of the wealth which lies under their land. That's mostly oil and gas. But also gold, and the largest diamond fields on Earth.'

'He thinks these guys may have been planning to break free of Moscow, at last?' asked Arnold. 'He thinks the Russians just put down a goddamned revolution?'

'He thinks something was brewing up there. And he feels the full list of who was apparently killed in the air crash will provide some important clues.'

Arnold was pensive. He took another luxurious pull at his Meursault de luxe, as he called it, and said, quietly, at least quietly for him, 'Listen, you guys . . . that's all three of you. I'm going to tell you something about the Russians. You all remember the Cold War, which you doubtlessly assumed was all about the rampant spread of communism and missiles?

'Well, ultimately it wasn't. The great fear in Russia, always has been, was the starvation of its people. Could the gigantic collective farms ever produce enough grain and vegetables to feed the population?

'Mostly the answer to that was no. Year after year, there were dreadful crop failures, and year after year they just somehow muddled along, suffering the most awful privations, sometimes even buying from the West.

'But the great fear of the free world, during the 1960s through the 1980s was that a First Secretary of the Communist Party would suddenly believe that a vast number of his people might starve to death.

'*That* was the great fear of the West. That a Russian leader had to find food to avoid the total collapse of the Soviet Union.

'And, kids, there's only one way for any national leader to get food. He either needs to buy it, or steal it from someone else, marshall its massive Red Army, and march into western Europe in search of food.'

'Sir, are you suggesting what I think you are?' said Jimmy.

'I'm suggesting that yesterday's Russian grain crisis is today's Russian oil crisis. If somehow they lost the Siberian product, I do not know what would happen. But I know this. The Kremlin has been nurturing for several years a user-friendly, modern face. And for them to take action this savage, this darned drastic . . . well, they sure as hell know something about Siberia that we don't. And whatever that may be, it sure scares the bejesus out of them. Russia seems very worried about her oil industry in Siberia. And I think that may lead the Kremlin to start searching far afield for new supplies, something that Russia has not needed to do in the past.'

'Christ, I'd sure hate to wake up and find out they'd conquered Saudi Arabia or somewhere,' interjected Jimmy.

'I don't think we'll find that, kiddo. But we got to watch them, and watch their movements internationally. We got enough trouble with China trying to buy up the entire world's oil supply, without the goddamned Russkis joining in.'

'Well, sir, Lenny's going for the passenger list from the non-existent aircraft in the tundra. It'll sure be interesting to find out precisely who the Kremlin admits is no longer alive.'

Arnold smiled and passed around the menus. 'Order anything,' he commanded. 'I've ordered us another bottle of this Meursault because I know Kathy will probably have fish. For us, my boy, I've ordered an excellent bottle of 1998 Pomerol – remember, all of you, that was the year the frost and rain hit the left bank of the Gironde and the great chateaux had a very difficult time.

'But on the right bank, the sun shone sweetly and the harvest was bountiful, and the wine all through St Émilion and Pomerol was rich and plentiful . . .'

'Jesus,' said Kathy, 'Would you listen to him? He thinks he's at the Last Supper.'

'I hope to hell he's not,' said Jimmy. 'This is just great – and all because the ole Kremlin staged one of its periodic mass murders.'

'Every cloud,' replied Arnold philosophically, 'somehow has a silver lining. Even that big bastard darkening the east side of Red Square.'

0900 Monday 4 October
Russian Naval Headquarters, Moscow

Three of the four men who had attended the meeting in the rotunda of the Senate building were now seated around a much smaller table in company with the Russian president. Prime Minister Kravchenko, Foreign Minister Nalyotov and the Energy Minister, Oleg Kuts.

'Very well,' said the president. 'Send for Admiral Rankov, will you?'

A navy guard turned smartly on the marble floor of the grandiose room and marched towards the huge double doors. Moments later, the mighty figure of Admiral Vitaly Rankov strode into the room. The veteran naval commander, in his new status as Deputy Minister of Defence, wore no uniform.

He was dressed in a dark grey suit with a white shirt and military tie, and he still looked as if he could pull the bowside five-oar in a Russian Olympic eight.

Despite a passion for caviar served on delicious blinis, and Siberian beef topped with cheese, plus all manner of desserts, Vitaly Rankov somehow remained fit. For a very big man, he was also trim, something that probably had a lot to do with a lifelong iron regime on his killer rowing machine. His eyes glued to the flickering computer as he hauled himself into Olympic selection, Vitaly could stop that digital clock at 6 minutes and 18 seconds for 2,000 metres. World class and his regular time in the run-up to the 1972 Olympics in Munich.

Today, at 60, the towering Vitaly Rankov fought a daily battle to 'break seven' – the young oarsman's mantra – and even this morning, fighting through the final 'yards' on his stationary machine in his basement, he hit the 2,000-metre line in 6.58. Nearly killed him. But here he was.

'*Dobraye utra* – good morning, Admiral,' the president of all the Russians greeted him.

'Sir,' replied Vitaly sharply, pushing his great shock of grey curly hair off his forehead. He took the chair left vacant on the president's right and nodded to the other three ministers, all of whom he knew relatively well.

'As I mentioned to you on the telephone,' said the president, 'this is a matter of the utmost secrecy. Our Intelligence Service leads us to believe the forces of Argentina are preparing to launch another attack on the Falkland Islands.'

This was easily the biggest lie the president had told this week, but it was still only Monday and the untruth was essentially kid's stuff compared with his record of the week before.

As it happened, the young Lieutenant Commander Rankov had received his first command – of a missile frigate – back in 1982. And like all of his colleagues he had watched with rapt fascination as the Royal Navy had fought that epic sea-battle off the Falkland islands, during which they had lost seven warships, including two Type-42 destroyers. Two ships still remained on the bottom of the ocean, while another, HMS *Glasgow*, had taken a bomb amidships, straight through her hull and out the other side.

Admiral Rankov looked quizzically at the president and said sternly, 'I'm not sure the result would be the same today, sir. The British have been very, very short-sighted about their war-fighting capability. The Argentines may actually be successful this time.'

The president nodded, and continued. 'At present we are only discussing a sudden pre-emptive strike which would certainly overrun the very flimsy British defences of the islands. But I would like your opinions upon the likely outcome if the British again sailed south with the intention of blasting the Argentines off their territory.

'Let's take a worst-case scenario,' said the president. 'The Argentines occupy the islands, and the airfields. Their marines are in tight control. There is no internal resistance. The British send down an aircraft carrier packed with fighter bombers and whatever guided-missile frigates and destroyers they have left, OK? Who wins?'

'A very complicated question, sir. We don't know much about the relative strength of the Argentine fleet, nor its land forces, although they're quite formidable in the air.

'All battles depend to a large degree on the will and brilliance of the overall commanders. In 1982 that Royal Navy admiral out-smarted the Argentine forces, held his nerve, made no real mistakes, and in the end clobbered them. He was the first admiral whose fleet ever defeated an air force. Knocked out more than seventy Argentine fighter-bombers.'

'Yes. I read that during the weekend,' mused the president. 'But, Vitaly, could you put your finger on perhaps one single aspect of the war at sea which cost the Argentines victory? One critical path along which they failed?'

Admiral Rankov pondered the question. He was silent for a few moments, and then said, 'Sir, the critical path for the Argentines was always simple: if they had taken out either of the Royal Navy carriers, before the British had established an airfield ashore, the operation would have been over. You always need two decks in case one goes out of action even for a couple of hours – otherwise you lose all the aircraft you have in the air.'

'Why would that be so important?'

'Because that would have robbed the British land forces of adequate air cover. That would have meant their army would have refused to go ashore. Because without air cover they would have had Dunkirk all over again, being pounded by Argentine bombs instead of Hitler's.'

'Hmm,' said the president. 'And why did the Argentines not go for the carrier? And end it?'

'Mainly because they couldn't get to it. The South Atlantic is a *very* big place, and that Royal Navy admiral was a *very* cunning commander. He made damn sure they would never reach it. He never brought the carrier within range, except at night, when he knew the Argentine air force did not fly.'

'Well, if the same war happened again, how would they get to the carrier this time?'

'With great difficulty, sir. Unless they had a very quiet, very skilfully handled submarine which could locate and track it. But that's extremely hard to do, and I don't think the Argentines have the skill.'

'Does anyone?'

'Possibly. But the Royal Navy commanders are traditionally very good at this type of thing. Getting in close to a ship of that size would be damn near impossible. All carriers are permanently protected by an electronic ring of underwater surveillance. I suppose the Americans might be able to get in and perhaps fire a torpedo, but even that's doubtful.'

'How about our own navy? Could *we* do it?'

'The real issue is, sir, could we do it without getting caught and sunk? I would not put my life savings on it. Especially against the Royal Navy . . . but you know, sir, I think the problem this time might not be quite so grave. Because I reckon that recent advances in the design of rockets, missiles and even bombs has been so great that any commander would prefer to sink a carrier from the air. And that's where the Brits might be expecting any attack to come from.

'Carriers – the damn things carry about a billion gallons of fuel. If you can get in close enough, with a modern supersonic sea-skimming missile, that's the trick.'

'So where does all this leave the Argentines – same as before?'

'Not if they can get a submarine in, maybe seven miles from the carrier, and take an accurate GPS reading on its precise position in the ocean. Then they could vector their fighter-bombers straight at it.'

'And do they have *that* submarine capacity?'

'I don't think so, sir. The Royal Navy would almost certainly locate and sink them.'

'If Argentina were to recruit an ally, to help them with this critical aspect of submarine warfare, who do they need?'

'The USA, sir.'

'How about China?' asked the president, shrewdly trying to keep his admiral off his own critical path.

'China! Christ, no. The Brits would pick them up before they reached Cape Town.'

'How about France?'

'Possibly, but they lack experience. The French have never fought a war with submarines.'

'Neither have we.'

'No, sir. But I'd still make us the second choice if I were the C-in-C of the Argentine navy. We still have top-flight commanders, and we probably have the ship which could do the job . . .'

'Oh, which one?'

'Well, I'd go for one of our Akula Class nuclear boats myself. Hunter-killers, about 9,500 tons, packed with missiles and torpedoes, excellent radar and sonar. The most modern ones are ten to fifteen years old, but lightly used and very quiet.'

'Do you know the ships personally? I mean, are they ready to go?'

'One came out of refit last spring. She's on sea trials right now, just completing. A very good ship, sir. I went out in her a month ago.'

'Aha, and what's her name, this Akula Class hunter-killer?'

'She's the *Viper*, sir. *Viper K-157*.'

'Thank you, admiral. That will be all for the moment.'

1630 Monday 11 October
Florida Garden Confiteria
Cordoba Avenue District, Buenos Aires

The Florida Garden *confiteria* had always been a favourite haunt of the military junta in Buenos Aires, back in the years when they had ruled Argentina so spectacularly badly, the late 1970s and early 1980s. It was a kind of glamorous escape for them from the fierce undercurrents of unrest which were edging the great South American republic of Argentina towards outright revolution.

It was a sanctuary from the hatred of the populace; a sanctuary with sweet tea, sugary pastries and piped tango music. And it still stood today, still frequented by Argentine military personnel and right next to the venerable old Harrods building, as a faded symbol of a long-gone friendship.

And in many ways the year 2010 was not much different from 1982. The shattering defeat of that year still rankled with the Argentine populace even after all this time. And the vision of the Falkland Islands – their very own *Malvinas* – still stood stark and taunting before them: high, wide and handsome, and very British.

The inflamed, reckless ambition of a junta of long ago was just as virulent in 2010. But now it lurked in the minds of a new breed of Argentine military officer, a breed that was better equipped, better trained, and better educated.

Which was why, on this cool sunlit Monday afternoon, two senior Argentine officers, one a general, the other an admiral, plus a medium-rank cabinet minister were sitting quietly at a corner table in the *confiteria*, awaiting the arrival of a Russian emissary. This was a secretive mission, an appointment arranged by the Russian Embassy but without any of its regular officials present. The Argentines had been urged to find as discreet a spot as possible.

Now they waited, staring out through the wide windows onto tony Cordoba Avenue, expecting their visitor to walk down the street from the Claridge Hotel. The secretive circumstances had made the men curious and the suspense mounted in the atmosphere of expectancy.

And they were not kept waiting long. At 4.32 p.m. the stocky, quietly dressed Gregor Komoyedov arrived. He was in his mid-fifties, wearing a dark blue suit, white shirt and dark red tie, carrying, as arranged, a copy of the *New Yorker* magazine. He stepped into the crowded *confiteria* and looked around. The Argentine minister, Freddie – he was one of innumerable natives of the country who had British ancestry – turned and held up his hand. The Russian nodded and made his way through the throng to the corner table.

Freddie stood up and introduced General Eduardo Kampf and Admiral Oscar Moreno. All three of them were wearing civilian clothes, and they each shook the hand of the Russian Minister for Foreign Trade, chosen by his president on the basis of his superior worldliness.

'I expect you, being a Russian, would like some coffee,' said General Kampf, smiling.

'That would be very civilised,' replied the Russian. 'Perhaps we should speak in English – your second language, I believe . . . ?'

'No problem,' replied the general. 'And I should say that we are extremely anxious to hear about your business here – your embassy was very close-mouthed about it. For a minute we thought you might be declaring war!'

'Ah, you military guys, that's all you think about. My own background is deep in the Russian oil industry, strictly commercial. To us, war is unthinkable, mainly because it gets in the way of making money!'

Everyone laughed – the Argentines mainly because they were not yet aware of the colossal insincerity of that remark. But old Gregor was a wily Muscovite wheeler-dealer from way back. He knew how to coax a subject along gently.

The coffee and pastries arrived, and, at a nod from the admiral, the piped tango music began to play a tad louder. 'I don't think we shall be overheard,' he said. 'And I am looking forward to your proposition?'

Gregor smiled. 'But how do you know I have one?'

'Because you would not be here otherwise, having flown halfway around the world – on obvious orders from your president – in a dark and clandestine manner.'

'Well, let me begin by assuming that you all know of the recent massive oil strikes in the *Malvinas*,' Gregor said, skilfully banishing the British name for the islands from his vocabulary.

All three Argentines nodded.

'And I imagine that you continue to feel the same sense of injustice that you felt in 1982. After all, the oil is yours by rights, and most fair-minded people in the world understand that. How London can possibly proclaim they own those islands, eight thousand miles from Britain but a mere three hundred miles off your long coastline . . . well, that's a mystery no one really grasps. But the British have some inflated views of both their past and their present.'

'The Americans understand,' said General Kampf.

'They'll understand anything they choose to,' said Gregor Komoyedov. 'Just so long as there's a good buck in it for them, ha?'

'They're going to make a good buck in the *Malvinas*,' added Freddie. 'We understand Exxon are in there already, in partnership with British Petroleum.'

'I did hear . . .' said the Russian, leaving the sentence hanging. Then he decided to plunge straight in. 'There was some talk the Argentine military might be assessing the possibility of a new campaign against the *Malvinas* – a sudden brutal pre-emptive strike, and an occupation of the islands which could easily withstand a counter-attack from the Royal Navy.'

'I wish,' replied Admiral Moreno, a surprised look on his face.

'But no one's told *me*.'

'Well, perhaps I transgress into military secrets which are none of my, or my country's, business.'

'Perhaps you do,' said the admiral. 'But please continue . . .'

'If, for instance, you *did* find yourself owning the oil, then you would find a very willing partner in the Russian government – to help you drill, pump and market it in the most profitable way.

'We could do for you what the Americans did for the Saudi Arabians. We have the know-how. And our pipeline techniques are probably second to none, since we already pump directly out of the West Siberian Basin. And we are used to working in extreme weather conditions.

'No one could help you quite like we could. We would take over the operation completely, and pay you a generous royalty for every barrel. We would allow you to oversee the daily output, and we would build you a tanker terminal in order to maximise the exports. Our aim would be the US market along their Gulf Coast.'

'The snag is, of course,' replied Freddie, 'that we do not own the *Malvinas*, nor have I discerned any anxiety on our government's part that we *should* own the *Malvinas*. I mean, there are periodic bouts of anger in the media, about how our birthright to those islands has somehow been grabbed away from us by an outmoded colonial power.

'And we do get outbursts from politicians who maintain that we should try again to negotiate a treaty with the British, one which would ultimately make the islands ours. But nothing definite . . . no, nothing definite at all.'

The men around the table fell silent. Admiral Moreno gestured to their waiter for more coffee, and since Gregor Komoyedov was plainly enjoying the sweet little pastries he signalled for a few more of those as well.

The sugar intake further galvanised the man from Moscow. 'Gentlemen,' he said, 'do you have any idea what recent London governments have done to the British military? They have crippled their regimental system, the one which has terrified their opponents for about three hundred years. They have cut down on the numbers of armoured vehicles, tanks and artillery. Much of their equipment, including combat clothing, is out of date. Even their small arms are suspect.

'The Royal Navy has been beaten down, their fleet reduced to a pale shadow of the one that faced down Hitler on the high seas. It would be fair to say the Royal Navy High Command is almost heartbroken at what has befallen it.

'A succession of incompetent politicians has progressively castrated the military in Great Britain. And we watch them very carefully. They do not have one single operational interceptor in their fleet, or their air force. They are unable to put a viable Carrier Battle Group together, not even to face a Third World air force.

'When we heard – perhaps wrongly – that there was talk here of a new offensive against the *Malvinas*, we were absolutely certain about one thing: if the Argentines attempt it, they will achieve it. But perhaps I have, as they say, jumped the gun.'

'I've often found myself thinking along these lines,' said General Kampf. 'But it's interesting to hear an outsider's viewpoint. You think that our military – our navy and our air force – have the capability to capture the Falkland Islands?'

'Yes, although that capability has one or two gaps.'

'Such as?' asked Admiral Moreno.

'We think your Achilles heel may be the lack of a top-class attack submarine which could range in close to the Royal Navy's carrier, running deep and quiet, perhaps revealing the carrier's position to your very fine fighter pilots.'

'You may be right about that,' replied Oscar Moreno. 'But remember, our Achilles heel last time, was the range of our aircraft. We could not refuel them sufficiently to get them round the back, to the east of Woodward's battle group. Therefore he could concentrate his defences to the west. I think this time we may have the range – but I cannot be absolutely certain. Failing to hit the Royal Navy carrier could still cost us any new war.'

'Not if you had just a modicum of underwater assistance from Mother Russia,' said Gregor, smiling. 'That would seal your overwhelming victory. Very probably on the first day of the war.'

And with that, Gregor Komoyedov stood up and wished them all goodbye, in Russian: *'Da svidaniya.'* Adding, quietly, 'Just a few things to ponder, gentlemen. If you would like to talk further I suggest that it should be in Moscow. Perhaps your C-in-C would like to arrange something with our ambassador here in Buenos Aires.

'Just mention the code word *Viper K-157.'* He stepped towards the café door and added, flamboyantly, his arms spread wide apart,

63

'VIVA LAS MALVINAS!!'

And the instant rousing cheers of the other café patrons echoed loudly in the ears of the wily Gregor Komoyedov as he stepped outside, summoned his waiting taxi for the 24 miles to Ezieza airport and an Aeroflot flight. Big European Airbus. Private. Not one other passenger. Direct to Sheremetevo-2, the sprawling international airport which lies 20 miles to the northwest of Moscow.

CHAPTER THREE

0900 Monday 18 October
The Kremlin, Moscow

General Eduardo Kampf and Admiral Oscar Moreno had spent a comfortable night in the sumptuous private apartment of the president of Russia, in the Senate Building.

Their journey from Buenos Aires had been conducted with such cautious precision – private aircraft, government cars, darkened windows, no uniforms – it would have been reasonable to suppose that no one knew the two top Argentine commanders were in Moscow except those who were supposed to know.

General Kampf was Commander of Argentina's 5-Corps, head-quartered at Bahia Blanca, close to the naval base at Puerto Belgrano, 280 miles south-west of Buenos Aires. General Moreno was Commander-in-Chief Fleet, a position once held by the hawkish Argentine patriot Admiral Jorge Anaya, the man who had taken his nation to war in the Falkland Islands twenty-eight years previously.

For the past week, both men had been cloistered in the Casa Rosada, the Presidential Palace on the Plaza de Mayo in Buenos Aires. Each morning, in company with the president of Argentina plus the nation's most trusted ministers, the officers had taken coffee out on the great columned balcony, gazing down on the place that had once held a million-strong crowd roaring, *M-A-A-L-V-I-N-A-S!! M-A-A-L-V-I-N-A-S!* when news of the Argentine troops landing on the Falklands had finally broken in the spring of 1982.

Both Argentines had served in the 1982 war against the British. Kampf had been a young lieutenant hopelessly trying to defend the garrison at Goose Green against the rampaging, slightly desperate Second Battalion of the Parachute Regiment. Moreno had been a lieutenant on board one of the old ex-US destroyers trying to protect the doomed *General Belgrano*. Both men had wept at the Argentine surrender on 14 June just ten weeks after the war had begun.

But now, cradled here in the immense stronghold of Russian military power, together with the president of Russia and his ever-faithful navy chief, Admiral Vitaly Rankov, things were looking sweetly different. And the wintry sun struggling into the grey skies above the onion domes of St Basil's Cathedral cast a sense of righteousness upon them all.

Of course the Malvinas are yours . . . What rights do the British have to them? Who do they think they are? And the oil? That huge field probably begins under mainland Argentina.

And there was the towering figure of this confident veteran Russian admiral, laughing loudly at what he called the wreckage of the Royal Navy: *'DESTROYED, WILFULLY, BY ITS OWN GOVERNMENT! HA HA HA!* Gentlemen, there is no way you can lose this battle.

'Firstly, I doubt whether the British could raise a battle fleet. Secondly, they hardly have an air-strike force to put on an aircraft carrier. And thirdly, even if they can find a few tired old Harrier jet fighters, with a little help from us you'll sink the carrier. And the Harriers will all run out of fuel and fall into the sea. Checkmate. Poor bastards.'

Even the Russian president laughed, and he was taking this entire conversation very seriously. 'Vitaly,' he said, 'I want you to explain to our guests exactly why we can make such a difference to the Argentine strategy if – and only if – the British elect to sail once more for the South Atlantic and fight to recapture their islands.'

'*Las Malvinas* are not,' interjected Admiral Moreno, '*their* islands. They are *ours*.'

'Of course,' replied the president, smiling. 'Thoughtless of me. I meant, should they wish to try once more to capture *Las Malvinas*.'

'General Kampf,' said Vitaly. 'As a senior military commander of land troops, you understand better than any of us that no one would dream of putting ashore an army several thousand strong on a fortified island – as the *Malvinas* will most certainly be – without proper air cover. Correct?'

'Absolutely not, Admiral,' replied General Kampf. 'That would be suicide. The troops would be strafed to pieces with no reasonable prospect of hitting back. Every man on the beach would be at the mercy of enemy air attack, and there'd be no British supply lines. The men would be cut off from their ammunition, food, shelter and field hospitals. For them to fight on would be impossible. I doubt whether any land-force commander would attempt anything so crazy.'

'And would the British high command be aware of this?'

'Of course. They'd never do it. No one in their right mind would.'

'So,' exclaimed Vitaly. 'You have a short sharp war, with one single objective: take out the Royal Navy carrier. Then the British will have no air cover for the men they intend to land on the beaches.'

'Correct. No carrier. No landing. The *Malvinas* will be ours.'

Admiral Rankov stood up, walked around the table and shook the hand of the commander of the Argentine land forces. 'General – how do the Americans say? We sing from the same hymn sheet!'

'But I think these facts dawned on the Argentines last time when they were unable to hit the carrier.' The Russian president had covered this conversation before, and he knew the answers. He was just feeding Admiral Rankov the lines he knew the navy chief wanted repeated.

'Oh, this time it will be very different,' replied the Russian admiral. 'You see, sir,' he said, turning to his boss, 'fighter aircraft are like motorbikes with wings. They go very fast and run out of fuel in less than ninety minutes. We do have extra tanker refuelling now, but a runway more than a thousand miles from the air base at Rio Grande is still a very difficult proposition. Not much time to waste searching vast empty seas for a wandering aircraft carrier.

'Only just time, in fact, for a fast one-shot strike on a known target, turn around and try to make it home on what's left in the tank. Last time, the Argentine air force pilots were often unaware of the damn carrier's location, and that Royal Navy admiral was amazingly smart at keeping it out of the way.

'The trouble was, Argentina had no effective submarine that could creep around, locate the carrier and silently stay with it. They still don't have a ship good enough to do that. But we do.

'The Russian submarine that we're planning to use can send a satellite communication to our friends in the Argentine air-control rooms which will put their fighter jets bang on target with accurate readings. Either that, or we can slam a wire-guided torpedo straight into the hull of the carrier. Whichever's easiest. The Royal Navy carrier will be history on the first day. These days the British simply don't have the muscle to stop it.'

'You hit it underwater? Or we hit it from the air?' asked General Kampf.

'Oh, probably you strike from the air,' said Vitaly. 'But possibly we might do the job from underwater. Our submarine would need to close to perhaps 7,000 yards to get a hit, and the British destroyers and ASW frigates would probably find us and make life very hot. A couple of active homing torpedoes make a very great – er – hullabaloo in the water.

'But your air force can launch an armada. The Royal Navy may hit some of them, but they won't hit them all. Most definitely not. Your guys will get bombs and missiles into that fleet, the carrier will explode – tons of jet fuel – and many sailors will burn or drown. But that's war. That's defeat. And the British forces will have no alternative but go home to England, while you throw a victory party in Port Stanley.

'I will come, bring the Red Army choir and some good Russian vodka. Celebrate for both our great countries. Ha ha ha! Then we can both make huge profits, hah? Make the stupid Americans pay top dollar for beautiful Argentine oil. And the Siberian traitors can go fuck themselves. Ha ha ha!'

The Russian president looked sharply across at Rankov as if warning him of the danger of that last statement. But it was clear that the Argentine military men had neither noticed nor understood. And just then the door opened and the ebullient figure of Gregor Komoyedov came exuberantly through the rotunda's enormous wooden doors.

'My friends!' he cried. 'How are my friends from the *confiteria*? So good to see you again. Are we partners yet? Or do I come back later?'

He bounded over to Admiral Moreno and gave him a mighty Russian bear-hug and a kiss on both cheeks before doing the same with Eduardo Kampf. Then he stood back with a great beaming smile on his face.

'Well, we are partners, eh?' he said, repeating his question.

The Russian president looked very slightly perplexed, as if Gregor Komoyedov might be rushing his fences.

But now both General Kampf and Admiral Moreno stepped forward, and between them they took each of the three Russians by the hand.

'Oh, yes,' said Admiral Moreno. 'We are most definitely partners.'

'*Pastries!*' yelled Gregor Komoyedov. 'Someone bring the sweetest, most lovely pastries for my friends from the southern oceans. And coffee. And vodka. The finest vodka!'

And the boss of all the Russians, smiling broadly, stood up and walked to the door to arrange for the refreshments, filling in for the Kremlin butler for the first and only time of his entire presidency. He could have kissed Gregor Komoyedov, that old Moscow smoothie.

Back in Buenos Aires, at the highest level of government, nothing was quite as innocent as General Kampf and Admiral Moreno had made out to the Russians. *What – us? Re-invade the Falklands? Hadn't really thought about it . . . not really one of our priorities . . . Argentine government has said nothing. 'And would you be interested if we could help?' Well . . . er . . . that's interesting. But we're quite unprepared for anything like that.*

Bullshit – as Admiral Morgan might have put it. They'd thought about it, all right. In fact, there was a group of Argentine military officers who had thought of hardly anything else for a quarter of a century. They'd seethed over the sheer humiliation of the 1982 war in the South Atlantic when 15,000 Argentine conscript troops and regular commandos had surrendered to a couple of hundred British paratroopers. They'd seethed, all right. And not one of them had ever forgotten or forgiven their imperious, victorious former friends from Great Britain. They called themselves *The Malvinistas*.

The British, of course, with a wealth of good intentions after Margaret Thatcher's great triumph, maintained for some years a tri-service force on the islands, under the rotational command of a two-star officer and with a joint headquarters. This remotest of British armed-forces garrisons was meant to be a stern warning to the Argentines not to try anything rash in the foreseeable future, and also to provide reassurance to the Falkland Islanders that Aunt Maggie's boys would come charging back at the drop of a tin hat.

For a start they built a new airfield, at Mount Pleasant, thirty-five miles west of the tiny capital city of Stanley. It was laid out on high ground, at an elevation of 242 feet, with two runways, one of them 8,500 feet long, over nearly two miles of flat blacktop. They also built a fine military complex for their shore-based troops – with a gym, swimming pool, shops, messes and club facilities. They even built a church.

But, as relations with Argentina began to improve, the threat of a renewed attack on the islands lessened. And Great Britain's government saw an opportunity for severe cuts in the British military presence there. They began to make significant force reductions, and as the years passed they cut back the little garrison in the Falklands – to the bone.

With demands mounting for British troops in parts of Africa, the Balkans, Afghanistan and the Middle East, the Falklands very nearly slipped out of the equation altogether.

In Whitehall, the 'mandarins' who ran the Civil Service would cheerfully have closed the entire thing down but for the political and moral necessity to reassure the Falkland Islanders that Great Britain really did have an abiding interest in their future security.

The other brake on outright British detachment from the islands and their inhabitants was the presence of the impressive structure of the Falkland Islands Memorial Chapel – due north of Portsmouth Dockyard – at Pangbourne Nautical College in the English county of Berkshire.

This church had been built as the ultimate symbol of British naval and military skill and courage in a modern war. It stands as a reminder of the sacrifices made in the South Atlantic: inside its portals, on two high granite walls, the name and rank of every British man who died in the Falklands conflict is carved into the stone – 250 of them.

Even the most self-seeking political number-cruncher could scarcely recommend cutting all military ties with the islands, thereby sending a message to all the families of those men that it had all been in vain. It would be like saying that the British didn't really mean it, or any longer need the Falklands. All those brave men had died for nothing. Names carved in granite for a cause made of gossamer.

And so the garrison remained. Because the British government accepted, albeit reluctantly, that it had to remain. They cut it back so that its operational capabilities were near-useless and soon it was regarded, by all of those who served in it, as the Forgotten Force. It was stranded in the South Atlantic for months at a time, vulnerable to an attack by just about anyone with a couple of spare missiles.

The discovery of oil, major reserves of oil, did not penetrate the minds of the bureaucrats and politicians, hard though that was to believe. Even the Saudis understood the urgent need to protect their oil with a heavily armed presence. Not, however, Britain's Labour government. Safe in the ironclad security of their own jobs, its functionaries whiled away the years in Whitehall, preparing to claim their secure retirement pensions and only scowling at the merest mention of the very expensive Falkland Islands.

Left largely to its own devices, operationally stripped to the bare minimum, the garrison was working for a government that believed Great Britain could not possibly be caught out again. Not so long as the new Mount Pleasant Airfield (MPA) was functional and capable of handling a rapid-reinforcement force at the first sign of danger.

But the government of 2010 appeared to have forgotten entirely that on 1 May 1982, the opening day of the Falklands War, it took about three minutes of precision-level approach and one British 1,000-lb bomb to render Argentine fast-jet take-offs and landings from the islands virtually impossible for the entire duration of the war.

Right now, in the autumn of 2010 there was just a company group of the 3rd Rifles – 140 men rotating every nine months. This force consisted of a small HQ and three rifle platoons. They had a few heavy machine guns but no mortars or anti-tank weapons.

The savagely diminished presence of the Royal Navy brought joy to the heart of Admiral Oscar Moreno. There was one ageing Fleet Auxiliary ship whose sole purpose was the resupply of groceries and fuel to South Georgia, the other British protectorate in the South Atlantic, some 1,100 miles away to the east-south-east.

And there was a 1,400-ton patrol ship, the HMS *Leeds Castle*, which was designed to carry a 30mm gun with a range of seven miles, a platform for a Sea King helicopter, and facilities for a detachment of Royal Marines. The helicopter was missing and so was the detachment of Royal Marines. But the gun was still there.

Both ships were stationed in Mare Harbour, a windswept little bay five miles south of the airport, where the Royal Navy's tiny HQ was based.

A few years back it had been decided that a heavily armed frigate, packing a lethal modern can't-miss guided-missile system, was essential for the defence of the islands. But these days the Falklands received only an occasional irregular visit from a Royal Navy frigate on task 4,000 miles to the north in the Caribbean.

The Royal Air Force presence had also been scaled right back. They kept a VC-10 refuelling tanker and a search-and-rescue Sea King helicopter. But they no longer had any lift capacity. For stores and supplies, the work had been contracted out to a civilian firm, which normally operated on oil rigs.

A decade earlier the Royal Air Force had been forced to withdraw from service a flight of four Tornado-F-3s owing to the prohibitive cost of continuing a service line for obsolete fighter aircraft. At the time it was intended they would be replaced by the air-defence version of the new Typhoon (the Eurofighter), which was still not operational despite having been the RAF's top-priority programme for twenty years.

It was not considered possible to send Typhoons to the Falklands. And the Ministry of Defence in Whitehall reckoned this was an acceptable risk.

They decided only one thing mattered: making sure the international airfield at Mouth Pleasant stayed operational. And for that they installed a Rapier missile system, manned by RAF personnel: two towed launchers, each mounting eight missiles for short-range air-defensive cover across the airfield. The Rapier missiles had a maximum range of around three miles and a ceiling of under 10,000 feet. Their surveillance radar was good for about twelve miles.

None of this had gone unnoticed by the *Malvinistas*. Thousands of evenings were spent by Argentine military personnel in the Florida Garden *confiteria*, gleefully for the most part, discussing the British defensive capability in the Falkland Islands.

They were older now. Mostly in their fifties and sixties. But some of them were pilots who had somehow bailed out of shot-down fighter aircraft at 600 m.p.h. There were others who had been pulled out of the Atlantic after the *General Belgrano* had been sunk. Still others had fought and been wounded in the freezing mountainous terrain of East Falkland – and, perhaps most bitter of all, there were the officers who had surrendered their beaten troops, unforgettably, humiliatingly, on the melancholy morning of 14 June 1982.

These were the core members of the *Malvinistas* who met in the café on Cordoba Avenue in downtown Buenos Aires. They were men who believed that there would be a next time, men who knew that any future attack would have to be a swift, violent strike, without warning. Surprise would be everything.

They were not remotely like the gung-ho amateurish group that had cheerfully gone into a major war against one of the best high-tech military machines in the world. By the time General Kampf and Admiral Moreno returned from Moscow with the one missing piece of the puzzle – the destruction of the British aircraft carrier – sorted, the Argentine high command had identified and selected a small group of carefully chosen officers, and had briefed them to begin detailed planning. Information was released strictly on a need-to-know basis.

This was a burgeoning Argentine army no longer packed with conscripts who knew nothing of combat. It had a command and staff structure based on the United States model, and its doctrine was based solidly on lessons that had been learned in 1982.

Conscription had been abolished in 1995, and since then a 55,000-strong regular army had been built, half the size, free of rookies and four times more professional than any force which had tried to hold the *Malvinas* twenty-eight years previously. It was far better equipped, better organised and better trained. Worse yet, for the Brits, the Argentine brass knew just about everything there was to know about the troops they regarded as occupying forces in the *Malvinas*.

The prime reason for this was the oil. The arrival of exploration, drilling and recovery teams, particularly in the North Falkland Basin and the Special Cooperation Area in the south-west, had opened up the region, wide, in the 1990s.

Most of the oil consortiums involved had established small bases in the Stanley area, and there had long been a regular flow of personnel to and from the islands. Many of them arrived on the Santiago-based Lan Chile airline which flew Boeing 737s regularly between Punta Arenas and Mount Pleasant.

This had enabled Argentine agents to move freely in and out of the Falklands for several years, observing the British garrison forces, identifying their strengths and many weaknesses, their equipment, their base area, their routines, their patrolling patterns, and many other military activities.

In the Florida Garden *confiteria* they knew more about the British Army and Royal Navy in the South Atlantic than the Ministry of Defence knew in London. And Messrs Kampf and Moreno had been telling a lie of the most majestic proportions when first they had assured their Russian visitor, Gregor Komoyedov, that no one in Argentina had given much thought to another assault on the *Malvinas*.

Now, armed with highly detailed charts and notebooks, General Kampf and Admiral Moreno were in conference in Bahia Blanca, the 5-Corps Headquarters where the principal military capability for the whole of southern Argentina was located.

With them were General Carlos Alfonso, the Army Chief of Staff, Admiral Alfredo Baldini, the Chief of Naval Operations, and the Air Force Chief, General Hector Allara, a former Mirage attack pilot who'd seen action over Falkland Sound in 1982.

All five men reckoned that they could be ready any time in the New Year. And all five men believed their attack should begin when the visiting Royal Navy frigate was well and truly on her way home, steaming hard towards the Caribbean, at least five days out of Mare Harbour.

General Allara was especially keen on this aspect of the strategy since his French-built Mirage jet fighter had been hit and destroyed by a Sea Dart missile launched from HMS *Coventry*, north of Falkland Sound, in the hours before the British destroyer had been sunk by Argentine bombs.

Hector Allara had bailed out into the water, and these many years later no one knew better than he that a well-handled Royal Navy guided missile ship was a serious opponent. He saw no reason to tangle with one, unless it was unavoidable. Sitting still and waiting for the British frigate to leave town, was, in his view, the most agreeable option.

5-Corps had under its command the 1st Armoured Brigade, stationed inland to the north-east at Tandil; the 11th Mechanised Brigade stationed far south on the coast at Rio Gallegos, 490 miles directly west of the Falklands; the 6th Mountain Brigade at Neuquen deep inland in northern Patagonia; and the 9th Mechanised Brigade at Comodoro Rivadavia, which stands on the coast 360 miles north of Rio Gallegos.

Thus 5-Corps had a light armoured battalion, medium artillery, air defence, army aviation and engineering, signals and logistics. And it had its one-third share of Argentina's 256 main battle tanks, 302 light tanks, 48 reconnaissance vehicles, 742 armoured personnel carriers and six attack helicopters.

The Corps's infantry division was armed with the most modern recoilless rifles, sub-machine guns, general purpose machine guns,

Browning M2 heavy machine guns, mortars, and anti-tank guided missiles. 5-Corps's artillery carried a formidable range of howitzers. They had low-altitude surface-to-air missiles, Bofors anti-aircraft guns and a whole range of other anti-aircraft guns.

More importantly, they knew how to use the entire arsenal. And right now their commanders were beginning to move their operations south, to the coastal regions down towards the Falkland Islands. This applied particularly to the Argentine Air Force which realised it must once more, for the second time in twenty-eight years, reactivate its sprawling Rio Grande airbase in Tierra del Fuego, the 1982 home of Commander Jorge Columbo's heroic 2nd Naval Fighter and Attack Squadron.

The base lay right on the coast at the mouth of the river, forty-two miles south-east of the Bay of San Sebastian, a big inlet, twenty miles across.

This was the base for Argentina's French-built Dassault Super-Étendard, the single-seat naval attack aircraft which delivered the 650-knot radar-homing half-ton anti-ship missile, the Exocet – the kind that incinerated the Royal Navy's Type-42 destroyer HMS *Sheffield* on the fourth day of the 1982 war.

The Super-Es, especially modified with extra gas-tanks fitted under one wing, had an 860-mile range – sufficient to get well within striking distance of the sea around the Falkland Islands.

Back in 1982 the Rio Grande base had been the start-point of the Exocet missile's deadly journey, but this time the strategy would be very different. Because this time the Argentine forces would hold the airfield at Mount Pleasant. Or at least they would if General Kampf had anything to do with it.

But any attacking air force needs a home base, on native soil, and Rio Grande would once more be home to a squadron of the fabled French-built Super-Es. From November the pilots and ground crew would live, work and train there until it became clear not only that Argentina owned and controlled the *Malvinas*, but there was no one lurking over the horizon who was still planning to do anything about it.

Right now the entire operation was just about as highly classified, utterly secret, as anything ever could be in a South American country. But Argentines talk, and they talk with emotion, fervour and optimism. Which was why, back in the Florida Garden *confiteria*, rumour was already rife about a new assault on the *Malvinas*.

By eleven p.m. on Friday 29 October a crowd had gathered in

front of the Casa Rosada presidential palace on the Plaza de Mayo. It was not yet in the tens of thousands, but it certainly numbered several thousand. As the weekend throb of the tango began to pervade hundreds of bars and clubs in Buenos Aires, there was, very suddenly, a rapidly spreading sense of heightened expectation and hope.

And as the moon rose above the dark, faded elegance of the old city, an ever-rising, rhythmic roar of unbridled passion could be heard from the Plaza de Mayo. It was a cry from a thousand hearts, a hymn to the slain Argentine warriors of 1982 . . . *VIVA LAS M-A-A-L-V-I-N-A-S! VIVA LAS M-A-A-L-V-I-N-A-S!*

1200 Monday 1 November
National Security Agency, Maryland

Lt. Commander Jimmy Ramshawe normally placed South America about eighth on his list of priorities. Nonetheless, he always enjoyed reading English-language newspapers from foreign capital cities. Sometimes he took a few days to get to them, but he always made sure that he did eventually.

Today he was scouring the *Buenos Aires Herald*, the English-language daily which specialised in politics and business news, and was renowned for its outspoken editorials written fiercely against whoever seemed to be screwing life up for the Argentines.

During the Dirty War of the 1970s and 80s, the *Herald* was so unremitting in its condemnation of military and police abuses, its editor had to go into hiding after threats against his family.

Of all the newspapers Jimmy Ramshawe was not really interested in, but could not afford to miss, the no-pounches-pulled *Buenos Aires Herald* stood right at the top of the list.

Scanning the headlines, Jimmy's eye caught one particular story which should have been confined to the business section but had been given enormous prominence on the front page of the paper. The headline read:

OIL STRIKE ON PATAGONIA COAST
HIGHLIGHTS MALVINAS OUTRAGE

'Hello,' muttered James. 'The bloody gauchos are at it again.' This was a statement of such astonishing crassness that Jimmy, whose Aussie brand of outback humour sometimes clashed with his high intelligence, was moved to reconsider his choice of epithet.

'Tell the truth, I'm not so sure what a bloody gaucho is, except that he rides a horse, carries a knife, eats a lot of beef, and doesn't give a rat's arse about anyone.'

As native Argentine horsemen and cowboys went, there was an element of truth in this. However, the badly missed point was the gauchos didn't give a rat's arse about the oil strike either. That was a matter for the big hitters of Argentine business.

The story in the *Buenos Aires Herald* speculated, with much apparent authority, on a possible rich field of oil and gas discovered a few miles to the north of the Patagonian port of Rio Gallegos. Rio Gallegos had long been a seaport for the export of coal from the huge mines 150 miles west of the city. There had also been oil discoveries in the region, of sufficient volume to justify a sizeable refinery there. But, according to the *Herald*, this new discovery was right on the coast and also stretched out under Argentina's coastal waters.

They quoted an executive from the Argentine state oil company who said: *'It cannot be a mere coincidence that the Patagonian oilfields plainly run from the coalfields to the coast, and then in a dead straight line to the Malvinas where the biggest oil and gas strikes in recent years have been confirmed.'*

The *Herald* reasoned: *If that is true, then the oilfields on the islands MUST be the property of Argentina, since we are the clear and rightful owners of the Malvinas, and the ONLY country with coastal waters and seabed above the oil.*

Argentina's claim on the islands has always been correct and unchallengeable politically – even the British understand that. It now appears to be also unchallengeable geologically. The rock strata that have housed the oil for thousands of years are purely Argentine, not British.

Their absurd claim to own the Malvinas would be as if we claimed their North Sea oil because a few Argentine families had settled on the east coast of Scotland.

Until now, the oil companies have always stated that the oil on the Argentine mainland and the oil in the Falklands are separate issues. However, last month's new discovery north of Rio Gallegos has joined up the last dot in a long chain of Argentine oilfields. The oil is ours, obviously ours. All of it.

And what is our government, and indeed our military doing about it? THEY OWE THE PEOPLE AN EXPLANATION . . . 'VIVA LAS MALVINAS!'

'Christ,' said Jimmy.

In an entirely separate story in the business section there was a long piece about the financial ramifications of the new strike – the likelihood of 500,000 barrels a day, the need for yet another huge refinery in Rio Gallegos, and the prosperity which the discovery would bring to southern Patagonia.

On the editorial pages, there was a piece by the editor of the *Herald* in person, pointing out the new strike had made the *Malvinas* even more difficult to reclaim. The British were now backed by the giant American oil corporation which had joined BP in the oilfields south-west of Port Stanley. They would probably dig in even more stubbornly, maybe even refuse to negotiate further.

'The British Government has never been anything less than dogmatic, unreasonable and forever obdurate,' he raged. *'Perhaps now is the time for Argentina once more to consider the military option.'*

'Christ,' repeated Jimmy. And then, slowly, muttering to himself, 'I'm telling you, that oil business causes more bloody trouble on this planet than any other issue in the entire history of mankind. Except religion.'

He pulled up a map on his big computer and punched the buttons for the program which would reveal the coast of southern Patagonia and its proximity to the Falkland Islands.

'I'll say one thing,' he muttered. 'It *is* a bloody straight line, and no error.'

He pondered the story, trying to work out whether it had anything to do with the United States and its national security. He decided against it. *If the ole gauchos wanna fight the Brits over those rathole islands again, well, let 'em. It really is none of our business.*

Nonetheless Jimmy logged the data in his special computer file, the one designed purely as a personal reminder, for any time he wanted to check the history of a global issue.

The impending row over the Falklands stayed on his mind for the rest of the day, and at the end of the afternoon he made copies of the articles in the *Buenos Aires Herald*. Then he posted them off, regular mail, to Admiral Morgan. He just scrawled FYI at the head of the first sheet and left it at that.

Seven days later, however, on Monday 8 November, there were two developments which caught his interest. The first was a memorandum from Ryan Holland, the veteran career diplomat from Mississippi who was now the United States Ambassador to Argentina. His communiqué had been sent directly to the State

Department, but it was then forwarded to the CIA and the NSA.

It read: *Continued Friday and Saturday night disturbances in the Plaza de Mayo, the huge square in front of the presidential palace in the centre of Buenos Aires. The crowd appears to grow in size every night. On Saturday the police estimate there were 12,000 people present, all chanting 'Viva Las Malvinas!'*

I mention this because there have been no such demonstrations here for many years. I cannot understand this sudden rise in public indignation over those damned islands. Though I did notice a hot editorial in the Herald *the other day, claiming the oil recently discovered on the Falkland Islands was in fact the property of Argentina.*

The Herald's *editor, a nice enough guy with a slightly hysterical streak, was actually recommending the use of military force again. I expect it will all blow over, but those crowds were very substantial, and loud, getting louder. At no time did the president appear on the balcony of the palace, and there was no indication of any official action being contemplated.*

One hour after Lt. Commander Ramshawe had read the communiqué, his direct telephone line rang. Admiral Morgan was at the other end.

'Hey, Jimmy, thank you for the cuttings from Buenos Aires. Very interesting. It's easy to dismiss stuff, easy to say it's not our business. But remember last time? We ended up to our armpits in that mess. The Brits and the Argentinians were really slugging it out, fighter bombers hitting the Atlantic by the dozen, warships hitting the bottom of the Atlantic. It was a very nasty bitterly fought war. And the USA was right in the middle of it, helping Ronnie Reagan's best friend Margaret Thatcher to win it.'

'Sir, I was only about four years old at the time.'

'Well, you should have been paying attention.'

'Yessir. But I'm definitely paying attention now. I just read a communiqué from our ambassador in Buenos Aires . . .'

'Ryan Holland, right? Cunning old guy. Doesn't make many mistakes, and, more important, doesn't waste a lot of time on rubbish.'

'No, sir. Want me to tell you what he says?'

'Sure. Always listen to Ryan Holland, my boy. He usually knows what he's talking about.'

Jimmy read the ambassador's memorandum aloud. And at the end of it, Arnold Morgan was very thoughtful. 'Kinda fits with what the *Herald* was saying, right? Growing indignation about the Brits' claim, not only to the islands but also to the oil.'

79

'Well, presumably we supported that claim in 1982 so we're kinda stuck with it now, huh?'

'Yes. We are. That's why these observations in Buenos Aires may well be important.'

'Well, Ryan says he is not seeing anything official.'

'It doesn't need to be official, does it?' said Arnold Morgan. 'Argentina has spent a lot of time being ruled by a military junta. And officers from all three services have enormous influence in that country.

'In 1982, a couple of admirals were almost entirely responsible for that war. And if there was anything similar going on right now it would be very difficult to run the plotters to ground. Doesn't mean it isn't happening, though, does it?'

'No, it doesn't. Just as the United Nations search team couldn't find Saddam's nuclear program in Iraq. Didn't mean he didn't have one, did it?'

'No, Jimmy, it did not.' The Admiral spoke thoughtfully. 'It meant the UN guys could not find it. That's all. *Can't find* and *doesn't exist* are not the same. And only a left-wing politican could think they were.'

'Do you think we ought to do anything?'

'Well, not in a big hurry. But I would not be surprised if something was brewing. And it might not hurt to have the CIA check out the military bases along that southern coast of Argentina. Just in case they pick anything up.'

'OK – I'll get right on it, and if anything shakes loose I'll keep you informed.'

'Right, and get some reading done on the 1982 war in the South Atlantic. You never know, you might be glad of the knowledge some day. Read Admiral Sandy Woodward's book. It's the most accurate and interesting account.'

'OK, sir. See you soon.'

For the following few days, Jimmy Ramshawe tried to understand the causes and results of the Argentine decision to make a military landing on the Falkland Islands twenty-eight years ago. It was, he decided, pretty damned obvious they had decided to go for it after a slashing British government defence review in 1981 which saw two Royal Navy aircraft carriers, the *Hermes* and the *Invincible*, sold to India and Australia respectively.

It was also, he reckoned, a blinding error of judgement on Argentina's behalf: to misjudge not only the dates upon which the carriers would actually *leave* England but also the fact that Margaret Thatcher was a very determined Prime Minister – a lady of whom President Reagan once said, 'She's the best man they've got.'

Anyway, as far as Jimmy could see, the invasion of the Falklands had been a total screw-up, bound for failure from way back and a harsh lesson for all those determined to pick a fight with an opponent actually much tougher than they looked.

It was a quiet time politically all over the world, coming up to Christmas. No one was getting wildly excited about anything, not even the Palestinians. Jimmy's studies were seriously interrupted only twice, both times by Lenny Suchov over at CIA headquarters in Langley, Virginia.

The first time Lenny revealed that the Russians never had issued another formal press release about the Siberians who had died in the plane crash in the tundra. At least, they had not issued one which named the dead. They only announced the wreckage had not been found, and there were elements of doubt about who had and who had not been on board. The military authorities therefore considered it 'inappropriate' to make any formal statement about the disaster.

As Lenny had predicted, no one in the media felt much like braving the Arctic weather and conducting their own search in northern Siberia. Especially as the government had cordoned off the entire area and banned private aircraft and private investigations.

'All that,' said Lenny wryly, 'to prevent a search for an aircraft that was not there in the first place. Clever, hah? No one could get caught doing one single wrong thing.'

This left, of course, only the missing persons and their distraught families. And three days after his first call Lenny was back on the line with a report, meticulously put together by the CIA's men in Moscow and Yekaterinburg. It contained the names of nine people who had just vanished.

One fact stood out: none of their families knew of a flight which would have taken their husbands, sons, fathers or brothers away to the far north. No one knew anything about a conference in Murmansk. And it was most unusual, apparently, for any of them to travel by Russian Air Force jet.

These were extremely distinguished and important men, all of them occupying positions of the highest order, whether corporate or governmental. It might have been only provincial government, but this particular province was bigger than the entire USA. And its main power-brokers had just vanished.

'Nine of them,' yelled the excitable Lenny. 'How you say? Vamoosed. And no one seems to know anything. The Russian Air Force claims to have lost its aircraft, won't even name the missing aircrew. And the government "wishes it could help". Yeah, right. I've known these bastards for too long.'

Jimmy sat listening pensively to the irate Lenny who was predictably furious at behaviour from the modern Russian government which mirrored that of the old Soviet Union.

At length Jimmy said, 'Lenny, are all the families agreed the missing guys were going to Yekaterinburg?'

The CIA spymaster checked his file. 'Yes, they're agreed on that.'

'OK, then whatever happened to them might very well have happened in Yekaterinburg, right?'

'Correct, Jimmy. And I can tell you are about to wander down the same investigation path I went down, and then steal my best lines. Selfish Australian bastard, hah?'

Jimmy laughed. 'Yeah, well, I was only going to mention that when the Russian government announced the plane crash, just one day after it apparently happened, they must have been damn certain right then the guys concerned were never going to be seen again.'

'Precisely,' said Lenny. 'So they were either transported away from Yekaterinburg and executed, or murdered right there in the city – right?'

'Any report of anything unusual happening in the downtown area . . .?'

'Keep quiet, Australian bastard – I'm coming to that! Now, I have one report from our agent, and we only got it because I asked him if he noticed anything. He did not think it important enough to mention by himself . . .'

'And did he?'

'He did. He remembers from his diary he was downtown in Yekaterinburg on Monday morning 27 September because he was having his hair cut. God knows why, he's damn nearly bald. Anyway, usually he parks his car and walks down Central Avenue and then cuts through one of the side streets to the barber shop.

'But on this day he remembers one side street was cordoned off . . .'

'Did he remember which one?'

'Silence, Australian bastard,' said Lenny, routinely. 'No, he didn't. But when I asked him he said he couldn't remember the name, but it was the street down the side of the big Sibneft office building . . .'

'Get outta there!' said Jimmy incredulously. 'Ole Sergei Pobozhiy's place, one of the missing guys, right?'

'How the hell do you remember that?'

'Mostly because I'm an Australian bastard, I suppose.'

'I wonder if you also remember my man in Noyabrsk, the one who tracked Roman Rekuts into town from the airport the week before, tracked him to another Sibneft office where Sergei was also in residence . . .'

'Jesus. And did he know why the street in Yekaterinburg was blocked off?'

'No. But he remembered there were several big military transporters in there, and the guys guarding the barriers on Central Avenue were army, not police. Trouble was, he might have gone down that street, but he did not need to. So he just kept going – but he noticed it was closed, right down the side of the Sibneft building.'

'You don't think they massacred those guys right there in the building in cold blood?'

'Don't I?' said Lenny. 'I am afraid you don't know them like I do.'

'What time did the Russian Air Force issue that press release, the one about the plane crash?'

'Midnight, Jimmy. Same day. And you know that was deliberate, getting the story played down in Russia. I'm sure they had it ready many hours before that. I mean, Christ! The president, or at least the prime minister must have been involved. And I checked both their timetables that day.

'The PM was watching an ice hockey game, and the president was ensconced in the royal box in Theatre Square.'

'Where the hell's Theatre Square?'

'Moscow, James,' replied Lenny, hautily. 'It's the address of the Bolshoi Theatre, home of the greatest ballet company in the world. Christ, there's a few gaps in your world knowledge . . .'

'Well, Lenny, old mate,' said Jimmy, reverting to his best Crocodile Dundee accent, 'We don't get a lot of *par day durr* in the outback. Upsets the koalas.'

'Fuck me,' said Lenny, with mock exasperation. 'Anyway, listen – what I'm trying to say is, that press release must have been agreed sometime in the afternoon. By which time, the highest level of government in Russia knew, beyond doubt, that those guys were all dead and they were not coming back. Ever.'

'Guess so. By the way, is anyone kicking up a major fuss about them . . . I mean, like a wife or a son?'

'I don't think anyone dares. But Mrs Anton Katsuba is about ready to make a few demands. She says her husband never went on any journey without telling her exactly where he was going. And since she's about twenty years younger than him, a very beautiful ex-actress, you can't blame him for that.

'She's called Svetlana, and they live in Yekaterinburg. He told her there was a meeting downtown at Sibneft which he thought would be over by late afternoon. Said he'd meet her at seven p.m. at the cinema. But he never turned up. Never called. Was never heard from again. Going to Murmansk? She told our man that was the biggest lie she'd ever heard.'

'Beginning to sound like the biggest lie I've ever heard,' said Jimmy.

'Anyway, my boy,' said Lenny. 'To return to the big picture, we plainly have a very disturbing situation between the Russian government and Siberian oil. There must have been a threat of some kind by the Siberians. A threat which apparently could not be tolerated.'

'Then I guess that's it for now – oh, by the way, I just heard they've released Masorin's body to return to Russia.'

'Have they? That's a pretty old corpse by now, Jimmy.'

'Yeah, but it's frozen. Poor old Mikhail's preserved, cold.'

'I bet he's not as cold as those other nine guys, buried somewhere in northern Siberia,' replied Lenny darkly. 'Stay in touch.'

The young Lieutenant Commander replaced the phone and returned to his studies of Argentina and the Falklands War.

Three hundred and forty islands altogether. Two big ones, East and West Falkland, divided by the wide seaway of Falkland Sound. Only 320 miles from the nearest point on the Argentine mainland. Less than 5,000 square miles in area, about the size of Connecticut, or Northern Ireland. The computerised facts popped out at him.

Jimmy scanned down the screen, muttering to himself snippets of key information in his usual quaint Aussie phraseology: *'Been British since Captain John Strong fell over 'em in 1690. Home to a coupla thousand sheep-shaggers. Nearly all of 'em Poms. A Pom colony with Her Maj Head of State. Same as Australia. Christ, Queen Elizabeth of the*

Falklands. When you think . . . her great-great-Granny Victoria was Empress of India. That's what I call a significant decline.

'Still, it says here the Falklands are home to the rare and bloody fragile Rockhopper Penguins, not to mention the ole Black-Browed Albatross. Wouldn't want to lose either of 'em, myself.'

He came to the section on oil exploration, staring for a long while at the numbering systems used for the quadrants and blocks contained in the massive 400,000-square-kilometre Designated Zone. This was over half as big as Texas and it surrounded the islands completely, ending sharply in the west, where Argentine waters began, over the *Malvinas* basin.

Many oil licences had been awarded, and indeed Occidental Argentina had been busy drilling in these waters under licensing agreements with the UK and Argentine governments. To the north, fourteen companies had been awarded production licences, directly from London.

And although everyone knew that in reality London controlled the whole operation, no one really cared – until the big on-land oil strike in late 2009.

At that point it became serious business, because oil located on land was about ten times easier to get at than deep-sea crude in offshore locations and thus was considerably cheaper. The Argentine oil consortiums never had a chance. Exxon Mobil was in there, quick as a flash, partnered by British Petroleum. Whatever oil there was immediately came under the control of the American colossus and the British giant.

By the end of the week Jimmy was an expert on the state of the Falkland Islands unrest. But his efforts seemed rather in vain, as nothing new surfaced, neither in Argentina nor Siberia, and phone calls from Lenny Suchov dried up.

The first fresh snippet of interesting news emerged a couple of days after the New Year, when Ryan Holland reported a massive New Year's Eve demonstration in Plaza de Mayo. About half a million people had crowded into the square before midnight, and they spent thirty minutes chanting '*Viva Las Malvinas!*' for no apparent reason. And shortly before midnight they had their way.

The president of Argentina, in company with two of his most trusted commanders, General Eduardo Kampf and Admiral Oscar Moreno, came out onto the balcony and faced the enormous throng of people, just as Juan Perón and his widow Isabelita had done decades earlier.

The president motioned the crowd to silence, and through a microphone wished them all the happiest and most prosperous New Year. He said, 'God bless you all, and God bless this great land of ours, this Argentina, this heaven on Earth . . .'

And the crowd rose up and chanted, shouting his name, shouting their loyalty to the republic.

And then, as the president was about to turn away, he did something which stunned everyone in the square. He suddenly seized the microphone again. With his clenched fist held high, he bellowed, '*VIVA LAS MALVINAS!*'

What followed was nothing short of pandemonium, a scene of patriotic fervour unmatched in the Plaza de Mayo since General Leopoldo Galtieri had stood on that same balcony in 1982. No one ever forgot how that president had faced one million people and sent them into a patriotic frenzy by shouting those very same words.

'*VIVA LAS MA-A-A-A-L-V-I-N-A-S!*'

Ryan Holland had watched the scene on television, noticing how Admiral Moreno and General Kampf enthusiastically patted the president on the back when finally he turned back through the palace door.

And in his report the US Ambassador noted: *I thought the entire performance seemed pre-planned. It was the most inflammatory action. The size of that crowd was too enormous to be ignored. And the photographs from the square were used on the front pages of every Argentine newpaper the following day.*

Television channels made it the lead item on their news programmes all day, and every single headline featured the word 'Malvinas'. Still, there have only been official denials in Buenos Aires: both government and military simply say that nothing unusual is going on. I'm surprised we haven't heard a word from London, but then again, they didn't say anything last time, remember?

I don't really believe Argentina's official line. Rumours here are rife. People suddenly seem to talk of little else except the recapture of those damn islands. I have not one shred of proof, but I shall be most surprised if something doesn't break loose in the next couple of months.

As it happened, something broke loose precisely six weeks later, on Sunday morning, 13 February 2011. At first light, a United States-built A-4 Skyhawk light bomber from Argentina's 2nd Naval Attack Squadron came screaming off the runway at Rio Gallegos and out over the Atlantic to make a rendezvous with a refuelling tanker forty miles off the coast of Argentina.

Full of fuel, with the sun rising way up ahead, the Skyhawk's pilot, Flight Lieutenant Gilberto Aliaga, set a course 110 degrees east-south-east for the 400-mile run to the *Malvinas* and opened the throttles.

Flying at 30,000 feet, the bomber took thirty-five minutes to come in sight of the jagged coastline of the Passage Islands, fifty miles ahead, guarding the western approach to West Falkland. He immediately swerved south-east and almost went into a dive, still making 600 knots.

Aliaga made a great sweeping loop, keeping his eye on the coastline of East Falkland on his port side. Now, coming in at low level out of the south-east, just above the waves and below the radar horizon, he 'popped up' as he swung around the coastline, ripping through the radar and taking a bearing on his target before diving back down.

Flying fast over open water, heading north-west now, he turned on his own radar and spotted his target one and a half miles out. He released two deadly 1,000lb iron bombs, which went flashing across the surface straight into the harbour where the only resident warship was in clear view. Instantly, Aliaga swung away to the south-west, completely undetected by anyone on land.

No one identified the bombs as they came hurtling at high speed across the water. The first anyone knew of it was when HMS *Leeds Castle*, moored alongside the jetty at Mare Harbour, exploded in a fireball at exactly 0755 on that bright, clear Sunday morning.

The blast tore the heart out of the ship, obliterating the engine room, and the ops room, located midships below the upperworks and the big radar mast. All on board, twenty-three men, were dead in an instant, incinerated when the half-ton iron bombs had slammed into the hull and upperworks on the starboard side and detonated with savage force.

HMS *Leeds Castle* was now essentially scrap metal. As warships go, she was very small, only 265 feet long, and the wallop in those big Argentine bombs could have sunk a man-sized destroyer. The few Royal Navy personnel sleeping in the accommodation block were jolted awake by the blast. They came charging out onto the jetty, half dressed and stunned at the sight before them.

The only warship the Falklands had was ablaze from end to end, a searing hot fire sending flames and black smoke from burning fuel

100 feet into the air. No one knew what was going on and what kind of accident could have wiped out the entire ship at one blow.

But this was no accident. The forces of Argentina had been preparing for this moment for almost three months. Just for openers, Admiral Moreno had sent a Lockheed P-3B Orion to track the 4,200-ton British Type-23 guided missile frigate *St Albans* as soon as it left for the Caribbean. Right now it was four days out and making twenty-five knots, 2,400 miles north of the Falklands, 300 miles off Rio de Janeiro. And irrelevant.

This attack was a proper military operation, conducted by excellent strategists, commanding officers who weeks previously had placed their assault crews and selected aircraft crews on immediate notice to deploy. Since mid-December they had all been sealed off from the outside world in carefully guarded camps and barracks – waiting for the highly dangerous British frigate to come and go.

The Argentine bombers earmarked for the attack had been flown down from their parent bases to Rio Gallegos where the forward tactical command headquarters had been established.

And even as the Royal Navy's makeshift damage-control units finally connected their hoses to quell the fires, two French-built delta-winged Mirage III Es, proudly displaying the livery of the Argentine Air Force, came sweeping out of the skies above the northern coast of East Falkland.

Each armed with twin 30mm cannon and two air-to-surface missiles, they flew fast at 20,000 feet, flashing over the settlement of Port San Carlos, which had not echoed to the roar of fighter-bombers for twenty-eight years.

The Mirage jets swerved overland, high above the foothills of desolate Mount Simon, and screamed over the landlocked end of Teal Inlet, crossing the lower slopes of Wickham Heights. And at that moment, Royal Air Force Sergeant Biff Wakefield picked them up on his Rapier missile radar system on Mount Pleasant airfield, twelve miles to the south.

He caught two 'paints' moving very fast, and he picked up a French radar transmission, precisely as Oscar Moreno knew he would. Sergeant Wakefield tracked the two 'paints' even though he knew they were well beyond the reach of his own missiles.

Outside, beyond his small concrete-built ops room, the two big Rapier missile launchers stood at permanent readiness. But there was no point activating them yet, the two Mirage jets were over

Berkeley Sound headed out to sea and off the screens. But Biff Wakefield kept them tracked as well as he could.

Little could he have known what lay ahead. Suddenly out of the skies north of Falkland Sound burst two more Mirage III Es, rocketing over the rocky granite coast. But not on the same easterly course as the other two. This pair was heading south-east.

And before Sergeant Wakefield's three-man team even had a chance to locate and identify the planes, the Argentine pilots unleashed two air-to-surface bombs each, all four of them aimed at the big short-range RAF Rapier launchers to the west of Mount Pleasant airfield.

They came homing in at more than 500 m.p.h., blasting both launchers to smithereens, followed by the second two Mirage jets which opened up with their 30mm cannon, riddling the area with shells that smashed through the window of the ops room, killing Sergeant Wakefield and both of his duty operators. Their radar surveillance was still aimed to the north-east in search of Argentina's fleeing decoys.

In the space of five minutes, Great Britain's seaborne defensive unit, HMS *Leeds Castle*, and the entire air-defence cover system for Mount Pleasant had ceased to exist. And that was by no means the worst of it.

Ninety minutes before first light, 500 marines from Argentina's 2nd Battalion had disembarked from landing craft on the deserted coast just west of Fitzroy. They had been marching steadily for a little over two hours, and right now were positioned on a bluff overlooking the airport. They were late, cursing their luck at not making it in the dark, but nonetheless ready for their daylight assault on the British garrison.

Meanwhile, the garrison ops room on the airfield which had been ignored in the air-attack on the Rapier launchers realised they'd been slammed by bombs or missiles. They could see the flames still leaping skywards from the harbour.

Captain Peter Merrill ordered his immediate-response platoon stood to. They had weapons and ammunition to hand, and the duty officer had them deploy instantly, initially to man all pre-prepared positions around the airfield buildings and control tower.

The captain alerted the company commander, Major Bobby Court, who ordered every man in his 150-strong force to get up, dress, assemble, and draw their weapons from the armory, full scales of ammunition from the stores' colour sergeant. The machine-gun section also drew their weapons, together with spare barrels and 12,000 rounds of boxed ammunition packed into belts of 250.

Twenty minutes later, with everything and everyone loaded onto army trucks, they began to move out of the garrison towards the airport buildings. And as they did so, they heard the opening bursts of gunfire erupt from the bluff to the west as the Argentine marines began to rain down fire on the vehicles of the British immediate-response platoon.

Led by Lieutenant Derek Mitchell the British soldiers poured out of the trucks and went to ground, desperately trying to locate where the small-arms fire was coming from. They had taken nine casualties in that opening burst and the stretcher parties were not yet assembled.

It took five minutes to identify the positions of the Argentine marines, and Lieutenant Mitchell ordered his men to fire at will. The Argentines could see they were up against a much smaller force than they'd expected, and they began to advance.

The British infantry held them as best they could, but the marines were well commanded by Major Pablo Barry. He split his force, ordering a separate company to move around onto the left flank of Lieutenant Mitchell's platoon.

That took fifteen minutes, and the moment they were in position Major Barry ordered the marines to fix bayonets, spread out in assault formation, and advance. By now the British immediate-response platoon had taken heavy casualties, and its numbers had been reduced by approximately half.

Which left around twenty-five British infantrymen to face 500 Argentines advancing from all directions. Right now they were still trying to fire at the first company which had engaged them.

With only fifty yards between the troops, the flanking marine assault party began to close in, opening fire, gunning down the British soldiers from this unexpected direction. They also used their bayonets to great effect. Overwhelmed by sheer weight of numbers, not one British rifleman survived the battle. Lieutenant Mitchell died from bayonet wounds to his back and lungs. The Argentines lost only twenty-three marines.

Meanwhile Major Bobby Court had the rest of his infantry company thundering into position, the big army vehicles transporting everyone to the airfield and its surrounds. They knew things had already gone badly for the immediate-response group, but they still had two heavy machine guns, which they carefully sited on the flanks of their defensive position. They might have been surprised and outnumbered, and they might have been totally unprepared to withstand an assault on this scale, but still the Brits were no pushover.

As the Argentine marines began their second advance towards the airport buildings, Major Court's machine guns raked the area, the fire converging across the front of the company. The invading Argentine marines took over fifty casualties on their first assault, retreated and gave the defenders time to organise a first-aid post and bring up reserve stocks of ammunition.

Again the Argentines attacked and were once more repulsed. Now they started to use their mortars, laying down indirect fire and still trying to penetrate the wall of metal spitting from the British machine guns.

Once more they took many casualties out there on that exposed ground. But they kept coming, using smoke bombs to disguise their advance, running forward, hurling grenades close-in to the trenches, all under cover of a mortar barrage.

And, as before, they eventually overwhelmed the defenders by weight of numbers. Only seventeen British riflemen survived, eight of them badly wounded. Major Pablo Barry immediately took charge, calling upon all civilians in the airport buildings to offer no resistance. The wounded from both sides were taken into the buildings where British and Argentine medical staff administered first aid to the casualties.

Major Court had been badly injured in the attack and died that evening in the passenger terminal. And just before he passed away, the last element of British resistance was removed as an Argentine Special Forces troop of seventy-five flew in from Rio Gallegos and immediately overwhelmed the small naval garrison at Mare Harbour with one volley of light machine-gun fire along the jetty. Only two of the seven sailors still on duty were hit, and Lt. Commander Malcolm Farley ordered his men to surrender.

Two hours later the big Argentine C-130s began landing at Mount Pleasant, carrying troops and light vehicles of the 4th Airborne Brigade based at Cordoba. Swiftly organised, they took it upon themselves to haul down every British flag at the airport and replaced them with the light blue and white bandera of the Republic of Argentina.

They then turned north and drove into Port Stanley, using

bullhorns to instruct the citizens to stay within their houses. As they'd been ordered, they were swift and brutal in their response to any objections to their presence, clubbing down five islanders with rifle butts and booting in the doors of any houses that looked as though they could be sheltering armed civilians.

At 1800 they ordered the Governor out of his residence and drove him and his family and staff to the airfield, shipping them out immediately by air to Rio Gallegos.

At fifteen minutes past six o'clock on Sunday evening, 13 February 2011, the Argentine flag flew over Port Stanley for the first time since June 1982, when Britain's 2nd Battalion Parachute Regiment had ripped it down and replaced it with the Union Flag of Great Britain. In London, it was ten o'clock in the evening.

CHAPTER FOUR

The most astonishing aspect of the lightning-fast Argentine military action on that Sunday in mid-February 2011 was the failure or inability of the British land forces to make any form of communication with their High Command. The same applied to the survivors in the Royal Navy garrison.

Under normal circumstances Lieutenant Commander Malcolm Farley would have contacted the closest naval operations base instantly, but Lt. Commander Farley had a 1,400-ton warship on fire right outside his front door, with many dead and some wounded. The nearest help was all of 2,400 miles away – the north-heading frigate – and his home base was 8,000 miles away in Portsmouth.

Major Bobby Court had similar problems. There had been a ferocious attack on the missile system which should have protected the airport and his men were under serious small-arms fire. Generally speaking, everyone was doing their best just to stay alive. The nearest help was thousands of miles away.

Neither Lt. Commander Farley nor Major Court lived to communicate with London and it was not until six p.m. that Sergeant Alan Peattie, who had manned one of the heavy machine guns and somehow emerged unscathed, called the British Army HQ in Wilton, near Salisbury. Here the duty officer, stunned by what he heard, hit the encrypted line to the Ministry of Defence.

At 10.24 p.m. the telephone rang in the British Prime Minister's country retreat, the great Elizabethan mansion, Chequers, situated deep in the Chiltern Hills north-west of London. The Defence

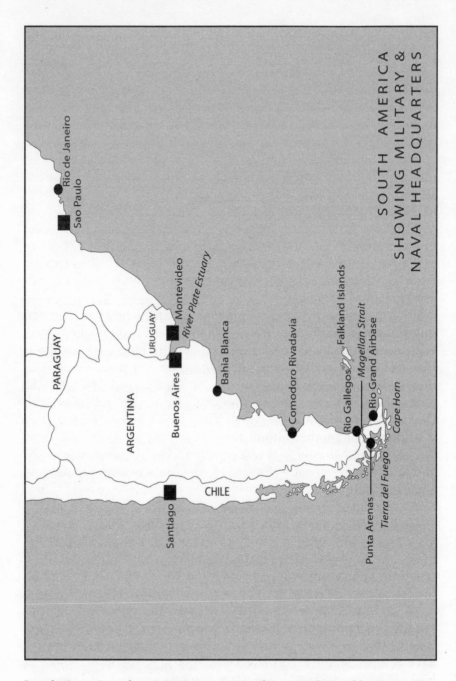

South America, showing Argentine military and naval bases.

Minister, the urbane former university lecturer Peter Caulfield, personally relayed the daunting news.

'*Argentine troops have invaded the Falkland Islands. The British garrison fell shortly before ten p.m. GMT. Port Stanley is occupied by Argentine marines. HMS* Leeds Castle *has been destroyed. Governor Manton is under arrest. The national flag of Argentina flies over the islands.*'

The colour drained from the PM's face. He actually thought he might throw up. Twice during the previous month he had been alerted to the obvious unrest in Buenos Aires, the crowds in front of the presidential palace's balcony on New Year's Eve.

There had been reports from the military attaché in Buenos Aires of troop movements and, more importantly, of aircraft movement at the Argentine bases in the south of the country. He also recalled ignoring mentions of Argentine anger at the oil situation on East Falkland.

He had spoken to the Foreign Minister three times in Cabinet, mildly asking whether there was any need to sit up and take notice. Each time he had been told, 'We've been listening to this stuff for over twenty years. Yes, the Argentines are less than happy. But they've been less than happy for the greater part of 180 years. In point of fact we've had exceptionally agreeable relations with Buenos Aires for a very long time. They won't make a move. They wouldn't want another humiliation.'

The Prime Minister had accepted that. But the decisions in the end were his, as were any glory and any blame. And this was a Prime Minister who was allergic to blame – at least, he was if it was directed at him.

He excused himself from the crowded dinner table, gestured to his secretary and walked slowly through the central hall, past the huge log fire which gave this historic place a faint smell of woodsmoke in every room, and into his study. Here he picked up the telephone, greeting the Minister of Defence curtly.

'Well, Prime Minster,' said the voice on the other end. 'Not to put too fine a point on it, but Argentina just conquered the Falkland Islands. Our troops defended the place as best they could, but we have at least 150 dead, and HMS *Leeds Castle* is still on fire with her keel resting on the bottom of Mare Harbour.'

'So it *is* true,' said the PM, feeling faint. His thoughts flashed, as they always did in moments of crisis, to the front pages of tomorrow's newspapers and tonight's television news.

'I'm sure you realise, sir,' continued the minister, 'we have no adequate military response within thousands of miles. I regret to say you are in an identical situation to Margaret Thatcher in 1982. We either negotiate a truce, with some kind of sharing of authority, or we go to war. I firmly recommend the former.'

'But what about the media?' the PM replied hoarsely. 'They'll be all over this like flies if they find out about the warnings we received from Buenos Aires. The Foreign Secretary will have to resign.'

'Prime Minister, I do understand your concerns. But right now we have to deal with 150 dead British soldiers, sailors and airmen on East Falkland. Arrangements have to be made. Someone has to speak to the President of Argentina. I am happy to open the talks – but I think you are going to have to speak to him personally. Meanwhile, I think the Foreign Office should start by making the strongest possible protest to the United Nations. I'm suggesting an emergency Cabinet meeting in Downing Street tonight, perhaps attended by the military Chiefs of Staff.'

'But what about the media?' repeated the Prime Minister doggedly, too shocked to be able to prioritise. 'Can we not stall them somehow? Call in the press officers and our political advisers? See how best to handle it?'

'It's a bit late for that,' the minister replied, a hint of impatience now creeping into his previously respectful tone. 'The Argentines will have the full story on the news wires, probably as I speak – *Heroic forces of Argentina recapture the Malvinas – British defeated after fierce fighting – the flag of Argentina flies at last over the islands. Viva Las Malvinas* – and all that. There is no way we can stop that.'

'Will the press blame me?'

'Undoubtedly, sir. I am afraid they will.'

'Will it bring down my government?'

'The Falklands nearly brought down Mrs Thatcher. But she instantly went to war, with the cheers of the damned populace ringing in her ears. And the military loved her.'

'They don't love me.'

'No, sir. Nor me.'

'Downing Street. Midnight, then.'

'I'll see you there, sir.'

The British Prime Minister walked back across Chequers's central hall with a chill in his heart. He was not the first PM to feel that and he probably would not be the last. But there was no room for manoeuvre in this situation. And it would require him to address the nation, immediately after the Cabinet meeting. He knew already that the press would give him a very, very rough ride . . .

'Surely, Prime Minister, you were aware of the unrest in Buenos Aires? Were you not told by your diplomatic advisers that all was not well in the South Atlantic? Stuff like this never happens without considerable preparation by the aggressors – surely someone must have known something was going on?'

But the one he really dreaded was 'Prime Minister, you and your government have spent years making heavy cuts to the defence budget, especially to the Navy – do you now regret that?'

He would take no questions at that first announcement, that was for certain. He needed time to think, time to confer with his media advisers, time to arrange his party line, time to deflect the blame either onto Whitehall or the military. But time, that was the most important thing. He had to buy himself some time.

Meanwhile, he couldn't show panic. He had to return to his guests. And he thanked God he had not invited anyone for this Sunday-night dinner who was connected in any way with the military.

Seated around the table were the kind of people a modern progressive Britain admired. Honeyford Jones, a hugely successful gay pop singer, who was reputed to be a billionaire. There was the international football striker Freddie Leeson and his gorgeous wife Madelle who not long ago had worked in a nightclub. The ageing film star Darien Farr and his wife Loretta, a former television weather forecaster. The celebrity London restaurateur Freddy Ivanov Windsor, who sported a somewhat unusual name for an English lout.

These were the kind of high achievers a contemporary prime minister needed around him, real people, successful in the modern world. Not those dreadful old establishment politicians, business-men, diplomats and military commanders so favoured by Margaret Thatcher.

On an impulse, the Prime Minister decided to tell them what had happened.

'I'm afraid our armed forces have had a bit of a setback in the South Atlantic,' he said gravely. 'The Argentines have just attacked the Falkland Islands.'

'Where's that?' asked Loretta.

'Oh, it's in the South Atlantic – a tiny British protectorate going way back to the nineteenth century,' he replied. 'Of course, we knew there was a lot of unrest in the area, but I don't think my Foreign Office realised quite how volatile the situation was.'

'Jesus. I remember the last time that happened,' said Darien. 'I was in my, like, dressing room on the set . . . and they announced on the television we'd been attacked . . . I was . . . you know . . . like, wow!'

'Oh, that must have been awful for you – in the middle of a movie and everything,' said Madelle.

'Well, we all knew it was very uncool,' Darien replied. 'You know, really, really bad, getting attacked by a South American country . . . but I mean everyone was totally, like, wow!'

'So what is it with these fuckin' Argeneeros, then?' asked Freddie. 'I mean what are they on about? First up, they got a bloody big country, ain't they? Second, do I look as if I care there's a war or whatever in the Falktons, I mean, like, who gives?'

The Prime Minister, for the first time in his premiership, suddenly wished he had chosen different friends for dinner. He stood up and said, 'I'm sorry. But I'm sure you all understand I have to return to London.'

Everyone nodded, and Loretta called out, 'Get on your mobile, babe. The army will get down there. Best in the world, right? Sort them Argeneeros out, no pressure.'

The PM shuddered as he made his way back across the central hall and outside to the waiting government limousine. He had staff to sort out the details of his return to Downing Street. He just climbed in the rear seat of the Jaguar and sighed the sigh of the deeply troubled.

Like all prime ministers, he loved the grandeur of this 700-acre country retreat. And he was aware of the immense decisions which had been reached down the years within its walls. He also knew, and the knowledge caused his soul a slight quiver, that Margaret Thatcher had sat in her study at Chequers to compose her personal account of the mighty British victory in the Falklands nearly thirty years ago.

He was assailed by doubts, the kind of doubts that cascade in upon a self-seeking career politician who does not possess the guiding light of goodness and purpose that had always gripped Margaret Thatcher. Gloomily, he gazed out at the Chequers estate gliding by outside, frosty in the pale moonlit night.

He truly did not know if he would return this way again, given the Brits' unnerving habit of unloading a prime minister before you could say 'knife'. Out of Downing Street in under twenty-four hours; glorious weekends at Chequers . . . well . . . those then became instant history. Pack your stuff and make a fast exit.

Traffic returning to London was light, and the PM had only an hour or so to ruminate on his recent exchange with Sir Jock Fergusom, chairman of the hugely influential Joint Intelligence Committee. In two very private phone calls, Sir Jock had tipped him off about the trouble brewing in Buenos Aires.

This hadn't been the kind of news a government wanted to hear, not with a general election coming up in less than seven months. No PM could afford to take his nation to war and then ask for everyone's vote. Even Winston Churchill had been unable to pull that one off in 1945, after the Second World War.

And if they could throw the Great One out, the PM thought unhappily, they could sure as hell throw *him* out. 'Jock,' the Prime Minister had said, 'let me have a nice little memorandum, would you? One which mentions the popular rumblings in Argentina about renewed military action over *Las Malvinas*. But in your opinion there isn't a shred of hard evidence on any of the diplomatic grapevines to suggest any such thing has a basis in reality.'

'Well,' replied Sir Jock, 'That is more or less true.'

'Absolutely,' replied the P.M. 'But it gives me a bit of cover if everything blows up and we're caught unaware. You will not regret this, I assure you.'

From this Prime Minister, that last statement meant one thing: *Sir Jock, old boy, stand by for an elevation to the peerage in the next Honor List.*

'Lord Ferguson of Fife, that's got a fine ring to it,' thought the JIC Chairman.

That memorandum, the one which would partly exonerate the Prime Minister, was tucked away in a desk drawer in Downing Street, in readiness for the day when it might be needed.

Driving swiftly through the suburbs of west London, the chauffeur had the head of the British Government home in his official residence before 11.30 p.m. And when he arrived there were three further pieces of news awaiting him.

First, the Argentine marines had pressed on to both of the major oil-drilling rigs on East Falkland, to the north of Darwin Harbour, and to the south of Fitzroy. According to the message from Exxon Mobil in Rio, they had arrested every last one of the British and American oil personnel and flown them out in an air force C-130

99

to Rio Gallegos. No one thought they would be returning any time soon.

Just as unwelcome was news of a further Argentine marine landing on the island of South Georgia, another purely British protectorate 1,100 miles east-south-east of the Falklands. South Georgia was the Alps of the South Atlantic, a far-flung remnant of the British Empire, a forbidding island of glaciers and towering mountains and the last resting place of the legendary British explorer Sir Ernest Shackleton.

The Argentines had first raised their national flag above the island when they'd landed there in 1982, and it had taken a very determined group of Great Britain's finest to recapture it.

Now the Argentines had not only done it again but they had also arrested all US and UK oil personnel working on the gigantic new South Georgia natural-gas strike zone, which Exxon Mobil and BP had been organizing for the past eight months.

To make matters infinitely worse, there was a disgruntled message from the President of the United States, requesting a call-back to discuss what Great Britain planned to do in order to rectify this disgraceful military aggression against the citizens of both countries.

The Prime Minister retreated immediately to his private office and put in a call to the President of the United States. And, as communications between the two allies went, this contact was not encouraging.

The President recommended immediate negotiations with Argentina. He did not recommend a war, but he wanted a deal done over the oil. In the event that the Westminster parliament felt they needed to declare some kind of military action against the new occupiers of this British colony, the US President would help but he would not send in troops.

'The Falklands are British islands,' said Paul Bedford. 'And if you guys really want them back, that's up to you. As your friends we're here to help. But I will *not* take my country into someone else's war in someone else's country unless the reasons are overriding as they were in Iraq. But we *do* want a deal over that oil, you hear me? You better speak to Pedro What's-his-name in Buenos Aires and see what you can agree.'

The British Prime Minister was highly sceptical about Pedro What's-his-name. Like most of his Cabinet the PM had never had a proper job in the private sector where money and results counted.

He was essentially a politician, a bureaucrat, paid for from the public purse and used to spending enormous amounts of government money living off the hog, surrounded by spin-doctors who tried to manipulate the press in his favour, day after day.

A down and dirty powwow with a South American president, ex-military, ex-cattle rancher, and horse-trader from way back, who'd just conquered over 300 British islands in about ten minutes – well, that was not really the PM's game. He knew nothing of the cut and thrust of big business, preferring to make obscure, abstract speeches about saving the starving children of Africa, and AIDs, and democracy. Stuff where you can't get caught out.

Jesus. What the hell did Bedford want from him? And what if he took the country to war? What if the British lost? What then? This was probably the worst day of his life. He'd always wanted a place in someone's history book. But not like this.

A further note on his desk reminded him that a few weeks ago an angry crowd in the Plaza de Mayo had carried in a huge cardboard banner showing him with a black patch over his eye and scrawled across it the words *Bandito de Las Malvinas*.

The PM did not speak Spanish but it was easy enough to get the drift of that one, and he had been none too pleased to hear the crowd had set fire to the placard, chanting whatever was Spanish for 'Public Enemy Number One'. The crowd had no idea that he was actually their best friend, that it was his swingeing cuts to the UK's army and air force and to the Royal Navy which would make a British reconquest of *Las Malvinas* darned nearly impossible.

And now what? Every member of his government knew what they had done. Though they would all duck and dive out of harm's way when the blame began to be hurled at them. Damn cowards. He'd see about that. He was not prepared to take the rap for this. No. He most definitely was not.

But the trouble was, everything was way out of his control. The world news was breaking from Buenos Aires, and the global media would be dominated by the devastating victory of the Argentines. He, Great Britain's Prime Minister, was a bit player at the scene of his own potential destruction.

The press would want answers from him to two key questions. Should someone have known this was about to happen? And what was he going to do about it?

To the first question the answer was plainly yes; and the most junior reporter would take about fifteen minutes to prove it. To the second, the answer was a plain, simple, unequivocal, 'God knows.'

By ten minutes to midnight, the PM's colleagues were arriving. The Foreign Secretary, Roger Eltringham, was first, followed by the Minister of Defence, Peter Caulfield. He had taken the time to call in the First Sea Lord, Admiral Sir Rodney Jeffries, and the Chief of the Defence Staff, General Sir Robin Brenchley. The Home Secretary was there, plus the Transport Secretary. The Lord Chancellor and the Chancellor of the Exchequer, both of whom could be counted on to have a joint heart attack at the very mention of war and its attendant expenditure.

The Prime Minister took Peter Caulfield aside to hiss that he might have gone beyond his brief to summon the military. But the Defence Minister replied, 'Sir, we're talking war here. We have been attacked. And we may be obliged to hit back. We need the military for advice and assessment.'

'Very well,' replied the PM, who had himself invited one press secretary and three of his personal spin doctors. He called the meeting to order and opened by stating, 'As you all now know, Argentina has attacked the Falkland Islands, apparently with some success, and now declares the islands – which they call *Las Malvinas* – free of British rule for the first time in 180 years.'

Roger Eltringham immediately informed the other Cabinet members he had sent the strongest possible protest to the United Nations, demanding the Security Council should take action of censure against the Argentine Republic. The attack had been nothing short of a pre-emptive and brutal military strike against a peace-loving sovereign people, loyal to the British Crown, and who now lay under the jackboot of a South American dictator.

The Prime Minister nodded his thanks and turned to Peter Caulfield, who said, 'I think you should perhaps decide whether or not you wish to retain the possibility of a military response, in which case I think we should first hear from Admiral Sir Rodney Jeffries, and General Sir Robin Brenchley. I say this because they may consider a military response impossible, in which case our options are very restricted.'

The Prime Minister winced visibly for two reasons: at being asked to consider the possibility of going to war, and at the prospect of being lectured by the general and some bloody battle-hardened admiral.

Slowly, he turned over the pages of the notes in front of him and then said, in a statesmanlike way, 'No country with our traditions and position in the hierarchy of the world's nations can afford to dismiss the possibility of a military response to an attack on its people. But before I make any decisions, I think Roger should enlighten us concerning the likely reactions of the rest of the world.'

Foreign Secretary Eltringham looked doubtful. 'As far as I can see,' he said, 'most of the world will be damn glad not to be involved. Our nearest neighbour France has sold the Argentines practically every piece of military hardware they own, particularly their Mirage fighter jets, the Super-Étendards and the Exocet missiles. And they will surely hope to sell them more. They also probably secretly hope we shall be defeated.'

'I thought we already had been,' interjected Admiral Jeffries.

'And just to conclude,' added Roger Eltringham, 'the only other nation with any real interest in this conflict is the United States. I can tell you right now they will not want to fight alongside us. But neither will they want to lose out in that oil situation down there. Like last time, they'll give covert help. But they won't commit their own forces in a ground or even a naval war.'

'I spoke to President Bedford a short while ago,' said the Prime Minister. 'And he said more or less what you just outlined . . . I suppose the question I must ask, is, do we have the capacity to fight a war in the South Atlantic, 8,000 miles from home?' Grudgingly, he turned to the two military men.

'Rather more pertinent, Prime Minister,' said General Brenchley, 'is whether or not you have the courage to stand up in the House of Commons and tell them we don't.'

The Prime Minister bridled. 'General,' he said, 'you and Admiral Jeffries are here to offer military advice, so perhaps both of you would restrict yourselves to that area. And perhaps you would answer my question. Do we have that capacity?'

His defiant glance was met with an equally hostile glare. General Brenchley loathed 'professional' politicians. 'No, Prime Minister,' he said gruffly. 'We don't. And if we went, we couldn't win.'

The Cabinet room went silent. 'Surely there's some course of action open to us?' said the PM.

'How about surrender?' grunted the general.

Admiral Jeffries chuckled sourly at the hideous but almost inevitable way in which all their chickens had come home to roost: the defence cuts year after year, the reductions in recruits, equipment, ships, aircraft, regiments, and the downturn of military morale.

Like General Brenchley, he sensed an onrushing feeling of power. If the military chiefs said no right here, there could be no armed response to the Argentine assault. They both knew that. So did the Prime Minister and his Cabinet colleagues.

General Brenchley stood up, towering over the table of politicians, none of whom had ever served in the military or had a proper job outside political parties, trade unions and general public rabble-rousing. Maybe a couple of lawyers, specialising in human rights, or some such bloody nonsense. All of them, in the opinion of the military, were, generally speaking, either beneath contempt, or hard on the border line.

But right now the military held sway. General Brenchley said coldly, 'Prime Minister, I feel I owe you an explanation. And I'm going to give it. You and your Chancellor, over the past several years, have made the following increases in government spending budgets: sixty-one per cent for the International Development Department, whatever the hell that is. Sixty per cent for the Home Office – that's several million more civil servants; fifty-one per cent for Education, mostly trying to teach the unteachable; and fifty per cent more for Health.

'On the other hand, the Defence budget has been increased by three per cent, which represents a massive net loss to us who try to serve in this country's armed forces. It used to be one civil servant for every eleven soldiers, it's now one and a half civil servants for every one soldier, which is, to be frank, bloody ridiculous.'

The words of the general stunned everyone around the table. But Robin Brenchley had the beleaguered Prime Minister on the run. And they both knew it. Right now, General Brenchley, Chief of Great Britain's Defence Staff, was unsackable, and he intended to make the most of it.

'Because you and your Chancellor regard us – disdainfully, for some reason – as spenders of the nation's wealth, you have systematically undermined every branch of the armed services, all in the cause of your constant desire to seek savings. Your disdain for us has infected all ranks – their morale, their sense of self-worth and their concerns for their future careers.

'Defence expenditure in this country has declined by thirty-five per cent. One-third of our personnel has vanished. Our conventional submarine force has gone from thirty-five to twelve. The destroyer and frigate force is down from forty-eight to twenty-eight, our infantry battalions are down from fifty-five to thirty-eight. Our tank strength has fallen by forty-five per cent. The number of effective fighter aircraft in the Royal Air Force remains at zero, where it has been ever since the Phantom was taken out of service.

'Prime Minister, five years ago, you and your Chancellor scrapped the only decent fighter-bomber the country possessed. Not only was it a highly effective all-weather interceptor, it could also operate as a ground-attack fighter, a recce and probe aircraft, and as a ship strike aircraft. Furthermore, it could operate from the steel deck of an aircraft carrier anywhere in the world.

'I must tell you, Prime Minister, the loss of the Sea Harrier FA2 capability represents the loss of our Fleet's ability to defend itself. This applies also to its associated land forces and their ability to defend against any form of sophisticated air attack.

'We have no new carriers in sight. Which means we are left with *Ark Royal*, small, twenty-five years old with only ground-attack aircraft and helicopters on its deck. And the *Illustrious*, at three months' notice, and even older.

'We do not even have the air-defence capability of the Sea Harrier FA1 which we had in 1982. Today we face a greatly improved Argentine air force. The FA2, which you so carelessly discarded, was, I must remind you, armed with a fully integrated missile system which could engage four aircraft, or even sea-skimming missiles, simultaneously, at ranges out to thirty-five miles, at speeds up to Mach-3. That little Sea Harrier effectively won the war for us in the Falklands in 1982.

'As you know, you and your financial ministers forced this brilliant little warhorse out of service well before the originally planned date, purely because of cost. And with a statement we all regarded as madness, your Defence Minister—' Barely pausing, the general rasped, 'Not you, Caulfield.' Then he continued, 'Your Defence Minister announced the Harrier's replacement to be the Harrier GR7/9. Understandable. That's the only fixed-wing aircraft we have left that can operate from the deck of a small carrier.

'But the GR7/9 is a small STOVL ground-attack aircraft with no radar. It can carry two advanced short-range air-to-air missiles (ASRAAM) for strictly visual launch. That means they're operational in daylight and good visibility only. And the damn thing flies for only one and a half miles. By the way it was "advanced" more than thirty years ago. Now the bloody thing belongs in the Victoria and Albert Museum.

'And you may require me to order the navy into battle – with THAT? And I should remind you, we don't have even one fighter-attack aircraft on the Mount Pleasant airfield. And if we did, it would sure as hell have been destroyed by now. So much for your economies. I suggest you stand up in the House of Commons later today and tell them what you have done.'

General Brenchley stopped, drew a breath and stared at the Prime Minister, waiting for a reaction. For the second time in a very few hours, the Prime Minister of Great Britain thought it entirely possible that he might throw up, right there, right then. He felt as though he had been hit by a truck, and this bombastic damn general was walking all over him. *Christ*, he thought. *If this man ever gets loose in the newspapers he'll finish me. He could actually bring down the government.*

But he had to hold his ground with all his strength. 'General,' he said, in his most conciliatory manner, 'I am certain that all my colleagues understand your point of view—'

'Not a point of view, Prime Minister,' interjected the general. 'Just a few plain, simple, irrefutable facts.'

'Of course – nothing you say is in dispute. It's just that this has all been so damned sudden, it came at us all like a bolt from the blue . . .'

'Did it?' said General Brenchley. 'Did it indeed, Prime Minister?' His voice dripped with irony.

'Well, certainly it has tonight. And I think it would be wise for us to fight the battle we're in, rather than several battles which have been fought, won and lost in the past. I mean that, of course, metaphorically.'

Peter Caulfield stepped in to save his boss. 'General,' he said, 'I think the Prime Minister is actually looking at a worst-case scenario. What happens if Parliament demands we go and retake the Falkland Islands with military force? We cannot just tell them it's impossible.'

'Well, it is.'

'General, I realise there are substantial difficulties. Of course, we all do, and most of them are certainly not your doing. But if Parliament demands we act, is there any hope we could pull something out of the bag like last time, in 1982?'

'We have two old aircraft carriers and four active squadrons of the Harrier GR7/9. I suppose we could muster a naval force at least to go down there. The GR9 can fly off a carrier. But without the Harrier FA2 we have no Combat Air Patrols (CAPs) – only last-ditch air defence for the fleet.

'By that I mean we have nothing to stop all incoming Argentine bombers, and some are bound to get through. I'm only talking about aircraft carrying two 1,000lb iron bombs, any one of which is capable of sinking a ship. They will explode this time too, like they did in HMS *Coventry* in 1982. She sank in twenty minutes.

'Our missile system has no time to do anything about it, except shoot down the A4 *after* it's delivered its bombs and is on its way home. By which time it's a bit bloody late.'

The general offered hardly a ray of hope. 'If we had the new aircraft carrier the government promised and just a dozen of those Harriers we'd probably beat them – high CAPs could swoop down on the A4s before they could attack. If we had *both* the aircraft carriers, as promised, and *two* dozen Harriers, we'd wipe them out. But we don't.'

'Any chance of the new Eurofighter being brought forward in time?'

'None. The bloody thing will be two years *late*, never mind one year early.'

'Will the army have a view?'

'Yes, a very simple one: they will refuse to make a landing without air cover – and the only air cover they have is the GR9, which can't see anything in bad weather and carries a missile which flies only a mile and a half.'

'And we cannot provide anything else?' asked Eltringham.

'Not against those French Mirage IIIs. But, Foreign Minister, in answer to the original question – yes, I suppose we *could* mount some sort of a show, although the soldiers don't even have decent boots, unless they bought them themselves.

'And there is one thing I want to make absolutely clear. If you propose to send several thousand of my troops and the crews of Royal Navy ships to what I regard as certain death, you'd better make up your minds about which of you will stand up in front of the British people and accept responsibility, as national leaders who were acting against military advice.'

No one in the Cabinet room was anxious to step into that role. And the Prime Minister himself now looked positively ashen.

'How good a story can we draft to make it look as though we are not too worried?' asked the PM. 'That there have been many months of negotiations with a view to Argentina taking over the islands – you know, makes geographic sense and all that. Could we make it seem the Argentines just got a bit overexcited and jumped the gun . . . but we were always in agreement with them, really?'

Admiral Jeffries looked up sharply. 'With a warship and an air-defence system blasted to hell, and 150 British servicemen lying dead on that godforsaken island . . . I don't think so.'

'Well, gentlemen,' said the PM. 'With the military situation as it is, we appear to have no options, except to negotiate and perhaps wring some kind of apology and maybe even reparations out of the Argentines, just to save our faces . . .'

'First of all, I do not think you will have even *that* option by the time you've read the morning papers,' said Peter Caulfield. 'The tabloids will be baying for blood. And this ridiculous nation, which is essentially one giant football crowd, is going to be baying for revenge. By the time it all gets into the House of Commons tomorrow you'll have demands for war, just like last time, from every possible corner of the British Isles.'

And Roger Eltringham, a renowned mimic, said solemnly, '"And here is an e-mail from 'Irate' of Thames Ditton."'

At which point, he put on his most exaggerated working-class English accent and said, ' "I've just about 'ad enough of this – bloody politicians sitting on their arses fiddling their expenses, while the rest of the world tramples all over us. Where's the Dunkirk spirit, that's what I wanna know? Let's get dahn there and sort 'em out."'

'Jesus Christ,' said the Prime Minister of Great Britain.

The following morning. London

The Times was swiftly into its stride, with front-page headline treatment which read:

> *Here we go again . . . 150 servicemen dead*
> ARGENTINA SLAMS BRITISH GARRISON
> TO CONQUER THE FALKLAND ISLANDS
> Royal Navy on 24-Hour Alert to Head South

The Sun went for MASSACRE AT MOUNT PLEASANT

The Mirror: SURRENDER! THE FALKLANDS FALL TO ARGENTINA AGAIN

The Telegraph: ARGENTINA RECAPTURES FALKLANDS
British Garrison Surrenders
HMS Leeds Castle *Destroyed*
150 dead in fierce fighting

By 7.30 a.m. there were 172 journalists, photographers and TV cameramen camped outside the main door of the Ministry of Defence in Whitehall. Forty-two political correspondents were practically laying siege to the gates of Downing Street.

The Prime Minister had already announced he would broadcast to the nation at nine a.m. The Minister of Defence would speak at a press conference in the briefing room in Whitehall at ten. And there was something close to a riot taking place outside the Argentine Embassy around the corner from Harrods in Knightsbridge where traffic was now at a complete standstill.

Pictures from the Falklands were scarce, and likely to remain so, since no foreign aircraft were currently permitted to land at Mount Pleasant airfield. The Argentine military had made it clear that any flight attempting a landing for whatever purpose, would meet precisely the same fate as HMS *Leeds Castle*. And that included any invasion of Argentine air space anywhere around *Las Islas Malvinas*.

The only communiqué the Foreign Office had received from Buenos Aires was a polite memorandum suggesting that the British military dead should be buried with the full honours of war in a hillside cemetery at Goose Green, alongside the fallen Argentine warriors of both 1982 and 2011.

The Argentine president hoped that when less troubled times came there could be a British ceremony of remembrance there, in which the Argentine military would very much like to participate. The president further wanted to assure the Westminster government that everything possible was being done for the British wounded, and that if necessary they would be flown to the highly regarded British Hospital in Buenos Aires. A list of their names, ranks and numbers was enclosed, as was the list of the dead.

In victory, grace and humility. And, boy, was this ever a victory.

The British government did not have the slightest idea what to do. An emergency debate was called in the House of Commons that afternoon, starting at noon. The Prime Minister's entire front bench of ministers was, to a man, dreading it. The Prime Minister himself loathed the House of Commons and attended it as rarely as possible, much preferring to run the country from his private office in Downing Street.

He did rejoice in one possible outcome of the debate: if Parliament voted to send a battle fleet to the South Atlantic, and he personally voted against it, nothing would be his fault, no matter what the outcome. Still, the calamitous possibility of being regarded as the most cowardly Prime Minister in the history of the nation was not terribly appealing.

Throughout his entire tenure in Number 10 Downing Street, this Prime Minister had one dominant *modus operandi*. He loved flowery speeches, particularly ones with big, bold new ideas, what he called 'great initiatives'.

His game plan was to stand up there, wearing his most concerned look and promise damn near anything: extra cash, extra committees, better police, more for the poor, better armed forces, a prosperous Africa – the kind of stuff which takes a long time to come to fruition.

Right now he was at that point in his premiership when only the very stupid, or very needy, still believed a word he said. And today's problem required him to step right up to the plate, make a decision, and have it carried out, on the double. None of the above three points of action represented his strong suits.

By twelve noon the chamber of the House of Commons was packed. Almost every one of the 635 members of Parliament were in their seats. To the Speaker's right were the Government benches, Her Majesty's Loyal Opposition to the left. The government Whips had informed the Speaker's office the PM would open the proceedings personally, and at three minutes after midday the Speaker called the House to order with the words, 'Silence for the Prime Minister.'

In the grand tradition of the Mother of Parliaments he rose from the front bench, where he was flanked by his Defence Minister and his Foreign Secretary. And standing in front of the ancient Dispatch Box on the huge table, he outlined the events of the last twenty-four hours to the best of his knowledge.

Details were no more forthcoming now than they had been the previous evening. Sergeant Alan Peattie had been permitted to make calls back to Army HQ in Wilton, and it was clear that he and his fellow soldiers had fought a gallant but losing battle against an Argentine force which outnumbered them by four to one.

The British position had been untenable from the first ten

minutes during which the assault force had knocked out Britain's entire sea- and air-defensive cover system with just a couple of bombs.

The House listened in silence as the Prime Minister went on to discuss their options, many of them strangely optimistic. Ending on a graver note, he concluded. 'Honourable members have been called this afternoon to debate this outrage by an armed aggressor. Ultimately this House must decide – do we negotiate a peace with the Argentines? Or do we do what we did last time, and sail a Royal Navy task force to the South Atlantic and defeat them in battle on the high seas, in the air and on the land?'

He sat down with the jingoistic cheers of the members almost raising the roof of the House. The Speaker rose from his chair and requested silence for the Leader of the Opposition, the somewhat colourful former Oxford University 400-metre champion, Adrian Archer.

And it was clear from his opening sentence where he stood – in the shadow of Margaret Thatcher. He railed against the 'pitifully weak' response of the Prime Minister and castigated the Labour government for its endless defence cuts, its inability to see what Britain really stood for.

'Honourable members, we belong to a tried and tested society, a society to which other weaker, poorer countries turn in times of need. Great Britain has always stood for a sense of fair play and, above all, it stands in favour of the rule of law. It does not and could never condone some damn quasi-Nazi rampaging over 2,000 of our citizens down in the South Atlantic.'

He paused for a second to collect his thoughts.

'Honourable gentlemen, if I may quote, more or less accurately, the great First Sea Lord of the 1980s, Admiral Sir Henry Leach. On the night when the Argentines invaded the Falklands in 1982, he told Margaret Thatcher that if we funked this, if we backed down now and did nothing – "Then tomorrow morning, Prime Minister, we shall both be awakening in a very, very different place."'

Looking around, he spoke slowly and clearly. 'Those words apply to each and every one of us here in the Chamber today.'

He sat down amidst thunderous applause from both sides of the divide, and the Speaker of the House motioned for Peter Caulfield, the Defence Minister, to be heard.

Caulfield stood and faced the opposition across the dispatch box. And, reading from notes, he outlined the sombre situation in which the government found itself. He pointed out that Argentina, with its national near-maniacal passion for the *Islas Malvinas*, had been smarting ever since the 1982 defeat. He stated that forces within the Argentine military, which had so often ruled the country, had been building up their armaments and scheming for this *coup d'état* for several years without much basis in reality.

'It's true, we are not so militarily prepared as the Argentines are. But they live less than 400 miles away. We are 8,000 miles distant. A war down there would just about double our national debt. It is not worth it for us to fight – it could not be worth it in terms of money and lives – and anyway, from my standpoint we'd have a very good chance of losing.'

At this point the Conservative MP for Portsmouth, the ex-naval Commander Alan Knell, waved his order paper in a request for Mr Caulfield to accept an interruption. And, in the established ritual of courtesy in the House, the Defence Minister said: 'I give way to the honourable gentleman' and sat down.

'I appreciate the position of the minister,' Commander Knell said, 'And of course I realise he is in fact defending an extremely weak Prime Minister. But my constituency on the south coast has many naval officers, and for years I've been hearing how appalled they are at the cuts to the Royal Navy budget. Would it be fair to say these idiotic defence policies have finally exposed this government for what it is? Perhaps the word "useless" might spring to mind?'

The Tory benches erupted in a burst of laughter and cheers, with members waving their own order papers. On the government side, Peter Caulfield climbed again to his feet, and continued amid heckling and jeering. 'The honourable gentleman knows as well as I do that sudden, unexpected military actions by a hostile and emotional nation can cast the very best planning into total confusion.'

Commander Knell, his voice easily rising above the din, yelled angrily, 'Yes, but we had a leader the last time that happened!'

At which point the Tory benches erupted with yells of support, while from the Labour benches a shrill cry of protest at this obvious rudeness echoed to the rafters.

'*ORDER! ORDER!*' bellowed the Speaker amid the uproar. 'I insist on order. The Defence Minister must be allowed to continue.'

By now, three more Tory MPs were on their feet and the Speaker chose Robert Macmillan, a distant relative of the former Prime Minister Harold Macmillan.

'Mr Speaker,' he said, 'I never thought I would stand here and hear a government minister suggesting that it was beyond our capacity to send a fleet down to the South Atlantic and reclaim our own territory from a foreign gangster. I mean, what's the point of having a navy if you can't use it? What's the point of having an army if it can't fight? And I see no point in having even a Defence Minister if the best he and his Prime Minister can do is stand up and point out we can't do anything against a country which, by any standards, is essentially Third World.'

Robert Macmillan's voice rose as he concluded, 'Margaret Thatcher once wrote of the morning we landed our troops at Carlos Water. An officer of the Parachute Regiment went and banged on the nearest farmhouse door. And, with the backdrop of the Royal Navy warships behind him, he said to the farmer, "I expect you're surprised to see us?"

'The farmer replied. "No, not a bit. We all knew Maggie would come." And, as Lady Thatcher wrote, "He said Maggie, but he meant all of us. He knew we would not abandon them."

'The question is: *Do we still have the guts for it?* Or has this weak, passive, utterly dishonest left-wing government stripped us even of that?'

Roars of 'Hear, hear!' – that traditional parliamentary shorthand for 'I agree' – rang out from the Tory side of the House. Derek Blenkinsop, the Labour member for East Lancashire, now rose from his seat.

'Mr Speaker, people lost sons, brothers and fathers in the last Falklands conflict. The 1982 war in the South Atlantic was absolutely ridiculous. We had ships sunk, sailors and their officers burned to death as our warships were bombed, we lost our bravest soldiers on the battlefield fighting for a barren, desolate bunch of rocks which mean nothing to anyone. How could that possibly be fair?'

The Speaker now pointed to Richard Cawley, the Conservative member for Barrow-in-Furness, home of Britain's submarine builders. 'Mr Speaker,' he said, 'most of the honourable members realise the Royal Navy's conventional-weapon submarine fleet has been cut from thirty-five to twelve. The new aircraft carriers may not show up until 2016.

'We have no Harrier FA2 strike force. That was scrapped four years ago and no longer exists. When it was withdrawn from service, that little fighter jet was generally regarded as the most capable, most respected all-weather, beyond-visual-range fighter in the entire European inventory. Its look-down, shoot-down, state-of-the-art Blue Vixen radar gave it the capability to detect and destroy four targets simultaneously.

'Its AMRAAM weapons system was designed to detect and engage small high-threat fast targets like sea-skimming missiles. It was the *only* UK weapons system capable of defending our fleet against the new generation of anti-ship weapons, including the Krypton and Moskit supersonic missiles. And now it's gone. And it was of course the first major step taken by this government towards British military impotence.

'I have no doubt that today you will be told we still have four squadrons of GR 7/9 aircraft. They can fly off an aircraft carrier, true, but their radar and missiles are not in the same league as those of the Harrier FA2, and they are less capable than the Harrier FA1 of 1982.

'This also applies to the new Typhoon, which for years has failed to come up to scratch in any of its trials. Aside from being grotesquely late in its production, when it *does* arrive it will be touch-and-go whether the damn thing hits the enemy or a friend.'

'Is the Government finally admitting we cannot go to war with the equipment the Ministry of Defence has provided? If not, what is the reason the Prime Minister seems so reluctant to go to the South Atlantic?'

The enormity of Great Britain's scandalous lack of naval air capacity was rapidly becoming obvious to the House, and MP after MP stood and regaled the House with descrptions of the sheer humiliation Great Britain would suffer in the world community.

These patriotic pleas for the Government to show some resolution were interspersed by those of other Honorable Members railing against the deprivations of the military under this Prime Minister.

One MP revealed the scale of the cuts to the military budgets which resulted in mass reductions in training exercises, especially overseas, huge fuel reductions, reduced track mileage for tanks and other armored vehicles, reduced amounts of training ammunition, less money for overseas training.

He explained how instant financial savings were made by delaying recruitment of trainees for six months of the year and then attempting a recruiting drive for the second six months, thus avoiding paying salaries for maybe 6,000 recruits for a six-month period. Which wouldn't work, of course, because too many of them would get fed up waiting.

One Member of Parliament pointed out the six British Military policemen who were killed in the conflict north of Basra in 2003/4, surrounded by a rioting mob of 500 Iraqis, because they only had radios which did not work in an urban environment. One mile away, he said, the Paras fought it out with terrorists for four hours, but had satellite comms and were able to call in reinforcements.

'The new British Forces radio system comes years too late,' he added. 'The soldiers' clothing is moderate, especially their water-proofs, and their boots are a disgrace, often splitting in half in the first couple of weeks. Almost all British troops heading for a theatre of war buy their own. I am not surprised,' he said, 'that this government is not anxious to go south and fight for the Falkland Islands.'

The discussion wore on into the late afternoon until finally a motion was agreed: *That the Government should instruct the British armed forces to prepare to retake the Falkland Islands by military force from the Argentines. And that the Ministry of Defence be ordered to show good cause within forty-eight hours if for any reason they consider the task untenable.*

The motion was carried by a majority of 159 votes. Barring a major objection by the Royal Navy, Great Britain was going to war against the Republic of Argentina.

The Prime Minister looked as if he had seen a ghost. Exposed in the House of Commons for his folly in listening to his Chancellor and ignoring the expertise of his generals and admirals, he found himself heading into a battle, which, if lost, would surely see him removed in utter disgrace from Number 10 Downing Street.

He was the man who might have penny-pinched his way to a military humiliation for Great Britain. What a total indignity for a politician as ambitious as the British premier. As Darien Farr and his lovely wife Loretta might have put it at the Chequers dining table . . . I mean, this was, like, wow!

0800 15 February.
Office of the C-in-C Home Fleet, Portsmouth Dockyard, southern England

The ministerial limousine was cooling its wheels outside the home of Admiral Mark Palmer, the Royal Navy's Commander-in-Chief, Home Fleet. This was a grand, imposing Queen Anne house hard by the jetties towards the end of the dockyard, close to the admiral's formal office on board the nearby HMS *Victory*, Admiral Nelson's magnificently restored Trafalgar flagship.

It was a place steeped in naval history. Portraits of legendary battle commanders and their ships adorned the walls. The whole building felt like an elegant ops room from the nineteenth century. If an admiral could not plan strategy in here, he probably couldn't plan it anywhere.

And, quite frankly, it gave Peter Caulfield the creeps. He never felt at home here, faced with the hard-eyed men who ran the Royal Navy, despite the fact that, as head of the Ministry of Defence, he was their lord and master.

He appreciated their courteous treatment of him, and their impeccable manners. But when he mentioned any course of government action of which they did not approve, their silent, penetrating stares made him feel, unaccountably, as if he was ripping the very heart out of England.

And this morning he was dreading the meeting even more than usual. He was shown into Admiral Palmer's drawing room and introduced to a heavily built, uniformed Naval officer, the four stripes on his sleeve indicating the rank of captain.

'Minister, I'd like you to meet Captain David Reader, commanding officer of our one serviceable aircraft carrier, HMS *Ark Royal.*

'She's over there at the minute,' he added pointing through the window. 'As usual David's brought her home safe and sound, with about a half-million pounds' worth of repairs to complete in the next couple of weeks.'

Captain Reader stepped forward and offered his hand, nodding coolly. 'Good morning, Secretary of State,' he said. 'Rather a rough ride you chaps endured in the House yesterday.'

Peter Caulfield stared past the captain's shoulder at the 20,000 ton 685-foot-long *Ark Royal*, moored on the other side of the harbour, the modern successor to the first *Ark Royal*, which had carried fifty-five-guns as the flagship of Lord Howard of Effingham against the Spanish Armada in 1588.

Somehow, even without one shred of knowledge of naval history, the Defence Minister felt like a little boy in the presence of the man who operated that towering modern fortress at sea.

Forcing his mind back to the conversation, he replied, 'Yes, it was a rather difficult time for the government. Strange as it may seem, we are incredibly concerned about loss of life in our armed forces, particularly in a potential war zone such as this one in the South Atlantic, which holds just about nothing for us.'

'Oh, I don't know,' Admiral Palmer interrupted, amiably. 'I think there's something to be said for honour. The Royal Navy's built on it, you know.'

Slightly embarrassed, feeling rebuked, Britain's Minister of Defence said quickly, 'Of course I understand that, admiral. But even with our honour at stake, do you really wish to see two or three hundred of our best troops killed or wounded, essentially for nothing?'

'My dear minister,' replied the admiral, 'we do not enter any conflict counting our dead before anything happens. We expect to enter a conflict and win; to misquote General Patton, we don't intend to die for our country. We anticipate making the other poor dumb bastard die for *his* country.'

'Yes, yes. Quite,' said Peter Caulfield. 'That's the way you must think . . .'

At that moment an orderly came into the room bearing hot coffee in a silver pot on a silver tray. There were three china cups and a plate of biscuits.

'I'll pour,' volunteered the admiral. 'Thank you, Charlie.'

'This is very kind,' said Peter Caulfield. 'And I shall do my level best to have this over in a very short time, so you won't have to give me lunch . . .'

'Come now, minister, we're all on the same side in the end. I would be most hurt if you weren't to stay for lunch . . .'

'Well, we'll see how things turn out. But, as you know, I have a very specific purpose here. I am compelled to ask you whether the Royal Navy believes it possible to sail to the South Atlantic, fight off the Argentine navy and their quite formidable air force, and then put a sizeable land force on the beaches somewhere on the Falklands and fight yard by yard for the territory? That's my question.'

'Do you want my personal opinion or my official response?'

'Let's start with the official response.'

'Very well, minister. I and all my officers are loyal servants of the Crown. If the Parliament of Great Britain decides we must go and fight for those islands, we'll go. It's not our place to argue the toss whether it's worth it, even whether it's right. We have all taken the Queen's shilling, as it were, for most of our service lives. If we are asked to go out and earn it, possibly the hard way, then so be it.'

'Captain Reader?'

'Same.'

'And your personal view, admiral?'

'We have a rather greater chance of defeat now than we had in 1982, and even that was a bit of a close-run thing.'

'And your principal reason for that view?'

'Oh, definitely the loss of the Harrier FA2, minister. With that, we always had a chance in the air. Now we do not even have a fighter aircraft.'

Peter Caulfield nodded. 'And may I ask the commanding officer of our aircraft carrier the same question?'

'Again, much the same, sir. Except to add that *Ark Royal* is a quarter of a century old. She's tired, she's feeling her age. Every time we go out we return with some operational defect. This time it's her starboard driveshaft. May need a new one.

'It's a very distant war for an old lady. Eight thousand miles down there, and if she goes wrong we'd be in shocking trouble, thousands of miles from a garage, in bad weather and under constant enemy attack.'

'But you'd still go if you were asked?'

'Yes, sir.'

Admiral Palmer stood up. He poured himself a little more coffee, and said, 'Minister, it's how we were all brought up. It's what I call the *Jervis Bay* syndrome. That was an old 14,000-ton passenger ship converted into an armed merchant cruiser for convoy escort in the North Atlantic in the Second World War. They mounted seven old six-inch guns on her deck.

'She was commanded by Captain E. S. Fogarty Fegen RN. And one morning they came in sight of the German pocket battleship *Admiral Scheer*. Instantly Captain Fegen ordered the seventeen-ship supply convoy to scatter, and, in an action he must have known was suicidal, he turned his ship to engage the enemy.

'It took the *Scheer* about thirty minutes to batter and sink the *Jervis Bay*, by which time the convoy had vanished, scattering far and wide, over the horizon. When rescuers turned up that evening to pick up survivors, Captain Fegen was not among them. They gave him a posthumous Victoria Cross for that.

'It was the same with Lt. Commander Roope VC, of the *Glow-*

worm, also in World War Two. In desperation, with his ship on fire and sinking beneath him, he turned and rammed the big German cruiser *Hipper*. Took her with him.

'That's what we do, minister. We'll fight, if necessary to the death, just as our predecessors did, just as we've been taught. And should our luck run out, one day, and should we be required to face a superior enemy, we'll still go forward, fighting until our ship is lost.'

Peter Caulfield stood up and walked to the sideboard to refresh his coffee cup. Stirring the liquid with a shaking hand, he tried hard to compose himself, his face turned away from the two naval commanders. Hoping his voice didn't betray his emotion at their unswerving sense of loyalty, he asked quietly, 'Then you will not declare the Royal Navy unable to sail to the South Atlantic to fight for the Falkland Islands?'

'No, minister, I will not say that. Not on any account. And neither would any other admiral who has occupied this office during the last two or three hundred years.'

'However bad it may look? However the odds are stacked against you?'

'No, minister. The Royal Navy will not refuse to go. *Jervis Bay* sacrificed herself to save that convoy. If, of necessity, we must do the same, to save you and your boss, we will not refuse to go.'

CHAPTER FIVE

Peter Caulfield left Portsmouth Dockyard shortly before noon and headed straight back to Downing Street. Missing lunch with the Chief of the Defence Staff, Sir Robin Brenchley, and the First Sea Lord, Admiral Sir Rodney Jeffries, who had arrived in Portsmouth in a staff car directly from Whitehall, had been a sensible move. The following two hours would be as grave and as depressing as the late afternoon of 21 October 1805, when Admiral Nelson had died on the lower deck of HMS *Victory* at Trafalgar. After all, the four naval commanders were discussing nothing short of the Royal Navy's total demise and the likelihood of possibly the worst defeat in the history of Britain's senior service.

'We don't have much,' said Admiral Palmer. 'So do we take everything down there, and leave just sufficient here to fight another day? Or do we just say the hell with it and take the lot?'

'We have so little, I'm afraid we'll have to take the whole navy,' said the First Sea Lord. 'If it's anybody, it's everybody. We don't have fifty destroyers and frigates any more, we only have eighteen and three of them are in refit. We hardly have enough to provide a proper escort for the carrier.'

'You say "carrier" in the singular,' said General Brenchley. 'I thought we had two?'

'One of them, *Illustrious,* is more than thirty years old. We can't take her – she'd probably never complete the journey, never mind fight a battle.'

'Can *Ark Royal* make it?'

'Just about,' said Captain Reader. 'But not for long: the wear and tear on any warship in a sea–battle environment, and in that South Atlantic weather, is very high. I'd give her six weeks maximum, and that's only if our luck holds.'

'If anything,' said Admiral Palmer, 'the aircraft situation is even more serious. I suppose we could rustle up a couple of dozen GR9s, but they cannot fly at night, and in bad weather they can't see a bloody thing.

'Robin,' he added, 'we have no air defence. None. And the quicker everyone accepts that the better. This damn government has dug a bloody great hole for itself and jumped into it.'

General Brenchley, the powerfully built son of a Kentish pub owner, had fought his way up the ranks of the British Army to its very pinnacle. He would have made it big anywhere. He was tough, inclined not to panic, inhumanly decisive, and had commanded his paras in both Iraqi wars. He had also been a close friend of Admiral Jeffries since childhood, both of them having attended Maidstone Grammar School in Kent.

Never, in their fifty-year friendship, had Admiral Jeffries seen the bull-necked army chief so utterly distraught. General Brenchley was pacing the room, shaking his head, torn between obedience to Her Majesty's Government, which he had sworn to serve, and the shocking possibility of casualties beyond the call of duty.

'Rodney, old boy, I suppose we have to decide,' he murmured. 'Will we allow X thousand men to die, or do we all resign and let this witless Prime Minister and his shoddy little group of ex-communist friends get on with it?'

An appalled silence enveloped the room. No one had ever heard him speak like that. The situation was worse than they'd thought. 'It seems to me,' said the First Sea Lord finally, 'that the PM is finished either way. If we and our principal staff quit, he'd have to resign because of the uproar. No politician could weather that storm. If we agreed to go and fight for the islands, and were defeated by a greater enemy, he'd also have to quit. Either way, he's done. But in the first instance we'd save many thousands of lives.'

'Not to mention what's left of the Royal Navy,' said the general.

'And yet,' said Admiral Jeffries, 'we are sworn to duty, in an unbroken tradition of obedience to the government or the Head of State which goes back centuries. And we ought not to be blind to the fact that we would both face lifelong disgrace if we quit and our successors somehow went down there and pulled the bloody thing off.'

'Rodney, despite this somewhat defeatist conversation, you and I are not going to quit. And we both know it. We're going to dig in and fight for the Falkland Islands as our Parliament has requested. We may think it's a lunatic request, we may seethe with anger at the criminal destruction of the services, but we're still going . . .'

'And if our enemy should be too strong, and our ship should be sinking, we'll bring her about, and if she still has propulsion we'll ram them – correct?'

'Correct,' said General Brenchley, gravely. 'We'll both, in the end, do our duty.'

0900 Tuesday 15 February
National Security Agency, Maryland

Lt. Commander Jimmy Ramshawe had spent twenty-eight of the last thirty-six hours pondering the military brilliance of Argentina's whiplash strike against the British defences on the Falkland Islands. The operation had been carefully planned. No doubt of that. How had the Brits not seen it coming?

Certainly the US Ambassador in Buenos Aires had been aware of the threat. His communiqué just before Christmas had stated that he would be surprised if something didn't shake loose in a couple of months. And Admiral Morgan had told Jimmy that he should always pay attention to the observations of old Ryan Holland.

But here we are again. The ole Brits caught with their strides down. And everyone in a bloody uproar about who's going to do what to whom. Are the Brits going to fight for their islands, or will they leave well enough alone?

'I've got a bloody powerful feeling the Brits are gonna fight,' he muttered to the empty room. 'And then the shit will hit the fan, because we'll be caught in the middle of it, and President Bedford will have the same problem as Ronnie Reagan – do we help our closest ally, or do we refuse because of our friendship with the Argentines?'

Admiral Morris, Jimmy's boss, was again working on the West Coast for the week, and Admiral Morgan had taken Kathy to Antigua in the eastern Caribbean for twelve days. Which left Jimmy bereft of wise counsel. So far as he could tell the United States had to protest to the United Nations today, about the seizure of the American oil and gas complexes in both the Falkland Islands and South Georgia.

'You can't have US citizens being frogmarched off the islands at bloody gunpoint, their equipment seized,' he muttered. 'I mean,

Christ, that's like the Wild West – Bedford is not going to have that. But that military strike was about oil. Buenos Aires thinks it belongs to Argentina and they won't easily give it up. That damn newspaper – the *Herald* – laid it out pretty firmly.'

Jimmy took a sip of coffee and flicked through to the file on the Falklands he had saved a couple of months ago. 'Well,' he mused, 'Exxon-Mobil and British Petroleum have sunk a ton of money into those oil and gas fields. The question is, will we go to war for it? Bedford won't, but Admiral Morgan might tell him to. And the Brits might think they have no choice. Strewth!'

Three hours later the US State Department complained formally to the United Nations about the wilful, illegal seizure of the Falkland Islands by the Republic of Argentina. And two hours after that, Ryan Holland requested an official audience with the president of Argentina in Buenos Aires. Thirty minutes later the British ambassador, Sir Miles Morland, requested the same thing. Neither embassy received a response.

In London the Argentine Ambassador was summoned to 10 Downing Street, and in Washington the Argentine Ambassador was summoned to the White House. The former was instantly expelled and given twenty-four hours to vacate the building in Knightsbridge or face deportation.

In Washington the American President gave the ambassador forty-eight hours to allow Exxon Mobil execs to restart the oil industry in both East Falkland and South Georgia, or else the US Government would begin seizing Argentine assets in the United States. In particular, the US would seize the grandiose embassy building on New Hampshire Avenue, Washington, plus the consulate properties in New York, Miami, Chicago, Los Angeles, Houston, New Orleans and Atlanta.

President Bedford also put in a call to the St James' Club in Antigua and requested Arnold Morgan to return to Washington as soon as possible, since the prospect of a war without the former National Security Adviser's advice was more or less unthinkable.

Admiral Morgan agreed to come home a couple of days early – so long as the President sent *Air Force One* to collect him.

Meanwhile, back in Westminster, the British Parliament had been alerted to gather to hear the Prime Minister speak at two p.m. on Wednesday afternoon. It was the first time in living memory he had attended the House two days out of three.

And he was not doing it out of a sense of duty. He and his spin doctors were desperately trying to halt the onrushing tide of editorials and features which by now had convinced most of the country that the PM and his left-wing ministers had ruined the great tradition of the British armed forces and that the UK might not have the military capability to fight for the Falkland Islands.

Defence correspondents, political commentators, editors and newspaper proprietors were finally telling their readers the simple truth: if you want to live in strength and peace, you'd better listen to your generals and admirals – and you better be prepared for war at all times.

The Times had produced a scorching front-page headline that morning:

YEARS OF NEGLECT DISARM BRITAIN'S MILITARY
Labour Ministers Stunned at Navy's Accusations

The *Daily Telegraph*, a Tory and military stronghold, had talked to General Robin Brenchley:

TOP ARMY GENERAL LAMBASTS GOVERNMENT 'STUPIDITY'
Brenchley's Warnings in new Falklands War

The following interview had nothing to do with the fighting ability of the soldiers and their commanders. It had to do with equipment, air cover, missile defences and ordnance. What the general called the 'criminal neglect of our requirements'. Without fear for his own career, General Brenchley described this British Prime Minister and this British government as 'the worst I have ever known'.

Brenchley's views were echoed over and over, in newspapers and television news programmes. Toadying up to Labour politicians seemed a thing of the past. It was as if the government had become a meaningless impediment to the gallant fighting men who would soon be sailing south to fight for the honour of Great Britain.

It was as if every chicken in the coop had come home to roost. The media gloated, slamming into a Labour Government which had thought it might somehow be able to wing it, feigning financial competence by increasing taxes, and capping military budgets to well below required levels.

They had then handed over all of the saved money to state

hospital bureaucrats, social security, disadvantaged gays, lesbians, homeless, single-parent families, unemployed, unemployable, the weak, the importent, the helpless and the hopeless. Not until this day had they truly realized the stark naivety of those policies.

And now, the Prime Minister's cronies sat packed into a tightly grouped little enclave of nervousness, while their leader stood before the House and tried to explain how Great Britain's military powers were not in any way weakened. And how the armed forces were absolutely ready to obey the will of the House, and head south to fight the jackbooted aggressors from the land of the pampas.

'I tell you now,' he said, in his customary shallow, cocksure way, 'in our many years in government we have prepared the navy and the rest of the military to fight a modern war. We have reduced numbers of personnel, but today we are more prepared for the kind of war we now face in the twenty-first century. Our professionalism is greater, our commanders have been given free rein to train our people to the highest standards.

'Our warships have state-of-the art weapons systems and no one would dispute our air crews are the finest in the world. I have spoken personally to all of our service leaders. I have explained that the will of the House of Commons, expressed in this place on Monday afternoon, must prevail.

'And, honourable members, I can say with enormous optimism they were completely in agreement with our decision. Indeed, several of them thanked both me and my government for the far-sighted changes we had made to the navy – by that I mean the two new state-of-the-art aircraft carriers and the superb new Typhoon fighter jets, which will soon be developed to launch from their flight decks.

'We are at war with Argentina over the Falkland Islands. And at this stage I see no reason to extend that state of war to the Argentine mainland. If, however, that day should come, then I am assured by all our commanders that we are ready, capable and certain that we shall prevail.

'But, like another Prime Minister, a lady from the opposite benches who stood in this very place twenty-eight years ago, I say again to the House, we in government cannot tolerate a brutish, unprovoked attack on our islands. We cannot and will not put up with it.

'As in 1982 the Royal Navy will sail to the South Atlantic. And they will bear with them a mighty task force. The Argentines will either surrender or we will blast them asunder on the land, in the air, and on the waters that surround the islands. But they will not get away with this . . .'

At this point, the entire House erupted with a roar that must have been heard outside in Parliament Square. Members stood up, waving their order papers, cheering lustily, in perfect imitation of a football crowd baying for revenge.

There was absolutely no political advantage for any member to stand up and challenge the validity of the Prime Minister's words. No one wished to hear them. This was an afternoon of the highest emotion – the hours of doubt were long gone. Britain's naval and military commanders had told the government they would go and win back the Falkland Islands. *Rule Britannia.*

So far as the MPs were concerned this was the Cup Final in the South Atlantic. Older members could somehow recall only the triumph, as Admiral Woodward's flagship *Hermes* came steaming home to Portsmouth. There was the gratifying memory of the big Argentine cruiser, the *General Belgrano*, listing, sinking, in her death throes. There were the pictures of the Argentine surrender, thousands of troops lining up, laying down their arms. And, of course, the timeless vision of the men of Britain's 2 Para, marching behind their bloodstained banner into Port Stanley, their commanding officer Colonel Jones slain but their victory complete.

Who could forget those distant days of pride and conquest? And who could resist a faint tremor of anticipation, as once more the sprawling, historic Portsmouth dockyard revved up for another conflict?

Not the veteran MPs of the House of Commons. Because the onset of battle seemed somehow to give them stature, to add to their sense of self-importance, if that was possible. But they left the great Chamber that afternoon with their heads held high, chins jutting defiantly, upper lips already stiffening. They were men involved with a war, a real war. They were men involved in life-or-death decisions.

If the honest opinions of the military were to be believed, however, it would be mostly death. After all, none of the MPs had sailed with Admiral Woodward into a gusting, squally levanter off the Gibraltar Straits in the spring of 1982. None of them had seen the entire ship's company of a homegoing British warship lining the port-side rails to salute the warriors heading south. None of them had heard the singing as Woodward's armada sailed by – the achingly prophetic notes of the hymn that morning, 'Abide With Me'.

None of them had seen the Paras, raked by machine-gun fire, fighting and dying on the flat plain of Goose Green. They had never heard the cries and whispers of the injured and dying in shattered, burning warships. And they had never seen the shocked faces of the doctors and nurses in the hospital on board *Hermes* as the burned seamen and officers were carried in.

They hadn't. But Admiral Mark Palmer had, and the memory of lost friends stood stark before him as he stared at the television, listening to the hollow words of the Prime Minister. The admiral winced at the sight of the ludicrous, complacent grins on the faces of the government ministers, nodding earnestly as their leader spun, distorting the military picture to the House of Commons.

Admiral Palmer was fifty-eight years old. He had served in the first Falklands war as a thirty-year-old lieutenant on HMS *Coventry* before she was hit and sunk just north of the islands in the late afternoon of 25 May 1982. He recalled the helplessness, the desperation, as they tried to manoeuvre the ship, its long-range radar on the blink, not knowing from which way the Argentine bombers would come.

Twenty-eight years later he still awoke in the night, trembling, his heart pounding when he heard again, in his dreams, the blasts of the bombs smashing into his ship, the screams of the injured. And he felt again the searing pain in his own burned face as the bomb blast hit him while he tried to supervise the 20mm gun on the upper deck.

Admiral Palmer was not afraid. His grandfather had fought at the Battle of Jutland in the First World War. In truth Mark Palmer was a modern-day Roope VC. He'd have rammed an opponent when all was lost, he would most certainly have died for his convoy, and, if required, he would have died to save this benighted British government which, like all his colleagues, he secretly loathed.

It was not a lack of courage, skill or daring that in his mind doomed this new operation in the South Atlantic. It was the hideous truth that their own government had denied his men the correct resources to fight a new war. So Admiral Palmer turned his back on the television and walked, coatless, out into the chill of the dockyard, appalled that the very best British people were somehow being led by some of the very worst. The brave and the honourable, sent to the meat-grinder by a group of self-seeking opportunists glorying in their limousines, chauffeurs and bloated expense accounts.

'Christ,' Mark Palmer muttered, alone in the cold dockyard. 'What a tragedy.'

He signalled for a driver before running inside to collect his greatcoat. Five minutes later he was on the jetty where HMS *Ark Royal* had suddenly become the centre of the universe. At least, the 20,000-ton light aircraft carrier was now the centre of his own particular universe, despite her age.

A team of engineers was still at work deep inside the propulsion area, checking and servicing those four hard-working Olympus gas turbines, and examining the two massive driveshafts which transferred more than 97,000 horsepower to the huge propellers.

The good news was neither shaft needed replacing. The bad news was the spare part to replace a cracked mounting had to be flown from Scotland, but not until tomorrow. And that meant the repair crew and the servicing engineers were still operational while the gigantic task of replenishing the ship's stores took place.

There was already an old-fashioned 'humping party' passing boxes hand over hand up the starboard forward gangway. Alongside them was a mobile conveyor belt with another crew loading enormous boxes of food – frozen, canned, dried and fresh.

In the middle of all this, the Fleet Maintenance Group and the carrier's own staff were at work across the starboard hull rectifying any defects, removing rust, repainting, checking every inch of the Battle Group's flagship, which within days would be heading to a theatre of war.

From all over the country, thousands and thousands of containers of stores were arriving from various depots, brought by train, by the Ministry of Defence's own transportation, and by commercial vehicles. And they were not just there for *Ark Royal*. In the dockyard countless other ships were lining up for the journey south. And all of them needed food, clothes, ordnance, ammunition, shells and missiles.

Massive amounts of fuel were arriving, diesel for the gas turbines, Avcat for the aircraft. And it was not only the warships that were being fuelled. The huge replenishment oilers of the Royal Fleet Auxiliary, which would keep them topped up on the journey south and in the battle zone itself, were getting their share.

Personnel from every branch of the navy were being drafted into Portsmouth. Every available unit of manpower was heading for the jetties, trying to clear the debris, helping with the loading, assisting the Supply Officers, who paced the loading areas, checking off their 'shopping lists' on big clipboards, calling out commands and instructions to the toiling, twenty-four-hours-a-day workforce.

Captain Reader came down to meet the C-in-C and together they paced the wide quay where *Ark Royal* was moored. By now the great arc lights along the waterfront were being switched on. Captain Reader and Admiral Palmer went aboard and took the elevator to the quarters of the commanding officer, while some swift refurbishment took place above them in readiness for the arrival of Rear Admiral Alan Holbrook who, as Task Force Commander, would fly his flag from *Ark Royal* throughout the operation.

His ops room, where he and his staff would plan the war, was located right above Captain Reader's quarters, though their duties would be entirely separate. The captain's task was to steer the 685-foot-long carrier safely around the South Atlantic, taking overall command of the 550-foot-long flight deck, the 680-man crew and eighty officers.

Admiral Holbrook would plan the deployment of the ships, the air and sea assault on the Argentine islands, plus the landing of the army and marine forces, in consultation with COMAW – Commander Amphibious Warfare – Commodore Keith Birchell.

The GR9 ground attack aircraft were due to begin arriving, straight onto the deck of *Ark Royal* from Yeovilton naval air station. Altogether there would be twenty-one of them, the full complement for a small carrier like *Ark Royal*, as opposed to the eighty-four which a big US Nimitz Class carrier could accommodate.

The non-arrival of the two new Royal Navy carriers, both 60,000-tonners, was widely considered to be a national disgrace. Despite the Prime Minister's somewhat glib self-congratulatory remarks about the new ships, the fact remained there had been government delay, delay and delay, and the earliest they were now likely to arrive was sometime in late 2015.

Every senior officer in the Royal Navy recalled the chilling words of the then First Sea Lord, Admiral Alan West, six years previously, when he had stated with quiet certainty that recent defence cuts 'have left the Navy with too few ships to sustain even moderate losses in a maritime conflict'.

With only a dozen destroyers and frigates ready for battle at any one time, the First Sea Lord considered the situation untenable:

simply not enough warships. And he knew what he was talking about: his own ship *Ardent* had been sunk in Falkland Sound. On 21 May 1982 a formation of Argentine bombers launched nine 500-pounders at the battle-hardened *Ardent* whose Seacat missile launcher suddenly jammed. Three of the bombs smashed into the Type-22 frigate, blasting the stern hangar asunder and blowing the Seacat launcher into the air. It crashed down, killing the supply officer, Richard Banfield, and the helicopter pilot, Lt. Commander John Sephton, who was manning a machine gun together with his observer, Brian Murphy.

Almost the entire stern section of the ship was now on fire, a huge plume of smoke lifting high above the Sound. Minutes later another formation of Argentine Skyhawks came screaming in over West Falkland and instantly spotted the blazing *Ardent*. Commander West ordered his helmsmen to turn their just-repaired 4.5-inch gun to face the enemy, and they opened fire with everything they had.

Commander West had cleared one of the ship's cooks to man one of the big machine guns and he actually downed one of the raiders. But nothing could save *Ardent* from this bombardment. Seven bombs slammed into her, almost lifting the ship out of the water.

The blasts, and the fires, killed or wounded one-third of the ship's company – the same number as in HMS *Victory* at this same time in the afternoon at the Battle of Trafalgar. Unlike Admiral Nelson, Commander West survived, and with the fires blazing all around him he once more ordered his gunners to turn and face the enemy.

But the ship could no longer steer, and by now the fires were roaring towards the missile magazines. Men had been blown overboard, and *Ardent* was shipping ice-cold sea water by the ton. She was sinking, and West ordered his crew to abandon ship. Not until the last man was taken off by HMS *Yarmouth* did Commander West, tears of rage and frustration streaming down his face, finally leave HMS *Ardent*. She sank early the next morning.

Alan West knew of what he spoke.

And when Admiral Holbrook arrived shortly before 1900 hours he shook hands warmly with the commanding officer and with his Fleet C-in-C, just stating solemnly, 'We haven't got enough, have we?'

'No, I'm afraid not,' replied Admiral Palmer. 'What we have, we take. But the GR9s are blind at night and in bad weather. If we need ship replacements . . . well, I'm afraid there won't be any.'

'Hmm,' replied Admiral Holbrook. 'We'd better move pretty sharply if that's the case. There's nothing quite so bleak as attrition you can't afford, eh?'

He gazed out onto the flight deck, scanning the area. 'It's a clear night,' he said. 'Are we expecting the GR9s soon?'

'Starting around 2100,' said Captain Reader.

'Helicopters?'

'Tomorrow morning.'

'How about marines? Will we have them on board *Ark Royal*?'

'Probably around 0600.'

Admiral Holbrook nodded. He was a slender, rather handsome man with well-combed wavy brown hair. As a commander he had served a previous captain of *Ark Royal* as Executive Officer, and had subsequently jumped over a few slightly more senior officers to make rear-admiral. The navy's high command wanted a new flotilla commander with first-hand experience of the only aircraft carrier likely to be operational for a long-range war.

Captain Reader told him his quarters would probably be ready right after dinner, and meanwhile perhaps they should have some cocoa and take a look at the available warships which would accompany *Ark Royal* on the long ride down the Atlantic. As with the previous Falklands conflict, the Americans would make Ascension Island available as a halfway house for resupply and refuelling.

Eight warships from the 4th Frigate Squadron would form the backbone of the task force, all of them Type-23 Duke Class ships built between 1991 and 2002. These were 4,200-ton gas-turbine vessels, all based at Portsmouth and right now undergoing similar resupply as their flagship *Ark Royal*.

In fact, HMS *Lancaster* and HMS *Marlborough*, both twenty years old, were unlikely to be out of refit to sail with the task force, but the Royal Navy was attempting to have every available warship in battle order.

This left the following six-frigate line-up, all of them carrying a more or less new, upgraded version of the old Seawolf guided-missile system:

HMS *Kent* – commissioned in the year 2000 and commanded by Captain Mike Fawkes, a forty-one-year-old ex-Fleet Air Arm pilot who had transferred to surface ships and impressed everyone with his handling of the ship during the second Gulf War. Married, with two boys aged twelve and fourteen, Mike Fawkes would assume command of the naval force, under Admiral Holbrook, if *Ark Royal* should be lost.

HMS *Grafton* – commissioned in 1997 and commanded by the urbane, smoothly attired Captain John Towner, whose dandyish appearance, complete with knotted white silk cravat, belied his technical expertise with the Plessey 996 search-radar system. At forty-five he was probably the best guided-missile officer in the Royal Navy and was known by his colleagues as Hawkeye.

HMS *St Albans*, commissioned in 2002, was the newest of the class. She was commanded by Captain Colin Ashby, at forty-nine the former commander of one of the old Type-42 destroyers and a veteran of the last Falklands War, where he had served as a sub-lieutenant on the flight deck of HMS *Hermes*. Captain Ashby's father, a Second World War battleship gunnery officer, had long had ambitions for his only son to join the navy. But after the eighteen-year-old Colin had managed to slam the family river cruiser into Rochester Bridge on the Medway River, breaking every cup and plate in the galley – well, after that Ashby Senior had insisted. And he lived to see his son become the first commander of the brand new HMS *St Albans*.

HMS *Iron Duke* was now seventeen years old. Her captain was Commander Keith Kemsley, at thirty-seven the youngest of the frigate COs and tipped by many to make it straight to the top of the Royal Navy ladder. An outstanding exponent of guided-missile warfare, and an expert in both ASW and gunnery, Commander Kemsley was by nature an aggressive war-fighter and, privately, Admiral Holbrook thought it entirely likely he might end up – dead or alive – with a Victoria Cross. A young Fogarty Fegan, was Kemsley.

HMS *Westminster*, one year younger than *Iron Duke*, was a very well-maintained ship under Commander Tom Betts, who ran his ship with considerable discipline and limited laughter. But the crew was highly efficient, particularly in the field of ASW. Commander Betts was himself a former torpedo officer with an expert's grasp of the complicated operational procedures with the Marconi Stingray weapons carried by *Westminster*.

HMS *Richmond* was commanded by Captain David Neave, former Executive Officer of the Type-45 destroyer *Dauntless*. Aged forty-six, he had always longed for a full command but had not considered the possibility of going to war within three months of his first appointment. Today he stood on the jetty watching stores being loaded into his ship, awaiting the new Westland Lynx helicopter which would arrive on his aft deck within the next hour.

And, essentially, that was it for the line-up of the Royal Navy's guided-missile frigate force which would face the Argentine air assault less than five weeks from now.

Two bigger 7,350-ton Type-45 destroyers were definitely in the group heading south. HMS *Daring* would sail from Devonport under the command of Captain 'Rowdy' Yates, from Sussex, a barrel-chested former centre-three-quarter for England Schoolboys and then for the Navy.

The brand new HMS *Dauntless* was going, despite still being on her sea trials. She would sail under the command of Commander Norman Hall, a former able seaman on HMS *Broadsword* who had come up through the ranks and was enormously popular with his 187-strong crew.

The twenty-five-year-old HMS *Gloucester*, commanded by Captain Colin Day, would also go, and all three of these destroyers were taking on board stores and ammunition on the quays near *Ark Royal*. The shore crews were attempting to have HMS *Dragon* and HMS *Defender* ready to join them. Failing that, two of the old Type-42s, probably HMS *Edinburgh* and possibly HMS *York*, which were smaller at 4,675 tons and equipped with the old Sea Dart missile system, would become part of the task force.

Sea Dart was a medium-range missile, best used against high-flying aircraft but pretty useless against an incoming sea-skimming missile. Also, its radar was suspect when aimed at low angles across the water and over the land. It was neither as modern nor as efficient as the new Harpoons on the Type-45s, which also carried the new European PAAMS surface-to-air system as their principal anti-air-missile defence.

HMS *Ocean*, the Royal Navy's 22,000-ton helicopter carrier and assault ship, was also going. *Ocean*, under the command of Captain John Farmer, would carry six Apache attack helicopters, a half-dozen big Chinooks, plus vehicles, arms and ammunition for a full Marine Commando assault. It could transport more than 1,000 troops comfortably, and 1,350 at a pinch. For this trip it would take the full 1,350.

A second specialist assault vessel, the 19,000-ton HMS *Albion*, would transport 1,000 troops, sixty-seven support vehicles, and a couple of helicopters. She would sail under the command of Captain Jonathan Jempson, whose legendary Royal Navy lawn-tennis partnership with Captain Farmer of *Ocean* had once seen them reach the second round of the men's doubles at Wimbledon.

The final significant ship was the almost-new 16,000-ton Landing Ship (Logistics) *Largs Bay*, built at the great Swan Hunter yards on Tyneside, and intended as the linchpin of a second wave of an amphibious assault. The ship could hold, if necessary, thirty-six Challenger tanks, 150 light trucks, 200 tons of ammunitions and 356 troops. Its reinforced flight deck could cope easily with heavy Chinook helicopters. It would sail under the command of Captain Bill Hywood.

Portsmouth Dockyard now resembled an industrial city, with transporters arriving by the dozen round the clock. Of course, the government's concept of a 'rapid deployment force' was a mere euphemism for 'cutting back on everything'. For military commanders it was a constant struggle to put together any kind of force when the entire operation was beset with shortages: not enough artillery, not enough warships, not enough tanks, not enough top-class combat clothing, not enough spare parts, everything scattered thinly, and – worst of all – not enough people.

There remained a governmental mindset in the United Kingdom, based on an idealised notion of hundreds of years of history, that the armed services could, at the drop of a hat, pull together a fighting force that would beat any other in the world.

It had been a very long time since that was true – if it ever had been – and with each passing year of left-leaning governments it had become less and less feasible. Certainly British troops and the Royal Navy had performed heroically well in the two conflicts in the Gulf. And there was much to recommend their performance in the operations in Bosnia. However, all these had been relatively 'low-tech' campaigns.

But in the year 2011, Great Britain had not gone into battle alone for almost thirty years when they had last fought for the Falkland Islands. And that had been a close-run thing. A look at Admiral Woodward's private diary revealed a somewhat disturbing sentence. On the night of 13 June 1982, he wrote, *'I do not have one ship without a major operational defect. I am afraid if the Argentines breathe on us tomorrow, we might be finished.'*

As it happened, the Argentines had surrendered the next day, and Britain celebrated a hard-won victory. But it might prove to have been her last, unless Westminster governments began to rectify the problems they had created.

Two more weeks went by before the troops began to show up in significant numbers. The first to arrive were members of the Royal Marine Brigade, plus their artillery support, the engineer squadron, their Logistic Support Regiment and the Air Squadron. Altogether 5,000 men from 40 Commando, 42 Commando, and 45 Commando began to embark the ships.

They were followed by a second 5,000-strong formation, the 16th Air Assault Brigade, including 1 and 2 Para, and a battalion from the Royal Green Jackets. This was part of the army's rapid-response force, equipped with Chinooks and Apache attack helicopters. It was a specialist force, trained specifically for this type of mobile operation.

They personally supervised the loading of their beloved Apache helicopters, which bristled with guns and rockets and would provide valuable air support against Argentine armour and ground troops.

The Artillery Regiment had their eighteen light field guns, which it was hoped could be deployed all over the combat area – if they could make a landing, that was . . .

On 4 March, a declaration signed by the British Prime Minister informed Buenos Aires that if the Argentine armed forces had not vacated the Falkland Islands completely in five days the British task force would sail from Portsmouth to the South Atlantic. There they would wage war upon the Republic of Argentina until the islands were cleared of this foreign invasion.

Suitably warned, still the Argentines made no response, despite much urging from the American State Department which was doing everything in its power to persuade Buenos Aires to back down and negotiate. The US government even offered to broker the talks which could be held in Washington until some satisfactory agreement was reached.

But Argentina was not about to negotiate. And the British Prime Minister was essentially in the hands of his own military high commmand. They had made it clear that once the task force sailed it would either fight or turn round and come home. The British forces involved simply were not strong enough to reach the South Atlantic and hang around indefinitely while politicians and diplomats argued.

The problems of food, fuel and supply lines were colossal, while many of the ships were old and likely to experience serious malfunctions. They could fight perhaps once, fiercely, for maybe a month, but they could not waste time.

'Prime Minister,' General Sir Robin Brenchley had said, 'to leave us down there for several weeks, fighting the weather, waiting for your clearance for battle, would be suicide for us – and perfect for our land-based opponents. So you'd better get used to it. Once we clear Portsmouth Dockyard we're going to fight, and if you can't cope with that you'd better call the whole thing off. Because if we get there and you put us in a holding pattern, we'll probably lose half this ageing fleet before we even start to engage the enemy.

'Try to remember,' he added as if talking to a child, 'all engineering problems, great and small, which would normally be carried out in a dockyard will have to be completed at sea. I cannot condone any delay.

'And if you try to put things on hold, you'll have the immediate resignations of both myself and the First Sea Lord, plus a dozen of the highest-ranked commanders. Our reasons will be unanimous: *the total incompetence of your government.*'

The Prime Minister was beaten and he knew it. 'Very well, general,' he said. 'I must agree. When the task force sails there will be no further delay. Your rules of engagement will be set out and will not be subject to change.'

Which essentially boxed everyone into an even tighter corner. Time was running out: the American diplomats were making no progress whatsoever, and Argentina had nothing to say to anyone.

At 0800 on 17 March 2011 the task force sailed. The dockyard was packed with well-wishers. Families of the men on board the Royal Navy ships lined the quays, many of them in tears. The band of the Royal Marines played 'Rule Britannia' over and over as the warships cast off their lines and headed out into the Solent, line astern.

Great crowds lined the seafront at Southsea, watching the ships sail slowly out into the English Channel and then on towards those great waters where devastating battles had been fought and won for centuries.

Admiral Alan Holbrook's flag flew from the mast of *Ark Royal* and the route they took was close to the shore, enabling the carrier to pass near the naval stations along England's south coast: Lee-on-the-Solent, Devonport and Culdrose. A constant stream of helicopter deliveries kept coming from the shore and stores and munitions were still being unloaded for those ships which had not yet been supplied in Portsmouth but were heading out later in the day.

And all along the historic coastline the crowds were out watching the warships on their way, clapping and cheering them in the gusty offshore breeze which carried their hopes and best wishes out into the Channel.

0900 17 March: 71.00N 28.47E
Depth 300. Course 225. Speed 22

She slipped swiftly through the cold deep waters off the most northerly coast of Norway: *Viper 157*, the 7,500-ton pride of Russia's ever-dwindling attack submarine fleet. The old Soviet Navy might have been in terminal decline but no expense had been spared in building this sleek black underwater warrior, completed a dozen years previously, lightly used and now 'worked up' to her maximum efficiency.

They had built her right in the cradle of Russian maritime engineering, the shipyards of Severodvinsk across the wide estuary of the Severnaya Dvina, on the often hard-frozen shores of the near-landlocked White Sea.

By general consensus *Viper 157* was the finest submarine ever built in Severodvinsk, constructed over a period of four years by the meticulous Severodvinsk nuclear engineers, many from the families of the same men who had built the enormous old Soviet Typhoon Class 26,000-ton ballistic-missile submarines back in the 1980s. She was nuclear-powered by a VM5-pressurised water reactor, which thrust 47,600 hp into her two GT3A turbines. A member of the excellent Akula Class ships, she was fourteen feet longer than the old Akula Is, and, at 360 feet overall, was the first of a new class of Akula IIs. The standard of engineering around her extra-long fin was unprecedented in Russian submarine building. She dived comfortably to a remarkable 1,500 feet, where she could make a good twenty-five knots.

Every possible radiated-noise level had been notably reduced. *Viper* was virtually silent at seven knots and under. Her sonar system was the latest improved Shark Gill (SKAT MGK 53), hull-mounted, passive/active search-and-attack. It functioned on low-medium frequency.

And her Raduga SS-N-21s packed a serious wallop, both as submerged-launch cruise missiles and surface-to-surface weapons, and her Sampson (GRANAT) missiles were fired from twenty-one-inch tubes, making Mach 0.7 for 1,600 miles, flying 200 metres above the ground and carrying a 220-kiloton nuclear warhead, if required.

She carried forty torpedoes, the twenty-five-foot long TEST-7IME fired from tubes fifty-three-centimetres wide. *Viper 157* was a Russian ship-killer, and each torpedo could travel through the water at forty knots for up to thirteen miles, packing a 220kg warhead – nearly 500 pounds of pure dynamite. Two of them would probably be enough to level the principal buildings of the Smithsonian Institute.

Viper had slipped her moorings in the Russian submarine base of Ara Guba shortly after midnight. Aside from the shore crew, just one lone Russian Navy admiral stood on the north jetty to see them off: the giant greatcoated figure of Admiral Vitaly Rankov, who had been personally briefing the captain and his senior officers for two days.

Free of her lines, *Viper* ran north up the long bay and headed up the channel into the icy depths of the Barents Sea. She dived in twenty-five fathoms, turning west towards the north Atlantic, beginning her three-month voyage through the dark seas.

The first few hundred miles would see her running down the endless narrow coast of Norway, leaving the southern city of Stavanger 1,100 miles to port. Here, *Viper* could move pretty briskly at 500 miles a day, but the narrowest point of the North Atlantic, the 800-mile-wide electronically trembling waters of the GIUK Gap, would force her to slow down.

This was the most sensitive 'submarine country' in the world. The line running from Greenland through Iceland to the northern coast of Scotland, and especially the stretch between Iceland and Scotland, was patrolled assiduously by submarines from the United States and British navies.

All through the GIUK Gap, the US Navy had installed an ultra-secret sound-surveillance system, a fixed undersea network of passive hydrophone arrays, sensitive listening equipment connected to operational shore sites which would collect, analyse, display and report any acoustic data relayed back.

These systems were laid in all key areas of the Pacific and North Atlantic, criss-crossing over the seabed and forming a giant under-water grid, but nowhere was the system more vibrantly sensitive than in the waters of the GIUK Gap. They say if a whale farts here, fifty American hearts will skip a beat as the undersea sound waves ripple down the SOSUS wires.

So, little imagination is required to picture the steely-eyed reaction in the US Navy listening stations when the steady engine lines of a possibly hostile submarine are detected.

The commanding officer of *Viper 157*, Kapitan Gregor Vanislav, one of Russia's most senior submariners, knew that once he ran south across the Arctic Circle he would be treading on eggshells.

No one would ever know what had really happened if his ship were sunk: the chances of a submarine being found in water two miles deep, somewhere in an area of several thousand square miles, was more than just remote. And no one ever wanted to admit the loss of a big nuclear ship, just as no one wished to admit they had destroyed it. Submarine losses are thus apt to remain very, very secret. All the more reason for Gregor Vanislav to be very, very nervous.

Making only seven knots, he reached the relatively shallow water of the GIUK Gap on the morning of 22 March. Now they really were moving on tiptoe, gliding above electronic lines on the ocean floor, as lethal as cobras, always alert to significant underwater movement and raising all hell in the American listening stations whenever they were triggered.

Captain Vanislav ordered *Viper*'s speed cut to five knots, and the most deadly attack submarine in the Russian Navy slowly eased her way forward, her great turbines just a tad above idling speed as she slipped further south down the Atlantic. Admiral Rankov had given Vanislav three commands on his way to the Falklands:

1) *Under no circumstances should you be detected along the route to the Falkland Islands.*
2) *Locate the Royal Navy task force and hold your position until hostilities begin.*
3) *Sink the* Ark Royal.

1130 (local time) Tuesday 22 March
National Security Agency, Maryland

Lt. Commander James Ramshawe was staring at the front covers of the major US news magazines. Without exception they featured large photographs of the Royal Navy task force sailing for the South Atlantic, most of which had been shot showing the decks of the aircraft carrier and the big assault ships lined with the GR9s and helicopters.

The President and the Pentagon had been alerted, as had the

NSA and the CIA, that the fleet's departure meant certain military action upon their arrival.

Jimmy poured himself a fresh cup of coffee, and continued to ponder the US coverage of the crisis. 'Jeez,' he muttered. 'Those bastards are actually going to fight for those islands all over again.'

He realised that this time a lot more was on the line than was immediately apparent. For a start, the US President was under enormous pressure from Exxon Mobil to do something about the Falkland Islands oilfields. They had paid an arm and a leg to the British government for drilling rights. And they'd had to make a massive investment in drilling-rig equipment, miles of pipeline, enormous pumps and transportation.

Exxon Mobil had two billion dollars tied up in that operation, and all of their guys had been frogmarched, at gunpoint, off the islands by Argentine troops. The oil giant wanted action. In fact the oil giant wanted President Bedford to get down there with a US Carrier Battle Group and 'roust these bastards back to where they came from'.

But President Bedford did not want to take his country into another war, especially with Argentina, a nation that had always extended the hand of friendship to the USA. The problem was that when Uncle Sam picked up his musket any ensuing war had to be won by the States, and the high command in the Pentagon knew how thoroughly the Argentines were prepared for this conflict.

The political ramifications of American boys fighting and dying on that godforsaken heap of rocks, which belonged to someone else in the first place, filled the President with horror – never mind the oil. And the Pentagon chiefs themselves were not mad about such an adventure either.

The US military was willing to assist Great Britain by running the base at Ascension Island, which would make resupply and refuelling much easier. They had even offered assistance with missiles. But President Bedford, like President Reagan before him, would not commit American troops, US Navy ships or US fighter-attack aircraft.

If truth were told, President Bedford actually felt somewhat guilty about the whole operation. Exxon Mobil was the biggest player in the Falklands oil business, and would thus be the biggest benefactor of any victory achieved by Great Britain.

Then there was the massive natural-gas strike on the island of

South Georgia. President Bedford had a disturbing vision of the British flag once more fluttering above Port Stanley, with the battered remnants of the Royal Navy fleet and its burned and wounded sailors huddled below it, men who would then have to turn south-east to South Georgia in order to save 10,000 British-national penguins and wrest 400 billion cubic feet of Exxon Mobil's natural-gas holdings from the hands of Argentine brigands.

It was not at all fair. He knew that. But then, nothing was, and the prospect of a couple of hundred body bags arriving back in the United States was more than he could risk. It would cost him his presidency.

Jimmy Ramshawe understood the high stakes. He had read, over and over, the carefully reasoned assessments of the forth-coming war by Ambassador Ryan Holland. He knew the heavy strength of the Argentine fighter aircraft – the Mirage jets, the Skyhawks and the Super-Étendards stationed at the newly active Rio Grande base.

And he knew that when battle commenced the Argentines would launch everything they had at the Royal Navy fleet. It would be an overwhelming aerial armada, and yes, the Brits would down several of them. But the Brits had insufficient air power: too many Argentine bombers would get through and they would blast the task force out of the game.

But no one understood the real issues here more thoroughly than Admiral Arnold Morgan. Recalled from his winter vacation in the Caribbean Island of Antigua, he had arrived on board *Air Force One*, and flatly refused to see the President until he had read the assessments of Ryan Holland and the summaries from the Pentagon.

'There's quite enough political assholes briefing you on subjects they do not understand,' he grated, 'without me joining them. Gimme two days and we'll talk.'

That had been Friday, 18 February and since then the President and the former National Security Adviser had been in constant communication. And, as ever, Arnold Morgan had brought a clarity to the situation which the President simply could not ignore.

'I understand why you do not want to take the United States to war,' said the admiral. 'But that is only the simple part of your problem. The difficult issue is that the Brits are going to get beaten. No ifs, ands or buts. They cannot win. They're too small a fleet, too thinly stretched, and they cannot defend themselves against iron bombs. Quite frankly, I'm astounded the Royal Navy agreed to go.

As for the British Army, God knows what's going to happen to them. Even if they manage to land on the Falklands to form an enclave preparing to march on the Argentine positions, if the weather's bad they'll get blasted out of sight because their GR9s can't stop an incoming enemy air assault. In my view we're looking at the possibility of the most shocking military defeat for Great Britain since Dunkirk.'

President Bedford walked across the Oval Office. He said nothing for a few minutes as he thought through the situation. 'I suppose we can't really ignore it, if that happens?' he finally asked.

'Christ, no,' replied Arnold Morgan. 'Refuse to help our best friends in the international community? A nation that stood shoulder to shoulder with us – twice – in the Gulf? Our one completely trustworthy ally in Europe? Hell – it would be construed as something close to treachery. No one would ever count on us again.

'And, of course, there's the oil. That's about as American as it gets.

'Mr President, to be honest, in the long run it might be a whole lot easier to join the Brits right off the bat, in the hope we frighten the shit out of the Argentines so that they'll withdraw from the islands in the face of our combined fury.'

'Something tells me, Arnold, they're not budging from that pile of rocks,' replied the President. 'And I don't think the oil and the wealth under the land is the true issue. I think they feel they are fighting some kind of a pampas *jihad*, battling for the birthright of every Argentine. They've been simmering over their defeat in the *Malvinas* for nearly thirty years. I agree with you. The Brits – and, in a sense, us as well – have our backs to the goddamned wall trying to fight these fucking fanatics.'

Admiral Morgan nodded sombrely. The President pressed a bell for another pot of coffee and waited for the admiral to finish his train of thought.

When he finally spoke, it was more like a father to a son than an ex-submarine commander to a US President. 'Paul,' he said, 'you and I have known each other for a long time. We both served in the United States Navy. And I want to ask you one question . . .'

'Shoot,' said the President.

'What would *you* do if you were in command of the Argentine military and wanted to win this forthcoming war in the fastest possible time?'

Paul Bedford didn't have to think twice. 'I'd take out the task force's Royal Navy carrier, the one with the entire air strength on board.'

'Yes, so would I. In fact I'd aim to hit *Ark Royal* and about a half-dozen other warships. I'd launch 100 fighter-bombers and send half of 'em after the *Ark Royal*. That way I'd put her on the bottom of the South Atlantic roughly four hours after the start of the war. Last time they had only five Exocet air-to-surface missiles. And Admiral Woodward kept *Hermes* well out of range during the daylight hours. This time it's all different. The Argentine air force is much bigger, much more efficient, and they have plenty of Exocets as well as a shitload of A4s.

'Christ,' said President Bedford. 'Now what?'

'Now what, indeed?' said the admiral. 'That's where we're likely to stand four weeks from now. So we'd better start thinking about it. Because the day's not far off when some comedian walks through that door and says that the Brits have just conceded defeat and the Falkland Islands remain in Argentine hands. The Chairman of the Joint Chiefs wants to know where we stand and the chairman of Exxon Mobil is fit to be tied.

'That,' added Admiral Morgan, 'would be a darned awkward moment.'

'You said that right,' said the President. 'OK, let's take a stroll along to the dining room, clear our heads and make a few decisions. You staying for lunch?'

'Depends what you're offering. Tuna sandwiches, forget it. Decent steak and salad, count me in. Tell you what, I'll even go for a roast beef on rye, so long as you run to mayonnaise and mustard. But, I repeat, we better start thinking. This Falklands bullshit gets more of a goddamned problem by the day.'

'If my wife catches me eating roast-beef sandwiches with mayonnaise she'll have a heart attack,' said the President, grinning.

'Then I guess we'd better be good boys and have two nice little grilled steaks with grass and fucking dandelions,' replied Arnold Morgan.

The two men stood up and pulled on their jackets. Leaving the Oval Office they walked along the West Wing corridor to the President's small private dining room where the butler had already set a table and poured them each a glass of sparkling water, knowing that neither man ever touched alcohol during the day.

The President sat down, his face set with determination. Something had to be done now.

'Well, oh Great Oracle,' said the President. 'What shall we do?'

'Dunno,' said the admiral, unhelpfully.

'You mean I sent the most expensive jet aircraft in the country halfway across the world to some goddamned Caribbean paradise to drag you off the beach with that goddess who married you, and at the end of it I get "Dunno?" Jesus Christ.'

Arnold chuckled. 'And the really bad news is I've just spent three weeks thinking about nothing else, night and day, and it's still "Dunno".'

'However,' he added, uttering the one word the President was waiting to hear. 'I know what we *cannot* do, under any circumstances. And that's rustle up 50,000 troops and somehow storm the place, with all guns firing, air, sea and land.'

'Why not?' asked the President, with pretended innocence.

'Because we don't even own the goddamned islands, and we would be universally accused of going to war over that oil and gas, which is a charge we've heard quite enough of for one century.'

'True,' said the President. 'Well, what's left?'

'Dunno,' said Arnold again.

'Jesus Christ,' said the President once more.

'Tell you the truth,' replied the admiral, 'I'd really like some time to talk to some of the Pentagon guys, particularly the Special Forces officers.

'What's strange is that there's one piece of information that seems to be too coincidental not to somehow fit into the big picture. I've been trying not to dwell on it, but we cannot ignore the fact that in the last few months we have witnessed two significant events.

'The first was the murder in the White House of old Mikhail what's-his-name, the Siberian. Which was a precursor of what the CIA believes to have been a larger-scale massacre of Siberian oilmen and politicians in Yekaterinburg.

'The only thing we can deduce from that is that Moscow seems overly concerned, to the point of neurosis, about oil-industry developments in Siberia. They must live under the constant threat of Siberia selling their oil not to Moscow but to their good and wealthy southern neighbours in China.

'Then the second major incident: the Argentine invasion of the Falkland Islands, carried out with scarcely a warning and conducted with massive confidence and total disregard for the possibility of a savage counter-attack by the Brits.

'Both of these things happened within a few weeks of each other, both of them brutal, ruthless, and done without apparent fear of consequences. And both of them were about oil and gas – the West Siberian reserves, which Moscow wants but may not be able to keep. And the Falklands and South Georgia reserves, which Argentina has grabbed.

'It may be a leap in my reasoning but I can't help thinking that somehow those two events may be connected in some way. That would sure as hell be bigger trouble than either you or I, or anyone else, could ever have imagined.'

The admiral's global grasp and perspective always astounded President Bedford. And as the two men slowly ate their steaks and dandelions their naturally talkative dispositions grew subdued in uncharacteristically sombre and silent contemplation.

CHAPTER SIX

HMS *Ark Royal* crossed the fifty-degree line of latitude in the western reaches of the English Channel, twenty miles south of the ancient naval city of Plymouth. The weather was foul, blowing a Force Eight gale, and the carrier pitched through ten-foot waves, the crests of which were beginning to topple, with dense streaks of foam marking the direction of the wind.

The rain, which had swept up the Atlantic in the approaching depression, was light but squally, sweeping across the deck in lashing bursts against the base of the carrier's island. The two Type 45s *Daring* and *Dauntless* ran port and starboard a half-mile off the carrier's bow.

Two miles astern of *Ark Royal* were three ships of the frigate squadron, *Grafton*, *Iron Duke* and *Richmond*, in company with a massive fleet oiler. Captain Farmer had *Ocean* positioned three miles off the carrier's port quarter, with Jonathan Jempson's *Albion* a mile astern, all of them making twenty knots.

Several hundred miles out in front were two 6,500-ton nuclear submarines, *Astute* and *Ambush*, both recently built in Barrow-in-Furness as the newest, state-of-the-art improvements on the old Trafalgar Class. *Astute* was commanded by Captain Simon Compton and *Ambush* by Commander Robert Hacking: both men were experts in navigation and weaponry.

Single-shafters with two turbines apiece, they each carried submerged-launch Tomahawk cruise missiles and thirty Spearfish torpedoes. They were equipped with the outstanding Thompson Marconi 2076 sonars, with towed array, and were probably the quietest deep-sea attack submarines, quieter even than the Russian *Viper 157*, which was still fighting its way down the coast of Norway.

The surface battle group pushed on down the English Channel towards the Atlantic, through driving rain and worsening weather. It was not yet storm force, but up ahead to the south-west the skies were darker and the clouds looked lower. The warships seemed to brace themselves for much rougher seas to come.

Admiral Holbrook had planned to visit the ships one by one and address the crews. But he elected to wait until the weather improved before making a succession of windswept helicopter landings on the flight decks of his various escorts.

They were in open water now and the waves were beginning to break over the bows of the frigates, but the Admiral reckoned they'd be clear of the stormy conditions within twelve hours.

With the coast of England finally slipping away behind them, the little fleet suffered its first equipment problem. Captain Yates's destroyer *Daring* developed a minor rattle in her gearbox, disconcerting though not life-threatening.

One day later, on the morning of Saturday 19 March, the flotilla steamed out of the rain and gloom into much calmer waters, proceeding under blue skies which would, with luck, hold fair for the 1,000-mile run down to the Azores.

Admiral Holbrook decided to visit *Dauntless* and *Daring* in the morning, and then fly back to *Iron Duke* and *Richmond* in the afternoon. And to each of the four groups of highly apprehensive sailors he delivered the same somewhat brutal message.

'Gentlemen, there's no point in beating about the bush. We are going to war, and it is likely that some of us may not be returning. I expect to lose ships, and people. And I am obliged to remind you that for several years now you have been paid by the Royal Navy to prepare for events such as this, to fight a battle on behalf of your country. Royal Navy seamen have long had a phrase for it – *you shouldn't have joined if you can't take a joke.*

'With regard to our enemy, the Args have two twenty-six-year-old diesel-electric submarines, both somewhat tired and slow. We ought to detect them far away and deal with them accordingly. They also have an even older, even slower submarine which one of their commanders ran aground in the River Plate at the end of last year. All considered, I do not regard the Argentines as a major subsurface threat.'

This raised a tentative laugh, but all in all Admiral Holbrook's

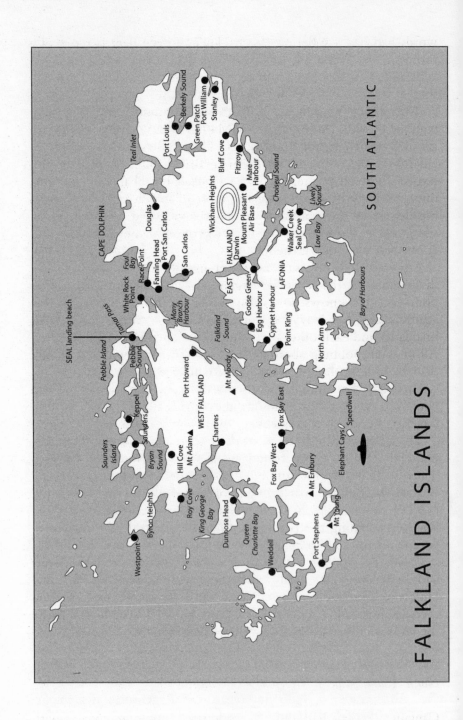

FALKLAND ISLANDS

SOUTH ATLANTIC

Berkely Sound
Port Louis
Green Patch
Port William
Stanley
Bluff Cove
Fitzroy
Mare Harbour
Choiseul Sound
Wickham Heights
Mount Pleasant Air Base
Lively Sound
Walker Creek
Seal Cove
Low Bay
CAPE DOLPHIN
Douglas
Port San Carlos
FALKLAND
Darwin
EAST
LAFONIA
Foul Bay
Race Point
Fanning Head
San Carlos
Goose Green
Egg Harbour
Cygnet Harbour
Point King
Bay of Harbours
White Rock Point
Many Branch Harbour
Falkland Sound
SEAL landing beach
Tamar pass
Pebble Island
Pebble Sound
Port Howard
Mt Moody
North Arm
WEST FALKLAND
Fox Bay East
Keppel
Saunders
Speedwell
Saunders Island
Bryan Sound
Hill Cove
Mt Adam
Chartres
Fox Bay West
Elephant Cays
Bryan Heights
Roy Cove
King George Bay
Dunnose Head
Mt Embury
Westpoint
Queen Charlotte Bay
Weddell
Port Stephens
Mt Young

148

words had had a sobering effect. 'Their surface fleet is more of a problem,' he went on, but added quickly, more encouragingly, 'although I expect our SSNs to have dealt with it before we get there.

'I'm talking about their four German-built destroyers, all of them equipped with Aerospatiale MM40 Exocet surface-to-surface missiles, which is not good news. They have another couple of elderly destroyers, one of them a British-built Type-42 with Exocets. The other one, *Santissima Trinidad*, is probably out of commission. They have nine frigates, most of which carry an Exocet missile system. Two of them are only ten years old. We must be on our guard at all times, absolutely on top of our game. And if we stay at our best we'll defeat them.'

Admiral Holbrook saw no point in dwelling upon the awful discrepancy in the air war, Argentina with perhaps 200 fighter bombers, God knows how many Super-Étendards, all land-based, against the Royal Navy's twenty-one GR9s with no viable radar, unable to find each other, never mind the enemy, in bad visibility. All of them bobbing about in the South Atlantic with no second deck to land on should *Ark Royal* be damaged.

Each day the admiral addressed a different ship's company and conferred with his captains as they made their passage south, covering hundreds of miles every twenty-four hours.

The aircrews continued to work up their attack force, with take-offs and landings being conducted all day and into the evening. They were rarely interrupted, except, on several occasions, by Russian long-range maritime patrol aircraft, known by their old NATO designation as Bears. They mostly just flew along the horizon watching the British ships, and every time the task force commander hoped to hell they were not talking to the Argentines.

Once the task force was south of the Spanish coast the Bears vanished altogether. But still the deep frown on Admiral Holbrook's brow never eased as he and Captain Reader discussed the appalling task ahead of them, knowing well that this might be the last battle that a Royal Navy fleet would fight.

231440MAR11 50.47N 15.00W
North Atlantic. Speed 7. Depth 500. Course 195.

Captain Vanislav had thus far conducted his long voyage with exemplary caution. He had run *Viper 157* swiftly for two days down the Norwegian coast, then cut his speed dramatically as he angled on a more westerly course out into the Norwegian Sea, gliding delicately above the SOSUS wires of the United States Navy.

Viper had crept down through the GIUK Gap making only seven knots as she moved over the Iceland-Faeroe Rise in 850 feet of water, straight down the ten-degree westerly line of longitude. They had pressed on over the Iceland Basin where the Atlantic suddenly shelved down to a depth of nearly two miles.

Then they had run on 500 miles south-west, down the fifteen-degree line of longitude until they approached the Porcupine Abyssal Plain 120 miles west of the Irish Trough. And right here they ran into one of those deep-ocean phenomena – a school of whales in front of them that would show up on the sonar like an oncoming battle group.

No one was overly concerned, since such events were fairly common in the deep waters of the North Atlantic, and the whales eventually swerved away. Almost simultaneously, however, something much more serious happened. One of *Viper*'s indicator buoys came loose, and made the most frightful racket rattling against the hull for two minutes until its mooring wire broke.

Viper was directly over a deep-water SOSUS wire, and two operators in the secret US Navy listening station on the craggy coast of County Kerry in south-west Ireland detected the noise instantly.

Almost immediately, with the loose buoy transmitting on the international submarine distress frequency, *Viper*'s comms room sent a short-burst 1.5- second transmission to a satellite, just to let the submarine's home base know right away they had not actually sunk.

The Americans heard all three bursts of noise.

'*Sounds like a submarine in trouble, sir. Russian. Nothing else correlates. I'm checking. It's a Russian nuclear – probability area small.*'

'*Degree of certainty on that?*'

'*Eighty per cent, sir. Still checking. She runs at the northern line of a ten mile by ten mile square. But right now the contact's disappeared.*'

'*Keep watching . . .*'

Everyone knew that the Russians were perfectly entitled to be running a naval submarine down the middle of the Atlantic south of the GIUK Gap. Just as the Americans or the British were.

But this particular submarine had not been detected for several hundred miles, which suggested it did not want to be. Then, as suddenly as it had appeared, it vanished, which made it even clearer that it had no intention of being located and was probably operating clandestinely, on a classified mission.

Everyone in the US listening station knew there were several possibilities. The Russian ship could easily have been on a training run, or testing new equipment on a long-distance voyage. Maybe the US operators had picked her up at the end of the training run as she made her turn. But if so, why was she not making proper speed north for everyone to locate her?

The US Navy Lt. Commander did not like it. Any of it. And he put an immediate signal on the satellite to Fort Meade:

231610MAR11 South-west Ireland facility picked up a two-minute transient contact on a quiet submarine. Data suggests Russian heading south. Abrupt stop. Nothing on friendly networks correlates. Fifty square mile maximum area. Still checking longitude 15. 200 miles off west coast Ireland.

The US Navy's Atlantic desk in the National Surveillance Office drafted a request to Moscow to clarify the matter. No reply was forthcoming but on the other side of the continent, in the heart of the Kremlin, Admiral Vitaly Rankov paced his office furiously, cursing the slipshod carelessness of *Viper*'s crew.

Thirty-six hours later, on the morning of 25 March, Lt. Commander Jimmy Ramshawe sat down to his usual scroll through the pages on the NSA's Internet site. Scanning through the message from County Kerry, the fifth line stopped him dead. It contained the word 'submarine' and from all the things Arnold Morgan had taught him he knew that submarines raised a red flag:

'Ramshawe, my boy, when you see the word "submarine", think only one thing: sneaking conniving little sons of bitches, hear me? When you see the words "Russian submarine", take that to the tenth power, and throw in the words "devious, furtive, shifty, underhanded" and "villainous". Because they are always, always up to no good.'

Jimmy logged into his classified intelligence CD-ROM and accessed the section on Russia, running through the classes of submarines which might be on the loose. Most likely, he thought, were the Akula Class boats, and there were eleven of them, with three laid up. Four of the old Akula Is were confirmed in the Pacific Fleet, three on the quays at Tarya Bay, and one visiting the port of Petropavlovsk on the Kamchatka Peninsula.

That left three, all in the Northern Fleet either in the base at Ara Guba or operational in the Barents Sea to the north of Murmansk. These were the newest, the improved Akula IIs – *Gepard*, commissioned in 2001, *Cougar*, commissioned in 2005, and *Viper*, commissioned in 1996.

'Well,' muttered Jimmy, 'our operator in Ireland reckoned it was a Russian nuclear, so it probably was one of these three. Still, I wonder what the little son of a bitch was doing heading south down the Atlantic.'

The word 'Atlantic' reminded him of the Royal Navy task force heading for the Falklands. He immediately checked its whereabouts . . . *800 miles north of Ascension . . . that's bloody miles from the Russian submarine, damn nearly 3,000. Can't see a connection there . . .*

Nonetheless, he decided to call his boss, Admiral George Morris, whose antennae rose instantly. 'Come along and see me, James,' he said. 'And bring a hard copy of that signal from Ireland, will you?'

Three minutes later they were both standing in front of a large wall computer screen, staring at a map of the Atlantic, at the area where the Russian ship had been detected.

'Strange place to be suddenly heard, then just as suddenly disappear,' mused the Director. 'He obviously did not want to be located – and when he was, it was a pure accident.'

'Can't tell if the bugger turned around or kept on going,' said Jimmy.

'No,' replied the admiral. 'No one can tell that. And no one's heard a squeak from the damn thing since? Guess we just have to wait till he makes another mistake. Because it sure as hell was a mistake. That was one creepy little son of a bitch, and he did not wish to be detected . . . let me know if Moscow offers an explanation.'

'You want to touch base with the Big Man, sir?'

'Jimmy, I'm real tied up this afternoon. But maybe you could have a quick word with him – you know how he is about submarines . . .'

'OK, chief. I'll give him a call.'

Twenty minutes later Admiral Morgan, in cheerful mood, answered the phone in Chevy Chase. 'Don't tell me,' he said. 'The Russian secret police just committed murder in Buckingham Palace.'

Jimmy chuckled. 'Not quite, sir. But I just received a signal from our listening station in south-west Ireland. They think they picked up a Russian nuclear submarine running south a couple of days ago.'

'What submarine?' snapped the admiral, all traces of bonhomie suddenly gone from his voice.

'Well, the most likely was one of their Akula Class boats. Not the Akula Is, which are in the Pacific. But one of three operational Akula IIs, much newer, all based in the Northern Fleet – either *Gepard, Cougar* or *Viper* . . .'

'Are they all accounted for?'

'Not reliably. Just before I called we located *Gepard* on an exercise sixty miles north of Murmansk, and we have a record of *Cougar* in workup after a refit just outside Ara Guba ten days ago. Nothing on *Viper*. But they have those big covered docks up there, so I guess it could have been either of 'em.'

'Where did the guys in Ireland detect the ship?'

'Coupla hundred miles west of County Kerry. In deep water – they heard a lot of clattering, then an international distress signal. Then they picked up a satellite signal, a short burst in Russian. Surveillance says it confirmed they were not sinking. Then it went quiet. I checked with the station: they record no other ships within a hundred miles.'

'Wonder what the hell scared her?'

'Can't help you there. I talked to the operator. He said they picked something up right out of the blue. From nowhere. And it vanished just as sharply. Never came back.'

'Hmm,' said Arnold Morgan. 'Sneaky little sonofabitch, right?'

'Yessir.'

'Tell you what, Jimmy. It's 11.30 – you want to come over for lunch? I'm fooling with a theory which just might fit right into this. But it's so goddamned outlandish I'm kinda nervous about mentioning it. It's not something I want you to act on, it's something I want you to have in your mind – in the back of your mind, right? Just for that moment when something pops out at you, when some tiny bit of data seems to shed some light.'

'OK, I'll just tell Admiral Morris. I'll be there by 12.30 and I gotta be back for 1600.'

'Don't get excited. You'll be back before then. This isn't a goddamned banquet, it's a quick sandwich and a cup of coffee. Don't be late . . .' Bang. Down phone. The Admiral, even in retirement, still didn't have time for 'goodbye'. Not even for the young naval officer he treated like a son.

Jimmy's elderly but perfectly tuned black Jaguar, its top down, came squealing into the admiral's drive three minutes before 12.30, nearly mowing down a couple of Secret Service agents in the process.

'Christ, sir, you'll kill someone in that damned thing,' one of them observed. 'I just hope it won't be me.'

'Don't you worry about me, Jerry,' called Jimmy. 'I've got eyes like a bloody dingo, and reactions to match.'

'What the hell's a dingo?'

'Australian prairie dog, a right little killer – stealthy, like me.'

'Stealthy! You're about as stealthy as a train crash,' replied the agent, laughing. 'Go straight in. The admiral's waiting.'

Inside the house, sitting quietly by the log fire in his book-lined study, was the most feared military-intelligence expert in the world. A man whose influence and expertise had once caused world leaders to shudder, and who, even now, was capable of wreaking havoc and inspiring fear among governments not entirely in step with the United States.

Admiral Morgan looked up from the editorial page of the *New York Times* with a scowl on his face. 'The sad and lamentable left,' he growled. 'Still fighting for the same tired old causes, years out of date, discredited, long dismissed. But only in the biggest newspaper in the entire goddamned country . . . hi, young Ramshawe, sit down.'

'Morning, admiral,' said Jimmy, brightly.

'Morning! Morning!' snapped the old tyrant of the West Wing. 'Right now we're nearly a half-hour into the afternoon watch. Eight bells before this coffee arrived – want some?'

'Thank you, sir,' said Jimmy. 'I mean Arnie. It's just damn near impossible to believe you've retired.'

'Don't you start off – you sound like Kathy.'

'It's just that everyone seems to think you're still in charge. And George Morris says that's what the President relies on.'

'Well, I'll have to whip him into line next week,' said the admiral, 'Because we're taking a short vacation in Scotland, kinda make up for my severely interrupted rest on a Caribbean beach last month.'

Jimmy poured himself a cup of coffee from the heated glass pot on the sideboard, freshened Arnold's cup as well, and fired out a couple of 'bullets' from the blue plastic container which contained the sweeteners.

The admiral flicked them into his steaming coffee. Then he told Jimmy to shove another log on the fire, and to pay attention. He would have told the President of the United States, or Russia, or China, to do precisely the same thing. It was part of his charm.

'Now listen, Jimmy. With the exception of George, I don't want you to repeat this conversation to anyone. I have mentioned it to the President, who was having his lunch at the time and damn nearly choked on it. And I'm going to tell you, because I know you will store the information and be watchful for correlating facts.'

'Right, sir. I'm listening.'

In his usual brisk style, Arnold Morgan went through the sequence of recent events around the globe, as he and Paul Bedford had done not too long ago. 'The murder of the Siberian politician in the White House, which was followed up a few weeks later by some kind of a massacre of all the big players in the Siberian oil industry.

'Drastic action, James. We're talking mass murder. The old tried and trusted methods of the Soviets. Remove the men, you remove the problem. But this Russian president is damned smart, and he's a long-range thinker. On the one hand Moscow is buying Siberian oil for an extremely low price, and taxing them, and on the other, Siberia's neighbours to the south, China, are offering a much better deal, and are even arguing about the direction of the new Far Eastern pipeline. And if the Russian president dwelled on the Siberian problem for long enough he probably concluded it was an ongoing pain in the ass. And if he took it to its logical conclusion, he probably foresaw the day when Russia might be confronting the Siberians, who will want independence – and their oil sold on the open market.'

'I guess so. And I doubt it's escaped him that China is scouring the entire bloody planet in search of oil supplies.'

'No, Jimmy, that will certainly not have escaped him. And now I'm going to ask you a very serious question . . . where has the biggest oil and natural-gas strike in the world in the last two years?'

'Not sure, sir.'

'I'll tell you. It's in the Falkland Islands. And what happened last month?'

'The Argentines invaded and conquered the Falklands and grabbed the oil.'

'From right out of nowhere, Jimmy. From right out of nowhere. For the first time for twenty-eight years there was a sudden rise in the political temperature in Buenos Aires. Now here's the thing, Jimmy. Why undertake such a drastic and reckless operation. Why now?'

'I give up,' Jimmy said, grinning. 'But I'm guessing that the clandestine Russian submarine somehow fits into this?'

'I don't know how exactly, but let's assume for a moment that Russia was involved. How about if Russia said they'd take care of the oil, drill for it, market it, build the pipelines, and cut Argentina in for a very generous piece of the deal? In return, they would make certain that any Royal Navy task force was eliminated, and the islands would remain sovereign Argentine territory.'

Jimmy hadn't expected this. 'Jesus Christ. Are you basing this on definite knowledge, sir?'

'Certainly not. I'm basing it on a series of wild deductions, hunches, guesses, and blind political bias.'

Jimmy had to laugh, despite the obvious gravity of the situation. 'Of course, sir. Stupid of me not to have realised.'

Arnold, however, did not smile. He stared at Jimmy darkly, and said, 'It might just explain that fucking Russian nuclear submarine of yours, apparently making a beeline south down the Atlantic towards the Falklands.'

'Fuck me,' said Jimmy, momentarily lost for words. At least, *normal* words . . . 'You're telling me that nuclear ship might be going to help Argentina defend the Falklands? Maybe attack the British? Christ. That's World War Three.'

'James,' said Arnold paternally, 'You don't have to do much to cripple the Royal Navy's task force. A couple of well-aimed torpedoes, straight into the guts of HMS *Ark Royal,* and that little conflict is over. She'll hit the bottom of the South Atlantic taking all the British fighter planes and half their helicopters with her.

'If the British Army is already ashore, they'll be massacred from the air and then taken prisoner. The fleet, with no air cover, will be hammered sideways and the survivors will be forced to return home – and no one will ever know what happened to *Ark Royal.* At least, no one who matters. The Russian SSN won't even surface. She'll just turn north and creep quietly home. And the world will believe the Brits lost a fair fight against Argentina, a fight which she should never have entered.'

'Fuck me,' said Jimmy again, even more emphatically this time. He shook his head, and then, hesitating, said, 'You know the big trouble with that little scenario? It doesn't have any weak points!'

Arnold guffawed. 'Well, except that we don't actually have one shred of evidence which makes all those little facts and circumstances hang together.'

'What is it you always say, Arnie? You do not accept incompatible facts, right? I'd say the line-up you just gave me is one *highly* compatible group of facts.'

'Jimmy, they are so far-reaching I hesitate to continue. But they have been on my mind, even before you mentioned the submarine west of Ireland. I suppose no one from the Russian navy has offered confirmation or even denial about the whereabouts of the Akula II submarines?'

'Not a word, so far as I know.'

'Again, that makes me think I may be right. Because if they'd sent a nuclear sub on a training exercise down the Atlantic, they'd have told us. The Cold War's over, you know. We're supposed to be buddy-buddy with Moscow. But when the Kremlin starts clamming up, on any subject, you just *know* there's something going on.'

'I guess there is,' said Jimmy. 'But if you're right, this is a huge development. I mean what if the Brits catch 'em, and sink the sub. I mean, where the hell does that put *us*?'

'Jimmy, I'll just have our sandwiches sent in – Kathy's out, which means we get roast beef with mayonnaise and mustard. Our housekeeper is on pain of death not to mention it . . . I'll be right back with some more coffee, too. And then I'll tell you where we stand.'

Jimmy took off his jacket, tossed it over a chair in the hall, and sat down again in the warm study. He glanced at the third lead story on the front page of the *New York Times*.

No Political Solution Yet –
Argentina Occupies the Falkland Islands

At that moment the admiral returned. 'Ignore that rubbish,' he said, 'Kipper knows more about it than they do.'

'Who the hell's Kipper?'

'Kathy's new dog. A King Charles spaniel. I think he's as silly as a sheep. But he might learn, which is more than they will at the *NYT*.'

'Where is he?'

'Gone out with Kathy. Virginia somewhere.'

Arnold sat down, and said quietly, 'We can't leave the Brits to suffer defeat at the hands of an armed aggressor.

'I know Argentina will blather on about the *Malvinas* belonging

157

to them. But that's just horseshit. The Falklands Islands are a legal British protectorate, full of British citizens, and they are ruled and financed by Westminster. The Argentine action, whether they admit it or not, is that of a gangster.

'And we cannot support that. Neither will the United Nations. Neither will the EU. The trouble is, we'll be expected to do something about it.'

'So now what?'

'I'm toying with the idea of forcing an Argentine surrender on the islands with Special Forces only. Maybe we could eliminate the Argentine air force and retake the island with just a force of landed US Navy SEALs working with the British SAS.'

Jimmy gaped at him.

'But they'll need air cover, just like the Brits, won't they? And then you'd be talking aircraft carriers, fighter-bombers and F-16s all over the place. That's war, real war. And where will the SAS come from, anyways?'

'The SAS *and* the Special Boat Service – a kind of SAS with flippers. To be honest with you, I'd be surprised if they were not already in there, or at least well on their way...'

For five more days, the Royal Navy task force steamed south, running into relatively calm waters north of Ascension on 28 March. At this point, *Viper* was still more than 2,000 miles behind. However, with SOSUS inactive in the southern reaches of the Atlantic Ocean, the submarine was now moving swiftly, often at twenty knots, 500 feet below the surface, hugging the eastern edge of the Mid-Atlantic Ridge.

Captain Vanislav had no intention of going anywhere near Ascension, and would pass its line of latitude, eight degrees south of the equator, some 1,000 miles to the west off the jutting, most easterly headland of Brazil.

Meanwhile the British task force was moving into the anchorage at Ascension Island, which had been rapidly transformed from a US communications and satellite tracking station into a forward fleet and air base. On that, President Bedford had been as good as his word.

Waiting there were piles of extra stores that had been flown out from the UK, and within a few days the Royal Navy's under-strength task force would at least be equipped with the supplies that they would need for the forthcoming conflict.

However, the two nuclear submarines, *Astute* and *Ambush* did not stop off at Ascension. They pressed on south. *Astute* was carrying sixteen members of 22 SAS, and *Ambush* had sixteen members of the SBS on board. These were the iron men of the British armed forces, who would land on the islands alone and under cover of darkness, equipped with radios, computers and satellite-communication systems. For a couple of weeks they would communicate back to the task force the troop placements of the Argentines, working in conditions of extreme danger. The night landing on the Falklands would be the most lethal part of the operation.

It would have to be by boat, fast hard-deck rubberised Zodiac outboards launched off the decks of the submarines, and driven in from four miles offshore, quite possibly having to keep under the Argentine radar.

The SAS would make a landing on the craggy coastline beneath the 800-foot-high Fanning Head at the north-eastern end of Falkland Sound. They would work from there, moving around the island only after dark.

The Special Boat Service troops were scheduled to go in somewhere on the coast of Lafonia, probably in Low Bay, which was situated to the south of Mount Pleasant airfield across Choiseul Sound. Their task was to scout out the territory for the British military landing, consisting of roughly 10,000 men. The land they would investigate was not hospitable. It was flat, with little cover and rock-strewn, but a place from which the British land forces could at least locate their enemy quickly by air, sea and land.

The military chiefs in Whitehall had discussed the possibility of a landing by parachute drop, but the risk was simply too great because no one knew exactly what the Argentine troops could see and what they could not. Things were tough enough without risking some of the best men in the landing force being shot to pieces the moment they landed. The solution was obvious. If the advance Special Forces were going in at all, they had to go in by sea.

The embarked SAS troop was commanded by thirty-year-old Captain Douglas Jarvis, a member of a venerable racehorse-breeding family from Newmarket in Suffolk. He had considered becoming a bloodstock agent but his elder brother had inherited the racing yard, and his sister Diana had insisted on selling the family stud farm, of which she owned fifty per cent.

Which left young Douglas with a bit of money from his quarter-share of the stud farm, a diminished family, and not much in the way of career choice. As it was, he was 'fed up to the back teeth with bloody racehorses' and managed to pass selection for entry into the Royal Military Academy at Sandhurst.

He was commissioned into the Second Battalion of the Parachute Regiment, and five years after that he was accepted into the SAS as one of an intake of only six from 107 applicants. Douglas Jarvis was generally considered to be one of the toughest young officers ever to wear the beige beret of 22 SAS.

A lifelong fox-hunter, steeplechase rider and amateur boxer, he once made the front page of England's horseracing daily, the *Racing Post*, when, at the age of eighteen, he had forged his entry to the annual Stable Lads Boxing Championship and flattened four stable-staff hard men from desperate inner-city council estates to win the heavyweight championship.

The committee took a poor view of the well-born son of a stable proprietor plundering the Championship which traditionally belonged to horse racing's 'other ranks'. Douglas was disqualified, and he grudgingly handed back his silver trophy. The authorities were not able to take away his steam-hammer right hook, however, and years later he was narrowly defeated on points in the Sandhurst Middleweight Final. But he won the Trophy for the Royal Military Academy's bravest loser.

The lean, wide-shouldered Douglas remained a legend in his native Newmarket, especially when he won a coveted Military Cross for leading his paras fearlessly in a pitched battle against insurgents in Basra during the 2003 Iraqi War. He shared the front page of the local paper with a sixteen-hand dark bay colt named Rakti who had won Newmarket's prestigious Champion Stakes and had been trained locally by Douglas's cousin Michael Jarvis. *THREE HEROES FROM NEWMARKET* proclaimed the newspaper, presumably referring to the trainer, the horse and Douglas.

'Jesus Christ,' said one of 2 Para's best young commanders.

The beautiful Diana Jarvis adored her kid brother. In recent years she had become something of a socialite, fox-hunting in Ireland and occasionally assisting a French trainer with the purchase of expensive thoroughbred yearlings at the major sales in Saratoga and Kentucky. But she and Douglas stayed in touch and saw each other whenever possible.

Neither of them married for a while but suddenly last year Diana had packed her bags to emigrate full-time to Kentucky. There she would marry an American who owned a huge breeding farm in the heart of the Blue Grass Country. They had been meeting for a couple of years at the Keeneland Sales.

Six weeks later she became Mrs Rick Hunter of Hunter Valley Farms at a small ceremony in the Lexington registry office, followed by a reception for thirty or forty friends and neighbours. Douglas was unable to attend, and it took Diana five more months to discover that her new husband, like her brother, had in his time been a member of his country's Special Forces. From time to time she picked up a few wry references to bygone conflicts, particularly when Rick's vice-president of thoroughbred operations, Dan Headley, came to dinner. She soon found out that Dan had once been in the US Navy as well.

The towering, superbly fit Rick had willingly told her he had been a Commander in the United States Navy, but only reluctantly admitted that he had also served a short tour in the Navy SEALs . . . 'Just a small Special Forces group, kind of like your brother's SAS guys.' The enormity of that particular sin of understatement was lost on the new Mrs Hunter, but Captain Jarvis, had he known, could have reliably predicted certain aspects of their future married life.

Right now, Douglas Jarvis was 500 feet underwater, speeding south down the Atlantic, 1,500 miles off the coast of Brazil and deep in conversation with *Astute*'s commanding officer, Captain Simon Compton.

They were in the ops area of the navigation officer, Lt. Commander Bill Bannister. Spread on the table was a large navy chart of the waters around East Falkland, and they were all looking at the northernmost points along the giant headland guarding the entrance to Falkland Sound.

This was a great craggy coastline, with high cliffs forming a seaward crescent facing to the north-west. The outermost top end of the crescent was Cape Dolphin, sitting on the end of a barren peninsula some two miles long. 'Militarily worthless' in the judgement of Douglas Jarvis.

The other end of the crescent was formed by Fanning Head, which really did guard the entrance to the Sound. It had once been 800 feet high, with sensational views over the water. Today it still had those sensational views, but now it stood only 787 feet high, its summit having been blown away by the guns of the Royal Navy frigate HMS *Antrim* during the first Falklands conflict.

'You think the Argies might be up there again?' asked Captain Compton.

'They might,' said Captain Jarvis. 'But only if they think we might do what Admiral Woodward did last time – send the fleet straight under their Fanning Head garrison at the dead of night. All lights out.'

'Hell, they can't believe we're *that* bloody dreary, can they?' said the CO. 'They must think we'd try something new.'

'You would think so,' replied Jarvis. 'But, for some reason, all our satellite interceptions suggest that they know a lot about us. Which is strange – they don't have much satellite observation themselves, if any, and we know for sure the Americans are not helping them. But someone is, though God knows who. So it wouldn't be surprising if they closed Falkland Sound to us completely. They may have mined it anyway, of course, but they didn't last time. All they need, really, is a powerful missile-and-gun position up on Fanning Head, with modern radar. It's something we must consider very seriously, as it would leave us incredibly vulnerable.'

'Yes, I agree. Where does that put us?' The CO had quickly grown to respect the SAS captain, as had everyone on board.

'Essentially we have to appreciate the logic of their position. An Argentine stronghold on top of that headland closes the north end of the Sound to us.' Jarvis pointed at the map. 'It means we have to go right around the back of West Falkland or swing way south down the Atlantic and come at them from the south-east.' He stabbed the map quickly. 'With very little time, trouble and cost, they can establish a powerful position on Fanning Head, which would plague us throughout this conflict. There's no other option, Simon: we have to land at the base of that cliff and, if they've set something up there, take the bastard out – not exactly by storm, but we'd still need to blow the fucker up somehow.'

'Christ, who's going to do that?'

'I am,' said Captain Jarvis. 'With seven of my best troopers.'

'You're going to climb that rock face?'

'In the absence of a chairlift, I suppose so. Where do you think we are, Courcheval?'

They returned to the chart and Captain Compton began talking the SAS boss through their route into the Falklands waters.

'We come in from the north-west, dive in about 200 feet of water, all the way to this light blue area where the ocean starts to shelve up. See these numbers here in metres? The ocean floor rises

162

up to only 120 feet, then stays at around 100 feet all the way in to Fanning Head. This narrow seaway into the Sound is only seventy feet deep, so we can just about stay underwater until we're a mile or so offshore, so long as we watch out for this fucking great rock marked here – only fifty feet below the surface with no warning light or even a buoy.

'Right here we're in the shadow of the cliff. And at 0200, it'll be as black as your hat. I'd prefer to launch the boats in here – just behind Race Point you'll have a mile longer to walk, but that's probably better than having your bollocks blown off by a radar-guided Argentine missile.'

Douglas Jarvis grinned. 'I assure you, Captain Simon, if anyone's going to have their bollocks blown off it will not be me. You think I could call my sister in Kentucky and tell her the Argies have gelded me? That'd be a family disgrace where I come from.'

'Well, I suppose you *would* have to be scratched from the Derby,' laughed the CO.

'Now, this submarine is seventy feet high, keel to mast. We need 100 feet minimum depth. If it's less than that, we surface, since I do not wish to see either you or your bollocks scraping along the seabed, specially if it's rocky.'

Both officers laughed again, and even Lt. Commander Bannister, who'd been frowning over the dangerous exploits ahead, joined in the nervous merriment.

'Let's get some coffee,' said Captain Compton finally. 'And then you can tell me where you want the second half of your troops to land.'

The Lt. Commander vanished in search of coffee, and Captain Jarvis continued looking at the chart of the jagged coastline. 'Simon,' he said, 'the second part of the SAS recce entails a thorough look at the Argentine defences around Mount Pleasant Airfield.

'I've eight men detailed to carry it out, and I cannot see any other way to get there except to walk. From this landing beach it's about forty-five miles through the mountains, and they'll need three days in these conditions.

'They'll be hauling a lot of weight on their backs and they can only move at night. I think we should land on Fanning Head more or less together but separate the groups by just a couple of miles, to avoid putting all our eggs in one basket.

'We'll take the Zodiacs in together, so you can make the fastest possible getaway. My guys are priceless, but I think the Navy values a £500 million nuclear submarine even higher.'

'Well, we don't have many,' said Captain Compton, but just then they were interrupted by a seaman handing over a hard copy of a satellite signal from the comms room.

'*311300MAR11. Argentine warships heading for battle stations around the Falkland Islands. Two destroyers and three frigates cleared Porto Belgrano 0500 today. Satellite intercept confirms destination East Falkland. All warships carry modern missile radar systems. Anticipate wide Falklands surveillance by Argentines, surface and air. Holbrook.*'

'Very timely,' said Captain Compton sharply. 'We stay deep, all the way in.'

The same signal was received by Captain Robert Hacking on board *Ambush*. He was in conference with the SBS team leader, Lieutenant Jim Perry, dealing with exactly the same subject: where to land the sixteen Special Forces men in Team Three, the guys who would hit the beach on the rough coast of Lafonia and work under cover of darkness.

As in *Astute*, the *Ambush* team was in the navigation area, poring over the chart, wondering where the nearest Argentine defences would be situated along this truly desolate part of the island, south of the airfield.

The deep inlet of Choiseul Sound was seventeen miles long and in places three miles wide, separating the 'business part' of East Falkland, where the oilfields and the airport and the military garrison were located. Indeed, Choiseul Sound very nearly bisected East Falkland altogether, prevented from doing so only by the narrow isthmus at Goose Green.

Much more pertinent, however, was the fact that the Sound was so damned shallow. There was a kind of navigation channel along the northern edge passing the entrance to Mare Harbour.

But even in this channel there was never as much as 100 feet depth, and the rest of the seaway was nearer thirty feet, in some places only ten. It was strewn with uninhabited small islands, submerged rocks, kelp beds and God knows what. It was a submariner's nightmare. No go. No even *think* about.

And somewhere in these treacherous waters Lt. Jim Perry had to find a place to drive the Zodiacs up the beach. He preferred to prevent his team from getting wet, since there was nowhere for them to dry out. And already, according to local forecasters, it was raining, with squalls out of the south.

Like Captain Jarvis's men, Lt. Perry's team had a formidable task. After the landing they had to establish a 'hide' – about a quarter-mile behind the beach, from where they could move out and watch, log and record all Argentine activity: the times and strength of shore patrols, if any; the proximity of the nearest Argentine military garrison; the regularity of sea patrols moving along the shore, if any; the times and depths of high and low tide for the incoming British landing craft; sites for missile batteries; helicopter landing areas; sites for shore radar systems which would scan across the flatlands to the north.

And all of this without being caught. When Lt. Perry's Zodiacs came in for the landing, one of them would be dragged up the beach and hidden, just in case a fast getaway was required.

Privately, Lt. Perry thought he might decide not to bother with the getaway Zodiac, which was very heavy, cumbersome, and an all-around nuisance for mobile troops. If the men of the SBS were caught they would expect to eliminate their enemy and carry on with their tasks. Running away was not in their training manual.

Both Royal Navy submarines continued their run south for seven more days. At noon on Friday, 8 April they were 100 miles north-west of the Falkland Islands, Captain Vanislav's *Viper* was still three days behind, and the task force, which had cleared Ascension on 3 April, five.

New intelligence from the US Navy in Ascension confirmed that an Argentine destroyer, an old Type-42, was moored at the quays in Mare Harbour, while two guided-missile frigates now patrolled two miles off Mengeary Point and Cape Pembroke, the two headlands guarding the entrance to the harbour and main town of Port Stanley.

The newest Argentine destroyer was currently making passage north, about three miles offshore. At the time the American signal was sent, she was moving quickly – around twenty knots – right off McBride Head, thirty miles east of the entrance to Teal Inlet. At the north end of Falkland Sound, another Argentine guided-missile frigate appeared to be almost stationary.

According to the satellite signal, this ship had come in from the north-west and had entered the Sound through the narrows below Fanning Head. When Simon Compton showed the signal to Douglas Jarvis they agreed it suggested that the Argentines seemed to plan to guard the Sound by sea, rather than build a missile launcher at the top of the cliff.

But still, the SAS leader could not take that chance. The Argentines were well prepared, smart and fiercely determined. They could still end up using Fanning Head to their advantage so Douglas's plan remained unaltered during the final miles of their long journey through the South Atlantic. The more disturbing aspect of the signal from Ascension, perhaps, was the news of the departure of three more Argentine warships from Porto Belgrano, all making direct course for the Falkland Islands.

Any chance the Royal Navy thought they might have had of the task force making a covert entry into these waters was plainly shot. The Argentines seemed to be aware of every move the British fleet had made on the voyage from Ascension, and they assumed, of course, the imminent arrival of Royal Navy nuclear submarines. For their part, neither *Astute* nor *Ambush* knew of the existence of *Viper 157*. Yet.

In the normal course of a Royal Navy commanding officer's duties, he would have received the information about the enemy destroyer off McBride Head and the frigate at the north end of the Sound and then he would have moved in and put both of them on the floor of the South Atlantic.

But this was different. The submarines were obliged to stay put quietly, to do anything to avoid getting caught. They had one responsibility right now: the insertion of the Special Forces could not be revealed to the enemy at any cost.

The slightest indication of a British attacking presence would be likely to double and treble Argentine awareness, and the number of their defensive positions. Right now the less they knew the better. So Captains Compton and Hacking moved stealthily, cutting their speed, reducing their engine lines on any probing sonar which might be transmitting on the north side of East Falkland.

The courses of the two submarines diverted thirty miles north of Fanning Head where the fifty-ninth degree line of longitude bisected the fifty-first degree line of latitude. *Astute* steamed on south, making only five knots, and *Ambush* made course 120, for her longer 100-mile journey around the east side of the island to Choiseul Sound.

The water was still almost 400 feet deep and would remain so for *Ambush* almost all the way. However the Atlantic began to shelve up here for *Astute* and for most of her journey inshore the depth would be around 200 feet, growing shallower every mile.

For the final run across Foul Bay, *Astute* would come to periscope depth in 100 feet of water, protected on three sides by huge cliffs and shielded from the Argentine frigate by Fanning Head itself.

Captain Compton ordered the ship to PD at 1826 hours, by which time the SAS team was preparing to exit the submarine. Each man was dressed in full combat gear, including the windproof, rainproof Gore-Tex light smock which covered their regular thermal clothes. SAS combat teams always wore the best waterproof boots that money could buy, and they carried in their bergens light thermal weatherproof sleeping bags, plus a quilted combat jacket in case the weather turned bad.

Each man had his own automatic rifle and ammunition, with a couple of hand grenades clipped to his belt. There was 'sticky' explosive for the possible attack on an Argie garrison at the top of Fanning Head. And there was plenty of concentrated processed food, plus water and medical supplies. The transmitter, laptop computers, cameras, and radios were all shared among the troops. They forbore from bringing their usual heavy machine gun, since their mission was supremely clandestine and the object was to stay undetected rather than mow down the enemy.

The success or failure of the entire British operation might depend upon their efforts of observation, assessment and transmission of facts. Every member of the submarine's crew knew the critical nature of the SAS operation, and every member of Captain Jarvis's team knew how high the stakes were.

At 1930 hours Captain Compton ordered the submarine to the surface, about one mile east of Race Point, tucked right behind the granite fortress of Fanning Head. They were still in 100 feet of calm water, and the moonless night was already pitch black. The most dangerous part of the operation was about to begin.

Astute's deck crews jumped instantly into action, hauling the half-inflated Zodiacs out of the entrance at the base of the fin. A jury-rigged davit was raised above the companionway to haul up the four 250 horsepower outboard motors. The engineers were already out on the casing, ready to fit the engines onto the sterns of the two boats.

Deck crews were loading the boats even as the electric pumps drove in the final pounds of air pressure into the hulls. A heavy boarding net and two rope ladders were rolled down the submarine's starboard-side casing for Captain Jarvis and his men to embark.

They trooped out of the fin, carrying their bergens and weapons which were loaded into the boats at the last minute before they were lowered gently into the water. Unrecognisable now because of the camouflage cream which coated their faces, the men waited in the cold still of the night until Captain Compton gave the order to embark the Zodiacs. And then they moved swiftly down into the boats, just as they had practised so many times during their week's training at Faslane.

No one spoke during the deafening silence of the night exit. The boats would run without lights, guided only by the big softly lit navy compass on the small dashboard around the wheel. The course was 185, almost due south, and the water would not be much deeper than ten feet all the way in, but the Zodiacs, at any speed, drew no more than eighteen inches.

The first two away were those of Captain Jarvis's group, heading in towards Fanning Head. The second pair, which would leave four minutes later, were for the group which had to walk forty-five-miles across the mountains to the airfield. Sergeant Jack Clifton, twenty-nine years old and about eight months away from promotion to Staff Sergeant, would lead the mission. Tonight he hoped to be ashore by 2030 hours and knock off the first fifteen miles before dawn.

The navy helmsman ran Douglas's Zodiac slowly towards shore at around five knots. The big Yamaha outboards which would cheerfully have shoved her along at forty knots, were barely idling at this slow speed, and the noise was negligible. Someone would have had to trip over the Zodiacs in order to locate them.

As they approached the shore their speed increased slightly. A seaman hauled up the engines on the automatic lift, and the Zodiac came scudding into the shallows and up the shingle beach.

The seaman on the pointed bow jumped onto dry land, holding the thick painter and hauling against the very slight waves which lapped the stern of the boat. One by one the SAS men leaped ashore.

It was an awkward manoeuvre in the pitch dark, but they hit the beach running. And, more importantly, all had dry feet for the two-week-long mission that lay ahead of them.

The seaman holding the painter now shoved his full weight against the bow of the boat and, assisted by a rising tide, heaved at the Zodiac until she floated. Then he clambered back onto the bow.

'Good job, Charlie,' said the helmsman, increasing the outboard's revs. 'Now let's get the hell out of here.'

Douglas counted his seven companions and made sure everyone was ashore and ready to go. Then he checked his compass and began to move west, leading his team over the rocky, already rising ground in the foothills of the eastern side of Fanning Head, which jutted skywards some two and a half miles away.

Despite all the evidence, it was still possible that an Argentine battery was already in place on the top of the mountain and that the area was being patrolled from a small base established on the peak. The guns of HMS *Antrim*, the ship commanded by Brian Young in 1982, had made the new Argentine operation easier, since the shells fired then had blasted a hollow on the summit which formed a natural area of cover.

Douglas planned to climb 500 feet up the east face tonight and establish a downward-facing 'hide' around 100 yards from the top, on ground which was near- impossible for the Argentines to patrol.

From there they could observe all troop and artillery movements and, far below, any patrolling warships. The trick was not to get caught, and when the British fleet arrived Douglas Jarvis and his men would eliminate the entire Argentine operation at the top of the mountain. When the island finally fell, as they were confident it had to, the SAS team would wait to be airlifted off by helicopter back to one of the ships.

And so they half-walked and half-climbed up through the darkness which enveloped the silent mountain. As they progressed the terrain grew steeper, and even with their new night vision, established after thirty minutes in the pitch black, it was still difficult to see between the rocks, boulders and crags which formed these lower reaches of the escarpment.

A huge cloud bank hung over the Falkland Islands. There was not a sliver of moon, and the stars were invisible, it was raining lightly, and a chill southerly wind was blowing. But the SAS men kept going, climbing steadily, until just before 2230 hours they reached an unmistakable rock face, not quite sheer, but close enough.

Douglas, a former team leader with the Sandhurst Mountaineering Club, had once climbed Mont Blanc in the French Alps. He now worked his way along the rock face looking for a gully, or an outcrop he could go for. After about half an hour, he found what he was looking for and set off with his bodyguard, using crampons when necessary, hammering the little steel footholds into the rock as quietly as he could. It took him about forty minutes to reach a point some eighty feet above his team.

The bodyguard, carrying two 100-foot climbing ropes, made them both fast to a jutting rock. The ropes dropped silently down the cliff face, one for safety, which the men would tie around their waists and shoulders and which would be hauled up by the captain as each man climbed.

Finally, Douglas Jarvis and his seven-man team were established on a thirty-five-yard-long deep ledge, which at one point seemed to burrow back ten feet into the cliff.

The ledge faced the wind, which was bad, but it looked a lot easier to climb onwards and upwards from there, which was good news. Captain Jarvis whispered carefully that everyone should eat something, have some water, and rest until 0200 hours, when four of them would continue up to the peak and check the place out.

By 0300 hours all that had been guesswork so far was confirmed. There were four Argentine military tents inside the hollow at the top but, so far as Douglas could see, no one there was awake. He and his men were face down behind a clump of windswept bracken, peering through night glasses. There were signs of a fire but the place was quiet.

The SAS men strained their ears, listening for a sound, any sound, from a guard or a lookout. But there was nothing. The Argentine troops had decided, not unreasonably, that their chances of being disturbed up here were close to zero. It had, after all, taken two helicopters to get up here in the first place, and it would take at least two more to airlift the guns, missile batteries and radar installations into position later that day.

The SAS men crept back to camp. Now for the tricky part. Captain Jarvis and his boys had to sit tight and observe, undetected. They already had one piece of critical information: the Argentine troops had in fact established a position at the top of Fanning Head. And they would transmit that information, encrypted, one hour from now, directly to *Ark Royal*, from right here on their secret rainswept ledge below the summit.

Not all that far away, Sergeant Clifton's team was walking quietly through the night. They had carefully tramped away from the shoreline and down the valley behind Port San Carlos and, two hours after they had disembarked from the Zodiac, they reached the narrow, rushing river.

Jack Clifton's map showed a bridge half a mile downstream and they crossed there, continuing along the valley towards the distant peaks of Usborne and the Wickham Heights, the last of which they would have to cross, probably two days from now, in order to advance downwards towards the Mount Pleasant airfield. There they would establish a hide from which they could see everything that was happening at this newest Argentine air base.

Around the same time that Sergeant Clifton and his troops crossed the river, Captain Hacking had concluded a long sweep around East Falkland and was feeling his way through thirty-five fathoms of rock-strewn inshore waters on the way in to Lafonia. There was a southern branch of the ninety-foot-deep channel which ran up to Choiseul Sound, and this would drive *Ambush* to the surface since no submarine CO liked to have less than ten feet of water below the keel.

The third group had elected to land on a tiny inlet on the east side of Lively Sound. The submarine came to the surface south of the headland, and the two Zodiacs made a two-mile run around the shoreline and dropped the men off on the north shore of the cove.

It was dark on the beach and raining, and there was a large amount of equipment to unload. In addition, three inflatable dinghies had been towed behind, and a pile of heavy wooden paddles. Lt. Perry, who led the group, had known all along they would almost certainly have to cross Choiseul Sound alone. It would be madness to land on the 'Argentine side' at the dead of night, risking running into an armed patrol.

'We need light rowing boats to cross that channel in the dark,' he had already pointed out back in England. 'For recces to the far shore two and a half miles away.'

They hauled the dinghies up on to the beach and dragged their equipment with them. The boats were light and had no engines but were made heavier by their firm wooden decking. Teams of four each carried one boat across the hard rocky ground, all the while searching for a sheltered spot for their hide which had to be established by dawn.

Twice during the first twenty minutes of their short journey they saw military aircraft coming in low over Lafonia and heading north-east, which gave everyone a precise idea of the location of the airfield. Maps and charts were good. Seeing something for real was always, somehow, better.

The land was flat here and there was little vegetation to shelter them, but there were various outcrops of rocks at the landward end of the beach. One of these did not quite make a cave, but four huge boulders formed only a very narrow opening to the sky, eight feet above the ground.

The partial shelter was not perfect because it was not big enough for the men and the boats, but it was a lot better than open ground. They moved in quickly and quietly, hauling out various scattered rocks and pebbles with a couple of shovels, unloaded waterproof groundsheets and sleeping bags. They stacked the boats at the entrance with the third one turned upside down on top of the other two. The dinghy's grey underside seemed to blend right in with the boulders. At least, it did in Lt. Perry's narrow-beam torchlight. And the young team leader decided they would risk lighting the Primus, brew some tea and soup, and conduct a patrol at 0100 hours, to ensure their first ops area was deserted.

Their biggest problem was that they had to operate in both directions. They had to establish the first landing beach on the southern side of the five-mile-wide Lafonia Peninsula, somewhere in Low Bay, remote from Argentine defences. And then establish a second beachhead across Choiseul Sound, much closer to the action, from where the British troops could launch their main attack on the airfield, Argentine garrison and the harbour.

But Lt. Perry and his men knew what they were doing and they knew the dimensions of the various terrains they were looking for.

As Admiral Arnold Morgan had rightly predicted in faraway Washington the previous week, Britain's Special Forces were in. And not one member of the now-massive Argentine invading force had the slightest idea they were there.

CHAPTER SEVEN

The three British Special Forces recce teams were not merely surprised by the level of Argentina's naval and military build-up on the Falkland Islands. They were stunned. Veterans of two wars, in the Persian Gulf and Iraq, they thought they'd seen it all. But this was incredible. Clinging to the cold, wet rock face of Fanning Head, Captain Jarvis's men watched the Argentines airlift not only multiple-launch missile systems but heavy 155mm howitzers as well.

All of them were ferried from the supply ships coming in at night to Mare Harbour, and were then transported by helicopter across the mountains to the summit of the towering headland where Douglas Jarvis and his men lay hidden.

Any British ships that tried to make passage through the narrows into Falkland Sound below would be on a suicide mission.

Sergeant Clifton and his boys arrived in the southern foothills of Wickham Heights around midnight on Sunday night, after a forty-five-mile trek and a total of twenty-five hours walking. Below them, Mount Pleasant Airport was well lit and extremely busy. All through the night they had both seen and heard military aircraft arriving and taking off.

No one knew yet what was actually incoming, nor indeed outgoing. But whatever it was, it was big. This was one of the busiest airfields Jack Clifton had ever seen and through the night glasses he could make out several parked military helicopters and a line of fighter aircraft, as well as several army and air force trucks parked near the terminals. There seemed to be people everywhere.

Down on the south shore of Choiseul Sound, Jim Perry's team had crossed the channel for the second time, rowing the little boats hard across the tide, hardly daring to take a rest in case they were swept off course.

It was a tough pull, but they had discovered a lonely, uninhabited little island right on their route. It made a useful stopping point just after the first mile, a place to get their breath back after rowing hard for twenty minutes.

On the far shore they had a carefully selected landing point, a 1,000-yard spit of rock and sand jutting out to the east, about four miles west of Mare Harbour, and 150 yards from the actual mainland. They made this their forward base, mostly because it seemed to have plant life – some high bracken and a few scattered gorse bushes. A cluster of thick tussock grass grew over some hefty boulders, and inside the thicket there was a place to hide the boats.

Lt. Perry had personally hacked out a pathway into this unlikely undergrowth, and last night, Saturday, they had left four men out there with sleeping bags and groundsheets, to continue monitoring Argentine aircraft through the day, coming into and leaving the Mount Pleasant air base. They had taken it in turns, two on duty, two off. And there was hardly a moment for twenty-four hours when they were not writing and recording. The verdict of trooper Fred Morton: *the Argies must have more fighter aircraft than the fucking Luftwaffe in 1940.*

As an assessment that was a tad wild, but it revealed one thing of critical importance. The Argentines did have a formidable air-attack capability and they were most definitely planning to launch opening strikes against the Royal Navy from this stronghold on East Falkland.

Worse yet, at first light Lt. Perry's spotters had made positive identification of three incoming Argentine Skyhawk A4s, which could deliver 1,000lb bombs at very high speed. Everyone thought back wistfully to the now-discontinued Harrier FA2, which *could* have stopped the Skyhawks before they had a chance to launch.

0400 Monday, 11 April
51.45S 56.40W. Speed 15. Depth 300. Course 180

Viper 157 was still in more than 200 fathoms when she arrived on station fifty miles off the northern coast of East Falkland, her mighty nuclear-powered turbines still running sweetly after an 11,000-mile voyage from the frozen north.

Captain Vanislav's orders, delivered by Admiral Rankov in person, were to patrol the waters east of the islands, awaiting the arrival of the Royal Navy task force. He was then to track the carrier with the utmost stealth, stay in satellite communication with the Rio Grande airbase, and sink *Ark Royal* with torpedoes one hour after the Argentine air assault was launched.

This would all have been much more difficult had the task force already arrived on station. The Royal Navy fleet would be on high alert and extremely sensitive, not to say trigger-happy. The slightest mistake from the crew of *Viper* would probably cause the roof to fall in, and not just metaphorically. The Royal Navy anti-submarine capability was legendary so Captain Vanislav had given himself all the advantages of being in place first, in position, quietly awaiting the arrival of the enemy, transmitting nothing, moving slowly, betraying no sound, no radar 'paints' in the dark undersea night of the South Atlantic.

This was the area through which the British task force had to pass if they were to fight this war.

Captain Vanislav knew what to do. What he did *not* know, however, was the precise position of Captain Simon Compton's *Astute,* now patrolling some fifteen miles out to the west.

Astute's towed array was operational and she was listening for engine lines from an Argentine submarine, as she had been for the past two days and would continue to do until the task force arrived. Captain Hacking had *Ambush* doing precisely the same thing.

But there were no Argentine warships anywhere outside the close-in coastal waters around the Falklands. Out here, where the seas were mostly deserted, there was no trace of any intruder.

At 0438 hours, however, a decision was made in *Viper* which in retrospect would be judged as careless. Almost everyone on board knew there was still a slight noise in the indicator-buoy stowage area, suggesting something was still loose and had been so all the way from the North Atlantic where the errant buoy had broken away.

So, in the middle of this dark overcast night, Captain Vanislav elected to surface and have the problem fixed. And *Viper 157* blew her ballast and came sliding up out of the deep. The process looked smooth – it *was* smooth – but in the underwater darkness of the South Atlantic the sound of the high-pressure air expelling the ballast was loud, especially to a patrolling Royal Navy SSN who had been listening for something like this for days.

In HMS *Astute* there was a flurry of activity in the sonar room. Chief Petty Officer Roddy Matthews suddenly thought he might have heard a slight rise in the background noise. 'Only a small increase in the level,' he murmured. 'Wait . . . it might have been rain, swishing on the surface. But I thought I heard something . . . give me a few minutes.'

The sonar operators froze. No one spoke while hearts momentarily paused. And three minutes later, at 0441, Matthews spoke again. 'I have a definite rise in the level . . . *Christ! It sounds like a submarine blowing ballast . . .*'

At 0451 a lightning bolt of tension shot through the sonar room – there was now a note of urgency in CPO Matthews's voice. '*Captain – sonar . . . I have definite sounds of a submarine surfacing – several miles away.*'

'*Sonar – captain . . .* I'll be right there.'

The CO ran into the room. Roddy Matthews said: 'It's not very close, sir. But no one could miss it. That was a submarine surfacing.'

Three minutes later the trail went cold and the sounds of the Russian submarine slipped away. It was the last time she would be detected in these waters, because in the next couple of hours Captain Vanislav would slow down to five or six knots as he'd been instructed by Admiral Rankov. And then *Viper* would be as silent as *Astute* and *Ambush*. Or very nearly so.

Captain Compton put a satellite signal on the net to the advancing Royal Navy fleet, directed to the admiral's ops room in *Ark Royal*. It read: *110458APR11: SSN Astute picked up unidentified submarine surfacing app. 51.50S 56.40W 0451 today. Estimate 45 miles offshore. Request orders should possible Russian prowler stray again into Falklands battle zone. Compton, CO Astute.*

Admiral Holbrook relayed it on to the UK, to Fleet Headquarters at Northwood. Admiral Palmer was in the situation room in conference with the First Sea Lord, Admiral Sir Rodney Jeffries, and the two men both gazed somewhat quizzically at the signal from the depths of the South Atlantic.

'Possible Russian SSN? Christ, what's that about?' Admiral Palmer looked extremely disconcerted.

'Well, before we give it serious thought, I think we should alert the Americans. They may know more than we do about a Russian prowler, and they may have an immediate answer.'

Sir Rodney nodded, handed the signal to a young lieutenant and requested it go immediately to US Naval Intelligence in

Washington. Five minutes later it was circulated to Fort Meade, and four minutes after that the NSA duty officer called Lt. Commander Ramshawe at home.

Jimmy was just out of the shower, intending to leave almost immediately for the office. With the Royal Navy about forty-eight hours from a head-on armed confrontation with the armed forces of Argentina, he and Admiral Morris were regularly meeting in the Director's office shortly after 0530.

He listened carefully to the signal which had come from Royal Navy HQ, Northwood and snapped, 'Get it on my desk and on Admiral Morris's desk right now. We'll both be there inside an hour.'

In fact he was there inside forty-five minutes, and having read it carefully could think only one thought: *I have to tell the Big Man. He'll probably have a fit if I wake him at 0530, but not as big as the one he'll have if I don't.*

'This better be fucking critical,' growled Arnold Morgan down the telephone, not caring one way or another who was on the other end of the line.

'It is, Arnie,' said Jimmy, all business. 'I think that Russian submarine, the one we concluded was almost certainly an Akula Class boat – *Gepard, Cougar* or *Viper* – just showed up in the middle of the battle zone, forty-five miles off the eastern side of East Falkland. Royal Navy SSN picked something up on sonar, surfacing, a couple of hours ago.'

'Tell me you're kidding.'

'No, sir.'

'Is George in yet?'

'No, but he'll be here in ten.'

'I'm coming over right now.' Bang. Down phone.

For some obscure reason, the admiral's flat refusal to utter the words 'Goodbye' or even 'Thanks for calling' always took Jimmy by surprise.

He was not, however, as deeply startled as Mrs Kathy Morgan who nearly fell out of bed when her husband bellowed at the top of his lungs, one hour before the sun rose over the Potomac, *'CH-A-A-A-A-RLIE!!! QUARTER DECK TEN MINUTES WITH CAR!'*

'God almighty,' she said. 'Did you have to do that?'

'Oh, don't worry,' replied the admiral. 'Charlie's used to it – gotta go.'

Downstairs Charlie did indeed hear the admiral's bellow. The people who lived three houses away probably heard the admiral's bellow.

Fully dressed, in readiness for just such a call, the chauffeur rushed outside, pulled the car up to the door, engine running, and was waiting patiently when the admiral came piling out into the dawn nine minutes later, dressed immaculately: dark grey suit, white shirt, Annapolis tie and highly polished shoes. Since his days as a midshipman, Arnold Morgan always shaved right before he went to bed, just in case there was an emergency. As this most definitely was.

Forty minutes later he was in Fort Meade, being escorted up to the Director's office on the eighth floor. When he arrived, Jimmy and Admiral Morris were standing in front of the illuminated computer screen on the wall, staring down the 56.40W line of longitude.

'George . . . Jimmy,' said Arnold, nodding curtly, heading straight for the big chair he had once occupied and shooting a laser glance at the coffee pot. 'Two bullets, Lieutenant Commander, one calculator and your full attention.' To Admiral Morris, 'You got him under control, George?'

'Absolutely.'

'Excellent. Date of the Akula detection off the coast of Ireland?'

'23 March, sir.'

'Time?'

'Sixteen-ten, sir.'

'Latitude?'

'Fifty-one thirty north, sir.'

'Date and time of detection in the South Atlantic?'

'Today, sir. 11 April, 0500.'

'Latitude?'

'Fifty-one fifty south, sir.'

Arnold hit the calculator buttons. 'Over 6,000 miles running south,' he muttered. 'You got an accurate mileage, Jimmy – taking in the distance west?'

'Yessir. Seven thousand, two hundred and eighty-two point nine five.'

'Vague, Ramshawe, vague. Try to be more precise, would you?'

'Yessir.' Lt. Commander Ramshawe was well up to this game.

'Nineteen days, eh?' said Admiral Morgan again hitting the buttons. 'He must have been making an average of 15/16 knots all the way.'

'Sixteen point four, sir. It was only eighteen and a half days.'

'Shut up, James.'

'Yessir.'

Arnold chuckled and sipped his coffee. 'It's gotta be the same boat. And it's gotta be Russian since nothing else could possibly have been anywhere near. And there's no point trying to call the Russians. Rankov would never return this call. He'd guess right away the Brits had picked up his fucking submarine.'

'And anyway, we may not want to alert them to the fact that we know something's going on,' replied Admiral Morris.

'No. I suppose not. Unless we want to try and frighten them off. I could get the President to make the call and feign absolute fury, demanding that the Akula be removed instantly from the Falklands battle zone.'

'Yes. We could try that. But you know, Arnie, I'm not sure it would work. The Russian president would just say he had no knowledge of any submarine in the South Atlantic, and then Rankov would tell everyone to be even more careful. We might never see the damn thing again.'

'But what if the "damn thing" took out the Royal Navy carrier?'

'If that's his plan, there's not a whole lot we can do about it. Short of going down there and hunting it down.'

'We don't have time,' replied Arnold Morgan. 'The British task force arrives on Wednesday, and the Brits cannot afford to waste their own time. That's a very weak fleet they have down there, and they've no replacements. If I were Holbrook I'd start firing as soon as I was in range before it all starts falling apart.'

'It's kinda frustrating, isn't it?' said Admiral Morris. 'We ought to have been able to stop this and we certainly ought to be able to sink this Russian intruder, but we can't.'

'Nonetheless,' said Admiral Morgan, somewhat grandly, 'I think in the end, like the Russians, we're gonna be in this thing up to our fucking jockstraps.'

0320 Wednesday 13 April
100 miles west of East Falkland

HMS *Ark Royal* steamed into the old Falkland Islands Total Exclusion Zone, which had served Admiral Woodward so wretchedly with its absurd *Don't shoot till they shoot* doctrine in 1982.

Today, however, there was no Total Exclusion Zone. The Royal

Navy had informed the Prime Minister and his politicians that since they had to begin operations with so many disadvantages they would shoot at anyone they damn pleased.

Mercifully, a thick blanket of fog covered the ocean, which at least provided some cover from air attack. But it also rendered all British flying impossible.

Admiral Holbrook and his staff were restless. They knew there might be a Russian submarine in the area, and in addition everyone was worried about minor repairs which had to be carried out on at least three of the escorts before battle could commence. With this in mind, they made course south across the old TEZ, heading straight for the Burdwood Bank.

This was a large area of fairly shallow water on the edge of the South American continental shelf. It was 200 miles long, east to west, by about sixty miles wide, north to south, sitting 100 miles south of East Falkland.

On its southern side the bank sloped steeply down into waters two miles deep. To the north, around the islands, it was only around 300 to 400 feet deep. But on the Bank itself the seabed was only 150 feet from the surface, and no submarine could run across it at speed without leaving a considerable wake on the surface.

Deep in the fog of the Burdwood Bank, Admiral Holbrook's task force would conduct their repairs, refuel, and make ready for battle. Both the Royal Navy submarines were headed inshore to patrol the coast and if possible sink any Argentine warships, none of which had yet been seen by the task force.

When the fog lifted, the Royal Navy would turn to the north and come out fighting. Their tactics, broadly speaking, would be to immediately launch missiles at any Argentine warship which came within range, get the GR9s away in an attempt to slam the airfield and the harbour, and pray to God they could hit the incoming Argentine air attack. And hit it early.

In the dark hours before that, *Ocean, Albion* and *Largs Bay,* which carried 2,700 troops, as well as helicopters, light trucks and ammunition, would already have headed north for the craggy south-eastern shores of East Falkland. There they would begin the amphibious assault, the drastically difficult task of landing a 10,000-strong army on the deserted beaches of Lafonia, as selected by Jim Perry and his team.

For two days and two nights, however, the fog bank never moved. The winds were light and sometimes it rained, but visibility stayed constantly poor. The CO of *Viper* had picked up distant sonar traces of warships in the area, and realised that he himself might just have been detected.

Nothing was definite, either way, but Captain Vanislav stayed in deep water, very slow and very quiet, waiting for the satellite signal which would tell him the time and date of Argentine's aerial onslaught from Rio Grande and Mount Pleasant.

When the Royal Navy ships moved, he was confident that he would pick them up. Right now in the fog he could only wait twenty miles north of the Burdwood Bank where he suspected they were. But he was not about to venture into those shallow waters where he would most certainly be detected.

Back in Washington there had been no feedback whatsoever from Buenos Aires. President Bedford had carried out his threat and closed down Argentine consulates all over the country. London had received no communiqué from Argentina either, even after the ambassador and all the diplomats had been expelled.

At 1530 on Friday afternoon, 15 April, with the repairs completed, the wind got up, and so did the sea. The skies cleared and the sun fought its way through the dank clouds of the South Atlantic.

Admiral Holbrook, regretting the loss of the fog cover, placed *Ocean, Albion* and *Largs Bay* on immediate notice to begin their journey into the landing beaches on the coast of Lafonia. The two Type-45s, plus HMS *Gloucester* were ordered to prepare to move forward at midnight to form the task force's first 'picket line' to the west of the fleet. This was the first line of defence, well up-threat from the main force and one of the loneliest places in all the ocean.

A clear and moonlit night followed the temporary departure of the fog, and at 1950 hours the assault force steamed away from the warships which would ultimately fight the battle. Captain John Farmer, on the bridge of *Ocean*, had *Albion* and *Largs Bay* line astern as they moved north through the dark, making twenty knots in a long rising sea, a cold south-westerly gusting in off their port quarter.

The guided-missile frigate *Richmond*, under the command of Captain David Neave, accompanied them, acting as 'goalkeeper' out to the left just in case they were spotted at first light and needed missile cover against incoming Argentine Super-Étendards.

The journey itself was uneventful. The ships travelled with very few lights and within four hours were within reach of the landing beaches, where Lt. Jim Perry and his men awaited them. *Ocean's* comms room had been in contact for the previous half-hour and details of the landing area were now with the commanders of the amphibious craft.

By midnight the three ships were in position to unload their cargoes. Captain Neave stood guard, facing westwards in the ops room of *Richmond*. The frigate, its missile radar on high alert, was steaming at only three knots in approximately six fathoms of water in the middle of Low Bay, fourteen miles wide at its seaward end.

At five minutes past midnight the huge stern doors of *Largs Bay* were lowered and the first of the landing craft, packed with marines, began to float out. One by one they made their way to the bay on the south shore of the desolate Lafonia peninsula where Jim Perry's SBS men were waiting to signal them in through the shallows.

Back on the Burdwood Bank, at precisely this time, the picket ships were lining up to leave on their four-hour journey to their lonely outpost. None of their commanding officers were especially looking forward to the experience. They knew they were the chosen few, because in the Royal Navy one wasn't really regarded as grown-up until one had commanded a picket ship, out there on one's own, not really covered by the weapons system of the rest of the force.

In fact, with a battle group stretched as tightly as this one was, those on picket duty were principally covered by their fellow picket ships.

Historically, picket ships were the very first to get sunk by an enemy: they were deliberately placed in harm's way. For the attacking force, the idea was to take at least one of the pickets out, thus punching a gaping hole in the defences through which to drive a main attack.

Both the British commanding officers of the Type-45s knew this perfectly well. And it was a thoughtful Captain Rowdy Yates who had HMS *Daring* under way first on that moonlit night, in the sombre hours before the dawn of the second battle for the Falkland Islands.

He would continue to position his ship way out to the right, more than twenty miles up-threat from the aircraft carrier. HMS *Gloucester*, commanded by Captain Colin Day, would occupy waters a similar distance but far out to the left. Commander Norman Hall's *Dauntless* would occupy the centre.

They made their way off the Bank line astern, all three commanding officers on the bridge, staying busy, trying to fight to the back of their minds any fears inspired by the brutal reality of the early hours of this particular Saturday morning. In all three ships, the long-range air-warning radars were already on high alert.

Three decks below in the ops room, everyone was at battle stations, dressed in full anti-flash-gear – yellowish cotton head-masks and gloves designed to prevent skin from instant burning caused by the sudden flash-fire explosion of an incoming bomb, shell or missile.

In grim contrast to the bright moonlit night outside on the water, the ops room was a sinister place, a half-lit scene from a sci-fi movie, amber lights from the computer consoles casting an eerie glow, quiet watchkeepers making terse comments into pencil-slim micro-phones, keyboards chattering in the background.

The Principal Warfare Officers, so highly trained, so completely in control of their tasks, were always standing, moving, quietly watching everything and everyone. The supervisors walked softly behind the young operators, checking, double-checking, always ready with a word of encouragement.

And every time the ship hit a wave, making the dull, majestic thump it always did when the hull of a warship slammed into a wall of water, many hearts beat just a fraction faster.

No sooner had the three destroyers cleared the Burdwood Bank than Admiral Holbrook's second line of defence was under way. Two newer Type-42 destroyers, the Batch Threes, *York* and *Edinburgh,* had arrived in the middle of the foggy night on Thursday. And now they would continue their defensive formation in the centre of the second line, flanked by the frigates from the 4th Duke Class Squadron, *Kent, Grafton, St Albans* and *Iron Duke,* some five miles up-threat from *Ark Royal.*

Between the carrier and the frigates, Admiral Holbrook placed three ships from the Royal Fleet Auxiliary, principally to confuse the enemy radar. *Ark Royal* would be positioned astern of these, accompanied by her 'goalkeeper' *Westminster,* the no-nonsense missile frigate commanded by the austere and able Commander Tom Betts.

By some miracle, the navy had completed the work on both *Lancaster* and *Marlborough* in Portsmouth, and both of them had arrived in one piece on Friday afternoon. They would operate around the coast to the north, specifically trying to get rid of any

Argentine warships in the area and launch missile and shell attacks on any new Argentine positions at that end of the island.

The most impressive arrival of all, however, was that of P and O's huge ocean-cruise liner the *Adelaide*, which had been ordered to abandon her next journey to the Caribbean and get to Portsmouth for instant conversion into a troop carrier. She had arrived on Thursday from out of the eastern Atlantic, bearing 7,000 troops, her decks shored up to take the enormous weight of men, equipment and ordnance. Her galleys were now filled with rather more basic fare than the rich *gourmet de luxe* to which her cooks and stewards were accustomed.

As colossally useful as she was, *Adelaide* posed a problem. She had totally inadequate damage-control and fire-fighting arrangements and, just as in 1982 her sister ship *Canberra* had been, in the words of Admiral Woodward, 'a bloody great bonfire awaiting a light', so was she.

Admiral Holbrook hoped to unload her massive cargo of men and matériel into other ships as soon as it was humanly possible to undertake such a formidable cross-decking operation.

Meanwhile, the warships were on their way to the admiral's designated position 400 miles east of the Burdwood Bank, well out of Argentine air-range. *Ark Royal* brought up the rear with *Westminster*. Both ships were largely dependent on the accuracy of the new improved Seawolf missile system carried by the frigate. Commander Betts described it as 'amply competent to knock any Argentine fighter-bomber clean out of the sky, just so long as the chaps are paying proper attention'. That was Betts. No nonsense.

0300 Saturday 16 April
Rio Grande Air Base, Tierra del Fuego

Argentina's Aviation Force Two – the 2nd Naval Air Wing, in concert with the 2nd Naval Attack Squadron – had virtually evacuated from Bahia Blanca, the sprawling air station which sat at the head of a deep bay 350 miles south-west of Buenos Aires, sharing its geographical position with Puerto Belgrano, the largest naval base in the country.

These two bastions of Argentina's air and sea power were situated exactly where the South American coastline swings inward and begins to narrow down, running south-sou'west, 1,200 miles all the way to the great hook of its granite southerly point of Cape Horn.

The fighter aircraft from Bahia Blanca had been flown 1,000 miles south to Rio Grande, the mainland base from which Argentina would conduct its defence of its newest territory, *Las Islas Malvinas*, which lay 440 miles to the east.

Admiral Oscar Moreno, Commander-in-Chief of Argentina's Naval Fleet, a devoted lifelong *Malvinista*, had been instrumental in planning the entire naval attack strategy. And now he had his substantial squadron of fourteen Super-Étendards, with their Exocet missiles, in position on the huge airfield.

It was curious, but in the last conflict against the British the success of this missile had taken some people by surprise. Today Admiral Moreno was not quite so sure of its prospects. He knew the Royal Navy had spent years perfecting an anti-missile shield against the Exocet.

And he was well aware the British ships carried excellent chaff systems and top-class decoys, all designed to 'seduce' an incoming missile through a large cloud of iron filings, which the stupid missile registered as bigger than a warship and which therefore represented a more desirable target.

But the Argentine navy had a very large Exocet inventory and they were obliged to use them – unless it became obvious they were a total waste of time – against Admiral Holbrook's ships.

Despite his slight misgivings, Oscar Moreno still considered that if you hurled enough Exocets at the Royal Navy some might get through, and when they did the damage would be colossal, just as it had been in 1982.

With this in mind, he had flown four Super-E's into Mount Pleasant airfield, hoping that an assault which started on land would initially confuse the British warships' radars when they scanned the horizon and ran into the customary difficulties all search-radars encounter when looking across the water to a coastline.

Admiral Moreno understood these matters. And he knew he was facing the possible failure of his Exocet attack. Which was principally why he had removed the entire 3rd Naval Air Wing 650 miles down the coast from their base at Trelew to the new operations centre at Rio Grande.

With them the 3rd Wing brought their entire squadron of twelve Dagger fighter aircraft, an Israeli-built cheap-and-cheerful no-radar copy of the magnificent French Mirage jet. With a few minor adjustments, the Dagger could carry two 1,000lb iron bombs, slung underneath in place of the usual 1,300-litre centre-line fuel tank.

To compensate for the subsequent shorter range, Admiral Moreno had stationed six of them on the airfield at Mount Pleasant. At H-hour he would send them in, flying low-level, against the British ships, which were, he knew, totally vulnerable to bomb attack. This time there were no high-altitude Harrier Combat Air Patrols, with their medium-range radars, always ready to hit and down the Daggers. The most the ships' missiles could achieve would be to slam the aircraft *after* the bombs were away. And even that prospect was pretty tenuous.

The remaining six Daggers would take off from Rio Grande, rendezvous with one of the Hercules tankers and refuel in mid-air before pressing on with their bomb attacks on the British ships.

The Argentine air force was also working closely with Admiral Moreno, who, as the most fanatical of all the military *Malvinistas,* was rapidly acquiring Homeric stature in Buenos Aires.

At his request, the air force removed its 5th Air Brigade, usually based at Villa Reynolds, down to Rio Grande. This included its formidable force of fighter-bombers – two squadrons of Lockheed Skyhawk A-4Ms and one squadron of A-4Ps, a total of more than three dozen aircraft.

The bigger 6th Air Brigade had left its inland home HQ south-west of Buenos Aires at Tandil airbase and moved south to Rio Gallegos, which lies to the north of Rio Grande on the coast, a 496-mile flight from the *Malvinas*. The 6th Attack Group flew seven Mirage Interceptors, thirteen Mirage 111E fighter/attack aircraft, and a squadron of twenty Daggers, all bombers. The Mirage jets would mostly be used for high escort cover for the Israeli-built anti-shipping specialists – the Daggers, the ones with the 1,000lb iron bombs.

Admiral Moreno had requested ten Skyhawks from the 5th Brigade and six Daggers from the 6th to fly to Mount Pleasant in readiness for the attack at first light on the opening morning of the battle. Whenever that might be.

Now he knew. The previous afternoon the fog around the islands and on the Burdwood Bank had cleared, and the Royal Navy ships were on the move, in the dark. He could only guess that they would come out fighting at dawn and his task was to hit them first and hit them hard. With luck, the ships would be silhouetted against the eastern horizon.

A few hours earlier, at midnight, Moreno had been driven to the Roman Catholic church on Avenue San Martin, in the nearby town of Rio Grande. There, on his knees, he had prayed devoutly for the success of Captain Gregor Vanislav's torpedo attack on the *Ark Royal* . . . *'that we may restore once more these ancient Argentine territories of the Islas Malvinas to Thy Holy Will.'*

Presumably Admiral Moreno felt Great Britain's grand brick-and-stone edifice of Christ Church Cathedral on Ross Road, Port Stanley, complete with its superb stained glass windows, made no contribution whatsoever toward His Holy Will.

However, Moreno was now back from his prayer interlude, working hard on the split-second timing required for his dawn assault on the Royal Navy. Outside, massive refuelling operations were going on, both at Rio Gallegos on the airfield beyond his office in Rio Grande and on Mount Pleasant airfield itself.

The KC-130 Hercules refuelling tankers were ready to take off from both the southern airbases and would rendezvous with the fighter/bombers 150 miles offshore. Both the Daggers and the Mirage fighters had new flight-refuelling receiving gear which they had not enjoyed in 1982. That was the one shining fact to comfort Admiral Moreno: the extended range of his aircraft. There were no longer the endless concerns of the pilots running out of fuel before they made it home from the *Malvinas*.

By 0500 Admiral Moreno's navy and air force command HQ in Rio Grande had received an encrypted satellite signal from Moscow telling them that the Royal Navy task force was currently positioned 140 miles east of Port Stanley.

The signal made no mention of the landing operation taking place on the south coast of the Lafonia Peninsula, and contained no details of the deployment of the British fleet. That would all have to wait until dawn finally broke over the South Atlantic.

There was was, however, one commanding officer operating on the Argentine side who did know the whereabouts of HMS *Ark Royal*. Captain Gregor Vanislav's sonar had picked up the sounds of the British warships on the move as they came off the shallow waters of the Burdwood Bank, and by the small hours of that Saturday morning he had closed in.

Viper 157 now ran slowly, ten miles to the south-east of Admiral Holbrook's battle group. The submarine was transmitting nothing active 300 feet below the surface. Vanislav was just tracking the warships, listening to the pings of the sonar, waiting for the dawn when the sub could come to periscope depth for a seven-second visual sighting.

At 0515, shortly before the first light began to illuminate the horizon, Admiral Moreno ordered the four Super-Étendards on the runway at Rio Grande to take off on their 440-mile race to the *Malvinas*. They would rendezvous with the tanker, refuel and come hurtling over East Falkland, heading east at 600 knots and flying below the radar of the British ships.

At 0614 they came streaking over Weddell Island and crossed Queen Charlotte Bay and the narrowest part of West Falkland before flying low over the Sound and straight across Lafonia. All four Argentine pilots saw the three Royal Navy ships still anchored in Low Bay and their own air-force radar at their Mount Pleasant Airbase picked the Étendards up as they flew over.

Making eleven miles every minute the French-built guided-missile jets, flying in two pairs eight miles apart, rocketed out over the Atlantic, flying very low now. They were only fifty feet above the water, gaining the protection of the curvature of the Earth from the line-of-sight sweep of the forward radars of the three British picket ships.

They held their speed and course for the next nine minutes. At which time the second pair swung further left. The first two prepared to 'pop up' to take a radar fix on whatever lay ahead. None of the four Étendard pilots dared to turn on a radio, and the concentration required to stay that low without flying into the ocean was so intense they were each virtually isolated.

And now, forty miles out from Admiral Holbrook's picket ships, the first pair climbed to 120 feet, levelled out and hit the radar scans. Immediately the pilots saw two blips on the screens, and simultaneously they both reached down to the buttons that would activate their Exocets.

Deep in the heart of Captain Rowdy Yates's *Daring,* the ops room was on high alert. Everyone was wearing their anti-flash masks, the air-warfare officers were murmuring into their headsets, the supervisors were pacing, and all gazes were glued to the screens. They all knew dawn was breaking. They all knew an attack might be imminent.

It was 0632 when Able Seaman Price called out the words which sent chills through the hearts of every experienced officer and Petty Officer in the ops room. Young Price blew his whistle short and hard and snapped: *'AGAVE RADAR!'*

Daring's AWO, Lt. Commander Harley, shot across the room and demanded, *'Confidence level?'*

'Certain,' stated Price. 'I have three sweeps, followed by a short lock-on – bearing two-eight-four. Search mode.'

Captain Yates and Harley swung around to stare at the big UAA-1 console, and they could both see the bearing line on Price's screen correlated precisely with two Long Range Early Warning radar contacts forty miles out.

'Transmission ceased,' reported Price.

Harley called into the Command Open Line, *'AWO to Officer of the Watch . . . go to action stations!'*

He switched to the UHF radio, announcing to all ships, *'FLASH! This is* Daring *. . . Agave bearing two-eight-four . . . correlates . . .'*

And Price called again, 'AGAVE REGAINED! Bearing two-eight-four.'

The ship's radar officers confirmed the contacts, range now only thirty miles.

'That's two Super-Es just popped up,' called Captain Yates crisply.

'CHAFF!' roared Harley. And across the room the hooded figure of a Chief Petty Officer slammed his closed fists against the big chaff fire buttons.

Harley again broadcast on the circuit to the whole Battle Group. *'This is* Daring *. . . Agave radar bearing two-eight-four . . .'* But the picket ships were all up to speed, Commander Hall's ops room in *Dauntless* was instantly on the case, and Captain Day was only fifteen seconds behind as HMS *Gloucester* prepared to tackle the second pair of Étendards heading to their right, straight towards him.

For the next five minutes *Daring* had to place herself carefully between the four clouds of chaff which were blooming around her, taking account of the wind and the natural drift of the giant clouds of iron filings – which Harley hoped to Christ were confusing the life out of the radar in the nose cones of the incoming missiles.

Captain Yates called to the Officer of the Watch on the bridge: 'Come hard left to zero-eight-four . . . adjust speed for zero relative wind.'

At 0638, the Argentine pilots unleashed their missiles and banked right, not knowing for certain at what they had fired. Their Exocets fell away, locked onto their targets, and the two Étendards headed for home, flying once more low over the water but this time heading west.

And in the ops room of *Daring*, the familiar cry of a modern warship under attack was heard: *'Zippo One! Bruisers!* Incoming. Bearing two-eight-four. Range fourteen miles.' But the two amber dots flickering across *Daring's* screen were so small they could scarcely be seen.

'Take them with Sea Dart,' snapped Captain Yates, knowing his fire-control radar would have trouble locking onto the tiny sea-skimming targets at this range but hoping against hope the Missile Gun Director could get the weapons away.

Eventually he did, but only one of the Sea Darts struck home, blasting the Exocet out of the sky. The second one was completely baffled by the chaff and swerved high and left, crashing harmlessly into the sea six miles astern of its target.

Commander Hall's *Dauntless* never did get her Sea Dart missiles into action but the chaff did its work and both missiles that had been aimed at the destroyer passed down the port side.

Captain Day's *Gloucester*, out to the left of *Ark Royal*, found herself facing four incoming Exocets, and her Sea Dart missiles, given more choice, slammed two of them into oblivion. Again the priceless chaff did its work: the remaining two Exocets swerved right into a huge cloud of iron filings and careened into the ocean with a mighty blast, two miles away off the destroyer's starboard quarter, prompting a roar of delight from the seamen working on the upper decks. Argentina nil, Royal Navy eight.

But not for long. Two formations of four Skyhawks and four Daggers were on their way off the runway at Mount Pleasant. The British frigates, armed with only Harpoons as a medium-range missile, were still seventy miles too far east to attack the airport, and the GR9s were only just ready to fly off the carrier, thanks to an early-morning fog bank.

The returning Étendard pilots, flying slower now, had already been in contact with Mount Pleasant and had passed on the range and positions of the three British ships they assumed they had located. They also alerted the base to the possible location of three, possibly four other large Royal Navy ships anchored in Low Bay.

And meanwhile the Daggers and the Skyhawks continued their fast low-level journey, flying fifty feet above the waves, well below the British radar. They headed straight for the Royal Navy picket ships, the Type-45 destroyers *Daring* and *Dauntless*, and the older *Gloucester*.

They lifted above the horizon and into range of the ships' missile systems at a distance of around ten miles. But the visibility was poor, and within sixty seconds they would have overflown the entire picket line.

All eight of the Argentine aircraft had their bombs away before the Sea Darts could lock on. Desperately, the three Commanding Officers ordered their missiles away and with mounting horror the observers on the upper decks saw the big 1,000-pounders streaking in, low over the ocean.

That was the way a modern iron bomb arrived. It was going too fast to 'drop'. It came scything in at a low trajectory, its retardation 'chute out behind it, slowing it down. The bombs were primed to blast on impact.

All Royal Navy commanders knew the best defence was to swing a targeted ship around, presenting not its sharp bow to the incoming attack but its beam. That way there was a fighting chance that the damn thing might fly straight over the top, as such bombs frequently did.

But there was so often no time. And there was no time right now on Admiral Holbrook's picket line. As the Skyhawks and the Daggers screamed away, making their tightest turns back to the west, eight miles from the destroyers, the lethal Sea Dart missiles came whipping in. The first one from *Daring* slammed into a Dagger and blew it to smithereens. The second smashed the wing off a fleeing Skyhawk and sent it cartwheeling into the ocean at 500 knots.

Three more Sea Darts missed completely, but Colin Day's first salvo downed another Dagger and blew a Skyhawk into two separate pieces. This was the very most they could do. They had no other defence because, high above, they had no Harrier FA2 Combat Air Patrol, which could have downed all eight of the Argentine bombers twenty miles back.

Meanwhile the first two bombs from the lead Skyhawk slammed into HMS *Daring* with colossal force, one of them crashing through the starboard side of the hull and detonating in the middle of the ship, instantly killing everyone in the ops room and twenty-seven others. It split the engine room asunder and a gigantic explosion seemed to rip the entire ship apart.

The second bomb, meeting the ship on the rise, crashed through the upperworks, blasting the huge pyramid-shaped electronic-surveillance tower straight down onto the bridge. Everyone inside was either killed by the explosion or was crushed, which brought the death toll to fifty-eight, with another sixty-eight wounded. There were huge fires, the water mains were blown apart and HMS *Daring*, shipping sea water at a ferocious rate, was little more than a hulk on her way to the bottom.

HMS *Dauntless* was hit by three bombs, two of them in the same spot, which just about broke her back, one single explosion destroying the engine room and causing an upward blast that caved in the entire upperworks. More than 100 men were dead, and almost everyone else was wounded. The destroyer would sink into the freezing ocean in under fifteen minutes.

Captain Day's *Gloucester* fared best. She took only one bomb, on her starboard bow. But it was a big 1,000-pounder from one of the Daggers and it smashed deep inside the ship before exploding with a blast which obliterated her foredeck, ripped apart her missile-launch systems and blasted overboard the for'ard Vickers 4.5-inch gun. *Gloucester* too instantly began to ship water from the gaping hole on the waterline on her starboard side, and there was a fire raging dangerously close to the missile magazine.

At this point hardly anyone, aside from the ship's companies in the pickets, knew what had happened. There was no communication from either *Daring* or *Dauntless*, but Captain Day sent a signal back to the flagship reporting his own fairly drastic damage, which might yet cause *Gloucester* to sink.

However, the loss of life on his ship was negligible compared to the losses suffered by the others, just twelve men killed and fifteen wounded. It took only another minute for the lookouts on the frigate line positioned just a few miles behind them to see three plumes of thick black smoke and flame on the horizon.

Captain Day, who was closest, now reported that *Dauntless* was sinking. He was out of contact with *Daring*, and two of the frigates, *Kent* and *Grafton*, were nearer. The CO of *Gloucester* knew the fire was slowly inching towards his missiles. When it got there it would blow the entire ship into oblivion.

His fire-fighting teams were down there trying to work in incinerating heat, but they were fighting a losing battle. At 0642 Captain Day gave the order to abandon ship. And Admiral Holbrook ordered his frigates forward to assist with the rescue of the wounded.

The trouble was, information was very limited. Holbrook did not know that eight more Skyhawks had already taken off from Rio

Grande, had refuelled and were heading east at maximum speed. The admiral understood the likelihood of further attack, of course, but without a Harrier CAP he was reliant on his down-range helos as well as the medium-range radar of his destroyers' missile systems, and the Argentine pilots were flying below that.

There was, however, quite sufficient information for one particular commanding officer. Captain Gregor Vanislav, still moving at minimum speed out to the east of *Ark Royal*, had already picked up on his sonar the savage iron-bomb detonations which had devastated the British picket line.

And now, shortly after 0700, he came quietly to periscope depth for a visual sighting of his quarry. He could see the *Ark Royal* out on the horizon through the telescopic lens, and there was no doubt in his mind. This was the Royal Navy's only active aircraft carrier. He'd come a long way for this, and now he intended to carry out the instruction issued to him with such firmness and clarity by Admiral Vitaly Rankov in person.

The carrier had moved three miles further east and was now well astern of the other warships, in readiness for its lower-deck hospital to begin receiving the wounded from the burning destroyers. Right now this was the only hospital the task force had: the other main medical facilities were in *Ocean* and *Largs Bay*.

Captain Vanislav, now almost stationary, was no more than three miles to *Ark Royal*'s south-east. His plan was to circle the carrier, staying deep and slow, 500 feet below the surface, a depth at which his Akula Class submarine was more than comfortable. He intended to launch his attack from two miles off *Ark Royal*'s starboard beam. The assault would be made easier by the fact that the carrier was scarcely moving and there would, he knew, be a great deal of diversionary action taking place. His last satellite communication, relayed from Moscow, had made that absolutely clear.

'Down periscope . . . helmsman, steer course three-zero-five, speed four . . . bow down ten . . . 300 . . .'

At this speed the *Viper* was absolutely silent, undetectable as it crept through the water, slowly drawing a bead on the 20,000-ton Royal Navy carrier. The submarine was transmitting nothing, her captain relying on a visual fix when his ship was in position.

At 0708 *Viper 157* was precisely where he wanted her. They came to PD for one final look. Even then, for the fleeting seconds when his periscope was jutting eighteen inches out of the water like a miniature telegraph pole, Yanislav was not detected.

Admiral Holbrook had already signalled for two escorts, the Batch Three Type-42s *York* and *Edinburgh,* to position themselves on his port and starboard quarters and use intermittent active sonar since the US had alerted them to the bizarre outside possibility of a submarine threat – and from Russia, at that! But there was plainly no point in having both destroyers passive, eight miles up-threat from the bombs and missiles.

But the destroyers were still a couple of miles short of this new station, and the British admiral had so much on his mind after the destruction of his picket line, he was was giving scant regard to the very real danger of a torpedo attack on his own flagship.

Right now there was something close to havoc in his ops room. Everyone was handing out advice – how best to deal with the crisis on the picket line, the urgency of getting the GR9s into the air and launching a major bomb and missile attack on the airfield from whence, it was assumed, the Skyhawks had come.

No thought was being given to the classic evasive manoeuvres a big warship might take to avoid a submarine attack – moving in a zigzag pattern, varying speed drastically from twenty-five knots to six, forcing any tracking submarine to show its hand by compelling it to increase speed.

Captain Vanislav intended to fire three torpedoes at his massive target from a range of 5,000 yards. Right now the Russian sub was a little over five miles away, and ready for its final approach. *Viper*'s CO ordered her closer.

Meanwhile the two flights of Skyhawks were clear of the Falkland Islands and were heading at wave-top height towards the British battle group, making more than 600 knots. The frigates *Kent* and *Grafton* were still about two miles short of the disaster area, with *St Albans* and *Iron Duke* further to the left and about three miles astern of the other two.

The four lead Skyhawks cleared the horizon and could now see the blazing destroyers. But their targets were two miles back, and all four of the Argentine fighters unleashed their 1,000lb bombs straight at *Kent* and *Grafton*.

Both frigates acquired targets and opened fire with their Seawolf missile systems. They hit the first two Skyhawks and missed the others before attempting to swing around to the right.

Grafton did not move fast enough and took two bombs hard on her port beam. Both bombs smashed into the interior of the ship, detonated and blew apart the ops room, the comms room and the engine room, killing thirty-two men and wounding forty. The ship was crippled. In fact, she would never sail again. Like *Daring* and *Dauntless* she was on her way to the bottom of the sea.

Much luckier was Captain Mike Fawkes's *Kent*. She swung around fractionally faster and while two of the bombs sailed right past on their way to *Grafton*, two of them came screaming over the top, fifty feet above the upperworks.

The second four Skyhawks now cleared the horizon and the first ships they saw were the two rear frigates, Captain Colin Ashby's *St Albans* and Commander Keith Kemsley's *Iron Duke*.

The very accurate short-range Seawolf systems on both frigates locked on immediately and both ops rooms had the missiles away in a matter of seconds. But again, not before the Skyhawks' iron bombs had been released. And there was absolutely nothing the Royal Navy commanders could do. The first two bombs smashed into *St Albans*, one through the portside bow, one amidships. The second two, on the rise, slammed down the communications tower and blasted the radar away from *Iron Duke*.

The carnage in *St Albans* was shocking. Forty-seven men were killed instantly. Somehow the Captain survived, perhaps protected from the blast by his own high television-style screen. But the ops room was on fire and three other survivors helped Captain Ashby to get out, leaving behind them a scene from hell as the bodies of the computer and missile operators burned.

The missiles from the two stricken ships knocked down two more Skyhawks. The trouble was, without a squadron of Harriers there was no early air defence from a high CAP, and no early warnings from the non-existent Harrier pilots. As General Sir Robin Brenchley had warned the British Prime Minister not so very long ago in the small hours of a February morning in Downing Street, the loss of the Harrier FA2s represented the loss of the Royal Navy fleet's ability to defend itself.

And with a total of six warships ablaze in the South Atlantic – four of them sinking – and at least 250 men killed and even more wounded, many of them badly burned . . . well, this was a catastrophe which had, perhaps, been very well foreseen by the navy but which had been totally ignored by their political masters.

Eight miles astern of the wrecked warships, Captain Vanislav came to periscope depth for his final visual. HMS *Ark Royal* was less than four miles away, moving slowly, her starboard beam exposed to the submarine's line of sight.

The CO of *Viper 157* prepared to fire. He would launch his big TEST torpedoes quietly at thirty knots, running in towards the carrier, staying passive all the way.

0725: '*Stand by one!*'

'*Last bearing check.*'

'*SHOOT!*'

The Russian torpedo came powering out of its tube, seemed to pause for a split second as its engine fired, and then went whining off into the dark waters.

'Weapon under guidance.'

'Arm the weapon.'

'Weapon armed, sir.'

Ninety seconds to go. 'Weapon now 1,000 metres from target, sir.'

'Weapon has passive contact.'

At that moment *Viper 157* fired her second torpedo, and within seconds it too was streaking straight at the massive starboard hull of the carrier.

With the lead weapon only 800 yards out *Viper*'s third torpedo was already under way. At this precise time the sonar men inside the *Ark Royal* picked up the incoming ship-killers. At least, they picked up one of them . . .

'*Admiral – sonar . . . TORPEDO! TORPEDO! TORPEDO! Bearing green zero-zero-four . . . REALLY CLOSE, SIR, REALLY CLOSE!*'

That meant about 500 yards, which put the lead torpedo about thirty seconds from impact, directly off the beam. It was out of the question to fire back – the old 20,000-ton carrier was simply not built for close combat of this type.

Someone bellowed '*DECOYS!*' But that was at least two minutes too late. The Combat Systems Officer alerted all task force ships still afloat that the flagship was under attack, along with everyone else. But he never even had time to yell '*UNKNOWN SUBMARINE!*' before the big TEST-7IME Russian torpedo slammed into the hull amidships – and exploded with stupendous force.

The second torpedo struck home further for'ard, and the last one almost blew off the entire stern area, fracturing both driveshafts, rupturing the flight deck, and blasting four helicopters over the side. It was a classic submarine attack, conducted with the utmost stealth and executed with total brutality. When Captain Vanislav came to PD for the last time, what he saw in those seven seconds would remain with him for however long he lived.

Gregor Stanislav could see the aircraft carrier had been ripped almost in two, her back broken by the blast of the first torpedo, her entire stern sagging back into the water. Even as he watched, a huge fire suddenly broke out right below the 'island', the big chunky superstructure on one side of the flight deck.

The near-immediate inferno had almost certainly been caused by a ruptured aircraft fuel line, and now Captain Vanislav could see British seamen jumping from the flight deck into the ocean, their clothes on fire. It reminded him of the gruesome pictures from the World Trade Center disaster in New York nearly ten years ago. Surely none of the 1,000-strong crew, apart from those working high in the tower, could possibly have survived.

The huge warship was swiftly ablaze from end to end, but the fires would not be long-lasting since the ship was also sinking. For the moment, however, the only part not burning was the upper floor of the island where presumably the admiral and the ship's captain were still alive. *Ark Royal*, now with thousands of gallons of jet fuel blazing, was one huge inferno, and Captain Vanislav, a very senior Russian career naval officer, almost went into shock at the sight of the disaster that he had caused.

The only thought in his mind was a feeling of profound regret, and a realisation that if he could live the last ten minutes over again he would not do what he had done. Because, having seen the reality, he would have been incapable of committing this act against a British ship whose crew, so far as he knew, wished him no harm. Captain Vanislav ordered his ship deep again, and with a surprisingly heavy heart accepted that his grotesque mission had been accomplished. He turned north for Mother Russia.

Meanwhile, on board the carrier, Admiral Holbrook was still alive, but the heat was becoming too intense to bear. He and Captain Reader were together until the last, knowing, as the flames leaped towards their quarters high above the flight deck, that their only chance was to jump before they were burned to death.

It would be like leaping from the George Washington Bridge. But others had done it. There was no other way down, except to walk down the companionway into the flames, and there was no time to wait for helicopter rescue even if that were possible.

The two senior officers walked outside and climbed to the platform area above the admiral's ops room. They were both still wearing their life jackets and anti-flash gear, hoods and gloves, standing there in the stifling smoke as the great ship, now in her death throes, suddenly lurched violently, thirty degrees to starboard. This reduced the distance down to the water, but confirmed the unavoidable fact that *Ark Royal* was sinking. The GR9s, most of them in flames, were slewing across the flight deck and falling overboard.

So far as the two officers could tell there was no enemy in sight. The rails were growing hot, almost too hot to hold, and they just stood there until Captain Reader said quietly, 'We never had a chance, did we?'

'No, David, we never did. And I'm not sure we'll ever know what hit us.'

Ten seconds later, as the ship listed even further, they both jumped, and hit the water, now forty-five-feet below, feet first. Both men miraculously survived the fall, but not the almost freezing water. When the destroyers moved in to pick up survivors two hours later, both senior officers were found floating but no longer alive.

Anyone in water that cold has approximately two minutes to live, which meant there were no survivors from the crew of the Royal Navy carrier. Historians would in future regard it as the greatest single Royal Naval disaster since the old 41,000-ton battle cruiser HMS *Hood* had been sunk by the *Bismarck* in the Denmark Strait seventy years previously. Fourteen hundred and twenty men were lost that day, but even the *Hood* had three survivors.

It rapidly became apparent to all the British officers that the flagship had been hit and almost certainly destroyed. Captain Mike Fawkes, on the bridge of the amazingly lucky frigate HMS *Kent*, now assumed command of the remnants of the fleet.

But there was not much of it left, and the rescue operation was by now the most colossal task. No one knew what was happening on the landing beaches. It was obvious the British Army forces must now be devoid of any air cover whatsoever, and their situation, exposed on the shores of Lafonia, had to be critical.

In fact, during the final moments before *Viper* had fired her salvo two of the GR9s had got off the deck and had been making their way towards Lafonia when the ops room in the frigate *Kent* informed them of the disaster that had befallen the carrier. This, of course, left the British pilots stranded with nowhere to land.

They both made a swing around the south-eastern coast of East Falkland and came in over the landing beaches where they ejected, sending their aircraft on to ditch in the South Atlantic. This avoided the possibility of Argentina claiming them as spoils of war, which would most certainly have happened if the aircrew had requested permission to land at Mount Pleasant.

Both pilots survived the landing, right behind the beach, but they quickly understood this was no place to be. Four minutes after their arrival, two Argentine bombers came in low and hit the assault ship *Albion*, which had mercifully already unloaded its marines.

Then two more fighter-attack aircraft came in low and strafed the beach, firing four rockets in among the parked Apache helicopters. Then a bomber came in and hit *Largs Bay* with a 1,000lb bomb. The British soldiers and marines, like Admiral Holbrook's sailors, were sitting ducks under the onslaught of the Argentine bombs and missiles.

The success of those opening raids on the Lafonia beachhead was entirely due to the brilliance of Admiral Oscar Moreno and his army counterpart, General Eduardo Kampf. They had guessed, correctly, that the marine battalions which had landed during the night would immediately set up a missile 'shield' against attack from the Argentine joint-force land base at Mount Pleasant, fifteen miles to the north across Choiseul Sound.

This they had already accomplished. The big Chinooks that had been landed from HMS *Ocean* had been ferrying the Rapier batteries into the rolling hills to the west of Seal Cove. From there they would be well placed to down any incoming Argentine jet fighter or attack helicopter flying in low from the north after take-off from Mount Pleasant. It had taken them several hours to install, and the 2,700 landed troops all felt considerably safer.

But both Admiral Moreno and General Kampf had fought and lost in the 1982 conflict. And both of them clung, in their own minds, to the rare Argentine successes against the invading Brits during that earlier campaign.

One of these had been conducted by three Skyhawks, bombing the British landing ships *Sir Tristam* and *Sir Galahad* as they had lain at anchor in Port Pleasant bay. The key to this successful attack was that the Skyhawks had come in from the open ocean and then streaked straight up the bay and unleashed their bombs, which killed fifty still-embarked soldiers and inflicted terrible losses on the 1st Battalion Welsh Guards.

Admiral Moreno understood this monstrous chess game, and he knew the answer was to come in from out of the Atlantic from the south-east, away from the British Rapier missile defence. He was accurate in his assessment, and once again, the British landing ships, stationary in calm waters, were easy targets.

Admiral Moreno planned to go on launching his air attacks from Rio Grande all day if necessary, with Skyhawk and Dagger bombers and Super-Étendard guided-missile aircraft. All day, until the British flew the white flag. As he knew they must, sooner or later.

On the beaches the troops tried to dig in and find cover, manned their machine guns, and tried desperately to get Rapier batteries into position to fire out over the sea. But time was short. Indeed, time was running out.

One hundred miles offshore the aircraft carrier had sunk. Captain Mike Fawkes, now effectively an acting admiral, assessed the carnage inflicted upon the fleet, assessed the weapons with which he could still fight and the inevitability of the Argentine bombing attacks against which he had no defence.

At 0800 on that Saturday morning, after just two hours of ferocious battle, Captain Fawkes, with tears of sorrow and anger streaming down his face, sent the following signal to Britain's Joint Force Command Headquarters at Northwood, to the west of London:

160800APR11. From Captain Mike Fawkes, HMS Kent. *Flagship* Ark Royal *hit and sunk. Type-45 destroyers* Daring *and* Dauntless *hit and sunk. HMS* Gloucester *burning and abandoned. The frigates* Grafton, St Albans *and* Iron Duke *all destroyed. More than 900 men believed to be dead in* Ark Royal, *250 in the other ships. Medical facilities now non-existent. We are defenceless against Argentine bombing. The land forces ashore are without protection. None of us can survive another two hours. Can see no alternative but to surrender.*

CHAPTER EIGHT

Captain Fawkes copied his Northwood signal to the Marine Brigade Commander on the beach at Lafonia where his HQ had just been established. Things were bad: five fully fuelled Apache helicopters were on fire and forty-seven men had been killed in the rocket and strafing attacks.

The scale of the damage to the assault ships *Albion* and *Largs Bay* was as yet unclear. But there were two huge plumes of black smoke rising to the south, and Brigadier Viv Brogden was uncertain whether *Ocean* could possibly now survive another attack from the Argentine bombing force.

The signal from Captain Fawkes added another nightmarish dimension to the myriad problems. With the navy out of action, the fact was, the British landing force was now effectively stranded, 8,000 miles from home and with no cover from the air or even from the sea. Evacuation was out of the question, and their fate was effectively sealed: surrender, or perish under Argentine bombing, here on this godforsaken beach. And all that fighting, for what?

Never in a long and distinguished career had Brigadier Brogden, a decorated Iraqi War veteran, faced such an insoluble conundrum. It was plain the remainder of his 10,000-strong force, currently marooned in the cruise liner *Adelaide*, could not possibly make a landing. Not without naval escort or air cover. The army commanders would never permit that, and *Adelaide* had no defences of her own.

Brigadier Brogden ordered his satellite-communication team to open the line for transmission. His signal, also to Joint Force

Command, Northwood, read: *160816APR11, Brigadier V. Brogden RM. Lafonia, Falkland Islands. Helicopter attack force destroyed. Forty-seven dead. Fifty wounded. Believe two assault ships also hit and burning six miles south. Like Captain Fawkes, we have no defence against bomb and rocket attacks. Landed force of 2,700 men now faces unacceptable losses. Agree with Captain Fawkes. Surrender is our only option.*

The two signals from the South Atlantic landed within fifteen minutes of each other in the headquarters of the Joint Force Command. General Sir Robin Brenchley, Chief of the Defence Staff, was in the war room when the duty officer brought in the first signal and handed it to the C-in-C Fleet, Admiral Mark Palmer. He read it, and passed it to General Brenchley who stared at it with undisguised horror. He had, in his soldier's soul, expected something like this over the next three or four days. But he hadn't been prepared for recommendations for total surrender after just two hours of battle.

He looked up and said quietly, 'Gentlemen, you are about to bear witness to possibly the most humiliating surrender in the history of the British armed forces – certainly since General Cornwallis asked for terms from the Americans at Yorktown in October 1781. General Cornwallis, however, had the excuse of running out of appropriate ammunition and artillery. I am afraid we never had either, even before we went.'

He passed the signal back to Admiral Palmer who stared again at the sheet of paper which heralded the destruction of his beloved Royal Navy. 'My God!' he kept saying, over and over. 'This is beyond my comprehension.'

General Brenchley, part of whose job was to keep the Minister of Defence, Peter Caulfield, informed, seemed to be transfixed by the signal. He just stared at it, knowing the words had somehow made him a prophet but nonetheless hating the experience, realising that he must now inform the Defence Secretary that all was lost.

'Anyone here know the correct procedures?' asked General Brenchley. 'No one ever really taught me what to do in the event of a surrender of our deployed forces.'

'Well,' said Admiral Palmer, 'I suppose we inform first the Ministry and then the Prime Minister. I think he must be told of the necessity to inform the Argentine government that Great Britain is no longer able to pursue the war and would like to sue for peace and a swift cessation of hostilities.'

At that moment the duty officer returned with the signal, just in, from Brigadier Brogden on the beaches in Lafonia. He once more handed it to Admiral Palmer, who just stared and passed it to General Brenchley.

'Good God!' the general breathed. 'There's no braver chap than Brogden, but the damned landing force is marooned with no air cover and no sea cover. They'll be bombed to hell. Someone had better get this on a fast track. We could lose 2,000 men in the next two hours.'

He picked up the nearest telephone and looked around the room, growling, 'You deal with the Ministry, I'll talk to the PM . . .' And then, to the operator, 'Downing Street – fast.'

Twenty seconds later, everyone heard him say, 'Operator, this is General Brenchley, Chief of the Defence Staff. Please connect me to the Prime Minister immediately, whatever he may be doing.'

It took four minutes, which seemed a lot longer in the Northwood operations room. Finally the Prime Minister came on the line and said calmly, 'General Brenchley?'

'Prime Minister,' the general replied, 'it is my unhappy duty to inform you that the Royal Navy has been badly defeated in the South Atlantic. Also, the land forces which landed on East Falkland early this morning are now stranded and are taking quite heavy casualties. Both battle commanders are defenceless against the bombing, and are recommending an immediate surrender.'

'A *what*!?' exclaimed the PM. 'What do you mean, surrender?'

'Sir,' said the General, patronisingly, 'it is the course of action battle commanders usually take when victory is out of the question and casualties are becoming totally unacceptable. It applies mostly to forces which are not actually carrying out a defence of their own country. That, of course, requires a different mindset.'

'But surely, general, our casualties cannot be *that* unacceptable. I mean, my God! Do you have any idea what the media would do to my government if we suddenly ordered our forces to surrender?'

'Yes, sir. I imagine they would probably crucify the lot of you. And for that they would receive the inordinate thanks of every single man who has been obliged to fight this war for you – all of them were improperly equipped, insufficiently armed, and inadequately protected.'

'General, for the moment I will ignore your insolence and remind you that I have been elected by the people of this country to look after their interests. *I* am the elected head of government –

I imagine the final decision on any surrender will be mine alone?'

'Absolutely, Prime Minister,' replied the general. 'But if you do not surrender, you will have the resignations of all your Chiefs of Staff on your desk in a matter of hours. Which would make us free to explain to the media precisely why we had taken that course of action.

'So my advice is to signal to the Argentines, formally, that the armed forces of Great Britain no longer wish to pursue the war.'

The Prime Minister gulped. Before him he saw his worst-ever nightmare – driven from office by the public, and by the military, for failing in his duty to protect the country. Disgrace piled upon disgrace.

Nonetheless he elected to remain on the attack. 'After all, general,' he said, 'professional soldiers and sailors are paid to run these risks and possibly face death. Are you quite certain they have done their absolute best? I mean, it must be centuries since a British Prime Minister was obliged to report the surrender of our armed forces to any enemy?'

'Would you care to know the state of the battle down there?' asked the general.

'Most certainly, I would,' replied the PM, a tad pompously. 'Tell me how it is, as we speak. And I warn you, I may judge the situation rather more harshly than you do. These men owe a debt of honour and duty to the country they serve.'

General Brenchley wasted no time. 'The Navy's flagship, the aircraft carrier *Ark Royal* has been hit, burned and sunk – no survivors among their 1,000-strong crew. All three of our picket-line destroyers are on fire, two of them sinking.

'The frigates *Grafton, St Albans* and *Iron Duke* have been bombed and destroyed. Admiral Holbrook and Captain Reader perished in the carrier. Altogether the navy estimates 1,250 dead and possibly 200 more wounded, many of them badly burned, many of them dying in the water. That's as we speak, by the way.'

The Prime Minister of Great Britain, the colour literally draining from his face, put down the telephone, rushed from the room and somewhat spectacularly threw up in the sink of the second-floor staff washroom, leaning there for fully five minutes, trembling with fear at what he now faced.

Back in Northwood, General Brenchley said, 'Something's happened. The line's gone dead.'

'Fucking little creep's probably fainted,' murmured Admiral

Jeffries, not realising how astonishingly close to the truth he was.

General Brenchley demanded to be reconnected, and when the Downing Street operator came on the line, he just said, 'General Brenchley here. Please put me back to the Prime Minister, will you?'

It took five minutes to locate the PM who was now using the other washroom sink to wash his mouth out and his face down. And three minutes later, he once more picked up the telephone. 'I apologise, General,' he said. 'Been having trouble with these phones all morning.'

'Of course,' replied Brenchley. 'Now let me inform you about the first-wave assault-troop landing. In the hours of darkness we put 2,700 troops ashore, plus helicopters, vehicles and a couple of JCBs.

'The Argentine bombers came in shortly after dawn and hit two of the big landing ships. We have no casualty reports yet, but both ships are burning. Right afterwards the Argie fighter-bombers hit the beachhead with bombs and machine-gun fire, killing forty-seven men, injuring another fifty and wiping out five of our six attack helicopters.

'We have no defence against their bombs. And if we continue to fight, I suspect there will be no survivors on that beach within two or three hours. They have no naval support, no air support, no possibility of reinforcements, and no means of evacuating a fortified island on which they are outnumbered by around seven to one.

'Prime Minister, we're looking at a massacre, and I will have no part of it. I'm a soldier, not a butcher. I am suggesting you contact the Argentine government and request terms for the surrender of the British armed forces in the South Atlantic. And I suggest you do so in the next ten minutes.'

'But what about Caulfield? What does he have to say about it? What about my ministers? I must have a Cabinet meeting.'

'Very well, Prime Minister. You have thirty minutes. But if by then we have taken significantly more casualties, we shall again advise most strongly that you contact Buenos Aires and sue for peace on behalf of my troops, who should be ordered to raise the white flag. Any other course of action on your part will cause me to offer, publicly, my resignation. And perhaps you can talk your way out of *that*.'

'Don't do that, general. I implore you. Think of the government . . . think of the national disgrace . . .'

'Prime Minister, at this precise moment my thoughts are entirely with burned and dying seamen in the ice-cold South Atlantic, and with mortally wounded young men dying on the beaches of Lafonia. I am afraid that at this time I have no room in my heart for anything else.'

In fact, the PM thought he might throw up all over again, right in the middle of the vast Cabinet table. But he braced himself and asked to be connected with the Ministry of Defence.

Back in Northwood, his eyes brimming with tears, General Sir Robin Brenchley put down the telephone and turned away from his colleagues, wiping his sleeve across his eyes. Everyone saw it and no one cared. He was by no means the only man in the war room so personally and overwhelmingly affected by this morning's events in the South Atlantic.

There was more information beginning to trickle through now from HMS *Kent*, the acting flagship for the remnants of the fleet. It seemed the warships' missile directors had downed six Skyhawks and two Daggers. But war of this type was about attrition. Argentina's big land-based air-assault force, both navy and air force, could afford the loss of eight fighter aircraft and their pilots.

It looked now as if Great Britain had lost its entire flight of GR9s, two ditched in the South Atlantic and nineteen lost in the carrier; her two best destroyers, the Type-45s, were gone, plus *Gloucester*, three guided-missile frigates had been destroyed; two 20,000-ton assault ships, one of them brand new, were ablaze; almost every attack helicopter was either on fire or had been lost in the assault ships; and the flagship, *Ark Royal*, which represented the only British airfield for 4,000 miles, had sunk in 600 fathoms. Total casualties: 1,300 and rising by the hour. Great Britain could not afford that.

Perhaps the only nation in all the world which could have absorbed that kind of punishment and still have come back fighting was the United States of America. And right now she was not playing. The shocking news, flashing around the globe from the Falkland Islands, was that British resistance must be at an end. Which indeed it was. Almost.

Four hours previously, 300 feet from the summit of Fanning Head, Captain Douglas Jarvis and his seven-man SAS team had been in their granite cave making satellite contact with the SAS commander on board the carrier. They had been forbidden to attack anything until hostilities formally commenced. And, in the opinion of Major

Tom Hills who was currently masterminding the SAS reconnaissance operation, this was likely to happen in the next hour.

When news of the opening attack by the Super-Es was first transmitted on the fleet network, Major Hills unleashed his tigers. *'Attack and destroy the Argentine position at the summit of Fanning Head,'* he ordered.

Captain Jarvis needed no further encouragement. His team was ready. Two of them would remain in the cave manning the communications, trying as they had been for the past two hours to make contact with the British landed assault forces on the beach at Lafonia.

The other six would climb stealthily upwards to the stronghold on the top of the mountain which effectively controlled the gateway to Falkland Sound. At least it did for the next twenty minutes.

At which point, Douglas Jarvis located the tent with the radio and satellite aerials erected outside, hurled a hand grenade straight through the opening, and dived behind a rock as the blast killed all three occupants and blew to pieces the entire Argentine communications system on Fanning Head.

The noise was shattering in the early morning light, high above the ocean, and it seemed to echo from peak to peak among the not-too-distant mountains. From four other tents the Argentine troops came running out, fumbling to get a proper grip on their rifles. They never had a chance. The men of 22 SAS cut them down in their tracks, all sixteen of them, the complete crew of Argentina's Fanning Head operation.

Immediately Captain Jarvis set about his real task of the night. He hurled a hand grenade into the big Chinook helicopter which was parked on flat ground right behind the tents, presumably for lifting heavy artillery pieces and missile batteries to and from Mare Harbour.

He and his five explosives experts attached 'sticky' bombs to the missile launchers, dynamite to the howitzers and gun barrels, and RDX high explosive to the missiles themselves. Fifteen minutes later, the explosion which ripped across the summit of Fanning Head was every bit the equal of those which were currently sinking the Royal Navy's destroyers.

The shallow cave in which Douglas and his boys sat cheerfully eating chocolate bars and drinking water literally shook from the violence of the blast.

'OK, chaps,' said the captain. 'Fire up the comms and let's tell Major Hills what we just did.'

The trouble was, his young comms man, Trooper Syd Ferry, was having no luck reaching anyone. All night long he had been trying to touch base with Lafonia, and the last time he had spoken to SAS HQ in *Ark Royal* the bloody line had suddenly gone dead.

'Fuck,' said Syd. 'There's more electronics in that damn ship than they have in Cape Kennedy. And we can't even make a phone call.'

'Keep trying,' said Douglas. 'If we have a link problem, try the destroyer *Daring*. We've got a secondary unit in there, a Lieutenant Carey. Do your best, Syd, we need orders and we need an escape route. We can't hang around up here. The Argies must have heard or seen something, and the bastards will hunt us down like rats . . .'

Syd's best, however, was not nearly good enough. No one was ever again going through on the military link to either *Ark Royal* or *Daring*. Syd kept sending his signal and the response was always silence.

Ten minutes later Captain Jarvis decided they had to pull out of the Fanning Head area, fast, before someone decided to come looking for whoever had just blown up the top of the mountain.

'Christ,' said Syd. 'We're not climbing down that rock face in broad daylight, are we?'

'No,' replied Jarvis. 'We don't want to end up on an exposed beach. We'll go up and west, down the other side of the headland. According to this map it's still pretty steep, but not like that cliff face. We'll walk for maybe five miles, just get out of the immediate search area. Then we'll sleep for the day and make our move at night.'

'Any idea where to?' asked someone.

'Absolutely none,' said the captain. 'But we can't stay here. Come on, let's get our stuff – that's everything – and get moving. We can dump things when we're a few miles away.'

'You thinking of making for the coast again, sir?'

'In the end, yes. Because if we can't whistle up a helicopter rescue we'll have to leave by sea.'

'But we can't tell anyone where we are,' said Trooper Syd. 'The comms are down. And we definitely don't have a boat.'

'We can get one,' replied Douglas. 'I mean steal one.'

'Well, what happens if the Argentine Coast Guard catches up and wants to know who we are?'

'Well, we just eliminate them in the normal way.'

'Oh yes,' said Syd. 'Silly of me to ask.'

'We are at war, trooper. And the enemy's the enemy.'

What neither of them knew was that, as it stood from about half an hour ago, Great Britain and Argentina were no longer at war. The British Prime Minister had been obliged to accept the advice of his military and end the one-sided debacle before more military and naval personnel were killed. The PM asked Peter Caulfield to contact his opposite number in Buenos Aires and offer the immediate surrender of the armed forces of Great Britain, on the land and the sea and in the air.

The Argentine Defence Minister, Rear Admiral Juan José de Rozas had been courteous in the extreme and had made no further demands, save for the raising of a prominent white flag over the beach at Lafonia and a formal e-mail from the Prime Minister confirming that the Falkland Islands were no longer under British rule, and that henceforth they would be known as *Las Islas Malvinas,* a sovereign state of Argentina, governed and administered entirely by that nation.

An immediate complete cessation of all hostilities was formally agreed for ten a.m. Falklands time on Saturday, 16 April 2011. Admiral Oscar Moreno, already in line for the next Argentine presidency, was given the news on the direct line between Buenos Aires and Rio Grande.

He instantly ordered all his pilots back to the base at Mount Pleasant. He also instructed two warships to make all speed to the battle area where HMS *Gloucester* was still burning, in order to assist with rescue operations and evacuation to Argentine hospitals by air from Mount Pleasant as soon as possible.

Sergeant Clifton's SAS team above the airfield was informed by the Royal Marines' commanding brigadier on the beach at Lafonia that all was lost, and that they should surrender immediately. Fortunately this comms line had been established in the moments before the first rocket attack on the Apache helicopters.

Not so the line to Captain Jarvis and his men, who had been working via a direct link with the SAS ops room on the carrier, in readiness for their task as a gunnery guidance team when the ships' bombardment of the Argentine positions began.

The fact was no one knew quite where SAS Team One was. The Argentines were furious about the destruction of their expensive stronghold on the top of Fanning Head and even more so about the cold-blooded killing of their missile personnel serving on the heights.

General Eduardo Kampf, extremely upset about the incident, had ordered an inquiry, informing the commander on the ground at Mount Pleasant he wanted a search conducted in the area. He added that he was certain a British Special Forces team had been involved, and his orders were simple: hunt them down and execute them.

This briefing had taken place in the twenty minutes before the formal surrender. Attack helicopters were already in the air and on their way to Fanning Head, none of which was especially good news for Douglas Jarvis and his boys.

They went to ground as only a camouflaged SAS team could, swiftly becoming invisible in the sparse vegetation of those bleak high hills of the Falkland Islands. When they saw the Argentine helicopters moving into the area they kept their heads well down.

The Argentine Air Brigade, which manned the Bell UH-1H attack helicopters, landed on Fanning Head and were shocked at what they found: the bodies of nineteen men, most of them half-dressed, and the charred remnants of the missile systems and artillery pieces. So far as they could see, it was a classic pre-dawn sneak attack by Special Forces and they reported those findings back to base.

When General Kampf heard what had happened he was even more angry. He told the commander at the Mount Pleasant base: 'Treat the British with courtesy. Make maximum effort with the wounded and dying. Try to assist the ships if possible and prepare to receive prisoners of war.

'The only exception to the regular guidance of the Geneva Convention is that Special Force, probably SAS, which sneaked up there and murdered some of our top missile men in cold blood. Find them, and show no mercy. I do not regard them as prisoners of war. I regard them as thieves in the night, murderers. Whatever you deem necessary please carry out as you wish. In the utmost secrecy, of course.'

Again, none of this was good news for Douglas Jarvis and his boys.

Trapped in the western foothills of Fanning Head, out of contact with their headquarters, they were forbidden to use a mobile phone because it could so easily be traced. And now they had not the slightest idea what was happening, whether on the islands, at sea with the battle group or on the landing beaches of Lafonia.

Douglas had few options except to make his way furtively out of the Fanning Head area and try to find a seaport with some kind of fishing trawler and attempt a getaway. Trouble was, he'd have to take the boat's crew with him, otherwise the boat would be missed and they might end up being strafed by the Argentine coastguard. Right now there was a *lot* of bad news for Douglas Jarvis and his boys.

1130 (local time) Buenos Aires

The Argentines lost no time in announcing their victory. *Agence Argentina Presse* released the government's statement to the world's media as it stood – no comments, no interviews and no follow-up. It read simply:

At 1000 hours today, Saturday 16 April, at the request of the Prime Minister of Great Britain, Argentina accepted the unconditional surrender of the British armed forces in the Battle for the Las Islas Malvinas.

Argentina suffered relatively minor losses of just eight downed fighter-bombers, while Great Britain's losses were enormous. The heroic pilots of Argentina hit and sank a total of nine Royal Navy warships, including the flagship aircraft carrier Ark Royal.

Great Britain's entire force of GR9 fighter jets were all destroyed. More than 1,250 Royal Navy personnel are believed dead, with many more injured. The gallant commanding officers of the Argentine navy are currently in the area of the sea battle, assisting the Royal Navy with their wounded.

In the early hours of this morning, British forces numbering almost 3,000 made a landing on the beaches of Lafonia. They brought with them attack helicopters, heavy-lift troop-transport helicopters and missile installations. At 0945, after fierce fighting, this force surrendered to the armies of Argentina.

A white flag of surrender still flies over those landing beaches and we are currently in talks with London as to the immediate future of the prisoners of war. We have been asked to be merciful, and your government will comply with this British request.

A communiqué has been received from the British Prime Minister confirming that their former colony, once described as the Falkland Islands, has now and shall be in future known as Las Islas Malvinas and shall constitute a sovereign state of Argentina, under Argentine law and Argentine administration. The national language shall henceforth be Spanish.

All islanders who wish to remain after the change in national structure will be welcome to do so, and the government of Argentina will work closely with the former administrators to ensure the most peaceful transfer of power.

The important oil and gas fields, seized by the Argentine army in February, shall remain the property of the Republic of Argentina, and there will be future announcements as to their administration.

The statement was signed by the President of Argentina. And countersigned by Admiral Oscar Moreno, Commander-in-Chief (Fleet), and General Eduardo Kampf, Commander of 5 Corps, which had secured the islands and had been deployed to confront the British in the Battle for Mount Pleasant Airfield, had that been required.

No statement ever flashed around the world faster. (It has been said that King George III fell back in his chair and almost fainted when he heard of the loss of his American colonies six months after the surrender at Yorktown.)

Several dozen of the world's news editors very nearly did the same thing when news of the British surrender reached them about an hour and a half after it had taken place. They were reacting out of sheer excitement about what it meant for their headlines.

There were several military experts in London, Washington and Moscow who had long considered the outcome to be inevitable. But to other nations the news came like a snowstorm engulfing residents of Tahiti Beach.

Shock. Horror. Panic. Brits pounded by the Argentines. The Third World Strikes Back. Headline writers hauled out their big guns and turned them to face the public. Then, in a hundred different versions, they let fly.

BRITS BLASTED IN BATTLE FOR THE FALKLANDS
– New York Post
PAMPAS PILOTS PULVERIZE BRITS
– Boston Herald
GALLANT GAUCHOS SLAM THE ROYAL NAVY
– Washington Times
MASSACRE IN THE MALVINAS AS BRITS SURRENDER
– Clarin Buenos Aires
VIVA LAS MALVINAS – IT'S OFFICIAL!
– Buenos Aires Herald

In Spain it was *VIVA LAS MALVINAS*. In France it was *FRENCH JETS HELP ARGENTINA WIN THE FALKLANDS* (never mind their European Union partners in London). Russia's *Izvestya* was subdued: *SHORT NAVAL BATTLE FOR THE FALKLANDS ENDS IN ARGENTINE VICTORY*. In Iran and Syria, the theme was *BRITAIN'S LAST COLONY FALLS TO*

ARGENTINA. South China's *Morning News* announced *THE END OF THE EMPIRE – MALVINAS RETURN TO ARGENTINA*.

Great Britain's Prime Minister had instructed the Ministry of Defence to break the news of the calamity in the South Atlantic to a stunned nation; a nation which in the past 230 years had known setbacks in war, had withstood bombs and attack, had suffered and retreated in the Crimea, at Gallipoli and Dunkirk. But it had never experienced decisive, overwhelming defeat and unconditional surrender to a foreign enemy.

Two hours after that seven p.m. news bulletin the Premier himself broadcast to the people on all television and radio channels. Six spin doctors had worked ceaselessly in a bold but futile attempt to distance their man from the disaster.

He made a rambling speech, referring to 'unending courage' and 'gallantry beyond the call', wittering on about meeting 'an enemy who had secretly been preparing for several years'. *Let down by his admirals and generals, not kept fully informed by the Intelligence services, unaware of the limitations of the fleet.* BLAH, BLAH, BLAH.

'*No prime minister can make decisions when the information is not thorough . . . no one regrets this catastrophe more than I . . . no one could have foreseen these consequences . . . I do expect some very major military resignations.*' (Not his own, of course). And . . . '*I shall personally be taking charge of the evacuation back to Britain of our wounded, and also of the reparations which I have already insisted will be paid to families who have lost their loved ones.*'

Right after that he recalled every member of Parliament to Westminster to begin an emergency sitting of the House of Commons at midnight.

1200 (local time) same day
Chevy Chase, Maryland

Admiral Morgan was not surprised at the outcome of the war, but he was slightly surprised at the speed with which it had been accomplished. He first heard the news shortly after eleven a.m. on Fox News, but the updated version of the bulletin at noon contained another surprise. According to the best naval sources available, it seemed the aircraft carrier *Ark Royal* had been sunk in less than fifteen minutes.

This was extremely fast for a big ship hit by either bombs or missiles. There were few examples of the time taken for a major warship to sink finally beneath the waves after a hit by an Exocet. But certainly in 1982 it took Britain's HMS *Sheffield* three days, and in that same war the *Atlantic Coveyor* burned for twenty-four hours before she blew apart and sank. Both ships took an Exocet above the waterline.

The *Ark Royal*, however, appeared to have gone down in under a quarter of an hour. But her comms room had had time to broadcast to the fleet she had been hit – three explosions had been reported. The flagship then went off the air immediately, and another CO positioned within three miles had reported fire broke out 'at least six minutes after the ship began to list'.

'I'd be surprised,' muttered Arnold, 'if she was hit by bombs or missiles. That ship went down too damn quick, like she was holed below the waterline or somehow had her back broken – or both. I'd guess the fires broke out in the engine room and then spread fast. Those damn carriers are full of fuel.'

He wandered outside, absent-mindedly inspecting his daffodil beds. In his hand he carried a recent message from Jimmy Ramshawe informing him that the two Russian submarines *Gepard* and *Cougar* had been sighted in the Murmansk area in the past two or three days.

'I wonder,' Arnold Morgan murmured, turning back towards the house, 'whether our old friend, the elusive Mr Viper was in attendance when the Royal Navy carrier was sunk. I'd sure as hell like to ask Vitaly Rankov, but there's no point seeking the truth from a lying Soviet bastard, right?'

Thoughtfully he answered his own question. 'Right, no point at all.' Walking back to the house, his mind turned once more to the dark cold depths of the South Atlantic where, he guessed, *Viper 157* would now be running slowly north, away from the evidence, her work done.

No sooner was he back inside than the telephone rang in his study. He checked the call-identity monitor and recognised the private number of Lt. Commander Ramshawe.

'Hi, Jimmy, told you it wouldn't take long.'

'You sure did. Two hours flat. Game, set and match. Everyone back in the bloody pavilion.'

Arnie chuckled. 'I got a few thoughts for you to work on. First, thanks for the information on the *Gepard* and the *Cougar*. That leaves *Viper 157*, right? The *only* Russian nuclear submarine which could possibly have been in the South Atlantic, right? And twice picked up on her way there – once by our guys in Ireland, and again by the Royal Navy CO east of the Falkland Islands coupla days ago, correct?'

'That's what we have, Arnie. You hear anything more?'

'Only from my own highly suspicious mind, kid. That aircraft carrier went down awful quick. Fifteen minutes. And eyewitnesses are saying the fires started about six minutes after she began to list.

'The fires didn't sink her. What sank her was a damned big hole below the waterline. Nothing else puts a warship on the bottom that fast. And it must have been a *very* big hole . . . sounds to me like something broke her back. And there's only one thing coulda done that – a wire-guided torpedo from a submarine. And I'd guess she was hit by more than one.'

'We got a report of huge fires,' said Jimmy. 'Spread fast. Started below the island.'

'Fires don't sink warships,' said Arnold. 'They burn 'em. And if they burn 'em for long enough they'll probably reach the bomb and missile areas which will blow the ship in half. But that usually takes hours and hours. This baby was on the bottom in fifteen minutes. That's not a fire, that's a hole.'

'So who fired the torpedo, Sherlock?'

'I'd guess Comrade Moriartovich, sneaky little son of a bitchovich. Straight out of the tubes of the Akula-class hunter-killer *Viper*, which had been watching for several days, waiting for that fog to clear . . . just lurking, silent and villainous. That's who.'

'I didn't realise you spoke fluent Russian,' said Jimmy. 'But I'm with you. That bastard just slammed a couple of big ones straight into the Royal Navy's *Ark Royal*.'

'Well, the Argentines could not have done it, kid. They don't have a good enough submarine for that. But someone did, and someone did it for *them*. And if you want to know who, just watch to see who gets the biggest oil contract in the world in the next few months. The one for the oilfield less than a dozen miles from the airport on East Falkland.'

'Excuse me, sir. A matter of protocol. I believe they just became *Las Islas Malvinas*.'

'But perhaps, young James, only temporarily.'

'How do you mean? The Brits have turned it up, right?'

'Yes. But we are still left with a very clear situation. Those islands have been British since 1833 – everyone who lives on them is

British. They have been a legal protectorate of Great Britain for darn nearly 200 years. Argentina has been griping and moaning about it for a long time, but Argentina has *never* owned the islands. Spain did, once, but the Brits threw 'em out a long time ago.

'So what happens? Argentina suddenly decides to grab 'em, lands a military force, blows up the British defences, kills a hundred troops and takes over. They kick out the legal oil companies, two of the biggest, most respected corporations on Earth, both of whom have paid fortunes to be there, and then marches them out at gunpoint.

'Then they effectively say, "*You want us out, come try it.*" At which point they blast and kill another thousand or more troops and accept a surrender. That worked fine in the nineteenth century. Doesn't work now. There's the UN and Christ knows who else to answer to.

'It would be as if Paul Bedford and I decided we'd very much like to own Monaco, went over there in a couple of warships, kicked Prince What's-his-name in the ass, and took his fucking principality. Accepting the surrender of those poncey palace guards who prance around in fancy dress. It'd probably take us about an hour and a half. And no one could do a thing about it.

'But, Jimmy, you just can't pull that nineteenth-century shit any more. Not in the modern world. And I gotta talk to the President later this afternoon. And Exxon Mobil are fucking furious. They want their goddamned oil and gas back, and I don't blame them. And they wanna know whether the Godalmighty United States is going to just stand around while some fucking lunatic in a poncho rampages around all over their goddamned possessions.

'And the President is not going to like it. And a thousand fucking disaffected sons of bitches are going to be asking him what he plans to do about it. And he's not going to know and frankly neither do I. But someone's sure as hell going to need to do something. We simply cannot condone it.'

Jimmy Ramshawe was thoughtful, and there was a momentary silence between the senior world-Intelligence maestro and one of the sharpest young minds in the National Security Agency.

Eventually, it was Jimmy who spoke. 'Arnie,' he said, 'I forgot to tell you why I called. You scanned through the business section in the *Times* today?'

'Not yet.'

'There was an item there I thought was significant. One of the biggest international agricultural deals in recent years . . .'

'If you tell me it's Argentina and Russia I'll probably stand on my head . . .'

'Upside down, sir. You got it first time. Beef cattle. Millions of 'em.'

'You know what that is, Jimmy? That's the start of a new cooperation between those two countries. And it's going to end with oil and gas in the Falklands and South Georgia – if, that is, the Argentines are allowed to get away with what they have done.'

'You decided what to advise the President yet?'

'No. Because I want to hear what the British Ambassador has to say this afternoon. I've met him a couple of times, and he's coming in to the White House. Just the three of us. A lot will depend on what he says.

'And then, of course, we've got the complication of the goddamned United Nations. They've got a meeting of the Security Council tonight. I think the Chairman's from someplace west of the Blue Nile, Mgumboo Nkurruption or someone, so that's gotta be real significant.'

Jimmy burst out laughing. Arnold Morgan's opinion of African dictators who lived like pashas in impoverished countries, collecting millions of dollars of foreign aid every year – well, that opinion was on the withering side of discourteous.

'I suppose you never considered the Diplomatic Service, did you?' asked Jimmy.

'Not this week, kid. Keep me posted.' Crash. Down phone.

Three hours later Admiral Morgan drove himself to the White House, where Sir Patrick Jardine, Great Britain's Ambassador to the United States, was already in the Oval Office, chatting to the President.

Sir Patrick was a tall, somewhat gaunt figure, wearing an immaculately tailored Savile Row suit. A scion of the great Hong Kong financial empire, he was a career diplomat despite having inherited 4,000 acres of prime farmland in Norfolk.

The fifty-six-year-old diplomat had only one commercial customer, and that was one of the biggest brewers in England. Sir Patrick was what the Brits refer to as a 'Barley Baron', with his large swathe of relatively rare, flinty land which grew malting barley, the prime ingredient for beer. Whichever way the market fluctuated, it kept Sir Patrick very handily in Savile Row suits at £2,000 a time.

In his youth he had trained to be a barrister, passed his exams and then quit. 'I simply can't imagine spending the rest of my life defending scruffy, spotty, mostly guilty young thugs who should probably be locked up on sight,' he had told his father.

'Yes, I do see that's rather disagreeable,' said Jardine Senior. 'I think you had better go and work in the Foreign Office. Won't make you rich, but you'll have a pleasant enough time, unless you get mixed up in some bloody war.'

Now, thirty years later, the dread of the late Sir Arthur Jardine had come full circle. His son was not taking cover under the bed while gunfire rained plaster and furniture down on him in some besieged British embassy. But he was right in the thick of it and, for the moment, he was Great Britain's last line of defence in the struggle to persuade the USA to remove the Argentine army from the Falkland Islands.

Sir Patrick, however, realised there was only one reason he was currently sitting in this chair, facing the President of the United States. And that was the stolen oil and gas which belonged to Exxon Mobil.

He stood up to greet Admiral Morgan who made his usual entry without knocking, and held out his hand to the ambassador. 'Patrick,' he said, 'I'm afraid we meet again in rather trying circumstances.'

President Bedford was clearly very concerned by the entire issue of the South Atlantic and its myriad ramifications.

'Arnie,' he said, 'I've been talking to the ambassador for twenty minutes and I must say we have so far clarified nothing. But I think you'll be interested in the position the Brits are taking . . . Sir Patrick, why don't you outline the situation for Admiral Morgan?'

'Of course, and I'll be as quick as I can,' replied the barley baron. 'I'm sure you know the history. The Falklands have been British since 1833. Argentina has always wanted them, went to war for them in 1982, has been negotiating for them ever since, and a couple of months ago seized them by military force.'

'Yup,' said Arnold, nodding. 'A regular *coup d'état*, no bullshit.'

'Well, you probably also know we went through the usual channels of protest, and the United Nations practically ordered the Argentines to vacate the islands. However, a Security Council motion to censure them and even expel them from the United Nations was vetoed by Russia. So it didn't go through.

'Buenos Aires refused to discuss the matter with anyone, save to announce the *Malvinas* had always been theirs and that was an end to it.'

'So Great Britain – understandably – decided to take matters into their own hands, as they did in 1982?' Arnold asked. 'And drive the Argentines off with military force?'

'Not quite,' said Sir Patrick. 'On very firm advice from the Foreign Office, my government made no threat to the Argentines. We did not announce the formation of a Battle Group, even though Parliament had voted for such an action. We just got ready and set sail.

'Our fleet arrived in the area. In international waters, at least 100 miles off the east coast of the Falkland Islands. We launched no attack, we opened fire on no one. But at first light, flying from both the mainland and the islands, Argentina launched an unprovoked airborne assault on our ships and very nearly wiped us out. You might say it was their second great crime of the year 2011.'

'I suppose they'll say the presence of the Royal Navy fleet was in itself a major provocation – and, indeed, a threat to their own troops,' suggested Arnold Morgan.

'I suppose they may,' replied Sir Patrick. 'However, we were not in Argentine waters, and despite their act of banditry in February those islands belong to the Crown. They are packed with British institutions and people.

'Argentina had no right to have an army occupying the territory. No right at all. Under any law, local, national or international, their occupation was illegal. And the fact that the Royal Navy attempted to defend itself against a sustained attack is irrelevant. This was not a formal war. It was one country whose possessions had been ravaged by another, contrary to every known international charter and treaty of the last 100 years.'

'Yes, I see that,' replied Admiral Morgan. 'But I suppose there was also the issue of the 2,700 troops who landed on Lafonia.'

'Well, that ought not to be an issue. We are surely entitled to land anyone we wish on our own islands.'

Arnold grinned. 'Yes, I suppose you are.'

And the President interjected, 'Yes. But the Argies are so damned convinced of the righteousness of their claim, it makes things very difficult. And, of course, the pure damned geography of the place is kinda on their side. Britain having the Falklands as a colony is almost like China owning Nantucket.'

Sir Patrick smiled. 'Mr President, I sometimes think people do not understand how very British the Falklands are, aside from the fact the natives are to a man British citizens, mostly living in harmony around a damned great Church of England cathedral in Stanley.

'There are Departments of Mineral Resources, Fisheries, Treasury. There's an Attorney General, an immigration officer, a Chief Executive, a Customs office, government offices. There's a Chamber of Commerce, a Development Corporation, a Met Office. There's even a Falklands Island Company with offices in Stanley and Hertfordshire, England. It's all connected to London.'

'But not, on this occasion, *protected by* London,' said Arnold wryly.

The President ordered tea, lapsang souchong from China, which was both his own and the ambassador's favourite. Paul Bedford made a habit of checking out all visiting ambassadors' preferences, just in case Colombian coffee or something sparked an unexpected suicide attempt by an appalled Equadorian diplomat.

Sir Patrick informed the Americans that Great Britain would return to the United Nations and once more request some decisive action, which Arnold Morgan remarked had never been the UN's strong suit.

But what Sir Patrick really wanted was for the USA to make a stand, to growl that the actions of Argentina had been nothing short of international piracy and if Buenos Aires did not come to heel forthwith Uncle Sam would make life very, very difficult for them. The rule of law must surely, in the end, in a civilised world, take precedence.

Just before the ambassador left, Admiral Morgan reminded him that it was sometimes necessary to take draconian measures to uphold that rule of law. And that he for one was not averse to implementing them if required.

Sir Patrick, as he walked from the Oval Office, took great comfort in that closing statement from the admiral. And he hoped to hear favourably from the Americans in the next few days. Admiral Morgan decided, in this instance at least, not to raise the possibility of the *Ark Royal* having been sunk by the Russians.

But when Sir Patrick left, the President and his most trusted friend had much to discuss. Because deep in their hearts both men realised that, regardless of the strength of Argentine feelings, the South American country had incontrovertibly committed acts of international mayhem.

'Ask yourself, Paul,' said Arnold. 'How would it be if everyone rampaged around like that? If France suddenly turned its power on

Morocco and told Rabat "*We've always owned your country.*"? What if the Brits did it to Jamaica? If we did it to Japan? If Portugal did it to the eastern part of Brazil? There's no difference. What Argentina did was wrong. And all their pious territorial claims are still wrong, and still unlawful.

'For us, this is one giant pain in the ass. But it's still wrong. And we still have to face the goddamned oil corporation. And, of course, there's still the Russian connection – another vicious act of international barbarism that may have killed more than 1,000 people.'

President Bedford frowned. 'Can we take this step by step? I'll ask the questions, you give the answers – OK?'

'Fine.'

'Right. Are you proposing we come straight out and say publicly we do not approve of this in any way? And Argentina must retreat behind her lawful borders?'

'I think we come straight out and say it. But not publicly. I think we send a private communiqué to the president of Argentina. It must be signed by your good self, saying exactly that and citing it as the formal opinion of the Pentagon chiefs. Because *that*'s gonna wake 'em up for sure.'

'OK, Arnie. So either they don't answer or they tell us to mind our own business. What then?'

'Well, I guess we have to be prepared to give them an ultimatum . . .'

'Like what? Nuke Buenos Aires? Because I got a feeling that's what it's likely to take to get 'em to change their minds.'

'So have I. And no, not that. No nukes.'

'Well, what?'

'I know this is not traditionally my instinct, but how about we do something subtle, something which will leave them scared and uncertain.'

'You mean like some Mafia don, some sinister threat – the kind of thing gangsters pull?'

'How about we tell them we are proposing to make it our business to have them vacate the Falkland Islands? And if they have not begun to evacuate by next week they will surely feel the hot breath of Uncle Sam breathing down their necks. But we will tell them nothing more specific than that.'

'OK. Then what?'

'We do nothing publicly. But very quietly we move our Special

Forces into the area. And we have the Navy SEALs link up with the British SAS, and we begin to exact a very serious revenge.'

'Like what?'

'Well, the Argentines have a reasonable navy, don't they? How about we sink a few warships, and maybe knock out a few aircraft? The Special Forces could do that without any trouble. And we admit to nothing. The Argentines may guess we're at the bottom of it, but they'll never know for sure. And they'll never find a way to prove anything.'

'Arnie, you think we could actually inflict so much damage on their military that they'd be forced to throw in their hand?'

'They might. But, in any event, they'd never admit to their people what was happening to them. And we could certainly make it impossible for them to retain their army of occupation in the Falkland Islands. We could make it possible for the remnants of the Royal Navy to retake the territory, and in return to hand over the oil and gas to Exxon Mobil and BP. And we sure as hell could throw the Argentines out of South Georgia.'

'I do see the merit of it all, Arnie. But do you think we could *really* keep the whole thing secret?'

'We'd need two things to help us. We'd want the total cooperation and support of Admiral John Bergstrom who's in the final six months of his command as head of SPECWARCOM. And we'd need some silent support from Chile, like the Brits had in 1982. That would make a huge difference. Give us a forward base, way down there in the south of South America.'

'Do you see a lot of people dying?'

'Not really, Mr President. I see a lot of very expensive equipment getting trashed. And I see a very angry Argentina demanding to know what's going on. And I see us saying we know nothing about it. It must be the Brits, we say, and that's just Argentina's tough luck. Shouldn't have taken their island in the first place.'

'And how, great genius of my life, do you see it all ending?'

'Mr President, we make the Brits hand over the Falkland Islands to Argentina, peacefully, over a period of two years. With cooperation and a certain amount of chivalry.

'We make Argentina thrilled to get the hell out of this highly destructive row they're having with us, or at least with someone. And we make the Brits delighted to get shot of the goddamned islands and somehow save face in the process. That way everyone's happy – or at least happi*er*.

'Of course, part of our price is the restoration of the oil and gas to their rightful owners, Exxon Mobil and BP. But we make the Argentines signatories on the contract for fifty years and then cut them in for a decent royalty, which begins twenty-four months from restoration. That way we've got the oil companies off your back, Argentina has a piece of the pie, and everyone can go back to work.'

'The weakest part of the equation, Arnie, is the Brits, who basically get little from it.'

'True. But they get oil money for two years. Compared with the very obvious mess they're in right now that will be fine. And they will quietly claim ultimate victory, in what their press will call the Secret War. Which will suit us very well.

'And British Petroleum will have its oil and gas back. We'll probably throw in a few further sweeteners which Argentina will have to agree to. But they'll agree to anything, just so long as they can see the time two years from now when *Las Islas Malvinas* will formally become a sovereign territory of Argentina – without endless grief from us and the United Nations.'

'Very neat, but I'm going to throw one final monkey wrench into the works before we send for John Bergstrom. What about Russia? What about that damned submarine you just told me you think whacked the *Ark Royal*?'

'Russia will slink quietly away if Argentina does not end up owning the oil free and clear. You can trust me on that. It's all they came for.'

'And the goddamned nuclear submarine?'

'Well, Mr President. Since no one ever announces the loss of a nuclear ship which has hit the bottom of a vast open ocean two miles deep. . . . I actually thought that we might sink it.'

The President came about as close as he had ever done to shooting a hot jet of lapsang souchong down his nose. He groped for his handkerchief, and looked up with a conspiratorial grin.

'Why, yes, Arnie. What a remarkably good idea.'

Same day: midnight (local time), London

Like most of the Western world's newspapers, the British press had few, if any, morals. As in the USA, all their newspapers and almost all their television channels were thoroughly commercial operations, unconcerned with the public or national good, only with the sale of their product. And, generally speaking, the best way to take care of that was to frighten the living daylights out of the population whenever possible. Fear sells, right?

The day the Falkland Islands fell, Britain's media collectively went bananas. Headlines unknown for decades leaped into the minds of the editors. Words like *Defeat*, *Humiliation*, *Catastrophe* and *Disaster* crowded onto front pages and newscasts, all mixed in with *Royal Navy*, *warships* and *surrender*.

The top brass of the Ministry of Defence and indeed that of the army and navy were obviously sworn to silence. But an issue as important as this could scarcely be held in check. It seemed that all through that early evening in England, every retired officer from any branch of the armed forces was quite prepared to bring up the matter of the retired Harrier FA2 fighter jets.

The BBC's first words in their ten p.m. newscast were: 'Was this the war which should never have been fought?'

The early editions of the Sunday newspapers, traditionally on sale in London's Leicester Square at 10.30 p.m., were absolutely lethal to the Prime Minister and his Cabinet.

The *Sunday Times* splashed over eight columns on its front page:

ROYAL NAVY BLAMES THE GOVERNMENT FOR DISASTER IN THE SOUTH ATLANTIC
Falkland Islands fall to Argentina -
British warships 'defenceless'

The source, or sources, for this scything statement of fact was in truth a succession of off-the-record conversations with a half-dozen retired admirals and captains, three of whom had commanded ships in the first Falklands conflict.

Great Britain had gone to war 8,000 miles from home without the proper kit – and the British media sensed blood. They were going to ride this 'story' to the bitter end.

ROYAL NAVY SURRENDERS FALKLANDS
Can't Shoot, Can't Fight
Government Cuts Blamed
– *Sunday Mirror*

ARGENTINA WIPES OUT 'DEFENCELESS' NAVY
Falklands Islands fall in two-hour massacre at sea
– *Sunday Telegraph*

ARK ROYAL SUNK –
ROYAL NAVY
SURRENDERS
FALKLANDS
– *News of the World*

(This narrow headline ran alongside a huge picture of the British aircraft carrier in her death throes.)

The newspapers devoted pages and pages to interviews with Whitehall Press Officers and were currently engaged in a relentless, ghoulish search for photographs of the dead. By midnight reporters were besieging naval towns like Portsmouth and Devonport, trying to contact families whose sons and husbands might have gone down with the *Ark Royal*.

By first light the press would have done its work, sowing the seeds of doubt and suspicion in the minds of the British people. Was this government as bad as many people thought? Was it just a self-seeking bunch of incompetents, concerned only with their own jobs and careless of their duty to the armed services?

Prophetically, an enormous black rain cloud hovered over Westminster and the Houses of Parliament as dawn broke over London. At least, that was how it seemed. But inside the debating chamber that cloud seemed to hang over the Prime Minister alone.

He had taken his seat on the government front bench as, high above, Big Ben chimed midnight. He arrived, predictably in this parliament, to thunderous roars from the Tory benches of, *'RESIGN! RESIGN! RESIGN!'*

And, at the invitation of the Speaker, he had begun the proceedings with a frequently interrupted speech in which he had endeavoured to explain away the obviously shattering defeat of the Royal Navy in the South Atlantic.

No one was listening. The scale of the nightmare and the terrifying ramifications of the defeat were too great for any British government. And thanks in part to the media hysteria, the loss of those little islands 400 miles off the coast of Argentina was rapidly being perceived in the minds of MPs as the end of all life as they knew it.

When the PM finally did sit down, the Tory leader of the Opposition stood up and stated, 'Well, I'm sure the House would like to join me in thanking you profusely for shedding a glaring light on the obvious. Now perhaps you would tell the House what you plan to do about the recapture of the islands and the rebuilding of our armed forces?'

Another storm of derisive cheering broke out. The Prime Minister's Secretary of Defence, Peter Caulfield, climbed to his feet and revealed that in the opinion of his Ministry it was far too early to make any such announcements, but that the Cabinet would be considering all the facts later in the morning.

It might have been too early to ascertain the precise moment-to-moment ebb and flow of the short sea-battle. It was not, however, too early to discuss the consequences of the defeat and the surrender.

The debate was now open to the floor. The Tory MP Alan Knell demanded, 'Can there be any reason why the Right Honourable Gentleman should not immediately offer his resignation to his party and to the House?'

The Tory side erupted once more with howls of '*RESIGN! RESIGN!*'

The Speaker stepped in and demanded, '*ORDER! ORDER!*'

Richard Cawley shouted, 'I personally warned the Right Honourable Gentleman about the loss of the Harriers – and what the lack of a beyond-visual-range fighter jet would mean. I told him over and over that without that look-down shoot-down Blue Vixen radar in the Harriers the navy would be in shocking trouble. There are 1,250 of this country's finest men dead in the South Atlantic. And the blame can be laid at no other door than the one which opens into Number 10 Downing Street, his home and that of his benighted government!'

The cheer from the Tory benches ripped into the great vaulted ceiling of the House. Again and again the Speaker rose to demand *ORDER.*

And so it went on. Five more times the echoing chimes of Big Ben tolled out the hour. Until eventually the MPs staggered out into the morning air, the Opposition congratulating themselves on a debate well won. Government ministers were wondering whether indeed their leader would have to resign in clear and obvious disgrace.

The headline on the leader column of the *Daily Mail* was darkly amusing, parodying one of Churchill's most moving wartime speeches. It quoted the Tory party chairman, the drole and urbane Lord Ashampstead:

IF THIS PARLIAMENT SHOULD LAST
FOR ANOTHER WEEK (GOD FORBID),
MEN WILL STILL SAY, 'THIS
WAS THEIR DARKEST HOUR.'

In the dying moments of the debate the Tories had pushed for a vote of 'No confidence' in the PM. And this would take place later in the afternoon when everyone had taken a couple of hours' sleep. The Premier did not enjoy a huge majority in the House, and many people thought that this might well be his last day in office.

The fallout from those Argentine bombs had rippled a long way north in a very short time. And as the weary British Members of Parliament walked outside into the reality of the dawn, few of them risked a glance at the eight-foot-high statue of Sir Winston, glowering down with a withering gaze from his granite plinth right opposite the outer wall of the Chamber.

The gloomy heart of London could scarcely have differed more from the joyous heart of Buenos Aires at midnight. In the city on the wide estuary of the River Plate there were almost half a million people crammed into the Plaza de Mayo – eight different tango bands were trying to play in harmony with each other, and the entire Boca Juniors soccer team, a symbol of national obsession and sometimes of unity, was assembled on a stage erected in the middle of the celebrating throng.

The president was on the balcony of the palace, waving to the crowd in company with Admiral Moreno and General Kampf, whom he announced as the great architects of the Argentine victory in the islands.

To the north side of the square stood the grand edifice of the *Catedral Metropolitana* which housed the tomb of Argentina's thus far greatest warrior-hero, General José de San Martin, one of the early-nineteenth-century liberators of South America from Spanish rule.

It was as if the great man had suddenly risen up to lead the Argentine people once more in their joy as the enormous bells of the cathedral chimed out the midnight hour. The rising anthem of the victors once more rang out over the square; in part a lament for brave men lost and yet also a ferocious roar of triumph, tuneful and rhythmic in its unanimous delivery: '*M-A-A-A-L-V-I-N-A-S!* . . . *M-A-A-A-L-V-I-N-A-S!* . . . *M-A-A-A-L-V-I-N-A-S!*'

CHAPTER NINE

1500 (local time) Sunday 17 April
North of the San Carlos Settlement, East Falkland

Under the cover of a cold mountain fog, Captain Douglas Jarvis and his seven SAS troopers had moved almost six miles south of the western slopes of Fanning Head. As this Sunday afternoon grew increasingly gloomy they found themselves north of the San Carlos River which snaked across the rough rocky plain between the Usmore and Simon ranges.

The weather had palpably worsened since their arrival on the island nine days earlier. It was colder, wetter, windier – and the nights were closing in. Three weeks from now it would be winter, a vicious South Atlantic winter, with ice-cold gales and snow squalls sweeping up out of the south where the Antarctic Peninsula came lancing out of the Larsen Ice Shelf, only 750 miles from Port Stanley.

We have to get the hell out of here was the only thought in Douglas Jarvis's mind as they moved through the soaking landscape, the all-weather Gore-Tex smocks fastened securely around their hips, hoods down, gloves and waterproof combat boots pulled on tight, heavy bergens weighing heavier by the hour.

At 1520 Captain Jarvis raised his right fist in a signal to halt. The troopers, walking carefully in pairs, stared ahead across the rough country. In the far distance, still north of the river, they could see the lights of a farmhouse. At least, they hoped it was only a farmhouse.

Out to their left, beyond a line of grey jagged rocks, barely moving, they could just make out a large group of shadowy figures – woolly shadowy figures. 'Thank Christ for that,' muttered Douglas. 'A decent dinner. We've earned that.'

And, not for the first time, he appreciated the long evenings of detailed, meticulous teaching that the SAS instructors gave every last one of their 'students' before any of them left on a mission.

Back in Hereford, Douglas and his troopers had undergone intensive survival training to prepare them for the Falkland Islands. And one good lesson they had been taught was that around seven billion sheep regarded the Falklands as home, and had done for more than a hundred years.

For over a century sheep farming had been the principal commercial activity of the islands, with almost all the Falklands seaports established for the export of wool. In recent years, fishing and then oil had expanded the economy of the islands, but there were still a zillion sheep grazing these rough but strangely fertile pastures of damp grass and ever-flowing mountain rivers. Douglas Jarvis and his team had stumbled upon one of the historic areas of Falklands farming, north of the settlement on the San Carlos River where sixth-generation shepherds patrolled the gently sloping land that rose towards the hills.

They might be here for a while before rescue, and it was no bloody good whatsoever being starving hungry in the kingdom of the roast leg of lamb. In their bergens, the SAS men had knives and a razor-sharp butcher's axe. They had been given specific lessons on how to skin and swiftly cut up a carcass. Douglas himself knew how to sever the two hind legs and cleave out the shoulders. They all knew how to slice out the rack of chops.

'OK, Peter,' said Douglas. 'Move up to that boulder over there, and take out a couple of small ones.'

All eight men knew how to live off the land. It was a basic requirement for any SAS man. And the total silence from their satellite transmissions had made it amply clear that something had gone drastically wrong with the Royal Navy's attack, and perhaps even with the landing.

Trooper Wiggins shrugged off his bergen and unzipped his SSG-69, the renowned Austrian-built bolt-action SAS sniper rifle, which in trained hands could achieve a shot-grouping of less than forty centimetres at a range of 800 metres. Peter Wiggins's hands were well trained, and to quote his mate, Trooper Joe Pearson, he had an eye like a shithouse rat.

Trooper Wiggins moved swiftly through the grass to the boulder, and selected his targets, both of them within fifty metres. Two single shots, fired only seconds apart, cracked out from the rifle, and two good-sized lambs dropped instantly from a 7.62mm calibre bullet slammed into the centres of their tiny brains.

Three more troopers raced out to help collect their quarry and Douglas Jarvis pointed at a cluster of rocks and a few bushes further north in the rapidly darkening hills. They moved quickly, and no kitchen was ever set up faster.

Using their one shovel, they dug a hole three feet long by three feet wide by two feet deep. They shifted the wet earth easily, and while Troopers Bob Goddard and Trevor Fermer skinned and butchered the lambs Trooper Jake Posgate found round stones and dropped them into the hole.

Douglas lit a fire from brushwood right on top of the stones and the troopers used their butcher's axe to hack some bigger pieces of brush into small but burnable logs. The entire operation took almost an hour, and when the fire began to die on top of the almost red-hot stones they suspended two legs of lamb in the hole and spit-roasted them close to the stones. The glow from the fire could not be seen from anywhere except from directly above the hole – SAS survival manual, chapter three.

No Special Forces group had ever been hungrier, and no leg of lamb had ever tasted better, despite being a bit burned on the outside. When the SAS men had finished their supper they dumped everything into the hole, including the wool and the remains of the carcasses and filled it in, rolling a rock over the fresh earth. Only a very highly trained tracker would ever have suspected they had once been there.

By 2200 hours they were on their way, pushing through the darkness, heading south, down towards Carlos Water, hoping to find a boat which would get them to the probably unguarded shores of West Falkland. They still carried all their camping gear, rifles, sub-machine guns, and, wrapped in clear plastic bags, four shoulders of lamb, two legs and thirty-two chops. But they no longer had any explosives and they had no need to carry water. The wilds of East Falkland were awash with it.

Every hour they fired up the comms system and tried to raise the command centre in the Royal Navy ships and on the landing beaches. But it was only a cry in the night: there never had been a reply, and by now Douglas Jarvis realised that there never would be.

He did not dare attempt any direct communication with command headquarters in Northwood, because that would certainly have been located and monitored by the Argentines. The last thing they needed was a seriously determined search party trying to hunt them down and picking up a radio 'fix'.

0900 Monday 18 April
Stirling Lines, Hereford, England

Lt. Colonel Mike Weston, commanding officer 22 SAS, had been studying the POW lists from the Falkland Islands for three hours. They contained the names of the men who had conducted the airfield recce at Mount Pleasant under the command of Sergeant Jack Clifton: all eight of them were in Argentine custody and were now travelling by sea to the mainland.

Lt. Colonel Weston had twice spoken to his opposite number at the Royal Marine headquarters at Lymestone in Devon and it seemed all the SBS men who had landed at Lafonia under Lt. Jim Perry were also safe, travelling by sea to the mainland with the rest of the landing force. The Argentine military had intimated they did not intend to detain them, although their weapons had been confiscated.

An Argentine ship would land them one month from now at the great Uruguayan seaport of Montevideo on the north shore of the River Plate estuary. The Royal Navy would be welcome to pick them up there and transport them home. The assault ships *Albion* and *Largs Bay,* which had been hit and burned in Low Bay, were to be scrapped, while the *Ocean* had been confiscated, punishment for the destruction of the eight Argentine fighter jets in battle. She would be renamed the *Admiral Oscar Moreno*. Captain Farmer and his crew would be going to Montevideo.

But what was currently vexing Colonel Weston most was the fate of Captain Douglas Jarvis and his assault group which had last been seen blowing the summit off Fanning Head. The colonel knew that part of the mission had been accomplished, and he understood the impossibility of further contact since both SAS command centres at sea had been removed from the line of battle. He also doubted whether there had been any form of communication between the various assault forces in the final hours before the surrender on the Lafonia landing beaches.

Which left Captain Jarvis and his team in a very uneasy form of isolation. Colonel Weston did not like it at all. But he understood the danger that a long-range communiqué from Hereford via satellite might pose to the men. If the Argentines picked it up Captain Jarvis would be in serious trouble.

Even the most highly-trained SAS group could scarcely cope alone against a force of 1,000 men in vehicles and helicopters who were using infra-red search radars. Colonel Weston could not accurately assess the scale of Argentine anger about the destruction of their stronghold on Fanning Head, but he guessed they would not be overjoyed.

Thus he did not dare to open up a line of voice-contact communication to Douglas Jarvis, but he did enter a coded satellite communication urging Douglas and his team to keep their heads well down, and telling them that a rescue operation would be mounted. He also instructed them to open up their comms for one hour at 1800 each evening.

Which meant that, for the moment at least, the SAS team had to survive as best it could. But this was an outstanding group, and Colonel Weston personally believed if anyone could stay alive in such a hostile environment, it was probably his guys, the ones who had just blown up Fanning Head.

If the Argentines caught them they might very well execute them and say nothing. That way Hereford would never know their fate. Although he did not believe them to be dead, Colonel Weston nevertheless listed Captain Douglas Jarvis and Troopers Syd Ferry, Trevor Fermer, Bob Goddard, Joe Pearson, Peter Wiggins, Jake Posgate and the Welshman Dai Llewelyn officially 'missing in action'.

There had been several communications from SAS families in the hours after it was announced that the British had surrendered to the Argentines. The Regiment was prepared to confirm the identities of those men who were in the custody of the new owners of the Falkland Islands, which brought immense relief to all those waiting at home for news.

Missing in Action, however, was an entirely different problem, and no regiment liked to be drawn into these discussions. Thus the duty officers at Stirling Lines would say very little, except that the Regiment could confirm the surrender and confirm the SAS had knowledge of POWs, and was working to ensure everyone returned home safely. For those for whom there was no information whether friends and loved ones were dead or alive, they would confirm nothing, only stating they had no knowledge of the men losing their lives, and would try to keep everyone informed of future developments.

When Jane Jarvis of Newmarket called to inquire about her second cousin Douglas they said, with regret, that they were unable to confirm anything except to the next of kin. Then she rang Douglas's elder brother Alan, who had heard nothing. So she rang her other cousin, Diana Hunter, out in the lush grassland of Lexington, Kentucky.

1100 Monday 18 April
Hunter Valley Thoroughbred Farms

Mrs Rick Hunter was reading the latest issue of *The Bloodhorse*, scouring the results pages for winning sons and daughters of the Hunter Valley stallions. Rick himself was in bed upstairs having been up most of the night helping to foal a colossally expensive brood mare by the champion US sire A. P. Indy.

The mare, who in her day had won five Grade One stakes races at Belmont Park, New York, and Saratoga had experienced a long and arduous labour. But at six a.m. she had safely given birth to a dark bay colt by the superb Irish-based sire Choisir, a charging Australian-bred champion sprinter who had once heard the thunder of the crowd at Royal Ascot and Newmarket.

Diana had dressed, cooked Rick's breakfast, and taken a long walk through the paddocks to inspect the yearlings. She was now sitting in the high sunlit drawing room of the main house, with its views between the tall white Doric columns and out into the front paddocks where several million dollars' worth of brood mares and their foals grazed contentedly.

When the telephone rang, the former Diana Jarvis was delighted to hear from her cousin back home. The two of them chatted companionably for a few minutes, before Jane came to the point.

'Diana, I don't want to worry you unnecessarily, but I think you know Douglas was sent to the Falkland Islands several weeks ago. Well, I expect you know all about the British surrender . . . but I just called SAS headquarters at Hereford and they refused to confirm one way or another whether Douglas was dead or alive.

'In a sense that was good, but in another sense I thought it sounded a bit gloomy. They wouldn't tell me more because I'm not next of kin. But they'd probably tell *you* – so, I'm calling with the number.'

Diana's heart missed about seven beats. She had seen on the twenty-four-hour Fox News channel that the British had surrendered, and all she could remember was that 1,500 men were dead.

'Jane, is there any real suggestion the SAS men may actually have been killed?' she asked nervously.

'Absolutely not. But I read they have lists of the men who have been taken prisoner and, from what I can gather, Douglas is not on those lists.'

'Well, where do they think he might be?' asked Diana, her voice rising, panic beginning to well up inside her.

'They won't tell me, Di. But I thought you might want to call and see if you can find out anything.'

Diana wrote down the number and sat at the desk to the right of the French doors, her heart pounding, half with fear, half with shock. *Douglas, her beloved Douglas, he couldn't be dead, he couldn't be . . . nothing could be that cruel.*

The call went through quickly. Diana announced herself as Captain Douglas Jarvis's sister, his nearest relative, and she wished to speak to the commanding officer.

Two minutes later, Lt. Colonel Mike Weston was on the line. 'Diana,' he said, 'we met a couple of years ago, at Douglas's birthday dinner at the Rutland Hotel in Newmarket . . .'

No one ever forgot meeting the vivacious whip-slim horsewoman from Suffolk who rode with the maddest of the Irish foxhunters and was rumoured to have been pursued by at least three of the richest men in England.

'Of course I remember,' she half-lied, recalling vaguely a couple of very attractive cool-eyed SAS officers at the dinner, and guessing he must have been one of them. 'I was just enquiring about Douglas.'

'Well, of course it's good to hear from you, Diana. But you will appreciate this is a very highly classified operation and I am limited in what I can say. And I should state right away we do have an eight-man recce team led by Captain Jarvis which is currently listed as "missing in action".'

'Oh my God! Does that mean you think he's been killed?'

'No. Most certainly not. It means that his team almost certainly went to ground after the surrender was announced. Their names simply do not appear anywhere on the casualty lists of the dead and wounded or on any register of those reckoned to be still in hiding somewhere on the island. And they're not on the POW lists sent to us by the Argentine military.'

'Is that encouraging?'

'To the extent that none of their names appear anywhere, yes. If they'd been caught, killed, wounded or assumed to have escaped we would have a report to that effect. As it is, we have nothing.'

'If they are caught, will you be informed?'

'I cannot say that. It rather depends how badly the enemy wants them. But our soldiers are not usually captured by any enemy.'

'It's just that God-awful island, isn't it?' Diana said. 'There's no escape from it. I just can't bear the thought of Douglas dying in such a terrible place without anyone knowing what's happened to him.'

'Give me your number, Diana. I'll call you the moment I hear anything. And please, don't fall apart. Douglas has some of our best men with him, and no one's yet mentioned any of them might be dead.'

She gave the number of Hunter Valley Farms to the SAS chief, replaced the telephone, and raced upstairs to the bedroom, tears streaming down her cheeks.

She awakened Rick and blurted out, 'Ricky, the most terrible thing's happened. Douglas is trapped on the Falkland Islands. He's the leader of an SAS recce team, and he's listed as "missing in action".'

Rick, who had never told her any details of his own career in the US Navy SEALs, opened one eye, and in his deep Kentucky drawl murmured, 'Well, that's kinda bad luck on the Argentines. Those SAS guys are tough. Real tough. Glad I'm not looking for those suckers.'

Diana had no idea that five years previously her husband had led one of the most daring, bloody operations ever mounted by US Special Forces, smashing his way into a Chinese jail on a remote island off Hainan and liberating an entire US submarine crew. And she certainly had no idea how closely he had worked with the British SAS on that mission.

Rick Hunter knew all about the SAS, their skill, their brutal training, and the absolutely ruthless quality of their work. Now he smiled up at his wife, hoping to see a ray of humour cross her very beautiful, very worried face. But there was no such reaction. She simply collapsed into floods of tears and kept saying over and over,

'He can't be dead, he can't be dead. Please, please tell me he can't be dead.'

'Oh, I can tell you that, all right. If Douglas was dead, 22-SAS would know he was dead. They might not know if Douglas and his guys had killed a couple dozen Argies, which is a lot more likely. But they'd know if one of their commanders was dead. Hot damn, you can't kill those SAS guys, not if you don't have an atomic bomb handy. You can trust me on that.'

Diana forced herself to stop crying and after a moment she said quietly, 'I just hate the phrase "missing in action".'

Rick raised himself on one elbow and took her hand. 'Listen,' he said, 'you haven't followed this war as closely as I have. And so far the Brits have not admitted they even had Special Forces on the islands. Which means they had the guys in there real early, checking the place out, specially the enemy defences.

'Ninety per cent of the casualties were in the Royal Navy's warships. The rest on the landing beach. Now, we know Douglas was not in those ships. You don't take Special Forces 8,000 miles and then leave 'em on some kind of a cruise. You get 'em in there, into the islands.

'And Douglas would not have been on the beaches. The Brits leave all that amphibious work to the Special Boat Service, not the SAS. So wherever Dougy was, he wasn't on the beach. It's much more likely he and his guys are on the loose somewhere, and do not want to surrender despite the political situation.

'But they'll be armed to the teeth, and they're trained to live off the land, and from what I read there's several million sheep there. If I had to guess, I'd say Captain Jarvis was right now sitting with his feet up, in some cave in the mountains, eating roast lamb and reading the *Penguin News* or whatever the hell they call their local paper.'

Diana smiled through her tears. She loved her brother dearly, but this six foot, three inches ex-US Navy SEAL had completely taken over her life since the day she had first met him.

She had been watching the yearlings being auctioned at one of the big sales in Kentucky. A superbly bred chestnut colt, sired by a local stallion, was walking gingerly around the ring, tossing his head and glaring through an unmistakable white-rimmed eye, displaying front legs which, if they ever got him to a racecourse, would be like an equine Lourdes miracle – or at least a Charlestown, Virginia one.

After a few minutes, the colt was knocked down to an agent from the East Coast for $154,000. Diana shook her head, and the big man leaning casually on the balustrade next to her muttered laconically, 'Sold to the man with the white stick, guide dog and very dark glasses.'

She could not help laughing. Turning to the towering American, she offered a cheerful conspiratorial glance, which racehorse people do when they have witnessed another practitioner of their craft make a blunder well on the absurd side of dumb.

'That was hard to believe,' said the master of Hunter Valley Farms quietly. 'Son of a bitch could hardly walk, never mind run.'

'I suppose they thought he might straighten up and run a halfway decent mile for some trainer when he's three or something,' said Diana. 'He's bred to run.'

'Since he won't walk around the goddamned sales ring for his owner, beats me why anyone thinks he might run a mile for someone else. Still, guess he might make up into a useful nine-year-old . . . pulling a very light plough.'

Again, Diana Jarvis burst into laughter, staring into the smiling face of the former Commander Rick Hunter, who grinned his lop-sided grin and inquired, 'English?'

'Yes,' she said, holding out her hand. 'Diana Jarvis.'

'Any relation to the immortal Sir Jack?'

'He was my great-great uncle,' she said. 'But don't think I'm important. I have about 2,000 Jarvis relatives in Newmarket alone. We didn't just breed horses, you know.'

Rick chuckled, and said, 'I'm just going out to take a look at a filly my dad likes. Well, he likes the pedigree. We had a couple of very nice brood mares from the same family. This filly's by an English-raced stallion standing in Ireland, but the bottom line's all American, same family as Alydar. Want to come?'

'Yes,' said Diana. 'Thank you. Where's she stabled – does your dad breed right here in Kentucky?'

'Oh, sorry,' he replied. 'Kinda forgetting my manners . . . Rick Hunter – we own Hunter Valley Farms out along the Versailles Pike.'

'Hunter Valley! That's your family's place?'

'Sure is. My daddy's really retired now and I run the place with my good buddy Dan Headley, third-generation stallion man. We're selling tomorrow, but we're usually on the lookout for one new filly with a good pedigree who might make a brood mare later.'

'Well, I'm very glad to meet you,' said Diana Jarvis. 'Might even buy one of your yearlings for my French owner.'

'You mean he owns you . . . or a racehorse operation, or both?'
. Diana laughed. 'Not me, mostly because he's seventy-six years old
and has been married four times. But he has some very nice horses in
training in Chantilly. And he'd like to start a breeding farm.'

'And he's hired a very beautiful young Jarvis to carry him
forward,' said Rick, smiling. 'Come on, let's go see that filly . . .'

And so they had strolled out to see the baby racehorse and then
had gone for a cup of coffee, then, later, lunch, then, much later,
dinner. They talked on the phone and met at the autumn sales in
England and Ireland.

They never did announce an engagement. They just decided to
get married. Diana was thirty, Rick thirty-eight And they were
both completely in tune with the rhythms and the ebb and the flow
of the thoroughbred racing season. They were students of the form
book, experts on pedigrees, both with a keen eye for the
conformation of both young and mature horses. Rick Hunter could
scarcely believe his luck.

He did not often see her upset and he hated to see it now. But he
understood how close she and Douglas had been, and he knew how
unnerving it was to be uncertain whether a close relative was dead
or alive.

He climbed out of bed, and took her in his arms. 'Don't worry,'
he said. 'I'll make a couple of calls and see what I can find out. I'm
coming downstairs in a minute. Let's have a cup of coffee . . . give
me ten.'

When Rick reached the kitchen, he could see she was still hugely
upset. She poured the coffee and managed to spill some of it on the
table, just as Dan Headley poked his head around the door, saying,
'Hi, Rick. That Storm Cat mare just foaled, thank Christ. Colt, dark
bay, white blaze like his dad. He's standing – hey, Di, what's up? He
been beating you up again?'

All three of them laughed at this. Rick, the iron-man gentle
giant, who had been known to weep at the death of a favourite
Labrador, said, 'Di's just a bit upset because her brother's been
posted missing in action in the Falklands. But no one's saying he's
been killed or wounded, which normally means he hasn't.'

'That's Doug, right? The SAS Captain?'

'That's him, Dan. Tell her he's probably OK.'

'Well, Di, those Special Forces regiments keep very strong tabs
on their guys. I'd say if anything had happened they'd sure as hell
know. How many guys are with him?'

'Seven troopers, all veterans. None of them on the POW lists, or the killed and wounded lists.'

'SAS?' said Dan Headley. 'They're on the run. And now the Brits have surrendered, I wouldn't worry yourself. Chances are the Argentines won't catch 'em anyway. Hey . . . remember that Special Forces helicopter which crashed in the Magellan Strait in the last Falklands War? There were six or eight SAS guys in it, and they all just vanished. But every one of 'em got back to Hereford. Christ knows how. I just read a book about it.'

Diana was marginally consoled, and she felt better after speaking to these two former US Navy warriors. But she still asked her husband to make a phone call to anyone who might be able to reach Douglas.

0830 (local time) same day. SPECWARCOM HQ
Coronado, San Diego

It was a pressure day for Rear Admiral John Bergstrom, Commander Special War Command – Emperor SEAL, as it were – lord of the most feared fighting force in all the US armed services.

His old friend Admiral Arnold Morgan had been on the line at 0700 checking that he would be able to fly immediately to Washington – there was a general buzz around the SEALS California base that the US government was likely to intervene in the Great Britain-Argentina negotiations over the Falkland Islands. However, his new wife Louisa-May wanted him to attend a performance by the Bolshoi Ballet in Los Angeles this evening.

At 0845 his private line rang again. Arnold Morgan was calling from the White House where he was ensconced with the President.

'I don't know why the hell they don't just make you President and be done with it,' said the SEAL boss.

'Out of the question,' replied Arnold. 'I'm just helping out. Remember, I'm officially retired.'

'Sounds like it,' said Admiral Bergstrom. 'Peaceful days in your twilight years. This is your second call this morning. I guess you're planning to start a war somewhere.'

'Well, only in the most limited possible way.'

'Don't tell me. It's the Falklands, right? The US government cannot afford to let this bunch of Argentine cowboys rampage all over someone else's legal territory.'

239

'Well,' said Arnold, disliking the idea of being second-guessed by the suave and shortly-to-retire SEAL chief. 'I'll just say you're kinda on the right lines.'

'And what would you and the President like me to do? Send in a couple dozen guys and chase 'em back to Buenos Aires or wherever the hell they live?'

'Again, John, I'd say you were on the right lines. But both the President and I would like you to come in and have a private visit with us here in the Oval Office.'

'Tomorrow OK?'

'*Tomorrow?*' roared Arnold. 'This afternoon would be pretty damn late . . .'

'OK, OK. I'll leave now. Take off in one hour which will get me into Andrews at 1750.'

'Thanks, John. We'll have the helo waiting at Andrews. See you at 1800.'

'Bye, Arnold.'

'Jesus Christ,' said Rear Admiral Bergstrom, picking up the phone to dial his soon-to-be-furious new wife. But before he could do so, his private line rang again. Not many people had that number, so he always answered.

'Admiral, this is a voice from the past – Rick Hunter from Lexington, Kentucky.'

'*Hey, Commander Hunter!*' Despite the hurry, John Bergstrom was genuinely pleased to be talking to the best Team Leader he had ever had, a combat SEAL who had carried out three awe-inspiring demolition missions – one in the heart of Russia, another way behind the lines in Red China, and one in the middle of a brand new Chinese naval operational base in the steamy jungles of south-eastern Burma, or Myanmar, or whatever the damn place was now called.

'Now this is an unexpected pleasure,' said Admiral Bergstrom. 'I often think about you, Ricky. For a lot of years I believed it would probably be you taking over the helm when I finally vacated this chair.'

'Can't say I haven't missed it. Just guess I didn't feel quite the same after they court-martialled Dan Headley.'

'No, I understood then, and like a lot of other people I still understand. It was a source of the greatest regret to me that Lt. Commander Headley was driven out, and you went with him . . .'

'Sure. But life goes on. Dan's fine now. He and I run my family's

240

thoroughbred farm, Hunter Valley out here in the Blue Grass. We still have some fun.'

'Fun like you had when you worked for me?'

'No, sir. Not that much.'

John Bergstrom chuckled. 'Ever thought about coming back?'

'Not more than about twice a day.'

Both men were silent, as the tragedy of the past seemed to sweep over them. 'You were the best, Ricky. The best I ever saw . . .'

'Thank you, sir.'

'Now, perhaps you'd better tell me what you wanted from me?'

'Sir, a year ago I married an English girl, Diana Jarvis. Her brother Douglas is a Captain in 22-SAS. I've only met him twice, but he's a real good guy, an ex-para, won a Military Cross in Iraq.

'And right now he's somehow trapped on the Falkland Islands with his troop. Listed as "missing in action". I was wondering whether you could find out anything for us . . . Diana was very close to him and she's completely distraught. Thinks he might be dead.'

'Jesus, Rick. I'm leaving for Washington in the next five minutes. But I'll do what I can, and I'll get back to you tomorrow – I know the CO at Hereford pretty well . . . Captain Douglas Jarvis, right? Gimme your number . . .'

Ten minutes later, with the words of another distraught wife still ringing in his ears, Admiral Bergstrom was on his way out of the office, having escaped the rigours of Tchaikovsky's *Swan Lake*.

Thirty minutes after that he was hurtling down the NAS runway on North Island, San Diego, headed east in a US Navy Lockheed EP-3E Aries, non-stop to Andrews Air Base, Washington. He had dismissed Louisa-May and Pyotz Tchaikovsky temporarily from his mind.

But the memory of Rick Hunter lingered in the mind of the Coronado boss. *He was the toughest, strongest, steadiest SEAL leader I ever knew. Brilliant marksman, deadly, and fearless in both armed and unarmed combat, could probably swim the Pacific, and expert with high explosive. He must be nearly forty now, but I never met one that good in all my years with the SEALs. Shame about his brother-in-law.*

They rustled up a couple of ham and cheese sandwiches during the flight, and there was coffee supplied by one of his assistants, Petty Officer Riff 'Rattlesnake' Davies, an assault-team machine-gunner by trade, wounded with Commander Hunter on that last mission in Burma.

The five-hour journey dragged by. The admiral and Rattlesnake swapped yarns, mostly about the newly surfaced Commander Hunter. 'I guess you'll never know how brave he was,' said Davies. 'Jesus, when we came under fire in that boat from those Chinese helicopters I thought we'd never get out alive.'

'And there was Commander Hunter, almost unconscious in the boat, blood pumping from a major wound in his thigh, still blasting away with a machine gun, yelling orders at the rest of us . . . I never saw courage like that.'

'I know, Riff. Don't think I don't know.'

They landed on time, and the US Marine helicopter flew them directly to the White House lawn. Three minutes later Admiral Bergstrom entered the Oval Office and shook hands with the President and Admiral Morgan, who glanced at his watch and observed that it was two minutes and thirty-seven seconds past 1800, which made the SEAL chief from California late. Marginally. Nonetheless Arnold couldn't understand what was happening around here. *Nearly three minutes late for the Last Dogwatch! Jesus, standards are sure as hell slipping.*

All three men in the Oval Office had served in the US Navy, and Arnold's insistence on charting the time of day in strictly naval warship terms unfailingly made the President laugh. Which was just as well. Right now he did not have a whole lot to laugh about, since the top execs at Exxon Mobil were growing angrier by the day, complaining that 'these goddamned gauchos have somehow run off with about two billion dollars' worth of our oil and gas, and no one seems to be doing a damn thing about it.'

President Bedford could see their point. And it was a source of immense relief to him that his two guests were probably the only two men in all the United States who could do a damn thing about it. And, better yet, they were apparently ready to do so.

'Gentlemen,' he said, 'I'm glad to see you both. And I should say, right away, that this Falklands problem has been extremely difficult for me, for all the obvious reasons. Arnold is the only person with a really solid plan. And I think he should outline it for us both . . . I'll send for some coffee . . .'

'John,' Arnold began, 'you know the problem we have sending our armed services to fight someone else's war. The President does not want to do it, and I agree with him. However we have another problem damn nearly as big. Exxon Mobil think we have sat back and passively allowed the Argentines to run off with their very expensive oil and gas.'

'Yeah, I've been following it,' said Admiral Bergstrom. 'And I've been wondering what was going to happen. You want my guys to go in and blow the place up?'

John Bergstrom was a droll man, with a sardonic sense of humour that was a common virtue in his line of work. Nevertheless neither Arnold Morgan nor the President of the United States ever quite knew whether he was entirely joking.

The President laughed. Nervously. 'Go on, Arnold,' he said.

Arnold grinned too. But he remained serious. 'In order to get them to back down, we gotta first of all frighten them, then move in as the great conciliators. We need to be seen as the voice of reason, and we have to get that oil and gas back on the road.

'In broad terms, we want a deal where the Brits volunteer to give up their sovereignty in twenty-four months, in return for British Petroleum being allowed back in there with Exxon Mobil.

'But right now we have reason to believe the Argentines plan to hand that oil project over to the Russians and we cannot allow that. So we need to persuade Buenos Aires that unless they come to heel they will lose everything. And we gotta do that without the world knowing how hard we are putting the arm on them.'

'Will the Argentines realise how hard we're putting the arm on them?' asked Admiral Bergstrom.

'Yes, but they will not be able to prove it's us. I am proposing we launch a series of highly classified assaults on their military hardware – fighter aircraft, warships, missile launchers.'

'Lemme have a sip of coffee, Mr President,' said Admiral Bergstrom. 'I just realised what I'm doing here, and I'm trying not to go into shock.'

'You're here, John,' said Arnold, 'to tell us whether your guys could go into the islands, take out the very few warships patrolling those waters, and then get rid of all the fighter aircraft stationed at Mount Pleasant and that other airfield of theirs on Pebble Island.'

'You mean, presumably, quietly and without getting caught?'

'Correct. I mean to put the Argentines in a position where they know they are being badly knocked about militarily but do not wish to admit it, and will finally agree to negotiate – for both the territory and the oil and gas . . . I have a hunch the Brits will be happy to get out with a little pride and their share of the oil.'

'Anyone given any thought how my guys get in there?'

'Not really,' said Arnold. 'But obviously it can't be by air – we can't risk a parachute drop. So that means by sea, and since we can't send in a warship that means a submarine, I guess.'

'Uh-huh,' said John Bergstrom. 'Any idea how many guys this will take?'

'Not really. Would you think maybe two teams of sixteen?'

'That's not many – not to take out all the fighter jets on two airfields, not when you consider the recce.'

'No, it's not. But my first question is, John, can it be done?'

'Sure it can be done. My guys are specialists. They can do it, and they won't get caught. I would have just one request, and that's for you to arrange an immediate evacuation by air, if somehow they get cornered. I want to help, and I will conduct the operation, but I'm not sending the guys into the goddamned *Malvinas* on a suicide mission.'

Arnold Morgan knew Admiral Bergstrom was about to retire, and he smirked at the SEAL chief. 'I don't want to give you a chapter for your book,' he said. 'We're seeing the Chilean ambassador right here early tomorrow morning. We'll have an evacuation plan. First sign of serious trouble, the guys are out of there, direct to the Magellan Strait, land at Punta Arenas on the Chilean side.'

'Since we can't get a fixed-wing transporter in there, Arnie, guess you're talking helicopters?'

'Just one, John. We'll use one of the navy's new Sikorsky Super-Stallions, the CH-53E, holds fifty-five marines. We'll bring it in under fighter escort, and immediately out again. She's fast, and she's armed with three heavy machine guns. Flies above 18,000 feet. We'll be fine, specially if your guys have achieved even half their objectives.'

'Any thoughts how we get the guys in there?'

'The final part of the insert will definitely be by submarine and inflatables. And we do have an LA Class boat on the way down there. But we need to move fast. And I know you'll want a few days' training for the SEAL teams. We can't really afford another two-week journey after that – you think we could make a drop landing at sea?'

'The Brits did it last time off South Georgia,' replied Admiral Bergstrom. 'Which means we could do it. Just don't want to get too near the Falklands coast and wind up on the goddamned Argentine radar.'

'No. We *definitely* don't want to do that,' said Arnold. 'But we do have a time problem. The longer we leave this, the better organised the Argentine defences will be. So we'll leave it to you to move quickly.'

'Oh, Arnie. One thing more. To conduct an operation like this we're going to need kit, especially bombs – sticky bombs and C-4, that is. We'll need enough gear and food to let them live off the land, but they can't carry it all – not with a parachute drop into the ocean.'

'No. I was talking to the President about that. I think we'll go for HALO and drop some stuff in, soon as they pick a safe landing area.'

'OK. That'll work.'

'One other thing, John. Who's gonna lead this thing? We need a very special guy, an experienced veteran commander who won't make mistakes.'

'My guys don't make mistakes, Arnie.'

'I know they don't. But this operation is very sensitive. It's got to be carried out by ghosts. By a Ghost Force. Ghosts with hammers in their hands.'

Admiral Bergstrom turned to the President. 'I can't believe it, sir. We're being briefed by a poet.'

Paul Bedford chuckled.

'Do you have any thoughts about a team leader?' asked Arnie.

'I've got one thought. I know who I'd like. But I can't get him. He retired a while ago. Still, we got a couple of pretty good instructors who've been on missions. I'll probably recall one of them.'

'OK, we'll leave it to you . . . but just out of curiosity, who was your first choice?'

'I can't really say. He left the navy in rather controversial circumstances.'

'Oh, did he, now?' asked Arnold Morgan, slyly. 'Wouldn't be running a racehorse farm, would he? Not the great Commander Rick Hunter?'

'I wish,' said Admiral Bergstrom.

1930 Tuesday 19 April
Hunter Valley Farms

Rick and Diana were checking the stallion covering lists. There was a busy night ahead for three of the youngest sires, and big horse-vans were already lining up in the lower driveway, bringing in wildly expensive blue-blooded mares from local farms.

At the same time there were six mares who had been in residence for several weeks who were expected to foal tonight.

Rick and Diana usually had dinner at around eight o'clock, and then pulled on their jackets to tour what Rick called the Springtime Battleground, where the fortunes of the farm for another year were more or less decided.

Rick, who was once described as the fittest man who ever wore sea boots, had just completed two hours in the gym he had built in the basement of the house. He worked out there four evenings a week and ran a hard five miles on the other three days. When he had left the navy three and a half years ago he had vowed to remain at the peak of his fitness for as long as possible. Thus far he had never faltered.

He and Diana often rode out around the farm together and they were both used to long walks through the paddocks, looking at various yearlings and mares. But today had been trying. Diana was still upset about Douglas, and had not wanted to venture out despite the invention of mobile phones. Her husband had to restrain her from calling Hereford again and again.

'Leave it,' he advised her. 'The SAS CO will call when he hears something and Admiral Bergstrom will definitely be speaking to them. He promised.'

But Diana could not be comforted. The only thing she could think of was Douglas, dead on some frozen landscape in the South Atlantic. Soldier unknown.

When the phone finally rang at 19:41, she almost jumped out of the chair. Admiral Bergstrom for Rick Hunter.

'Good evening, admiral,' said the ex-SEAL commander. 'Any news?'

'Yes, I've spoken to Mike Weston in Hereford and he says they are sure that Douglas and his team are still alive. Otherwise the Argentines would have included them on the lists of the dead. Hereford HQ believes they have declined to surrender, because their mission was highly destructive – according to Colonel Weston, it was the only big hit the Argies took on the Falkland mainland.'

'Jesus. You mean they're on the run, through those mountains, trying to get off the island?'

'I do. And don't mention this to your wife in so many words, but Mike Weston did point out that the Argentines might very well be after them in a determined way.'

'That's less good news,' replied Rick, who'd had the same thought already.

'It is, but Weston said it would have to be a helluva good soldier who managed to kill one of *that* group. Apparently Doug Jarvis and his seven trained killers are what you might call state of the art. Hereford say they're not worried and expect to hear something positive any day.'

'Well, that's a relief, admiral. I guess the only problem is what kind of numbers the Argentines can throw into a hunt, right?'

'That, Ricky, is the problem,' the admiral agreed. 'There's not many of them, and they may be up against a determined enemy.'

'I guess right now there're no plans to go in and try to save them?'

'Well, certainly not from the Brits. But I think we may have to do something to help – the Argentines have, after all, stolen all that Exxon Mobil oil and gas. You wouldn't consider giving us a hand, would you?'

'Who, me?' Rick was stunned for a second but rallied quickly. 'What do you mean?'

'Well, Rick, I won't pretend we've ever really replaced you, because we haven't. And everyone was real sorry when you resigned your commission, although we understood. I just wondered if you'd consider helping us save your brother-in-law.'

There was a brief moment of silence. Then Rick spoke.

'Jeez. That's one hell of a question.'

'Wanna talk about it?'

'Well, sure, you're welcome to see us any time.'

'How about tomorrow?'

Slightly thrown by the speed of things, Rick tried to think quickly. Middle of foaling season, but fine.

'OK. What time?

'I could leave around six a.m. Get in there around four hours later – 1300 for you.'

'Fine. I'll meet you. Blue Grass Field, Lexington. US Navy jet, right?'

'I'm gonna be there, Rick. See you tomorrow.'

Diana, who had been hovering anxiously on the other side of the room, said, 'Who's coming?'

'Admiral Bergstrom. You'll like him. He's head of the US Navy's Special Forces.'

'Has he found Douglas?'

'No, but he's on the trail. The SAS are certain he's not dead. And

John Bergstrom is working on a plan to get them all out. The Brits can't do much at this stage.'

'But what does this have to do with you? And why is he coming here?'

Rick paused for a moment.

'Wants to talk to me about it. He and I worked on several missions together.'

Diana couldn't quite get her head around it all. She was still worried for Douglas.

'But you've retired from the navy and all that stuff.'

'Kinda hard to replace a top man,' said Rick, grinning.

1300 (local time) Wednesday 20 April
Blue Grass Field, Lexington

Rick Hunter was not tired, which was surprising since he had hardly slept all night. Twice he had been up and out to the covering shed where a young stallion was not only playing hell but, much worse, refusing to cover a mare, a service for which the farm was charging $150,000.

A couple of the more youthful stallion men were about to give up when the boss arrived. 'I know he's difficult,' Rick had told them, 'But, unlike any of you, that stallion often earns $300,000 a night . . . I don't care if he demands a candlelit dinner, a string quartet and a bottle of Chateau Latour for him and the mare . . . *IF HE DOES, THEN GO GET IT FOR HIM, HEAR ME!* But get that mare covered.'

Rick spent the remainder of the night thinking about his life as a US Navy SEAL – the training, the stealth, the terrible danger, the attacks, the supreme fitness, the camaraderie. *My God, what days they were – could I still do it? Just one more time? Was John Bergstrom joking when he asked me? Christ, guess I'll find out before too long.*

Now, standing on the airfield, he could see the Lockheed Aries at the horizon. The airport was quiet and he watched the US Navy aircraft come screaming out of the west, over some of the most famous thoroughbred racehorse pastures on earth. It flared out when it reached the runway and touched down gracefully. The pilot had, after all, spent a lot of his working life landing on aircraft carriers. Blue Grass Field was a lot more steady.

Five minutes later Rick was shaking hands with his old boss, Rear Admiral John Bergstrom, head of SPECWARCOM, who walked through the airport in civilian clothes, like just any other visiting horse-breeder.

They exchanged the warmest greetings, a thousand memories surging through them both. And by the time they had driven back to Hunter Valley it was more than clear that the Admiral did indeed want Rick to be part of a secret Falkland mission, bailing out the islands for both the Brits and the oil companies.

He also had the distinct impression that the temporary loss of Douglas Jarvis was precisely the kind of motive the Admiral had needed to try and persuade him to join the mission.

Before they entered the house, Rick held back the admiral, deciding to ask the big question. 'Sir,' he said, 'are you going to ask me to join you in the back room and help plan the assault?'

The admiral hesitated. 'Not quite.'

'You mean you want me to join the guys on the mission, and do whatever we need to get those Argentines into line, and the SAS out of there?'

'Rick, I want you to command it,' the admiral finally said.

'*What?*' Rick replied, stunned at the magnitude of the request. 'But I'm not even in the navy.'

'As an ex-SEAL commander, you could be back in by this evening. Guys like you have special rules in Coronado. I am perfectly empowered, any time I wish, to re-recruit one of my best men for a specific mission. Particularly someone with a record like yours.'

'Sir, you realise I would have to decline this out of hand were it not for the – er – complication of Diana's brother?'

Despite the gravity of the situation, the admiral was rather enjoying Rick's surprise. Rick Hunter, however, was frozen to the spot with apprehension and excitement. Every instinct told him this was nuts, that he could not leave the farm at this time of the year, he could not just pack up and go on some diabolically dangerous mission with the SEALs, and perhaps get himself killed.

And yet . . . and yet . . . the thrill of combat, the overpowering sensation of working with top guys against an almost certainly inferior enemy. Oh boy, how often had he dreamed of it these past years, tasted it, remembered the desperation, the fear and the triumph, and the friendship and the laughter. Hell, he thought, once a SEAL always a SEAL.

He thought of his Trident, his own personal badge of courage, tucked in the shirt drawer. The little badge he still polished when the mood took him. He thought of the work underwater, the rush of adrenalin when he and his boys had blown up two warships in Burma. And what about that power station they'd knocked down, and the getaway, under Chinese fire? Jesus Christ, he'd remember that day till he died.

John Bergstrom was smiling, as if he knew exactly what was going through the mind of his finest-ever SEAL. 'Nothing like it, old buddy, is there? Nothing quite like it.'

'No, sir. There's not. How long?'

'A few days' training. Then two weeks max, in and out.'

'How do we get in?'

'Submarine, then inflatables to the beach.'

'Sir, it's gonna take a submarine two weeks to get down there. How come you're saying two weeks start to finish?'

'You'll fly down, and join the submarine.'

'Where?'

'In the middle of the ocean. We're planning a drop zone in the Atlantic a hundred miles north of the Falklands.'

'Jesus, sir. I've never gone in by parachute.'

'I know. That's what the three days' training are for. You know the rest better than I do.'

Just then, Diana came out of the house and made her way over to the dark green four-wheel drive off-road vehicle which bore the logo of Hunter Valley Thoroughbreds.

'I'm sure this spot is nice and private,' she said smiling. 'But you might be more comfortable inside. I've made you some coffee and there's some lunch when you're ready.'

She looked beautiful in tight jodhpurs and boots, with a white shirt and light blue cashmere sweater.

She held out her hand to Admiral Bergstrom and cast him one of those half-smiles which had bewitched some of the wealthiest men in England. 'Afternoon, admiral,' she said. 'I've heard a lot about you. All of it good.'

'Diana,' he replied, 'so far, I'd say you make a perfect wife for the best commander I ever served with.'

'I'm trying my best,' she said. 'As a foreigner.'

'People from New York are regarded as foreigners around here,' Rick chimed in. 'Folk from Newmarket, like Diana, are more or less regarded as natives.'

'I'm doubly impressed,' said the admiral, smiling. 'Beauty and background – the unstoppable combination.'

The three of them walked back to the house together, and it was the admiral who brought up the subject of the missing Douglas Jarvis. 'I'm really very sorry to hear about this, Diana,' he said. 'But the good news is that Hereford has a much clearer picture now.

'It seems that Douglas and his team carried out the demolition part of their mission a short while before the Royal Navy and the British landing force surrendered to the Argentines. He was apparently operating in a remote part of East Falkland and was out of touch with his command centre in the aircraft carrier for a few days. The carrier was then sunk.

'So while the free world reeled at the British surrender, Douglas and his men were stuck up the side of some mountain, with only a vague idea of what had just happened. In Hereford's opinion, they are keeping their heads down, since they were apparently the only group which did manage to inflict serious damage on the enemy. Under those circumstances no Special Forces commander wants to surrender.'

'So the SAS are more or less certain they're not dead?' asked Diana, her face showing both worry and hope.

'Oh, no one thinks they're dead,' the admiral reassured her. 'It's just a matter of getting them out.'

'But who will get them out now the British have surrendered?'

'I'm afraid that will have to be us, Diana. The US had some serious oil and gas interests in those islands and no one's very thrilled the Argentines have seen fit to grab it all.'

Diana had really warmed to the SEAL chief and his calming words. But what could he possibly be doing, here in the middle of Kentucky, in the middle of the foaling season, having arrived in a private US Navy jet to speak to her long-retired husband? A tiny warning bell was going off in her head.

Long used to making firm decisions about the purchase of racehorses which cost hundreds of thousands of dollars, Diana Hunter decided on a direct approach. She went into the kitchen and collected a tray bearing a large, engraved silver coffee pot, a breeder's prize that Rick's father Bart had been awarded after a Hunter Valley-bred colt had won the Travers Stakes at Saratoga.

There was a fine framed oil painting of the colt on the wall behind the admiral. And out beyond the west-facing portico, in the stallion barns, the same hard-knocking racehorse was trying to make a name for himself in the less strenuous career bestowed only upon those who could *really* run.

'Admiral,' Diana said as she poured the coffee, 'why have you come to see us? What do you want Rick to do for you?'

John Bergstrom knew that to hedge or evade would be absolutely fatal. This very smart English girl would pick up those vibes in a split second. 'Diana, I want him to come to Coronado with me and help with this mission.

'Rick has a vested interest. He wants success as much as I do. Partly for me, for old time's sake, but mostly for you. He wants to get Douglas out of there, and my command has the people, the back-up and the necessary power to achieve that.'

He smiled at her and added, 'By the way, I have not really asked him yet to give me a definite yes or no. Perhaps you'd like to do that for me.'

Diana Hunter was so taken by surprise she had to sit down. But before she could gather herself to speak, John Bergstrom added, 'If Rick accepts, we'll get Douglas out. If he declines, I *hope* we'll get Douglas out. That's the difference.

'You're married to a Special Forces commander who's one of the best there's ever been. They didn't give him that Distinguished Service Cross for nothing.'

Lamely, Diana asked, 'What Distinguished Service Cross?'

'It's the second-highest decoration in the United States armed services, right up there with the Medal of Honor. Rick has it, bestowed upon him by the President. I don't just want him, Diana, I need him – and so, in a way, do you.'

'Rick,' said his wife, 'do you want to go? Do you think you *ought* to go?'

'How can I not go?' said the big ex-SEAL team leader, suppressing his personal excitement for the moment. 'How could I live with myself if Douglas died? I'd always think I could have saved him. And so would you.'

'But what about the farm? We're so busy.'

'Dad will come back to work for three weeks. He and Dan could manage. If necessary Dan's father would step in. Hunter Valley and its staff would cope, like they always have. And anyway, I'd rather lose a couple of foals than Douglas – wouldn't you?'

Diana did not answer. But she turned again to Admiral Bergstrom. 'Do you mind if I call you John?' she said.

'Not a bit.'

'Then, John, will you please tell me how dangerous this all is?'

'It's like everything. The better you plan, the more you think about the problems and the solutions, the greater your chances of success. Frankly, I am not too bothered about my guys getting killed by the Argentines, because it won't happen. They'll have a ton of back-up, by air and, if necessary, by sea.

'If it came to a choice between flattening Argentina's Mount Pleasant garrison and everyone in it, or losing my guys in battle, there's only one answer to that: "Goodbye, Mount Pleasant." This is a mission where we must be careful, but it's not nearly so dangerous as the last three operations Rick commanded.'

'What a horrible catch-22,' said Diana. 'If I object, and Douglas dies, it's true, I'll always think it was my fault for stopping Rick going in to save him. But what if I lost them both? What if neither of them came back? I would never forgive myself for letting him go . . .'

'Di,' said Rick, 'we've got to try. I can't just sit here and do nothing, when I have the commander of SPECWARCOM sitting right here damn nearly begging me to lead this mission. I think all three of us in the room understand that – especially you, Di. Now tell me, do I go with your blessing?'

'Yes, Rick, you must go with my blessing. But God help you both.'

Commander Hunter turned then to face his CO. 'Sir, you must ask me formally.'

'I understand,' said Admiral Bergstrom. 'And I will do so. Will you, Rick Hunter, accept a new commission in the US Navy, and, with all the privileges and responsibilities of your former rank of Commander, lead the US Navy SEALs in the forthcoming operation to the Falkland Islands?'

'Affirmative, sir.'

1500 Thursday 21 April
SPECWARCOM HQ Coronado

'Hello, Admiral Morgan? Hi, John Bergstrom here. Just wanted to tell you Commander Hunter has agreed to return to the navy for one single mission and lead the operation to the Falkland Islands.'

'Has he really? Wow, that's terrific, John. Well done. Silver-tongued bastard.' The admiral rarely bestowed such effusive praise, so this was an honour of the highest grade.

'Wasn't much trouble, Arnie. He misses it all like hell.'

'Don't we all? Where is he now?'

'He's right here, and still as fit as anyone on the station. He slotted right in, just like he never left. Some of the guys who'll go with him still remember him pretty well. Some of 'em are still in awe.' Bergstrom sounded pleased and Arnold Morgan agreed.

'So am I, John. How the hell he ever got out of that mess in Burma, I guess we'll never know. By the way, how does he feel about the air drop into the ocean?'

'I'll tell you later. He's just starting a two-day airborne course right now.'

'You worked out an assault landing plan yet?' Morgan wanted to know.

'Sure have. The guys move out of the submarine and straight onto Pebble Island. They fix bombs to every one of the fifteen fighter aircraft on the ground, with six-hour delayed fuses. Then they get out, by boat, back to East Falkland. That way they make the Argies concentrate their search forces up there in the wrong place. Go in with a bang. Immediately get 'em off balance.'

'Commander Hunter OK with that?'

'It was Commander Hunter's plan.'

CHAPTER 10

1500 Thursday 21 April
Naval Air Station
North Island, San Diego

Rick Hunter gazed up at the scaffold from which he was going to jump in just a few moments. It looked high – thirty feet to the platform.

There was a slight knot in the veteran commander's stomach. Standing here in this huge aircraft hangar, waiting his turn, was not much short of an ordeal.

Most of his younger colleagues were already experts, having completed the compulsory course at the new SEALs airborne training facility – regarded since 2009 as essential for modern Special Forces. But Rick had never done any parachuting, mostly because, as the most powerful swimmer on the base, he'd been too busy underwater.

And now the instructors were getting ready to begin the first jump.

'OK, sir, come on up.'

Rick walked to the iron ladder and began to climb. At the top he stepped onto the platform and looked over the edge.

'Jesus Christ,' he muttered. 'It looks damned high.'

By now they were buckling the harness around him and checking the line which was attached to the big fan. 'OK, sir,' snapped the dispatcher. 'All set. You're going to do about half a dozen of these, so let's get the first one over. It's dead easy – just step to the edge and jump out when I say "Go".'

Rick stepped. 'GO!' yelled the instructor, slapping him on the shoulder. And against all his better judgement Rick leaped into space, falling down dead straight until the fan up above whirred and then slowed him right down, ten feet from the ground. He never even fell over when he landed.

Another instructor moved over to unbuckle him. 'Knees together . . . feet together for the landing,' he snapped. 'Remember, sir, that's what we're doing. practising landings.' Rick was so pleased to be on the ground, alive, he actually smiled.

By the end of the afternoon, he was more or less jump-perfect and scheduled to face The Tower, which was more than twice as tall as the scaffold.

From the bottom it looked high and flimsy, and Rick stared straight up the iron ladder. The instructor said, 'OK, commander, up you go. And don't worry about this, it's a cinch.' But halfway up the ladder Rick made the mistake of looking down. He had to admit he was scared shitless.

'Look up, sir – keep looking up . . .'

He heard the voice, pressed on, and reached the platform.

'OK, sir. Harness on, all set – now remember what we're doing. We're practising the exit from the aircraft, the flight drill, and the ocean-landing drill. Now, get your lead foot firmly on the step, left arm at forty-five degrees. Hold on to the scaffold there, sir. Now, right arm across the reserve 'chute – that's it.'

Rick looked down, and he might as well have been on top of the Empire State Building. The people down below actually looked smaller.

'Right, sir. Nice firm step . . . jump clear – and GO!'

Rick closed his eyes and went, forcing himself once more into space.

'That's good, sir. Nice and strong, then the landing position as we lower you down . . . that's very nice, sir. Keep looking around, eyes up, then down – don't want you crashing into the guy below you, OK?'

The high fan whirred and 'bit', slowing the jumper right down, 'Looks good . . . very nice . . .' called the instructor on the ground as Rick landed gently. 'Three more of those and you'll be ready for the balloon.'

So at 0700 the following morning, Friday, Rick found himself staring up at an enormous balloon anchored in the sky, thirty feet above the ground. Way below it, at the bottom of the cable, was a flimsy-looking metal cage, big enough to hold six people.

Rick, the lone pupil, was guided in by the dispatcher. The single bar which served as a door was slammed across, and, on the signal, the cage began to move upwards with the balloon, its cable being slowly released, unwound from a winch truck.

'You'll feel it tilt all the way up there,' said the instructor. 'When it clicks off at the top, the angle will change and we'll level out at 800 feet. That's when we've arrived.'

For the first time, Rick debated with himself whether he shouldn't simply surrender. He was struck dumb by fear but he forced himself to control that. Through the low metal-grid rails he could see the ground slipping away beneath him, the cage shuddering and swaying as the balloon rose to the dropping height.

The master of Hunter Valley was not enjoying this. Up and up they swayed, the rising wind now whining through the bars of the cage. Rick hung on to the section of the 'wall' nearest to him, his knuckles milk-white in the eerie silence of the ride. He touched his parachute pack, gripped by the unnerving silence.

He could not for the life of him imagine how he was going to jump out of this cage and not plummet to his death. *No way. No fucking way. I might be crazy, but I'm not fucking nuts.*

Just then the cage swayed back into a level position. *Jesus Christ. This is it. I've got to get out.*

'OK, sir, check parachute lines on the static line right above your head . . . that's good . . . step forward . . .'

Rick stayed where he was, aware of the manifest truth that he could see half of California from up here.

'Right, commander, over here, sir . . .' the voice insisted.

Rick came forward, planting his lead foot, the left one, on the toe of the cage. The instructor checked the parachute line. Rick placed his left hand on the outside of the 'doorway'. Someone pulled off the bar, the single bar which stood between him and instant death.

'LOOK UP!' Instinctively, Rick obeyed.

'Now, when I tell you to go, you GO, right?'

'Yes.' *No!*

'GO!'

And Rick Hunter hurled himelf out of the cage – into thin air – and as he fell, he felt himself leaning back, his feet riding up in front of his face. Never had he experienced such a chill of fear.

Then, high above him, he heard a crack, and a billowing sound, and he began to swing back, and his feet began to ride downwards, and suddenly he was going slower and his body was at the right angle. Staring above him, he saw that the parachute had miraculously deployed and the canopy was right up there. He might not die after all.

And now, temporarily safe, he remembered the drills. He looked around him, to the left and to the right and especially downwards. He knew he was supposed to be going forward, slowly, so he pulled down on his forward lift-webs, adjusting his feet for the landing.

Down below he could already hear the instructors on the ground barking commands through their megaphones. *'ALL RIGHT, COMMANDER – ASSESS YOUR DRIFT . . . ADJUST FOR LANDING.'*

The ground was now coming up to meet him. Rick kept his knees together, shifting the angle of his feet, as he had been taught.

'LET UP NOW!'

Moments later he hit the ground, not too hard, and went immediately into the roll. But when he stood up the 'chute began to pull him across the ground, as the wind took it again.

'PULL IN LOWER LIFT-WEBS . . . COLLAPSE THE CANOPY' someone was yelling.

Rick obeyed, and broke free of the parachute. He packed up calmly and headed back towards the navy jeep, a slight swagger in his stride.

'How was it, sir?' asked the driver.

'No trouble,' he replied jauntily.

1100 Friday 22 April

With two instructors Rick climbed aboard the aircraft. It was raining lightly as they took off into the skies above San Diego to make Rick's first proper airborne parachute jump.

The main objective at this point was to become familiar with the noise, the turbulence and the need to watch the hand signals from the dispatcher and the lights above the door.

Strapped in, Rick braced himself as the troop transporter roared down the North Island runway, thundering and vibrating upwards through the low rain cloud and up to an operational height of just under 5,000 feet.

Rick felt the pilot bank right, crawling right around to the north of the city of San Diego. The noise of the engines was deafening inside the aircraft. Soon he heard the dispatcher, who announced,

'We've come full circle, we're right above the airfield again . . . coming up to the Drop Zone now . . . let's go to ACTION STATIONS . . .!'

Rick stood up, clipped on to the static line which ran along the fuselage of the aircraft, and moved towards the rear. The dispatcher had the door open now, and the scream of the wind made communication almost impossible.

'STAND IN THE DOOR . . .!'

Rick came forward, jaw jutting, secretly still a bit nervous but always the leader in his own mind.

'OK, sir, you know the drill. . . . you're clipped on . . . parachute ready . . . RED ON . . .'

Above the door the red light glared. Rick Hunter placed his lead foot on the step, keeping his eyes up, left hand angled out against the doorway.

'GREEN ON! GO . . .!'

Rick Hunter chuckled as he walked back to the jeep which had arrived to pick him up. He hadn't much enjoyed his short course in parachute jumping. But at least he knew how to do it.

Admiral Bergstrom had done the decent thing and permitted Rick Hunter a short lunch break at the SEALs compound, which the commander considered real sweet, since he, Rick, had just spent one and a half days executing lunatic leaps into space, somehow cheating death on a goddamned hourly basis.

Admiral Bergstrom had invited two VISs (Very Important SEALs): Lt. Commander Dallas MacPherson and Chief Petty Officer Mike Hook, both of whom had served with Rick in the desperate getaway from Burma, three and a half years previously. As they'd escaped in the inflatable boats both men had manned M-60 machine guns, hammering away at the Chinese helicopters.

Commander Hunter walked into the bright, white-painted conference room below Admiral Bergstrom's office and almost died of shock at seeing his old team-mates for the first time since the bloodbath in the Burmese Delta.

He threw his arms around Lt. Commander MacPherson and hugged CPO Mike Hook with equal warmth and friendship.

Admiral Bergstrom thoughtfully left them alone for ten minutes before he joined the group. When he did so, he began with a very short, dramatic announcement: 'Dallas, Mike, I want you to know officially from me that Commander Hunter has rejoined the United States Navy for the purpose of one highly-classified mission. And you're going with him.'

'*Me*?' said Lt. Commander MacPherson. 'I thought I'd done my main mission and I was going to be a senior instructor.'

'You are, Dallas. But first you're going to take a short trip to the South Atlantic. I should perhaps tell you that I asked Commander Hunter personally if he had any preference for a 2I/C and he said immediately, "Dallas MacPherson, if he's available." You should be very honoured.'

'I am, sir,' replied the Lt. Commander. 'It's just a bit of a shock, that's all. But I'm ready. Where did you say we're going?'

'South Atlantic. Falkland Islands.'

Dallas MacPherson, always prepared with a dash of old Southern charm, stepped forward and shook the hand of Commander Hunter. 'Death to the gauchos, right, sir? I been reading all about 'em. Battered the Brits and stole the oil, right?'

'That's correct. But we're not going down there to kill 'em all. We're just going to blow a few things up, get their attention, catch 'em off guard.'

'Hey, as I remember, you and I are pretty good at that.'

'As I remember, Dallas, we're not too bad. Not too bad at all.'

Lt. Commander MacPherson was the principal explosives expert on the base. A wide-shouldered career officer from South Carolina, he had started his military studies at the great Southern academy, the Citadel, but moved after just a couple of semesters to Annapolis. He made gunnery and missile officer in an Airleigh-Burke destroyer before he was twenty-five.

As careers went, that came under the heading of meteoric. But it was nowhere near good enough for Dallas. He immediately requested a transfer to the US Navy SEALs, and finished a sensational third out of around a hundred in the BUD/S indoctrination course.

A lot of people were amazed at such a stellar performance by such a very young surface-ship missile officer. Dallas, however, remarked that he thought he'd been stitched up. Opinion on his future was divided into two distinct camps. One group was convinced he would ultimately take over the chair presently occupied by Admiral Bergstrom. The other believed he was more likely to end up with a posthumous Medal of Honor.

Commander Hunter had always been in the first group, but did not entirely discount the possibility of the second outcome. Dallas MacPherson was as tough as hell and as brave as a lion. But it was his brains that Commander Hunter admired. And after the death-defying mission in Burma, he had developed an unshakeable respect for the wisecracking, fast-thinking SEAL whose expertise would, he knew, be critical to the mission in the South Atlantic.

The supremely athletic Chief Petty Officer Mike Hook was also an explosives expert. He came from Kentucky, like Rick, and would act as deputy to Lt. Commander MacPherson, in charge of the timing and fuses. They had worked together to create what must have been the biggest explosion ever seen in the Burmese jungle, petrifying the natives and shaking the entire delta of the Bassein River.

CPO Hook stepped forward and offered his hand to his old commanding officer. 'Look forward to it,' he told the racehorse breeder from his home state. 'You got any idea what we're gonna hit?'

'Couple airfields, few fighter-bombers,' replied the commander. 'Kids' stuff to guys like us.'

'How do we get in?' asked Hook.

'Submarine, then inflatables.'

'How do we get out?'

'Damn fast,' interjected Dallas.

Admiral Bergstrom stepped in. 'OK, men,' he said, 'Let's sit down right here and have some lunch, then we'll retire to one of the ops rooms, meet our colleagues, and get down to details. For the next hour I'd like us to restrict ourselves to basics: the insert, the objectives, the rescue, the mission, and the exit. OK?'

The three SEALs nodded. The admiral pressed a bell and an orderly entered the room with plates of salad, and warm crusty bread. Then he asked each man how he would like his steak cooked.'

'Jeez,' said Dallas MacPherson. 'I knew that word "rescue" was significant. This has to be real important. Medium rare, please.'

'Don't worry, old buddy,' replied Commander Hunter. 'They're not even captives yet.'

'You mean the Brits have left some Special Forces in there, and we gotta get 'em out?' asked Dallas, with truly astonishing perception

'Now how the hell would you draw such an outlandish conclusion?' asked the admiral, quietly.

'Well, we're sure as hell not going to rescue any Argentines,' Dallas replied. 'The Brits have surrendered the islands. The population is coming to terms with their new rulers, and I guess they're back in their homes and farms. And you said "rescue" – that means the Brits have left something behind. That leaves only one option – their recce team, which somehow got stranded, out of the mainstream, and is still in there, out of contact and refusing to surrender with the rest of the troops since no one knows where the hell they are. Probably SAS – right?'

Bergstrom's chair, no doubt, thought Rick Hunter.

And the admiral himself, as if by telepathy, smiled and said, 'Thank you, Dallas. You don't mind if I keep this chair warm for a few months, do you?'

Lt. Commander MacPherson grinned. He was well used to being a couple of jumps ahead, and he knew he had a long way to go to make rear-admiral. But he saw himself walking with kings, rather than courtiers, and was accustomed to achieving his objectives.

'Now, you need to be very careful,' said Admiral Bergstrom. 'For obvious reasons Hereford dare not risk locating them with a cellphone call. Because if the Argies picked it up Captain Jarvis and his team would be hunted down and taken out by sheer weight of numbers. But I have their call sign on satellite radio, and I think that's the way to go when you make contact.'

All three of the combat SEALs nodded in agreement. And just then the steaks came in, which kept everyone, even Dallas MacPherson, more or less quiet for a few minutes.

The lunchtime planning session, as conducted by the admiral, was restricted to the broad brush strokes: the final preparations, the ocean drop to the submarines, the arrival of the gear, by parachute, and the number of men who would conduct the opening attack.

'The SAS guys have been on the run for six days, probably living off the land, hiding out, and eking out their supplies. The place is awash with unpolluted fresh water, and it houses several billion sources of roast lamb. I think we should treat Captain Jarvis and his men as fully operational,' Rick Hunter said.

Admiral Bergstrom nodded in agreement but left the stage to Rick who continued: 'I think we should conduct our first objective as soon as we go in. That airfield in the north. I'd only need eight men, and from there we could link up with Captain Jarvis, after we find him and his men, and proceed to our next mission, all seventeen of us.'

Again the admiral nodded, and said, 'OK. I think that's sound. Let's finish lunch right away and move out to an ops room with a big computer screen. It's hopeless trying to work out a plan for a pile of remote islands unless we've got big accurate charts. Basement situation room. Block D. We can walk.'

Twenty minutes later they filed into the white concrete-walled ops room where Rick Hunter had sat three times before, plotting death, doom and destruction for the enemies of the United States.

Rick hit a few buttons on the computer and a detailed chart of the Falkland Islands illuminated almost the entire wall. Ocean depths, tidal directions and heights, navigation routes, guides, buoys, lights, lighthouses and shoals, sandbanks, rocks, wrecks and oil rigs. On land it showed accurate contours of mountains, a few roads, townships, sheep stations, airports, harbours and government buildings. All updated whenever possible by the Pentagon.

The SEALs gravitated towards it like a flight of homing pigeons: '*Christ, it's pretty damn shallow in there – how big's this damn place?*' '*Which side are we landing?*' '*Anyone know which area the SAS guys are in?*' '*Any warships in the north?*' '*Is that a garrison on top of this darn great headland?*'

The questions came raining in. A SEAL team couldn't ever have enough information, so they wanted to know everything. '*Is this a gate? Does it squeak?*' '*Who lives in this farmhouse?*' '*Will there be a moon?*' '*If it rains what's the ground like in here?*' '*Do we have details on Argentine patrols? Are they out looking for Captain Jarvis?*'

'Gentlemen,' said Admiral Bergstrom, 'I think we should establish our strategy and size of force immediately. Commander Hunter and I are agreed that the submarine will deliver his eight-man team to this area' – he pointed at the map – 'two miles north of the headland west of Goat Hill . . . right here – there's 100 feet depth through here – and the inflatables can run you straight through this gap, the Tamar Pass. You'll launch your attack across the strait and return the same way.

'Team Two is the underwater assault group which will hit the Argentine warships in Mare Harbour. According to our satellites, the Argies often have two destroyers plus two frigates in there. They patrol in the day and return at night. That's when we hit 'em, OK? That team will comprise eight swimmers, with four back-up – landing right here from inflatables in East Cove. Then it's an overland approach, and an underwater, delayed-time hit. Escape from East Cove to the submarine.

'The question I have is this: are we capable of knocking out the Mount Pleasant airbase, which is thick with Argentine troops? Just for the record, my instinct is no. But I want to hear your thoughts on this.'

'What's the size of the garrison, sir?'

'There may be up to 3,000 troops on the ground, plus maybe fifteen attack-helicopter gunships, fifty-plus armoured vehicles, and vast supplies of ordnance. They also have some heavy artillery and missile launchers in place, but that will not affect us.'

'Jesus,' said Rick. 'That's not really our game, is it? We can't send a dozen guys in to take down an army, sitting in the middle of an occupied island, with helicopters, rockets and missiles at their disposal. I guess we might blast a few aircraft out on the perimeter, but I don't think that's a good use of our time and skills.'

'As ever, Commander Hunter, I agree with you,' said John Bergstrom. 'And my update from Washington this morning was very encouraging. The president of Chile has agreed to give us every support, from his airfields, military bases and communications network.

'It's funny – the Argentines and the Chileans are near neighbours with much in common, but there's never been much love lost between them. They helped the Brits last time and they'll help us this time.'

'How many guys will you need for the main attack on Rio Grande?' asked Dallas.

'Probably forty.'

'But we only have twenty.'

'Correct,' said Admiral Bergstrom. 'But we'll send down another twenty to our forward base in readiness for the attack.'

'Forward base?' asked Dallas. 'Where's that?'

'Chile. We've been granted take-off and landing facilities at the Chilean naval airfield in Punta Arenas. Heard that this morning from Admiral Morgan, while your boss was hurling himself into the stratosphere.'

'So we all join the submarine,' said Commander Hunter. 'Then my group leaves for Pebble Island in two inflatables, while the submarine continues on to land the underwater guys on East Cove for the Mare Harbour attack. Then my guys find Douglas Jarvis and his team, and we make our way to a rendezvous with the submarine, and haul the inflatables inboard again – if there's time.'

'Correct.'

'And what about the East Cove guys? How far away are they? And when do they rejoin the submarine?

'Mare Harbour is approximately 135 miles away from the eastern headland of Pebble Island. But the water's relatively deep and the SSN will make it in a little over five hours.

'The ship will pick up each group as it completes its task. Maybe it'll be yours, maybe the others. Then, with all twenty-eight of you on board, including the SAS, it makes all speed for the Magellan Strait, 440 miles away, where we rendezvous with a Chilean freighter which will land you all at Punta Arenas to prepare for Rio Grande. All being well, Rick, you and your guys will leave almost immediately, by helicopter.'

'Time-frame, sir?'

'Both SEAL teams leave here by air tomorrow afternoon at 1600,' said the Admiral. 'And that will put you over the drop-zone north of the Falklands at 0700 Sunday morning – that's first light. We don't have a problem being seen that far north, and the submarine will have Team One right off Pebble Island by around 1700, just as the light starts to fade.

'The Pentagon has no record of any Argentine patrol up there for the past week after 1400. And anyway, we got depth to stay submerged right up to a couple miles offshore. At midnight there'll be a HALO drop straight into your landing beach from a United States military aircraft flying higher than 30,000 feet and transmitting only civilian radar.

'Rick, you've done this before, so you'll carry in the beam to guide the canister down. It'll contain all the explosive and detcord you'll need, timers, fuses, wire-cutters, screwdrivers, shovels, extra food, a powerful satellite transmitter, and a big machine gun in case of emergency. You can bury the canister, and load the stuff into the inflatables for the outward journey to East Falkland where – with luck – you'll find Captain Jarvis fairly quickly.

'Now. Details. First off, there's six A-4P Skyhawks parked on Pebble Island with nine of those Israeli Daggers. These are the guys that delivered the big 1,000lb bombs into the Royal Navy fleet. The airbase has a new, extended concrete runway, installed a couple of years ago by a consortium of the oil companies exploring offshore to the north. The new buildings, like the runway, were unused and have now been converted into an Argentine command head-quarters. They were unharmed during the recent conflict.

'There may be a seventy-five-strong force in there, that's aircrew, ground crew and guards. It's really the only stronghold Argentina has in the north. But the last thing they'll have on their minds is having the airbase assaulted. Remember, their enemy has very publicly left the area, and the Argentines still hold many prisoners of war.'

Rick Hunter nodded. 'Sir, there's four eight-man hard-deck inflatables on board this damn great navy submarine, right? Two for us, two for the others. Now, they are going straight into East Cove to do their business and then straight out again to the ship – that's a round trip of less than ten miles.

'On the other hand, according to this chart, our best place to meet the SSN, after we locate Douglas Jarvis, is going to be the south end of Falkland Sound and that sucker's fifty miles long, all the way down to Fox Bay.

'Now, Captain Jarvis is almost certainly on the west coast of East Falkland, probably trying to find a boat he can commandeer to get the hell out of there. So we are faced with a journey of around sixty miles from our landing beach all the way down the Sound, in a couple of high-powered Zodiacs which burn gas like a fucking 747. I just want to make certain we've got enough . . .'

Admiral Bergstrom referred to his notes. 'One of those inflatables, running at ten knots without making much noise, uses a gallon every forty-two minutes. You'll hit the beach with full tanks – that's twenty gallons – enough for fourteen hours or 140 miles. If, for any reason you have to floor it to make some kind of escape, which is unlikely, both boats carry two full four-and-a-half-gallon spare cans. Basically, the boats can make 200 miles apiece.'

'Thank you, sir. Just checking.'

'You're welcome, commander.'

'Tell you something,' said Dallas, 'With full tanks those boats are going to be darned heavy to drag up the beach and conceal while we blow up the airfield. But what am I thinking, sir? The commander could probably carry the damn thing by himself.' The enormous strength of the SEAL team leader was proverbial at Coronado and hardly anyone could ever compete with it.

Rick Hunter was taking careful notes. Without looking up he asked, 'We got an accurate GPS on the landing beach where the HALO's coming in?'

'It's 51.21.50 south, 59.27.00 west.'

'Midnight, right?'

'Affirmative.'

'We got a chart for the phases of the moon?'

'Right here.'

'What happenes if the sea conditions are very severe and we have to hole up on the landing beach for a day or even two?'

'Not a problem. Just keep the SSN informed on the satellite. And Captain Jarvis.'

The meeting had moved from its slightly haphazard start into a high-octane military planning session. And it stayed that way, an enclave of the most minute detail and forward thinking, until the five SEALs who would join Rick's team arrived at 1600.

There were two more demolition specialists, both Petty Officers First Class – Don Smith, from Chicago, another great bear of a man like the commander; and Brian Harrison from Pennsylvania whose exploits in the Iraqi war had gained him a major reputation.

Seamen Ed Segal and Ron Wallace, both from Ohio, had also served in Iraq and were experienced in combat and boat handling. The final man, Chief Petty Officer Bob Bland, from Oklahoma, was inevitably known as 'Pigling' but mostly behind his back since he had won the station heavyweight boxing championship and was apt to react on a very short fuse.

Bob's speciality was breaking and entering. Any fence, wire, wall, door or gate, old Pigling could get it open. His task was to cut the airfield fence silently, and then move on to attack a metal gate which barred their exit point. He would move out in front again for the final stage of the operation.

The twelve-man underwater group was in another section, going through the same process. They would not meet until the following morning shortly before final preparations for departure.

1400 Friday 22 April
East Falkland

Douglas Jarvis and his team had walked south for about fifteen miles. It was a frustrating journey, carried out in wet, squally weather down the landward side of Carlos Water. The objective was to reach the coast, but not to become stranded on the western fork which guarded Carlos from the open twelve-mile wide Sound. The SAS men did not on any account intend to be caught with their backs to the ocean.

And that had meant a walk of another few miles south to where the land became less of a peninsula, where they might hijack a fishing boat in a little place called Port Sussex.

They had arrived in a wide sweep of grazing land within clear sight of Mount Usborne and stared down at the deserted harbour. They could see moorings, possibly four of them, but no boats, which Captain Jarvis remarked was 'bloody dull'.

It was already growing dark, and there was just a scattering of buildings around the harbour, two of them with lights on. And the problem which faced the young commander was the same as always – could they bang on the door and announce themselves, running the risk of Argentina soldiers being in residence? Or even the risk of a swift phone call from any civilian occupants to the military HQ at Mount Pleasant?

Of course they could take out the enemy instantly. But what good would that do? The soldiers would be missed, then found, and a manhunt for the fugitive British Special Forces would begin in earnest. The men from Hereford were, as Douglas put it, buggered. Their options were narrow. There was little they could do, except feast on roast lamb whenever possible and try to steal, hire or borrow a boat to get away at the earliest time.

Tonight was plainly a roast-lamb situation. They also had to find shelter quickly. It was raining like hell and it would be completely dark inside an hour. Their waterproof clothing and boots had held up well, and no one was suffering from illness or injury, but it was all getting a bit depressing, with no discernible enemy, the constant threat of an Argentine manhunt hovering over them, and no sign of a proper objective. The only ray of hope seemed to be the vague, encrypted satellite promise from Hereford several days ago that a rescue operation was being mounted.

Douglas dispatched Troopers Wiggins and Pearson to what he called the 'local butcher', the 4,000-acre pasture to the east where sheep and lambs were grazing as far as the eye could see. And while they were gone, the rest of them groped around in the sparse undergrowth for a spot to 'light the oven'. They were getting very good at this, wielding the axe, chopping up the low bushes and the carcasses of the lambs, before lighting the fire in the hole they just dug in the damp ground.

Douglas toyed with the idea of moving quietly down into one of the empty buildings on the quayside, but again the risk was too great. What if a fishing boat pulled in during the night and they were discovered? What if any such fishing boat was accompanied by Argentine marines?

The truth was, the SAS team could cope with anything except discovery, because that might very well mean death from an Argie helicopter gunship strafing the area where someone had located them.

No. Tonight looked like another night in the open. And thank God for the excellent waterproof sleeping bags, and may the morrow bring a suitable boat into the hitherto deserted harbour of Port Sussex. Privately, Douglas thought it would be just a matter of time before an angry shepherd grew irritated by someone stealing his lambs and reported the matter to the authorities. They'd snatched eight of them by now and a good detective might easily put two and two together and make four.

He shuddered and checked the lamb, which was beginning to sizzle cheerfully, and once more they made their fast evening communication to their command HQ. As usual there was only silence in response. At Doug's orders, they left the radio switched on, ready to receive, although no one held out much hope any more. Rescue op or not, they would plainly have to rescue themselves.

And so they drifted off to sleep under the bushes, leaving one man at a time on a one-hour sentry watch.

And at thirteen minutes past 0100 Trooper Bob Goddard saw a sight which made his hair stand on end. Winding up the coastal track to the right of the long sea inlet of Breton Loch were the unmistakable twin beams of a pair of headlights, moving fast. He grabbed the night binoculars and stared at the green-hued landscape to the south.

Jesus Christ! It's an army jeep . . . and if it stays on that track it's going to pass less than a half-mile from right here.

Trooper Goddard shook Captain Jarvis, who almost leaped out of his sleeping bag in surprise, since long undisturbed nights were the rule around here in this desolate southern wilderness.

'God – what's up, Bob?'

'There's an army jeep, sir, moving fast, coming more or less towards us. Right now it's a couple of miles south of the harbour.'

Douglas Jarvis said softly, 'Wake everyone, get into combat gear, weapons ready, and pack up everything in case we have to move fast. If we have to we'll take 'em out, but I'd like to avoid that because if we do all hell will break loose.'

'OK, sir – binoculars are right there, near the sniper rifle.'

Swiftly the SAS men slipped into fighting mode, boots laced tight, gloves on, hoods up, ammunition belts slung into place. The sleeping bags and groundsheets were quickly packed by two troopers. The other six were ready to repel an attack – or to launch one of their own.

Douglas Jarvis watched the jeep pull onto the quayside and stop outside one of the houses which was lit inside. He saw two men jump from the front seats and bang on the front door, which opened immediately. Light spilled out onto the jetty. One man came out and moments later, a powerful searchlight on the roof of the jeep began to sweep the hillside, throwing a long beam past the boulders and scrubland below them.

By the captain's assessment the men and the jeep were about 600 yards away, and with every sweep the beam of the searchlight drew nearer their clump of bushes.

Down, guys. Stay well down. We don't want to make this any uglier than it is already . . .

As far as Douglas could tell, there were only two possibilities. Someone had seen them moving across the foothills of the mountain, or a shepherd had seen a couple of shadowy figures make off with a lamb.

And he was correct. Luke Milos, a sixth-generation Falkland Islands shepherd, had been darned near certain that he'd seen someone in the pasture running away, carrying something. And he knew the main Argentine garrison had issued a warning about wandering intruders – British troops unaccounted for in the battle – who might be armed and dangerous.

He had placed a call to the small Argentine military compound at Goose Green, which was situated on the narrow isthmus dividing Choiseul Sound.

An Argentine patrol was up there inside the hour, sweeping the hillside with a big mounted searchlight. Right now its beam was slicing into the bushes where Douglas and his men lay face down, pressed into the ground, gripping their guns.

As far as Douglas was concerned anything was preferable to a fight. But if there was one, the group would have two tasks: to kill every man in that jeep, and then make sure no one found any evidence of the slaughter. The first was easy, the second damn near impossible.

There was a dull ache of anticipation in Douglas Jarvis's stomach when he heard the jeep's engine kick over and the vehicle began to rumble towards them. Worse yet, he could hear the clatter of machine guns as the Argentine patrol raked every bush and rocky outcrop with real live bullets.

'Fuck,' hissed Douglas. 'Peter, Bob – take the guys on the left side of the vehicle coming towards us. I'll take the driver, Jake takes the one in the back seat on the right.'

No one spoke, but each man wriggled and crawled into position, spreading out and ready to open fire in an instant. Suddenly the Argentines went quiet. Then the searchlight went on again, and its beam swept the copse where the SAS men had been sleeping, 200 yards from the edge of the pasture.

The jeep roared forward again, and a burst of machine-gun fire ripped into the very spot the SAS team had vacated only minutes before.

'OK, fuck it, that's *it*!' snapped Douglas, 'Take 'em NOW!'

His own Enfield L85A1 'bull pup' assault rifle spat fire at fifty yards range, the heavy SS109 steel-core rounds ripping through the head and neck of the driver and the front passenger. Troopers Wiggins and Goddard put two lethal bursts into the rear seat from the left, while Jake Posgate slammed ten rounds into it from the right.

Doug Jarvis ran forward, closing in now from the rear of the vehicle, and fired another burst. But there was no more movement from inside the jeep. Four men lay slumped in their seats.

'OK, guys,' said Douglas. 'You see the nearest hillside over there – probably about a mile away if this damn searchlight is any good. I'm gonna drive over there and I'll drop off a trooper every 400 yards. That way we'll all meet when I find a spot.

'Then we're going to hide this bastard and its passengers. It won't stay hidden for ever. But it'll probably stay concealed for a week till someone finds it. By then we'll be long gone.'

They manhandled the two dead men in the front into the rear seat to join their equally dead comrades and then clambered into the vehicle and set off towards the distant slopes of Mount Usmore. It took a half-hour to find a secluded gully and they shoved the jeep down into it, about six feet below the track they were on. Douglas personally severed the wires that led from the battery that powered the vehicle's radio.

One hour later they had about a half-ton of gorse and tall grass piled all over the vehicle. Someone could have walked past it twenty times and never spotted it.

'That's it,' said the captain. 'Those guys won't be reported missing for several more hours. Meantime we'll head back to the coast for the next three hours. When it's light, we'll hide up somewhere and try to get past Port Darwin this evening. We have to stay right next to the sea shore. It's our only way out.'

1530 Saturday 23 April
US Naval Airbase
North Island

Commander Rick Hunter, in company with Lt. Commander Dallas MacPherson, Chief Petty Officer Mike Hook and the rest emerged from the room where they'd had their final briefing dressed in full combat gear. Their rucksacks were already loaded. They were armed and ready, and they carried with them the special heavy-duty hooded and flippered wetsuits that would prevent them from both sinking and freezing to death in the South Atlantic.

The parachutes and the reserves were already loaded. These would unclip and release the moment the men hit the water. The rest would be up to Captain Hugh Fraser's highly skilled submariners from the USS *Toledo* who would be working the inflatable boats in seas that would, with luck, be reasonably calm.

Rick Hunter walked out to the edge of the runway where the Lockheed C-130 stretched Hercules was already fully loaded and running its engines. He walked to the steps of the aircraft, followed by Dallas and Mike Hook. But before he began the climb towards the cabin he paused for a few moments to chat with Admiral Bergstrom who had materialised from nowhere.

'Sir, one favour . . .?'

'Of course.'

Rick handed him a piece of paper with a phone number in faraway Kentucky on it. 'Could you please call Di – just tell her I'm fine?'

'I'll do it this morning,' the admiral said, smiling. 'And Rick – good luck.'

Dallas stood grinning cheerfully as the officer from the Blue Grass walked confidently up the steps.

Inside the aircraft, the crew was waiting at the door. As Rick walked in, one of them said, 'OK, sir?'

'Let's go,' said the commander, walking back and strapping himself into his reserved seat. The great aircraft shuddered beneath him as it made its way to the end of the runway, swerved around and rumbled forward, its speed building, the noise of its engines shattering.

No one spoke until the fuel-laden Hercules had fought its way off the ground, hard into the south-west breeze gusting in off the Pacific. They all felt it gain height and then bank left onto its course of one hundred and fifty degrees, bound for the cold South Atlantic.

They climbed into the warm spring skies of the northern hemisphere. The Hercules, always a lumbering giant, seemed even noisier this morning due to the giant echoing gas tank set in the middle of the main cargo area. Right now they were flying through sunny clear skies. By the early hours of tomorrow morning, they would be close to the Antarctic convergence, flying in temperatures around eighty degrees below freezing.

No one spoke for half an hour at which point, Dallas turned to Commander Hunter and said, 'Sir, do you think we're supposed to be scared?'

'Us? No, not us. We're invincible.'

'No, sir. I'm serious. Is this really dangerous, or are we just dealing with a bunch of jokers?'

'I don't think anyone knows that, Dallas. But we have been tasked to find the lost Brits and slam the fighter aircraft. Nothing you and I can't deal with.'

'Yeah, but hold on a minute, sir. Let's say they send a chopper after us and start blasting away. What happens then?'

'Dallas, we are about to conduct a standard, classic SEAL operation: infiltration of enemy territory. If they are mad enough to come after us, we'll blow their fucking helicopter right out of the sky with the Stinger, right? Get your mind straight, kid. We're the US Navy SEALs and we're going in. Anyone gets in the way of our mission dies, right?'

'Yessir.'

Dallas fell silent, and the Hercules, guzzling fuel by the gallon every few seconds, kept rumbling south at 42,000 feet. They would refuel in Santiago. Rick noticed the veteran explosives expert Mike Hook was sound asleep. Ed Segal was lying back in his seat, his eyes wide open, his mind on the cold south.

The crew served them coffee at 1900, with hot soup and sandwiches at 2200, and most of them slept through the night until 0330 when they landed in Santiago. Refuelling took just thirty

273

minutes, and everyone seemed to wake up. The mood was sober, though, and no one had much to say.

At 0600 Rick Hunter and his team began to change their clothing. Their other gear and their weapons were already secured in the four big waterproof containers they would take with them on the drop. They pulled their heavy-duty hooded wetsuits over the special deep-water Gore-Tex body-vests and tight-fitting trousers they would wear for the jump into the freezing South Atlantic. Their last task before fitting the parachutes was to pull on their life jackets.

Two hundred and fifty miles ahead, the crew of the submarine USS *Toledo* were preparing for the pick-up under still dark skies with intermittent cloud cover. The hard-copy satellite message was unambiguous. It contained the accurate GPS rendezvous position, time and details, plus the code word *Southern Belle*.

Captain Fraser's crew were already lowering two diesel-powered inflatables into the water. It had taken a small crane to haul the deflated boats and then the engines up onto the sub's casing. And out on the deck it was more trouble than usual because of a heavy Atlantic swell. But Captain Fraser had preferred the boats to a Chilean helicopter that was apt to be both noisy and slow: he recognised the importance of scooping the SEALs out of the frigid ocean in the fastest possible time.

The Hercules flew on south-east, and 130 miles north of the Falklands the navigator hit the radar button and immediately got a 'paint' on the ocean thirty miles away. He switched the radar off instantly to avoid prying Argentine eyes, but Captain Fraser's ops room had picked them up. *Low-flying contact . . . 5,000 feet . . . speed 250 . . . course three-five-five . . . range thirty miles . . . IFF transponder code correlates Southern Belle . . .'*

All four of *Toledo*'s inflatables were now running free, right off the port side of the submarine. The drop was scheduled to take place 1,000 yards away, but for the moment the helmsmen kept their distance just in case one of the SEALs came plummeting down out of a cloud bank and crashed straight into the Zodiac.

Back in the Hercules, Rick Hunter and his men were struggling towards the door, carrying the waterproof containers. They could hear the dispatcher shouting: *'OK, get ready now . . . we're heading right towards the zone . . . another couple of minutes . . .'*

Mike Hook, behind the commander and Dallas MacPherson, was

looking scared, his face was white, his mouth dry. Rick noticed the tremor in his own hands as he hooked onto the static line and called for a bottle of water – he seemed to find it hard to swallow as well. Dallas appeared unconcerned, all business, while Ron Wallace was quiet and unsmiling. No one looked forward to a mission like this, one that started out on the frontiers of death.

Rick shook his head to rid himself of the sombre mood. His adrenalin was running now. He was scared, but the light of battle was in his eyes, some inherent gene of the Hunter family driving him forward even in the face of the most terrible danger. In one corner of his soul he enjoyed the thrill of it, charging out of that door at the head of a group of hard-trained SEAL assault troops. This was what he had missed, what he had joined for, and it sure beat the hell out of frigging around with baby racehorses.

'ONE MINUTE!' yelled the dispatcher above the roar of the engines. Rick squeezed his nose and blew hard to clear his ears as the aircraft lost height. He turned back to Mike Hook and gave him a reassuring look. 'Not to worry – just jump, right after me. Remember the drills and stay cool.'

Just then, the aircraft throttled back to a speed of only 130 knots, and the dispatcher opened the big door on the port side. The screaming rush of ice-cold air was a major shock, doubling the noise and tripling the scare factor. But Rick Hunter was not scared any more. Not at all. He felt only a sense of exhilaration, gripping the static line and watching the dispatcher, glancing downwards at the deep blue of the dawn ocean, the great white breaking swells. He could not yet see the US submarine.

'We're coming to the drop zone now, right on our nose – ACTION STATIONS . . .'

They could hardly hear the dispatcher above the howl of the wind, but everyone checked their static line and moved forward to the area immediately in front of the opening.

'STAND IN THE DOOR, NUMBER ONE!'

Rick came forward, his face grim, shrugging his shoulders like a heavyweight fighter in his corner preparing for round one. On another man this might have seemed like bravado, but it was not so for Rick Hunter. He was in battle mode – ready for this fight, ready to *go*.

'RED ON!'

The Hercules was now flying at dropping speed but the force of the howling wind outside the fuselage formed a wall of freezing air, a curtain of transparent steel. Rick thought he might be forced right back in again. Then he could see the glare of the red light above the door. They were right on the drop zone: he braced himself and stared out.

'*GREEN ON . . . GO!*'

The dispatcher slapped him on the shoulder, and Rick Hunter plunged out of the aircraft. He swept clear in the slipstream and then dropped swiftly sideways. He held his knees together, feeling the by now familiar sensation of rolling backwards. He hoped Dallas, Mike and the rest were also out. But then his parachute opened and he could not see anyone above him.

Back inside the cockpit the radio operator snapped into the secure encrypted VHF: '*Southern Belles go.*'

Toledo came back on 'cackle' . . . '*Roger. Out.*'

All the 'chutes deployed faultlessly, slowing down the headlong flight of the SEAL teams. Rick looked down and noticed that the sea looked markedly less friendly than it had from 1,000 feet. He guessed he was less than 200 feet above the surface, and he could see the outline of the submarine quite clearly now, all four inflatables still circling close to its port side.

The surface of the water showed deep troughs, and white lacy patterns and the wind was strong. As he descended, Rick could see it whipping the froth off the top of the waves, some of which were breaking, sending a cascade of broiling white water down the leeward side. The sea was running out of the south-west, as was the wind. Long studies of the charts had suggested this was bad news, since the roughest, coldest gales around the Falklands came raging in from the Antarctic shelf.

Rick didn't think this was a full-fledged gale yet, but it seemed to be building, and he wasn't sure how much he was going to enjoy the experience of sitting in a submarine in an Antarctic storm. Well, it would be a whole lot better than bobbing around in the South Atlantic in a wetsuit.

Now, dropping downwards to 150 feet, he pulled the rig forward under his backside until he was effectively sitting in the harness. He quickly banged the release button on his chest and freed the straps to fall away beneath his feet.

Hanging there now, holding on to the lift-webs above his head, Rick waited the last fleeting seconds, staring down at the shapes of the waves, which did not look good. Twenty feet above the surface, he could no longer *see* the submarine – or the inflatables. He just felt himself hurtling towards the ocean as if he had jumped from a diving board. He immediately breathed in deeply, held his breath, gripped the lift-webs tighter and thrust his legs downwards, underneath him, until his body was vertical.

Ten feet above the surface of the ocean, Rick let go of the parachute and crashed into the South Atlantic, submerging ten feet or so. He kicked his way to the surface, flippers gripping the water, and felt the freezing cold ocean against his hands and face.

His parachute had disappeared and he was gasping for breath as a massive rogue wave rolled right over the trough in which he now wallowed. Rick was a great swimmer, and he had a good lungful of air, but it seemed a hundred feet upwards before he broke clear of the water again and gulped in more air. He braced himself for the next oncoming wall of water, prepared to go under once more, but he need not have worried. Two pairs of brawny seamen's hands clamped onto his shoulders and hauled him out backwards, over the broad inflated sides of a Zodiac.

He landed on his back. 'Hold it right there, sir . . .' someone yelled unnecessarily. Then he felt the diesel engine accelerate, dragging them around in the direction of the advancing waves. Before Rick could raise himself up, Mike Hook, gasping and choking on sea water, landed on top of him. Then the diesel roared again, as the helmsman got the boat synchronised with the pattern of the waves and steered them toward Dallas MacPherson who was, unsurprisingly, yelling.

The inflatable was now rising up through six feet against the hull of the submarine where Rick could see a succession of safety and harness lines being lowered and grabbed by the seamen. Right now he had no idea what was happening but he could see the sailors moving around and securing the lines with sure, swift expertise.

'What happens now?' he said.

'Grab those boarding nets, sir. The guys will haul you onto the casing . . . don't worry – you can't fall . . .'

Just then the second boat arrived bearing Don Smith, Brian Harrison and Ed Segal. Seven minutes later, the first ten SEALs were being greeted by Captain Fraser.

It took another ten minutes for all of them to assemble inside the submarine. The last boat recovered the gear containers which had been dropped separately.

This had been a flawless ocean drop – no one lost, no one injured, everyone safe and feeling a massive sense of relief. This mission might be dangerous, but the part which had concerned them most was over.

0900 Sunday 24 April
Argentine Military Garrison,
Goose Green, East Falkland

'Sir, we're getting no reply on the radio. Nothing. It's dead.'
  'What time did they leave?'
  'Around midnight.'
  'Last contact?'
  '0105.'
  'Position?'
  'Quayside, Port Sussex.'
  'Contacts?'
  'Señor Luke Milos. He reported sheep-stealing. I just spoke to him, and he saw our jeep heading up the mountainside around 0130. He heard machine guns but they were ours. The men were sweeping the area with a searchlight and bursts of gunfire.'
  'Did he see which way the vehicle went?'
  'Only for around 600 yards up the hill behind his home. Do you think we should send a search party? Couple of jeeps?'
  'Well, they may be on their way back. It's very barren up there. I think we should leave it another couple of hours and then send a helicopter up to Port Sussex. That way we cover more ground faster.'
  'Yes, sir.'

1100: same day

Captain Jarvis and his SAS team had made it to the southern end of Brenton Loch and had gone to ground close to the water at the northern end of the isthmus that crossed Choiseul Sound. This rectangle of land was about five miles long and only a little more than a mile wide. The Argentine garrison at Goose Green was in the diametrically opposite south-eastern corner, a distance of perhaps five and a half miles from the SAS team. No more.
  The land here was flat, but the shoreline was craggy with a lot of rocks on the landward side of the pebbled beach. Jake Posgate had found an ideal spot, a group of eight huge, flattish boulders which overlapped, two of them resting on the 'shoulders' of three others.

This did not provide much space, but there was enough for eight hard-trained combat troops to hole up, mount their defensive position and remain invisible from any direction. The only way anyone could locate them would be to squirm straight into the low tunnel formed by the boulders – and then kiss life on this planet a very swift goodbye.

The main trouble for Douglas was the impossibility of cooking the three joints of lamb they still had, at least not until nightfall and even then it would be a bit risky.

But they had water and some chocolate and there was little to do except wait until dark. Then they could attempt to cross the isthmus and head down to the next harbour without being spotted.

So far the day was passing very slowly and very boringly. Suddenly, at 1110, they heard the rotor whine of a military helicopter, flying low, maybe a couple of miles to the east. Douglas himself wriggled out of their hide and, lying flat on the pebbles, saw it heading north and making a circular course back towards the coast.

'That's the enemy,' he muttered. 'They've decided their patrol has gone missing. Guys, we just became the target of an Argentine manhunt which is likely to get bigger and bigger over the next few hours.'

'What do we do?' asked Trooper Wiggins.

'Nothing. We stay right here, and hope to Christ they concentrate their search six miles north of here around Port Sussex. If our luck holds, they may not bother with this stretch of exposed coast till tomorrow. Meanwhile we'll make our move south soon as the light fades.'

'How close to the Argentine garrison do we go?'

'Probably within a mile. We'll just keep crawling along the coast and make darned sure no one sees us. In daylight we stay right where we are. Hidden.'

And that was precisely where they stayed until, at 1300, they heard another helicopter take off from the south end of the isthmus. Then the first one flew back and two more helos came in from the south. Captain Jarvis reckoned they were coming from Mount Pleasant.

'Jesus, we got 'em worried,' said Douglas. 'They now believe something happened to their guys. And they're about to scour this fucking island to find out who did it.'

'Who's more worried, us or them?' asked Bob Goddard.

'Us. By fucking miles, since you ask,' replied the team leader. 'This is beginning to look very, very hairy.'

'If they corner us, do we fight or do we surrender?'

'I guess we fight. Because if we surrender they'll shoot us anyway – for murdering their colleagues when the war we came for was clearly over. That's how they'd see it, at least.'

'No need to worry too much right now,' said Douglas. 'First of all they're not going to find us, secondly we know someone is certainly trying to rescue us, and thirdly we must have a chance of getting a boat out of here. We are British, and any citizen of these islands is effectively a British citizen in captivity. We just need a break – like a friendly trawler fisherman with a tankful of diesel which will get us to the Magellan Strait.'

'You sure about that rescue stuff?' asked Bob Goddard.

'No,' replied Douglas curtly.

They all fell silent, trying not to consider themselves trapped in this hell-hole from which right now there was no escape. And for three more hours they lay flat on the ground, awaiting the fading of the light.

At 1800 Trooper Joe Pearson switched on the satellite radio communication and put on the headset, as he did every night. In the background there was the familiar faint electronic 'mushy' sound but, as usual, no other variation.

Fifteen minutes later, Joe Pearson was almost nodding off to sleep when he heard it: a voice, indistinct, but still a voice.

'Jesus Christ, there's someone on the line!' he gasped.

'Careful it's not the fucking Argies,' snapped Douglas. 'Give it to me!'

Joe ripped the headset off and handed it to the boss.

And right away, Douglas heard the voice: *'Foxtrot three-four . . . Foxtrot three-four . . . Sunray SEAL team . . . Sunray SEAL team . . . do you copy? Come in, Dougy . . . this is Sunray SEAL team . . . do you copy?'*

'Foxtrot three-four . . . Dougy receiving Sunray . . . repeat, receiving Sunray . . .'

'Get to free-range dockside ASAP . . . we're coming in. Good luck. Over and out.'

The unseen line of communication from Douglas Jarvis's make-shift cave shut down. And the comms mast of USS *Toledo* slid silently inboard, seconds before the submarine sank below the surface.

Which left Douglas and his boys to work out the details. 'Sunray' was US/UK military code for commander. And the SEALs were plainly on their way. But 'Free-range dockside'? *What the hell was that all about?*

As codes went that one was relatively easy, since the line was fairly secure. And it took about four minutes peering at the coastal map of the western side of East Falkland for them to get it.

'Right there,' said Douglas, jabbing a forefinger down on the map. 'About fifteen miles east-south-east of here – tiny little place, sheltered inlet off Falkland Sound . . . see it? That's where we're going – Egg Harbour.'

CHAPTER ELEVEN

2000 Sunday 24 April
South Atlantic, north of West Falkland

The USS *Toledo* ran slowly inshore, 51.16S, 59.27W on the GPS, five miles north of the rough and rocky north coast of the island. They came to periscope depth and checked for deserted seas. Captain Fraser ordered the inflatable boats launched in twenty minutes as the submarine came creeping into waters only 100 feet deep.

Commander Rick Hunter and his team heard the CO order his ship to the surface. They watched the two Zodiacs being hauled out onto the casing, followed by their four engines, each of which was manhandled up out of the torpedo room on swiftly erected davits set inside the sail.

Commander Hunter and Dallas MacPherson led the other members of the team out onto the casing and they all stared in awe at some seriously worsening weather. Heavy swells were riding up the bow of the submarine. The wind was not yet gale force, but it was now almost certainly increasing and Captain Fraser advised them to move fast and make the run into the beach with all possible speed.

The embarkation nets and rope ladders were in place on the submarine's hull within two minutes. The seamen lowered the two boats down into the water, each one already containing its driver just in case it somehow broke free.

Commander Hunter would be last away, and Dallas MacPherson led the men down the ladders, four in each boat, carrying as much of their gear as possible.

At 2030 the helmsman turned the boats south and opened the throttles, driving towards the landing site – the headland jutting out into Pebble Sound. It was sheltered from the onrushing South Atlantic waves and could perhaps withstand a big nor'wester. But it was susceptible to a strong tidal pull through the narrows, which might make things extremely tough for the SEALs.

The near-gale-force wind buffeted the boats in which the SEALs crouched low, their rucksacks packed with ammunition, food, waterproof sleeping bags and the radio. The helmsmen were unable to make much headway in this sea but they pushed along at ten knots, aware that it would take a very alert Argentine surveillance officer to locate them out here in the pitch-black ocean.

Rick Hunter was personally acting as navigator, and he knelt on the wooden deck, staring at the compass. He was trying to locate the gap in the low hills on the shoreline up ahead, the Tamar Pass, through which they would find shelter and calmer seas – and the landing beach.

It took ten minutes to spot the flashing buoy on the east side of the gap and they raced through, much faster now as the water flattened, leaving the warning light 100 yards to their port side.

The landing beach was slightly more than a mile ahead, dead straight, and they came in at an easy speed, the engines cut and raised forty yards offshore to avoid grounding out on the shingled seabed while the men paddled in with big wooden oars.

They beached both boats and unloaded them separately, with each man moving to a pre-planned task, as precise as a tyre-change by a Grand Prix pit team. The disembarkation took less than forty-five seconds.

Rick Hunter quickly checked that all members of his team were present before they began the most serious part of the landing, which was to haul the Zodiacs out of sight. Each of the men gripped one of the boats' handles and heaved.

They moved the first boat back around seventy-five yards into the shelter of a few rocks and some sparse-looking bushes and went back for the second. Then they unscrewed the engine bolts and manhandled the engines flat onto the ground. They turned the boats upside down and placed them over the engines, propping up the bows to give the wheel clearance. It was a major effort but it removed the problem of metal engine-casings glinting in the sun and betraying their position.

Rick asked Don Smith and Bob Bland to cut some gorse to lay

over the upturned hulls and to weigh them down with rocks. Within another ten minutes the boats were secure and invisible from the air, ready for the attack – and, perhaps more importantly, ready for the getaway.

Using a flashlight they discovered they were in a relatively sheltered spot, in an uninhabited area. They pulled out the spade and dug in for the night. It was bitterly cold, but dry, and they could stay out of the wind in the lee of a long flat rock.

Commander Hunter ordered Ed Segal and Ron Wallace to stand guard for ninety minutes each, while the rest of the team snatched some sleep and then prepared to receive the HALO drop at midnight. Dealing with that would keep them up until dawn.

Right now, at 2100, the United States B-52H long-range bomber out of Minot Air Force Base, North Dakota, was refuelling in Santiago in readiness for the final 1,300-mile flight down to the Falklands.

This great gun-grey warhorse of the US military was 160 feet long and weighed 220 tons. Its distinctive nose-cone made it look like a great white shark with wings, and tonight, with its light load, it would fly high and fast at close to 500 knots, following the lofty peaks of the Andes. It would stay in Chilean airspace all the way, south until it angled east above the Magellan Strait, then straight to the open ocean and the Falkland Islands.

As it skirted Argentine airspace, the B-52 would be cruising at 45,000 feet, too high but fuel-efficient. It would be transmitting only non-military radar. Civilian aircraft, flying high at night, were not routinely checked out by airline authorities in southern Argentina, nor indeed by Chile. Ryan Holland had been very definite about that.

At 2120 the US Air Force Stratofortress came hurtling off the Santiago runway and set a course due south, which would take it 900 miles down the entire Pacific coastal length of Chile. They had flown on an extremely tight schedule from North Dakota, refuelling once at North Island, San Diego, where they had picked up most of the explosives for the HALO canister.

And at this moment the veteran front-line pilot out of the Fifth Bomb Wing, Lt. Colonel E. J. Jaxtimer, was running approximately seven minutes late. The B-52 would be directly over the SEALs' hide at 0007, though he hoped to pick up time during the high-speed run through the very thin air above the mountains.

Meanwhile the SEALs slept. And the night hours flashed by. At 2330 everyone was awakened. They ate some concentrated protein, drank fresh water, and prepared for the oncoming arrival of the 250lb computerised bomb-shaped canister, swinging downward beneath its black parachute, having dropped like a stone for almost 45,000 feet. That was the whole idea of HALO – high altitude, low opening, as untraceable as a falling meteorite for ninety-nine per cent of its journey, then too low to be located by anyone's radar.

Rick Hunter was checking the high-tech target-marker he would place on the ground, the device that would send a powerful laser beam streaking into the black sky to the east. This was the beam which would flash a pinpoint-accurate GPS reading to Lt. Colonel Jaxtimer and his team – 51.21.05S, 59.27W. The ops room of the Stratofortress would lock right onto it in the brief minutes before they jettisoned the canister out of the B-52's bomb bay.

The beam in Commander Hunter's target-finder was life and death for this mission. If it failed, everything failed. If it functioned, the Argentine air force could bid *adios* to their fighter-attack bombers parked on the airfield at Pebble Beach. Parked, incidentally, in this remote, inaccessible spot without even a semblance of a guard.

At 2345 the SEALs took up their positions. Commander Hunter placed the target-marker, accurate to within five yards, in the precise spot indicated by the GPS system. They made it secure in the shingle and drew out its collapsible aerial pointing to the east. Mike Hook stood with Rick, and the remaining men spread out in pairs to form a forty-yard-wide triangle around him.

Rick decided this was such a remote beach he would risk placing three dim chemical light-markers with each pair of SEALs in order for everyone to know precisely who was where – a considerable luxury on a pitch-black moonless night like this. It would give them the best possible chance of seeing the canister's arrival. The B-52 would 'see' nothing visually, but would rely totally on the laser beam from the target-marker.

At six minutes before midnight Commander Hunter activated the beam, hitting the switch which would send its laser-light flashing up into the dark skies, a lonely beacon in the heavens, ready to guide the precious canister down.

Lt. Colonel Jaxtimer, however, was still thirteen minutes out, which put the Stratofortress a little more than 100 miles to the east, at 61.10 west, flying high and fast towards the jagged headland of

Byron Heights, the north-westerly point of West Falkland's mainland.

On the ground the wind was rising out of the east, gusting a wicked chill across the exposed beach where the team from sunny Coronado was waiting, shivering and hopping around to keep warm.

Rick Hunter knew he would not hear the huge jet arriving eight miles above the Earth's surface, but they might catch an echo of the engines as the aircraft rumbled on upwind and out over the Atlantic.

At four minutes after midnight the laser marker suddenly started 'painting' on the aircraft's receiver. Three minutes to release, and the final seconds were ticking by automatically on the computer.

'We're locked on . . . red light, sir . . . bomb doors open . . . looking good . . . left . . . left . . . on track . . . five-nine-two-seven coming up . . . still looking good . . . that's it, sir . . . the bomb's away.'

Beneath the huge bulk of the B-52 the doors of the weapons bay in the central fuselage began to close behind the falling canister as it hurtled through the darkness, straight down Rick Hunter's laser beam.

On the ground the SEALs were just beginning to gripe and moan about the Air Force's lateness when suddenly they heard the far-distant growl of eight mighty Pratt and Whitney turbofan jet engines.

'It's gotta be them,' snapped Rick. 'Look up and for Christ's sake keep your eyes open – this thing could kill you.'

They all peered into the darkness, and it was Dallas who spotted the flickering ghostly shape of the parachute. 'Right here, sir,' he yelled, 'WATCH YOUR BACKS – THE FUCKER'S DOWN!'

Twelve feet from where Rick stood the huge canister crashed onto the beach with a shuddering thump. Two SEALs rushed forward to grab the 'chute and stow it under the boats. The rest of them grabbed the long leather-padded lifting bars on either side and began to carry it back to their hide. It was heavy but not as heavy as a Zodiac and they manhandled it with ease.

Inside was the required explosive for the destruction of the Argentine aircraft. That took up two-thirds of the canister, but there were also two extra shovels, eight extra machine pistols, and wetsuits for the short ocean crossing to Pebble Island. There were fuses and timers, plus wire and an extra radio transmitter. Best of all there was canned ham, baked beans, cheese, bread, cold cuts, coffee

286

and chocolate. Plus two Primus stoves with a couple of containers of fuel.

The SEALs immediately dug a large hole in which to bury the canister, which would not be found for at least a hundred years. And then they lit the Primus stoves and made themselves a midnight feast. The weather was growing worse by the hour and they all put on their waterproof smocks before turning in for the night, huddling against the rocks, hoping the weather would calm down before tomorrow evening's mission across the water.

But the weather deteriorated. Five hours later, when dawn cast a grim light on the grey beach, every member of the SEAL team was shocked by the seascape. Great white-capped waves were rolling through the Tamar Pass and onto the shore, whipped by the howling wind. The clouds were high, but the sun was low and hidden. The prospect of pushing an inflatable out into this particular sea was nothing less than daunting. The only sound to be heard above the wind was the long sucking noise of shingle, followed by the thumping crash of long rolling waves.

'We could,' said Mike Hook, 'drown our fucking selves before we get five yards. There's no way we're going anywhere in this. Not if they really want that airfield blowing up. My guess is not tonight, guys.'

He was right, too. For hour after hour the gale never abated. The sea came raging in through the narrows which separated this rocky outpost of West Falkland from Pebble Island. The tide seemed to turn in the late afternoon, and the wind whipped the water into a frenzy as it surged out between the two headlands.

'Jesus Christ,' said Dallas. 'If you tried to row across there, you'd get sucked right out through the entrance into the open ocean – I know this mission is supposed to be urgent, but we couldn't survive out there. No way.'

The better news was that the entire landscape around them seemed bereft of human habitation. Or any other inhabitants for that matter. Not so much as a stray sheep or even a goat from the local hill came wandering their way. They had chosen a desolate spot, plainly safe from prying eyes. In any event, with the machine gun rigged as it now was, they could hold off an army, tight against this rock, protected by solid granite on all sides except the front.

'What d'you think about the radio, Mike?' asked Don Smith. 'We safe to use it here?'

'Yeah. I'm sure we can. So long as we restrict ourselves to short bursts. It's darned tricky, tuning into someone else's messages, especially if they only broadcast for a few seconds. Anyway, even if the Argies did hear us, it'd be damned near impossible to locate us from that, unless you had really sophisticated equipment, which I doubt they do out here. You wouldn't expect anyone to be here, would you? No one in their right mind, anyway.'

'No one wants a postponement,' said Commander Hunter. 'But we'll have to bag it for another twenty-four hours because the journey has to be made at night. And we sure as hell can't do that. No one's gonna thank us for getting drowned.'

And so they waited it out for the day, with the sea remaining far too dangerous. They fired in a message to Douglas Jarvis on *Foxtrot three-four* to stay on hold for forty-eight hours, and once more waited out the night.

Not until noon, however, did the waves begin to die down, along with the wind. It remained very turbulent even in the relative shelter of Pebble Sound, and the waves still hit the shore with a thumping crash, but it was not like the previous night – nothing like the gale which had been building since the canister first hit the beach.

A blanket of fog closed in over West Falkland by 1300, and it was no longer possible to see across the stretch of water which divided the mainland from Pebble Island. This was a blessing, because they could relax and use the Primus stoves to make soup and coffee with not the slightest chance of detection by the Argentines who, they hoped, were not even looking anyway, with their British enemy long departed.

By 1400, Commander Hunter thought they'd be able to leave when the light began to fail at 1700 and row as fast as possible across the channel. As far as he could tell, the sea would flow in from their starboard quarter, giving them some assistance, but they would need to keep steering right in order not to drift too far off the headland at which they'd be aiming. The compass bearing would read three-zero-zero all the way. If they were lucky it might be possible to knock it off in two hours, but the wind, calmer now, was still out of the north-west and it would gust right on their nose.

At 1500, he radioed a satellite signal back to Coronado: '*Stormy petrels seaward 1700. Shingle forecast 1900.*'

They began changing into heavy-duty wetsuits for the journey. Each man would have flippers and his rifle would be clipped on, the idea being that if either or both inflatables capsized – a fifty-to-one chance at worst – the men would grab onto the unsinkable hull and be able to propel themselves forward with the big flippers.

Engines on the first leg of the journey were out of the question because of the noise, and the near-impossibility of rescue, so far away, ruled out the use of one-time survival suits. If the SEALs went into the sea they would have to fight their own way back to shore. The waterproof radio was sealed tight and placed in the care of Mike Hook, who anticipated no accidents. The sea looked fierce, but navigable.

At 1700 they carried the two inflatables down the beach and loaded in their equipment, and fixed engines for the getaway.

Hoods up, tight rubber gloves on, Rick gave orders for the four men in the second boat to watch him mastermind the first launch and then follow. His plan was to push the raised bow out into the surf, wait for the wave to thump and pass, then shove, running the boat forward through the frothy shallows. All the boat's crew would leap inboard and paddle like hell to beat the next breaking wave. 'What you wanna avoid, guys, is getting caught under the wave because it'll swamp the boat and you'll have to start again.'

Rick, for'ard on starboard, moved into the water, keeping in step with his partner on the port side. They watched the next wave crash twenty feet in front of them, felt it swirl past, knee deep. Then Rick yelled, 'G-O-O-O-O!' and all four of them pounded forward, racing through the undertow, watching the rise of the next wave up ahead.

'N-O-W-W-W-W!' roared the commander, and the three others leaped over the side, grabbed the paddles and straddled the inflated hull as if it were a horse, driving the thick wooden oars into the water and heaving, long deep strokes. They just made it, climbing the breaking wave, paddling with every ounce of their strength until they broke free at the crest and pushed on into calmer water.

Behind them the second boat was obscured, but as the wave crashed onto the shore they could see Dallas MacPherson and his men charging into the shallows and then diving over the side into the boat. For a minute, Dallas thought the wave had them and would send them tumbling back onto the beach.

But suddenly the second boat came barrelling off the crest, driven by brute force and determination but staying more or less dry. Free of the breakers now, Dallas and his men rowing with frenzied clumsiness, moving the boat forward.

'*Good job, kid!*' yelled Rick across the foggy water. 'Now fall in. Get that boat right off our starboard beam where I can keep a good eye on you.'

'I'll say one thing, Commander Hunter,' the officer from South Carolina shouted back. 'Even when I'm inches from fucking death in a hell-hole like this, you still think I'm as crazy as you!'

Rick's great roar of laughter recalled for both of them other times when they had cheated death together. And each of the other men sensed it as well, deriving comfort from the confidence it displayed as they settled into a steady rhythm, moving the boats forward through the drifting fog, leaving behind a small bubbling wake on the leaden surface of Pebble Sound.

They stayed close, separated by only fifteen feet. Rick Hunter called out the stroke rate: '*And NOW . . . and two . . . and three . . . and four . . .*'

Occasionally glancing at the tiny light on his compass, he would order a minor course change: '*Dallas . . . follow us . . . port side easy, and starboard side two hard . . . now altogether . . . and one . . . and two . . . and three . . .*'

They kept going for a half-hour, then rested. But Rick was afraid to wallow around for long because he knew the tide would drag them off course. They each had a drink and settled back to row for another thirty minutes, warm in their wetsuits but going slower than they had hoped because of the choppy sea, which kept shoving the light bows of the boats upwards.

By 2030 they were still going. It was now pitch black and there was no sign of land. Rick's GPS was telling him they ought to be on the beach by now, but visibility was so bad he didn't know how close they were. Eventually he called for the tired rowers to stop. They must have headlands on either side, so he was proposing to make a right turn and hope to hit a beach.

The weary SEALs nodded and Rick's boat scraped up onto a sheltered shingle beach just five minutes later.

Landing in the shallows, they dragged the boats out, unloaded the equipment and moved towards the low hills behind the shoreline. There was no sign of life, no light, no buildings. Visibility was still only about twenty yards, and they went back for the boats, then made camp for the night, brewing some more tea and heating soup, silently preparing themselves for the opening mission at the airfield.

At 2100 Rick Hunter sent in his signal to Coronado: '*Petrels nesting on shingle.*'

With sub-machine guns cocked and ready, the troopers had tea with bread and cheese at 2200, and for the third time Rick repeated his detailed briefing: 'We cut the wire right here and move forward onto the runway, all together. All the aircraft are parked 100 yards further on, to the right. We move down together unless there is an emergency or a patrol, in which case Bob and Ron peel off left and right of the concrete and take 'em out. The rest of us hit the deck, in the grass.'

'That applies both before and after we fix the aircraft?' asked Dallas.

'No. Only before. Ron and Bob are not explosives guys. During the operation Bob will man our big machine gun, the one that arrived in the canister – right here . . . that way he can cover all directions. His relief will be Ed Segal because he'll be leaving early . . . and, anyway, a patrol can come from only one direction, straight down here from the building. The trick is to stay quiet.'

'OK, sir. Got it.'

'Right,' continued Rick. 'Only six of you will work on the aircraft. Ed stands guard, while Bob cuts out the new exit.

'Now, the timers are set for sixty minutes after we've finished. That's our getaway window. And we're moving out fast to the west, on a different route back to the beach. There's a gate in the way, which Bob will have dealt with before we reach it. If we are caught on the fucking airfield we don't want to be restricted by having only one way out through the wire, because that's where any Argentine patrol will be waiting for us – if they've got any sense.'

Everyone nodded, and Rick pressed on, illuminating the map with his narrow flashlight.

'OK, guys, we charge through Bob's gate right here – and 400 yards along, here . . . On this track where we're headed the guys in planning have marked a very large low building, surrounded by wire, which they think is a huge ammunition dump. By the time we arrive there Bob will have cut an entry gap, and we'll proceed to blow it sky-high with the hand grenades. These places usually have a few minor explosions first and then it takes about four more minutes for the whole lot to go up, which gives us time to get clear.'

He looked around at the small group. 'With luck the Argentine patrols will think it was some kind of accident and no one will even guess we might have blown up the aircraft – and that's important.

Because until they see that ammo dump go up, they will not even suspect we were there.'

'How big an explosion is it, taking out one of those aircraft?' asked Bob.

'Not very, because it's internal,' replied Rick. 'Our aim is to split the engine in half. This makes a bit of a thump, but it's dull, muted, with hardly any flash. There's a good chance they won't even notice till the morning. If the guys at Coronado are correct, that ammunition dump is going to look, and sound, like Hiroshima for about twenty minutes. It's full of fucking bombs and missiles and Christ knows what else . . .'

The SEALs spent another five minutes looking at the map to memorise every detail. Then, gathering up the magnetic bombs and detonating gear, plus their own sub-machine guns, hand grenades and ammunition, they set off for the airfield, moving low through the elephant grass.

Using just the compass and GPS they followed the maps, which would lead them to the airfield and the destruction of the entire Argentine air operation on Pebble Island.

It took them a couple of hours to get there, moving quietly and well off the track through the pitch-black night. When they arrived they checked out the small settlement located close to the airstrip, on the south part of a narrow piece of land about five miles from the landing area.

Each house was marked on the map, but the entire place was dark: no lights, no sentries, only the homes of Falkland Islanders and farmers. Not one sign of an Argentine military presence.

The airbase, according to Coronado Intelligence, now contained less than seventy-five personnel. Rick's map showed – accurately, he hoped – the position of all fifteen aircraft on the ground, parked in lines of three west of the runway.

The problem was, as so often down here in the fickle, frigid weather systems of the South Atlantic, that the wind seemed to be rising again. Rick Hunter could feel it gusting across Pebble Sound, no doubt putting whitecaps on the low waves through which they had to drive the inflatables.

Out in front of the airbase where they now stood he could hear the wind tugging at the beach grass. The black sky overhead seemed ominous with its layers of dark cloud banks which completely blocked out the moon and stars.

The getaway would be increasingly difficult if this weather

continued, but the attack on the aircraft would take place under the best possible conditions, darkness and the howling wind obscuring the SEAL team's movements.

The rest of the group crouched against a grass hillock while Ron Wallace and Bob Bland moved forward to the tall unlit fence where they would clip a ten-foot gap in the thick wire netting.

According to Commander Hunter's map all the aircraft lay dead ahead, down the runway to the right. By some miracle, Ron and Bob found the fence twenty yards on, right where the map indicated it would be, and, five minutes later, all the SEALs moved forward through the gap.

At Rick's order they crept slowly and stealthily down the runway, counting the strides to 100, at which point they guessed the aircraft would be on the right. Another three minutes went by until Don Smith walked straight into an A-4 Skyhawk and uttered a short, sharp 'Fuck!'

Rick clicked on his flashlight and whipped the beam around. For the first time they could see their targets. He snapped softly, 'OK. Deploy.'

The SEALs with the explosives headed to the first two lines of aircraft. It was 0006, and Brian Harrison climbed the length of a plane and positioned himself on its wing, as arranged. Ed Segal was crouched low and Dallas placed his right foot in the middle of his back, pushed upwards and grabbed for Brian's hand. Two others seized his legs and pushed up. Dallas MacPherson was on the wing in four seconds flat.

Expertly he moved to the nose-cone panel where the avionics equipment was located as well as the front-undercarriage hydraulics. He placed a charge right in the middle, setting it for 120 minutes. Then he opened the panel of the port-side engine, the access point used for lubrication, and placed another small magnetic bomb right in there, angled to blow the engine block in half.

The nose-cone of the second Skyhawk was much more securely locked, so Dallas decided to blow both engines clean in half. While he set the charges he ordered a team member, 'Get in the fucking cockpit and cut and rip every wire you can see, and boot out all the dials on the instrument panel on the way out.'

Ron Wallace chuckled silently at the determination of the young SEAL explosives king, but he wondered what the point was of wrecking the instruments if the darned aircraft didn't have any engines. Still, Dallas was a thorough man.

Skyhawks three and four were tackled in the same way. But it was taking too long and Rick instructed them to take out the next four aircraft with one charge in the cockpit and another in the engine, which was much faster.

'Right now we've got forty minutes for the last seven bombers,' he hissed quietly. 'Dallas, you and Mike better take the far two . . . I'll take care of the next two right here. Three men with each aircraft, the timers are all preset for sixty minutes after we leave. Ed's got the chart on the little computer – he'll just hand you the correct timer for the final group, numbered one to seven on the casing.'

It took all of the forty minutes to complete the operation, but they made it. There had been no sign of a patrol from the airbase buildings, and the SEALs quickly gathered up the remains of their equipment – loose wire ends, cutters, screwdrivers – stuffed them in their rucksacks and ran behind Rick Hunter, crouching low and heading straight for the gate that Bob Bland had just rendered useless.

They ran, faster now, down the track, with Commander Hunter using the flashlight every few seconds for the briefest possible direction check. It took five minutes to reach the big shed, but not until they stood directly in front of it could they see the tall wire gate. Inside, Rick's flashlight picked out a large sign — a skull and crossbones with the word *'PELIGRO!'* – danger in Spanish.

'Holy shit!' said Rick. 'This is it.'

'You're right,' said Dallas. 'And we plainly have to give it proper attention.'

Everyone within range chuckled softly. Rick called out softly 'Bob? You in there?'

'Right here,' hissed back their resident burglar. 'I've severed the gate wire. The lock was too tough to crack in four minutes – but you can get in here.'

Rick and Dallas climbed through, smashed a window, and swiftly dropped two powerful short-delay charges inside. They climbed back out to the road, hurled four grenades through the broken glass and ran for their lives, diving into the grass as the smallish explosives went up.

They set off fast, charging down the track to put themselves as far away as possible from the shed before the stuff exploded. They were half a mile away when the ammunition dump blew.

The ground literally shuddered. The whole darned island seemed to shake from end to end and the flash from the explosion of about fifty 1,000lb bombs lit up the night. Three minutes later, looking back from a hill further on, the SEALs could see the raging fires in the shed at the perimeter of the airfield.

They could also make out headlights from two or three vehicles speeding towards the area, down the track. Rick stared at his watch and just faintly felt another shudder in the ground as all fifteen aircraft on the runway exploded with dull crumps.

None of them would ever fly again, but Rick doubted if the Argentine military would notice yet, given their proximity to the mightiest blast in the southern hemisphere since Krakatoa blew its stack in 1883.

'That's it for us, guys,' he snapped. 'Now, to utilise an old SEAL phrase, let's get the fuck out of here.'

He checked the compass and the GPS and led the way. They moved three times as fast as they had on the inward journey. Empty-handed except for their weapons and ammunition clips, they raced through the biting wind, charging over the flat, cold ground, straight for the beach.

The SEAL team covered the final half-mile in record time and hurled themselves into the shelter of the rocks. Dallas and Ron Wallace laughed with excitement, looking back at the brightly lit sky to the west to watch the continuing violent explosions.

The time was 0230 and the sea was pounding.

'We going, sir? In this?' Mike Hook sounded concerned.

'We're going, Mike. In this,' replied Rick. 'At first light someone's going to know we were here because they'll find the blown aircraft. It'll take 'em about an hour to have a massive search party operational, and they'll be combing this island with helicopters. I don't care where we are six hours from now, just so long as we're not on Pebble Island.'

During the next half-hour the SEALs ate on the run. Ed Segal made ham and cheese sandwiches, while the rest carried their gear down to the water's edge. They upended the boats and carried them both down to the same spot, checking the engine bolts on the stout wooden transoms of the inflatables, connecting the fuel lines and the electric wires to the oversized batteries. Finally they went back for the extra fuel cans and carried them down to the departure zone.

All were wearing heavy-duty wetsuits and life jackets, but in this surf there was no question of loading the boats in the water so they piled their gear into the inflatables at the seaward end of the beach. Then came the tricky part.

Once more Rick Hunter lined up his team. In the lead boat he was taking Mike Hook, Bob Bland and Ron Wallace. Don Smith would provide the heavy muscle at the starboard bow of the second boat with Dallas, the second team leader on the port bow. Brian Harrison and Seaman Segal would work at the stern.

With the inflatables now loaded with all the SEALS' worldly goods, they could not afford to capsize. Standing in the shallows, Commander Hunter went over the drill again.

'Wait for the wave to break and roll in, then haul the boat in till it floats. Take your positions and shove like hell, straight at the next wave . . . head-on to the break . . .'

Rick pumped his right fist and added, 'The moment you feel the bow riding up . . . *Get in! Up and over the side . . . Helmsman! Hit the ignition and open the throttles. The other three get on the bow, weigh the nose down. and for Christ's sake hang on to the handles.'*

Commander Hunter did not hear one, 'Aye aye, sir.' However, he *did* hear two 'Fuck mes', a couple of 'Holy shits!' and a *'Jesus Christ!'* Personally, he had but one thought in his mind: *if Di could see me now she'd have a heart attack.*

He made one final check. 'Everything loaded, no traces left behind?'

'Only the biggest fire since the Brits burned down Washington,' muttered Dallas in his Southern drawl, pronouncing the nationality of the armies of His Britannic Majesty as *Bree-yuts.*

Everyone grinned in the dark, and Rick Hunter said firmly, 'Boats to the shallows, we're going together . . . watch for the wave and when I shout "GO", MOVE IT!'

They seized the handles and hauled the boats down the slope into the inches-deep foaming water. Despite the lightness of the rubberised hulls, the SEALs were groaning at the weight now that the engines were in place. Rick and Dallas primed the fuel lines and quickly tested the ignition and starter motors. Ready to go, they stood, facing the incoming South Atlantic breakers and waiting for Commander Hunter to select the right wave.

All seamen know that the ninth wave in a series is often markedly bigger than the previous eight, and Rick waited, counting and watching for the big one. When it came, the water rushed in around the SEALs' knees and Rick gave the command.

'OK, guys, into the water and let the next wave suck out. We'll go on the following one . . . FLOAT THE BOAT!'

The next wave came in with a crash and the moment it started to suck out Rick Hunter roared, 'GO! GO! GO!' at considerable volume.

The inflatables surged forward for twenty yards as they hammered through the surf in the pitch dark, guided only by the phosphorescence in the ocean. They could see the next roller coming straight at them, maybe eight feet high. And they felt the bow rise as Rick bellowed above the buffeting wind, *'NOW! . . . GET IN! . . . FOR CHRIST'S SAKE GET IN!'*

All eight of them grabbed and leaped, floundering inboard with the boat's bow rising upward. Ron Wallace was first. He hit the starter and the big Yamahas roared. The other three dived onto the bow and hung on for dear life.

In the other boat, Ed Segal hit the starter two seconds after Ron. Both helmsmen lowered the engines fully and rammed open the throttles. They surged up the face of the wave, but in the rush for the bow, now rising at forty-five degrees from the horizontal, Mike Hook slithered over the side, half in the water, half out, hanging on with only one hand.

In an astonishing display of strength, Rick Hunter, lying flat on the short curved bow, grabbed Mike's elbow, left-handed, and hauled him back on board. The wave was breaking now and threatening to turn the boat over backwards, but Ed held the throttle open and they burst through the crest in a gale of wind-swept foam, roaring forward into the calmer waters beyond the surf.

Rick glanced right and saw Ron Wallace come surging towards him. The big Zodiacs bumped together.

'Hell, Rick, that was beyond the call of duty,' yelled Dallas.

'Duty?' called Mike Hook. 'He just saved my fucking life.'

'Shut up, Hook,' said the commander, shouting to make himself heard over the waves. 'Or I'll have you charged with desertion in the face of the enemy. Now fall in, guys, and follow me through the Tamar Pass. It's gonna be a little rougher out there, and we've got an eight-mile run along the shore into the Sound. Just follow our speed. We're staying real close to the shore.'

Dallas and his team fell in, line astern, and Rick ordered Ed to make for the flashing light up ahead at flank speed. 'This channel's deserted,' he said. 'We gotta make time while we can. It's 0400 and we need shelter before 0600 when it starts to get light.'

The twenty-four-foot Zodiacs headed for the Pass, making twenty-five knots in the choppy sea, slicing through the tops of the waves, riding the stump caused by the howling propeller.

Ed Segal, steering the lead boat, could see the flashing light coming up on his starboard bow, and he arrowed the Zodiac forward, coming off red two degrees to leave it 100 yards off his beam. And as he did so, they all felt the swell of the open ocean deepen. The bow rode up alarmingly.

They surged down into the trough. Ed Segal with a seaman's instinct, rammed back the throttle just in time, cutting the speed down to five knots, allowing them to ride up the incoming wave rather than plummet headlong into its front 'wall' and take a half-ton of green water on board.

'Great job, Eddie!' called Rick above the wind. He saw that Ron Wallace had similarly cut his speed. 'This won't last – it's just where the tide is rushing through this bottleneck. Soon as we break to the right, it'll flatten out a little . . . but it'll still be rougher than it was in Pebble Sound. NOW KEEP IT MOVING!'

In another age, Commander Rick Hunter would have stood shoulder to shoulder with Jones in the burning Bonhomme Richard.

They chugged through the seething tide for another 400 yards, then made their ninety-degree turn hard to starboard, pursued by a driving four-knot South Atlantic surge on their port quarter.

But Segal and Hunter were its masters. Rick ordered the helmsman to come off eight degrees from their due east, zero-nine-zero course.

'Come left, little more, Ed . . . This way we'll get a decent shove from the tide without being forced inshore all the time. Now make your speed fifteen . . . no more for the next half-hour. That's for seven miles, then we better slow down.'

Hard astern the sky was still lit up by the burning ammunition store, but right ahead there was only a heavy darkness, visibility not twenty feet, even with a bright western horizon. According to the softly lit GPS they were only 350 yards offshore, but the depth gauge showed 100 feet of water.

This was the most dangerous part of the operation – exposed off the north shore of West Falkland, easy prey for any Argentine warship or helicopter. The slightest suspicion of the SEALs' presence would have sent the entire Argentine army, navy and air force into a collective war dance, swearing vengeance. Rick Hunter shoved the thought firmly to the back of his mind.

Ed Segal and Ron Wallace kept going forward into the night, confident of the accuracy of the US military Intelligence info that these seas were utterly deserted for now.

It was the calm before the storm, lasting only for another four or five hours, until the air force ground staff realised that someone had blown the bombers on the Pebble Island airbase. And then all hell would break loose. Rick Hunter prayed that SEAL Team Two would blow up Mare Harbour sometime this morning and give his guys a bit of breathing room to get away.

They pressed on along the coast, gaining some shelter from the offshore wind which had now backed around to the south-west. But it was still freezing cold, and whoever had insisted the SEALs should wear their wetsuits for this entire operation deserved, in Commander Hunter's opinion, some kind of a medal.

And the Zodiacs were outstanding too, riding the stump of the Yamahas and driving smoothly along the wave-tops, drawing less than a foot of water. The trick was to get the speed dead right: thirteen would have been choppier as the boat sagged into the water, but eighteen knots would have thrown them 'out of tune' with the quartering sea. On second thoughts, Rick Hunter thought, both helmsmen, Ed and Ron, deserved medals as well.

Huddled behind the windshields and trying to keep down out of the cold, the US Navy SEAL team took another half-hour to make White Rock Point. They never saw a boat, never heard an aircraft, never even saw a light, neither onshore nor at sea.

They cut back the throttles at the sight of the flashing beacon on the Point and came trundling slowly over the shallow kelp beds, their engines slightly raised, and into Falkland Sound. Rick Hunter ordered a course change to one-seven-zero to bring them back into the south-running channel, and at this speed, on much calmer waters, they made hardly a sound, even in the silence of the night.

After two miles, running at only eight knots, Commander Hunter ordered another change: 'Two-two-five, Eddie . . . we want to head down the shore of West Falkland, slowly, for about eight miles. That's when we turn away and find shelter . . .'

'Where, sir?' asked Ed Segal.

'We'll head into Many Branch Harbour,' said the commander. 'That's to our right, a landlocked bay. If we get through to *Foxtrot three-four* – we'll be gone by 2030 tonight.'

0900 Wednesday 27 April
Argentine Military Garrison
Goose Green, East Falkland

'*Goose Green – Mount Pleasant HQ. We have reports of a massive attack on the airfield at Pebble Island. All fighter aircraft destroyed, ammunition dump still blazing, everything destroyed. No casualties, but Pebble airbase requests assistance for aerial surveillance. Proceed all three helicopters to Pebble Island immediately, with troops embarked. Repeat, proceed to Pebble Island. Runways and landing areas intact.*'

'*Will extra assistance fly up from Mount Pleasant?*'

'*Affirmative. Six helicopters and three fixed-wing aircraft, containing a detachment of seventy-five troops.*'

'*Do we have a warship in the area?*'

'*Negative. But destroyer scheduled to depart Mare Harbour at 1100 today.*'

'*We're on our way, sir.*'

That final piece of Argentine naval intelligence was never going to happen. Even as the radio communications flashed between Mount Pleasant and Goose Green, US Navy SEAL Lt. Commander Chuck Stafford and his underwater team were edging their way back to their base-camp meeting point on the shores of East Cove.

They had been holed up for three days, with all their gear and two inflatables, in a deep cave right on the shore, a cave which had the inestimable advantage of flooding to a depth of almost two feet at high tide. This meant the team kept everything in the boats and jumped aboard, all twelve of them, when the cave floor started to submerge.

Their getaway was timed for the rising tide at 1900, when there would be just sufficient water in the cave for them to escape fast, approximately ninety minutes before the tide peaked at 2030.

More significant, however, was the fact that the veteran explosives expert Chuck Stafford and five of his crack underwater crew had attached limpet bombs to all four of the Argentine warships currently moored in Mare Harbour, two old Type-42 destroyers and two guided-missile Exocet frigates.

The bombs were timed to detonate at 2230, which would give the fleeing SEALs ample time to make the three-mile journey over very rough ground back to their cave, and then get well under cover for the blasting of Mare Harbour.

★

While Lt. Commander Stafford and his team were heating up soup on their Primus, Commander Hunter's team were hunkered down forty miles away to the north-west, in a long narrow bay running to a cul-de-sac, south-west out of the main harbour, following the line of the shore.

They had found this utterly desolate spot after a two-hour search and had chugged into a fifty-foot inlet surrounded by rocky cliffs fifteen feet high. Rick Hunter had taken one look at it and ordered Brian Harrison to jump out and check out what he could see from the clifftop to the east.

The SEAL petty officer climbed the easy sloping rock face and was gone for fifteen minutes. When he returned he reported, 'There's a line of low hills about 200 yards from here. From the top I can see the Sound, way beyond the entrance to the harbour. Aside from that there's nothing, not even a house or a shed. And no sheep.'

Rick Hunter had already dismissed the idea of any warship coming after them: the water through the harbour entrance was too shallow. Even a patrol boat would think twice.

For the moment, the two teams of United States Navy Special Forces, the specialists from SPECWARCOM, were safely in their daytime quarters, unseen by and unknown to their enemy. Which was the way they liked it.

On the far-distant shore, however, Captain Jarvis and his team were slightly the worse for wear. They had made their way to a lonely hillside above Egg Harbour and positioned themselves in a gully from where they could see down to the waters of Falkland Sound. The damn place had little vegetation and they'd used up much of it on the first night, when they had cut the gorse and pulled up grass to give themselves concealment from aerial search.

Twice they'd almost been caught moving across the narrow isthmus near Goose Green, both times by vehicle patrols, but each time they had gone to ground, flattened into the earth, sub-machine guns cocked just in case. Both near misses happened in the late afternoon, and the patrols were moving too fast, but the second one passed less than twenty feet from where the SAS team were laying prostrate, face down in a ditch.

The Argentines did not see them and as the night grew darker Captain Jarvis steered his men across the barren wasteland of East Falkland to the tiny harbour where he expected the American – 'Sunray' – and his guys to show up.

The silence of Tuesday night was a major disappointment to the captain. No radio communication had been received and the SAS men were growing tired in their filthy, dirty clothes. But, thankfully, there was no injury or illness. Everyone felt scruffy but otherwise fine. They had maintained fairly high standards of diet and when it was clear that Sunray had gone missing, Douglas authorised a new sheep raid. At midnight they had all enjoyed excellent roast lamb and bars of some kind of compressed spinach that tasted like cow-shit. At least, according to Trooper Wiggins it did.

Up here in the hide above Egg Harbour they were nowhere near fresh water, and their own water supplies were running short. That night Troopers Goddard and Fermer went to sleep in the gully under the bushes with sheep's blood on their hands.

As Jake Posgate had remarked, 'It's like a scene from *Dracula's Revenge* up here.'

And so they slept, aware only faintly of the Argentine search going on for them because it was being conducted in a thoroughly half-hearted way. Just the occasional helicopter flying north, and nothing overhead along the Egg Harbour shoreline. Douglas guessed, correctly, that the jeep which contained the bodies of the four Argentine soldiers had not yet been found.

But this morning, Wednesday, the skies suddenly resembled some World War Three scenario. It was now 0930 and three helicopters had taken off in quick succession from Goose Green and headed due west, straight over the SAS hide at high speed, flying up Falkland Sound.

Three fixed-wing military aircraft had also flown just to the north of them, heading the same way, at no more than 5,000 feet. In the distance they could hear more helicopters clattering, just west of San Carlos Water and all apparently heading for the same objective.

'Jesus,' said Douglas. 'They must have found the bodies.' He was as yet unaware of the devastation on Pebble Island, and an hour from now he would be too far away to notice the imminent chaos in Mare Harbour. Right now he was merely counting off the hours to 2000 when he prayed he would hear again from the elusive 'Sunray'.

Some distance away, Rick Hunter too and all of his team watched the helos thumping through the leaden skies directly overhead. They were not surprised, however, only thanking God they had risked the heavy seas and put ten miles between themselves and the Pebble Island airfield.

Rick was thoughtful as they sat in the lee of the rocky overhang in their tiny bay. At 1030 it was still silent in Many Branch Harbour. No fishing boats. No boats of any kind. Although from the bluff, Brian Harrison reported a couple of trawlers heading north up Falkland Sound, maybe two or three miles from them.

In Mare Harbour, however, things were far from silent. Lt. Commander Stafford's twelve limpet bombs, stuck on the warships' hulls below the waterline, for'ard, midships and aft, all detonated together with a dull underwater *K-E-R-R-U-M-P!* causing the jetties to shudder and the harbour waters to rise up into a boiling maelstrom which crashed onto the shore, obscuring for a moment any view of the savage destruction of all four ships.

The Argentine naval personnel in the harbour looked on in horror, squinting through the spray and billowing smoke, unable to comprehend what was going on. Four warships, calmly moored at the jetties, with no enemy on the horizon, ablaze from end to end. And the skies were completely empty: no one had dropped a bomb, never mind four bombs.

The scene was one of total chaos and Argentine officers quickly leaped to the alarmingly false conclusion that someone's navy had lambasted the ships with guided missiles, well-aimed guided missiles at that. But no one had seen anything – no dart-shaped winged killer with a fiery tail hurtling out of the skies. And these ships must have been hit by more than one missile apiece since all of them were ablaze in three different places. Great fires were raging below the foredecks, huge flames and billowing black smoke were surging upwards from their engine-room areas, and one of the frigates looked as though its stern had been blown clean off the hull. This had been a big multi-hit, carried out by forces who clearly knew their stuff.

But whose forces? The surrendered Brits, what was left of them, were limping home. *Caramba!* Everyone in Argentina had seen the aerial photographs of the defeated Royal Navy fleet heading north back up the Atlantic. No, the Brits had not done this. Then who had? There was not a sign of a foreign warship in the waters surrounding the Malvinas within a 200-mile radius. And the skies were clear of military aircraft. Any aircraft, for that matter.

And if it was not bombs or missiles, then what was it? The Argentine naval officers, still staring in disbelief at the appalling scene of absolute devastation in the harbour, were baffled. They moved quickly into action, trying to organise stretcher parties to evacuate the wounded and to connect fire hoses to aim at the ships which were growing hotter by the minute.

They were trying to work out how best to evacuate the entire area when the first fire blazed into one of the ships' missile magazines and unleashed the kind of explosive power that could swiftly demolish a town, never mind a few stone buildings in a scarcely used harbour.

The scene was much like that which had faced the British in February when their 1,400-ton lightly-armed patrol ship *Leeds Castle* had been obliterated by Argentine missiles. As Saint Matthew wrote in Chapter XXVI of his Gospel, *Those who take the sword shall perish with the sword.*

And when it came to death, Lt. Commander Stafford's men had caused a lot more of it than Rick Hunter's team, and they made Douglas Jarvis's skirmish on the mountain look like kids' stuff.

There were crews of at least twenty-two officers and men on each of the warships, some on watch, some asleep, some working on maintenance in the engine rooms. Only nine in total survived the savage blasts, the echoes of which would be quickly heard around the world.

In the Argentine military headquarters at Mount Pleasant chaos reigned as commanders tried to make sense of the barbaric attacks by an unknown enemy. Just the previous day, the marine major Pablo Barry had flown in for a visit, and the entire officer community on sea, air and land was now looking to him for guidance. Major Pablo had, after all, conquered the damn place in the first instance.

But he was as bewildered as any of them. The news from Pebble Island was terrible, and the news from Mare Harbour was even worse, given the heavy loss of life. Major Pablo Barry stared out at the airfield in silent rumination. Lined up were Argentina's all-conquering Skyhawks, Daggers and Étendards, the most dangerous air-combat force in South America. And he did not have the slightest idea against whom to unleash them.

The situation was, in his opinion, extremely unnerving. Here they were being smashed to pieces by an enemy who was refusing to identify himself, an enemy they could not see. To Major Pablo, it was clear, those ships had not been hit by incoming bombs, nor by missiles. And, given the near-simultaneous attack on Pebble Island, there was no question of random, opportunistic sabotage.

No, thought Major Pablo. Those ships had been blown up inside the harbour, by bombs which must have been attached to the hulls. Nothing else fitted. Nothing else made the slightest bit of sense. Someone, somehow, had crept into the little dockyard, underwater, and planted bombs beneath the surface, all timed to go off at once. This had to be the work of highly trained forces; nothing else would fit.

Major Pablo now knew that someone had done something very similar to the aircraft at Pebble Island. The question was, who? Which country hated Argentina so badly that they would do such a thing? And how was it connected to the sheep-stealers up at Port Sussex? And where the hell were they? And where was the missing patrol? Major Pablo had about a thousand questions and no answers to any of them.

But shortly after noon someone helped him out with one piece of the puzzle. Luke Milos, wandering among his sheep up in the high pastures above his house, found the lost jeep.

The Argentine military had now been slammed three times, and Major Pablo considered it inconceivable that the three events were not somehow connected. Although what the sheep-stealers had in common with possibly two highly trained groups of Special Forces . . . well, heaven alone knew the answer to that.

But the major knew the sheep-stealers were very possibly the British SAS assault team trapped – and clearly surviving – on East Falkland after the surrender. Were the bombers of Pebble Island and Mare Harbour somehow connected? Did Great Britain have an ally who was prepared to fight on when all seemed lost? The key was to catch the sheep-stealers. The marine commander, conqueror of the Falkland Islands, was certain about that.

The major advised a general evacuation to the outskirts of the area, with all personnel warned to stay away from the airfield. He also decided that a search of Pebble Island was a total waste of time, and that the helicopters of Goose Green and Mount Pleasant should all return to the Goose Green garrison and launch their search for the SAS men from there.

Meanwhile he took a large chart of the Falkland Islands and stuck the point of his compass into the hill behind Port Sussex. From there he described a thirty-mile radius which ran way out to sea and took in all the little near-deserted harbours down the west coast of

East Falkland: Kelp Harbour, Egg Harbour, Cygnet, Port King, Wharton and Findlay.

'They're in there somewhere,' said Pablo the Conqueror. 'They're either in the hills or, more likely, on the coast. But we *will* find them.'

CHAPTER TWELVE

Wednesday 27 April

At 1400 Major Pablo Barry ordered all aircraft out of the Pebble Island area and back to base: three helicopters to Goose Green, the rest to Mount Pleasant.

At 1500 a military aircraft bearing General Eduardo Kampf and the C-in-C Fleet, Admiral Oscar Moreno, landed at Mount Pleasant for a high-emergency meeting with the commanders on the ground.

Major Barry spent a couple of hours debriefing them about the devastating events of the past twenty-four hours. And at 1700 they convened in an army situation room, inside the old Mount Pleasant airport passenger terminal, to formulate a plan.

Each of them was in agreement: the key to discovering the secret enemy was to round up the British rustlers and grill them – metaphorically, of course – before executing them all for the murder of four Argentine military personnel, several days after hostilities with Great Britain had formally ceased.

General Kampf was certain that any SAS group would make for the coast in order to seize their only possible chance of escape. The occupied fortress island of East Falkland had much in common with Alcatraz. It was surrounded by wide, dangerous waters, with no other way out.

'To remain here would mean certain capture,' said the general. 'These men are well trained and likely to be ruthless. I suggest they now have one aim in this life, and that's to beg, borrow or steal a boat. They have no other option, and even that might not work.'

'I agree,' said Admiral Moreno. 'If we want to find them, we have to comb the shore by land and air. It will require a lot of troops and we have as many helicopters as it takes.'

He glanced at his watch and said quietly, 'It's getting on for 1800 and growing dark. We must prepare to launch this manhunt at first light tomorrow. Therefore we should start to get organised right now – gas up the aircraft, establish pilot and aircrew schedules. That way we can go to work as soon as it's light over the airfields.'

If solutions were becoming simple in the front line of the Argentine military, back in Buenos Aires they were getting highly complex. The president of Argentina, in company with his principal ministers, had received this afternoon a somewhat perplexing note from the United States Ambassador, Ryan Holland.

It came directly from the White House, and it was signed by the US President himself, even though the letter itself had been crafted by the delicate hand of Admiral Arnold Morgan.

It read: *Dear Mr President: Needless to say, we in Washington have been deeply saddened to hear of your recent losses of aircraft and warships on the Falkland Islands. These were most unexpected attacks, and apparently without either reason or an obvious culprit.*

You will by now have received our electronic communiqué, with regard to reaching a satisfactory agreement with both Great Britain and the US oil companies over the future of the new Malvinas. Perhaps you may feel inclined to furnish us with a reply, with a view to opening negotiations with all interested parties.

The United States would be more than happy to both broker and host such talks. Yours sincerely, Paul Bedford, President, United States of America.

The Argentine president read the letter with equanimity at first, which was quickly replaced by a deep sense of foreboding. The first two paragraphs initially seemed unrelated to the other, but there was a certain tone, an implication.

'*Jesús Cristo!*' he breathed. 'Is this a threat?' He handed the communiqué to his Defence Minister, the trusted veteran Vice-Admiral Horacio Aguardo. Aguardo took several seconds to peruse it until he said, very firmly, 'Two things, *Señor Presidente*. First, the letter is almost certainly a veiled threat. Second, we are most definitely not going to have any kind of military altercation with the United States.'

'Are you telling me, the United States of America was responsible for the atrocities on the *Malvinas*?'

'Sir, I cannot say that. But this letter suggests the perpetrators of these military strikes against us may somehow answer to the United States.'

'As, indeed, we ourselves ultimately may do, if we are not very careful.'

'Sir, I thought we were all agreed before we went into this conflict with Great Britain, it would be a straight fight between us and our very weakened opponents. With just a little help from our friends in the frozen north. We did not anticipate any US involvement.'

'And until now we were right,' replied the president. 'Even now we cannot be sure they had anything to do with the actual attacks at Pebble Island and Mare Harbour.'

'Nonetheless, there is an undercurrent in that letter from the US President,' said Admiral Aguardo. 'You don't read it, you feel it. Because it is telling us if we don't come forward and toe the line, as laid down by the White House, something else will happen and we shall not like it.'

'I know. I know. It's hiding between every line of the letter.'

'Remind us, sir. What did that other communiqué from Washington suggest?'

'Well, the first one – delivered ten days ago – made it clear the USA did not approve of our military action, and when the time was right Washington would step in on behalf of Exxon Mobil.'

'Yes, of course,' said Dr Carlos Montero, the Minister for Industry and Mining. 'But was there any indication of Washington's solution to the problem?'

'Absolutely,' replied the president. 'The President of the United States proposes that Argentina and Great Britain enter into a joint governing and handover period of two years. After that, with proper institutions put into operation, the *Malvinas* become a solely owned sovereign territory of the Republic of Argentina.

'At that point we wave goodbye to our friends from Great Britain and Spanish becomes the official language of the islands, which will be ruled from Buenos Aires.'

'And the oil?'

'As a part of the agreement, that will immediately be handed back to Exxon Mobil and British Petroleum, on a fifty-year contract between them and the Argentine government. The Americans will negotiate us a very fair royalty deal lasting long into the future.'

'And how about for the next two years?'

'We will share that royalty with the government of Great Britain, sixty-six per cent for us, thirty-three per cent for them. They did, after all, manage the exploration and licensing for many years.'

Admiral Aguardo nodded, gravely. 'And how about our friends in the Kremlin?' he said. There was a moment of nervous silence.

'Well, they will have to understand that the sudden intervention of the Americans has rather changed the game,' replied the President.

'Yes – they probably won't want to raise their heads above the parapet,' said the admiral. 'After all, the entire exercise cost them no more than a couple of plane fares and three torpedoes, I believe.'

'Perhaps,' said the president. 'But I don't much like being manhandled into a corner by the Americans. And quite frankly I do not think we should jump just because Uncle Sam has growled. And he's done that pretty quietly.'

'So he may have, sir,' said the admiral. 'But he has big teeth, and he can be very vicious, especially when someone runs off with a couple of billion dollars' worth of assets which belong to a US corporation.'

'I am aware of that,' said the president. 'Nevertheless, I believe we have one chance, only one, to come out on top in this thing. We need to capture that Special Forces group which is rampaging around the *Malvinas*. If they will talk under . . . er . . . duress, we just might be able to hang the Americans out to dry in front of the United Nations – you know, launching clandestine attacks on us, murdering our seamen in Mare Harbour, assassinating our soldiers in Port Sussex.

'But I am inclined to agree. If we don't capture these men we would have a very difficult time persuading the Americans that the *Malvinas* and the resources of the islands rightfully belong to us.'

'Yes,' said Dr Montero. 'And then they might get very, very angry, and that would not be to our advantage, either economically or militarily.'

'So what do you think?' asked the president. 'Do we continue to defy them, refuse to answer their communiqué, and redouble our efforts to catch those fugitives in the islands?'

'That's a possibility. But if things do not work out, and the Americans demand justice for Exxon, what do we tell the United Nations?'

'We tell them as a result of a long-running territorial dispute between the Republic of Argentina and Great Britain, and as a result of broken-down negotiations, we found it necessary to assert our rights over our own sovereign territory.

'When the government of Great Britain decided to send a battle fleet down here, plainly to attack the brave servicemen of Argentina, we were obliged to sink it. This was a fair fight between two nations with very entrenched positions. In the end we won, the British were defeated, surrendered and went home. End of story.

'The assets of the *Malvinas* plainly belong to us according to the ancient traditions of the spoils of war. And we are always open to talk with the Americans. However, we are *not* prepared to be blackmailed by them.'

'One thing, sir,' added the admiral. 'What happens if our mysterious enemy strikes again, in secret, and vanishes just as completely as he has done this week? What then?'

'That depends on the degree of damage.'

'Well, say he wipes out the Mount Pleasant air and military base – destroys everything?'

'That would be very serious. And if we still had no idea who the culprits were, I think we would have to give very serious consideration to the proposals put to us by the President of the United States. Assuming, of course, he possessed sufficient influence to put a stop to these . . . er . . . most unfortunate events.'

Admiral Aguardo smiled a slightly lopsided smile. 'I don't think you'll find he has much trouble doing that, sir.'

'No. Possibly not. But I think we should try to bring this entire business to a close as soon as possible. Perhaps do nothing for a week, and then consider our position . . . but, admiral, it is imperative you urge our forces to catch those intruders on the *Malvinas*. And catch them fast.'

2000 same evening, Wednesday
Above Egg Harbour, East Falkland

Douglas Jarvis and his team were tired and hungry. They had run out of lamb, and with the sudden increase in military activity in the air the captain had decided their regular evening pastime of rustling sheep was unwise.

All day long aircraft had been coming and going, and the SAS team was still unaware of the events on Pebble Island, or at Mare Harbour. Douglas was certain the Argentines had now discovered the bodies in the jeep, and this plainly made the SAS men's position ever more dangerous.

So far he surmised the Argentines were confining their search to the immediate area around Port Sussex, but he expected the manhunt to intensify tomorrow morning at first light. He was confident about the camouflage which covered the hide. At least, he was confident the SAS team could never be seen from the air. But they were vulnerable to a massed ground search by hundreds of troops.

The trouble was they had nowhere to run. They had no access to any aircraft or any ship to get them off this confounded island. They had one chance – 'Sunray' and his team – and if *they* did not show up in the next few hours tomorrow might be the SAS men's last day on this Earth, since Douglas neither hoped for nor expected mercy from the Argentines.

Quietly, lying back on the groundsheet, he watched Trooper Syd Ferry switch on the satellite radio and pull the big padded headset down over his ears, as he did every night at this time. He saw Syd shake his head miserably at the same old, same old electronic noise.

Suddenly, at six minutes past eight o'clock on that chill Wednesday evening, Trooper Ferry sat bolt upright. 'Fuck me,' he snapped. 'I'm getting something . . . there's a voice, sir – it's a definite voice – and I'm bloody sure it's not Spanish . . . wait a minute – it's American . . . *yes, this is Foxtrot three-four receiving Sunray . . . Foxtrot three-four receiving Sunray . . . please hold for Dougy . . .*'

He whipped the headset off and handed it to Captain Jarvis. 'It's an American, sir, asking for Dougy again – dunno how he knows your name.'

Captain Jarvis came across the trench like a mountain lion, grabbed the headset and spoke into the comms system: *'This is Foxtrot three-four receiving Sunray . . . Dougy here . . . repeat, Dougy here.'*

The response was all business. *'Free-range dockside 2200 . . . left or right main jetty query?'*

'My right 200 yards looking at you.'

'Signal us in . . . flash three slow . . . two quick . . . copy?'

'Copy. Roger out.'

The newly-improved radio-surveillance system at Argentina's nearby Goose Green garrison picked up the signal. But it was heavily encrypted, both to and from the satellite. Doug Jarvis could hear a voice and its American accent, but the electronic words had been automatically dismantled, jumbled and put back together again when they hit Foxtrot three-four's receiver. It was a voice but an unrecognizable voice, machine-made, belonging to no earthly being.

Nonetheless, the radio operator at Goose Green had heard a transient satellite transmission at 2007, received not far away, somewhere on East Falkland. Of course, it could have been a straightforward communication from one farmer to another. Many of the islanders had quite sophisticated radio systems, but this had been encrypted, and sheep farmers did not need codes.

The operator reported the transmission to the duty officer, who reported it to the Mount Pleasant air-warfare HQ. Immediately, the entire Argentine military surveillance system went on high alert, island-wide, with every possible electronic sensor tuned to pick up and possibly identify the approximate position of the receiver, or maybe the transmitter, even if they could not decipher what the words were saying.

If Commander Hunter so much as looked at that comms system again, the entire island would quiver with electronic antennae. Commander Hunter, however, had no intention of even switching on his transmitter, far less speaking into it.

He and his team had cleared Many Branch Harbour at 1930 under cover of darkness, moving through the narrow seaway into Falkland Sound and making a hard right turn down the shoreline. When they contacted Foxtrot three-four, they were running the inflatables south, with no navigation lights, three miles off the settlement of Port Howard, which housed a massive 200,000-acre sheep station, the oldest farm in the Falklands.

There was a slight chop to the water but nothing of any consequence. The helmsmen held their speed at seven knots, making for North Swan Island, which sat more or less in the middle of the Sound eight miles north-west of Egg Harbour.

Commander Hunter knew that one mile off the north coast of the island there was a submerged wreck, marked by a flashing white light. When he saw that they would change course to one-three-five, which would take them directly down the two-mile bay into the Egg Harbour dockside. There might be a slight southward pull from the tide, but he would compensate for that and keep one eye on the GPS, watching for the five flashes from Captain Jarvis's light.

'He'll probably faint when he sees me,' thought Rick.

They chugged on through the deserted water for another twenty minutes, until Rick's lookout man, Mike Hook, thought he saw something way up ahead.

'I thought it was a green light . . . but it's a bit difficult through the night glasses . . . hey, wait a minute – there it is again . . . Christ! It's a green running light about two miles south . . .'

Commander Hunter reached for the night glasses and peered through their greenish hue into the darkness. 'I can't see anything,' he said. And then, 'Oh, Jesus. Yes, I can. Mike, that's not just a green running light – I can see a red one as well. Whatever it is, it's coming dead towards.'

'Do we fight or run?' asked the petty officer, tightening his grip on his sub-machine gun.

'Right now we run,' replied Rick. 'Because we can't just wipe out a local fishing skipper, who's British.'

'What if it's an Argentine patrol?'

'We wouldn't have time to take 'em all out before someone hit the panic button to HQ. That would probably make life very tricky. That's why we run.'

'Where?'

'We make a right swing, leaving that flashing light up ahead to port – we'll get into the shelter of North Island and hope to Christ no one sees us.'

'Fast or slow?' asked the helmsman, Ed Segal.

'Slow. I just want to disappear quietly from their radar, which will be switched on for certain. Fishermen have radar as good as warships.'

'Please God it *is* a fisherman,' said Ed Segal.

Nine minutes later, tucked into the lee of North Swan island, they could hear the beat of the oncoming diesel engines. They would not see the vessel until it was past. Unless, of course, it had come looking for them.

It hadn't. It turned out to be a local trawler with better things to do and it kept right on going, making for Port Howard on the West Falkland side of the Sound.

They waited for another five minutes and crept back out, line astern, past the marked wreck on the ocean floor and then south-east towards Egg Harbour. The trawler had not been a problem. It was the time which was bothering Rick. The last thing he wanted was for Captain Jarvis and his boys to be exposed on a beach, a couple of hundred yards from the three houses close to the harbour jetty. Especially at this time in the late evening when fishermen might be leaving for their night's work.

And yet he dared not hit the throttle, simply because he had no idea of the Argentine surveillance in Falkland Sound. *Jesus, twenty-eight years ago they lost a war right here . . . right now they gotta have something listening to all traffic through here . . .*

As it happened they did not. But still, Commander Hunter could not risk it, and the two SEAL inflatables just kept going at seven knots, knowing they would be nearly twenty minutes late at the RV.

Meanwhile Captain Jarvis was leading his men quietly down the hill to a point only thirty yards from the houses on the harbour. From there, they would continue down onto the beach, beyond the wall of the jetty, and out to the deserted stretch of waterfront where the SEALs would come in.

The curve of the shoreline was not perfect because it could be seen from the houses. But the other side, where the beach angled outwards, was worse and they would be in plain view of the occupants from their living rooms, never mind from right outside their front doors.

Unknown to Douglas, they would very soon face another, much more serious problem. Major Pablo Barry had ordered four patrols out of Goose Green to drive to each of the harbours on that west coast, from Kelp Harbour twenty miles south to Flores, taking in Egg, Cygnet, Port King, Wharton, Findlay and Danson.

At each of them Major Pablo had ordered two armed troopers to disembark and take up station on the waterfront. He would deal with the rest of that long lonely shoreline at first light, with search helicopters, but for now the Conqueror of the *Malvinas* was positive he had sealed up the most likely points of escape for the sheep-stealers.

And he was no fool. Guessing his quarry was in hiding somewhere in the rough hill country up behind one of the tiny seaports, he had the jeeps pull up two miles east of each waterfront and made the two-man patrol walk the rest of the way.

Douglas Jarvis and his team, heads down in their hide, had no immediate view of the ground to the south. The track along which the Argentine guards walked was completely obscured from them. They might have spotted them on the jetties, but there had been a half-dozen locals down there at various times, presumably waiting for the returning fishing boat.

So the two Argentine soldiers had arrived at twilight and somehow slipped into Egg Harbour unobserved. The SAS men meanwhile moved very quietly in the dark, coming down the hillside with the utmost stealth, in single file, staying low, crouching almost double, reducing any silhouettes which might be seen should the moon make a sudden break from behind the cloud.

They reached the hard-top along the dock without being detected and made their way carefully down the rough track to the beach to the right of the jetty. There was light in the houses, but no sound, and Douglas led his team along the beach, trying to walk slowly to avoid the crunch of the shingle.

It was five minutes before ten o'clock and the night was pitch black. There was no sign of 'Sunray' yet. Douglas let three more minutes go by until they reached the spot he had chosen, 200 yards from the jetty.

At 2159 he pulled out the flashlight and, with his back to the houses, shielding the beam, he aimed out to sea and flashed the light five times – three long, two short. He did not expect a response but he did expect a boat. His heart unaccountably pounding he tried to penetrate the darkness of the night, his ears straining against the soft breeze for the sound of an engine. But there was only silence.

Like Rick, he had switched off the comms system, knowing the danger of the last transmission. If anything had gone wrong he could not have been informed. Troopers Wiggins and Goddard stood on either side of him. Joe Pearson, carrying the radio, was right behind, in a huddle with Fermer, Posgate, and the two unarmed-combat experts Syd Ferry and Dai Llewelyn.

And the clock ticked on. At five past ten, Douglas again signalled with the five flashes. And again there was no response, no sight, no sound of 'Sunray'.

Sternly trying to control his anxiety and fighting down a feeling of dread, Douglas Jarvis said quietly, 'They're just a bit late – only five minutes – but retreat up the beach a bit. I'll stay here by the water with Syd and Dai while the rest of you get into those rocks behind. I'll signal again in five.'

They dispersed quietly, Trooper Wiggins positioning himself alone halfway between the three men on the shore and the four men keeping watch behind the beach. At ten minutes after ten o'clock Douglas signalled again. And this time the three long flashes were a little longer, and so were the two short ones. Douglas Jarvis was praying the SEALs would somehow see the light.

They did. Rick Hunter had ordered both engines cut, and the eight SEALs, about a mile offshore now, were paddling in, hard, with firm sure strokes. They all saw the signal, the five distant quick-flicking lights like a warning buoy on submerged rocks.

Trouble was, Argentine Trooper Ernesto Frasisti, staring out of the window of the house nearest the beach, also saw it.

'Carlos,' he snapped to his comrade, 'there's something out there. I saw a light on the water, along there, right of the jetty.' The two elderly residents of the house, who had made coffee for their visitors, both stood up. The old Falkland Islander Ben Carey, a retired seventh-generation fisherman walked to the door and stepped outside, staring along the beach into the dark.

'Can't see anything myself,' he told Ernesto, who spoke not one word of English. 'Might have been the moon or something.'

But Ernesto called to Carlos, 'Come on, we must check this out – bring a cellphone.'

The two Argentine soldiers walked down the track to the beach, following the same route as the SAS men. They crunched along the shingle loudly, both of them carrying switched-on flashlights. Out at sea Rick Hunter and his men, closer now, could see the extra lights.

'What the hell's that?' muttered Rick. 'Unscheduled lights. Don't like it.'

On the beach Douglas was horrified as the lights drew nearer. 'Must be local residents,' he whispered. 'I'm going to try and bluff this out, especially if they're English.'

He stood in the glare of the light as the two Argentines approached, dazzled by the beams and unable to see who was carrying them. But Trooper Goddard who was using the night glasses could see.

'Fuck me,' he muttered. 'These guys are Argentine military. Peter . . . Peter . . . they're armed soldiers.'

Trooper Wiggins did not hesitate. Ernesto Frasisti was almost level with Douglas who still could not see his uniform against the beam of their flashlights. The Argentines were baffled by the sight of this unkempt beachcomber and that bafflement, that split second of confusion, cost them both their lives. Trooper Wiggins cut them down in their tracks with two bursts from his sub-machine gun. The only other sound was the dull crunch of the pebbles as they fell.

Quickly, all five of the rearguard SAS ran forward and gathered around the two bodies. Douglas, slightly shaken at his obvious brush with death, could only think, *What if they'd fired first?*

Instinctively, he swung around and shook the hand of Peter Wiggins. But other thoughts were cascading into his mind. What if 'Sunray' was out there, and had seen the lights and even heard the gunfire?

He grabbed for his flashlight and hit the buttons, firing five more quick beams out to sea. Still pulling hard on the oars in the inflatables, and still more than a half-mile from the shore, Rick Hunter caught the message and made one of those decisions that had made him a legend in Coronado. Every impulse he possessed was telling him, *Speed, nothing more – just go, go, go!*

'FIRE UP BOTH ENGINES!' he yelled. *'And floor those throttles – make straight for that last signal . . . NOW! NOW! NOW!'*

Segal and Wallace hit the ignition and rammed open the throttles. The bows of the Zodiacs arched upwards and the two Yamahas howled, forcing them through the water. Seconds later both boats surged up over the stump and settled onto their fastest angle, flying across the top of the choppy waves. Don Smith and Bob Bland were both upside down, their legs waving in the air, flung back by the sheer force of the power-drive to the beach alongside Egg Harbour.

The SAS men could now clearly hear the roar of the motors as Commander Hunter gunned his SEALs into the shore. Douglas hit them with five more quick-fire beams as they reached the shallows.

'ENGINES UP!' roared the SEAL chief. 'ENGINES UP!' And the two Zodiacs came slicing in to the beach where Troopers Ferry and Llewelyn, up to their thighs in water, grabbed the painters and hauled the boats in.

'OK, guys – grab your stuff and get aboard. Four men to each boat – eight of you, right?'

None of the SAS men had any idea who this giant officer was, with his face painted black and his 'drive-on rag' wrapped around his forehead. He looked like Geronimo's personal trainer.

'Captain Jarvis, your very bossy sister sent me to get you and I've crawled over broken glass to make it!'

Douglas Jarvis stared in amazement at the tall figure. 'Ricky?' he said. 'Jesus Christ! Is that you? I thought you'd retired. What the hell are you doing here?'

'Damn good question, old buddy. But I just told you: Di sent me to get her kid brother home.'

'How'd she know where I was?'

'I think she phoned your Prime Minister. You know Di. Fearless.'

Doug Jarvis flung his arms around his brother-in-law. 'Jesus, Rick, you'll never know how glad I am to see you.'

'I bet I do,' chuckled the big SEAL leader. 'And by the way, those two guys right there spread out on the beach – are they just resting, or are they dead?'

'Dead. Argentine military. Kinda jumped us. Had to blow 'em away before they did the same to us.'

'Yeah, I know the feeling,' replied Rick. 'Better load 'em in the boats. One in each. Don, Brian – give the guys a hand. Dump 'em inboard and then let's go. Fast, before someone comes looking.'

'You don't wanna just leave the dead guys, Rick?'

'Hell no. If we do, they'll get found in an hour. If we take 'em out to sea and dump 'em, it'll probably take a week. Missing soldiers are nowhere near as urgent as murdered ones, right?'

'Right,' said Doug, 'Let's dump 'em, like the man says.'

And so they all clambered aboard. Two of the SEALs shoved the boats out, stern first into the tide. The helmsmen dropped the engines and backed out into deeper water, while the two boat-men, Mike Hook and Don Smith, hauled themselves up onto the bow.

Moments later they were heading directly out to sea, back into the south-running channel of Falkland Sound, all sixteen of them – plus the late Ernesto and Carlos whose journey would be somewhat shorter.

'How far, Rick?' asked Douglas, when the introductions were more or less complete.

'Thirty miles. We'll be running down the Sound between the islands at around ten knots all the way to our meeting point. That's a spot just south of Elephant Cays, north of Speedwell Island. Way down at the south end of the Sound. You probably saw it on the map.'

'I did,' said Douglas. 'What are we meeting?'

'US navy submarine. USS *Toledo*. She had another pick-up around at East Cove at 2100. That's 100 miles away from our meeting point. She'll be there, right off the Elephants, at 0200, in about two hundred feet of water.'

'Beautiful,' said Douglas. 'They got any showers on board?'

'That submarine's got more bathrooms than the Waldorf Astoria,' said Rick. 'Get you guys smartened up. I forgot to mention, Dougy: you look like shit.'

'And of course you look absolutely fucking wonderful, all dressed up for the enclosure at Royal Ascot, right?'

Everyone laughed until Ed Segal asked, 'Rick, you got any idea what's up ahead?'

'We got a clear run steering course two–two–five,' said Rick. 'For about nine miles. Then we have to jog left through a narrow seaway off Great Island. There's a wreck to the south, and a goddamned sandbank the size of the Sahara.'

'Two–two–five?' asked Bob Bland, double-checking the course like all good navigation officers do.

'Right. Just gotta be careful around the island. It's uninhabited, unmarked, and totally fucking unnecessary, but it's there.'

And so they slipped quietly across the pitch-black waters of Falkland Sound, unseen by anyone, making a steady ten knots. It was a little after 2300, and simultaneously, USS *Toledo*, making a swift twenty knots at 150 feet below the surface, was somewhere off Sea Lion Islands, the most southerly point of the Falklands, fifteen miles off the mainland. On board were the twelve US Navy SEALs who had blown to smithereens every ship in Mare Harbour.

And right now this particular Dirty Dozen had it all over the sixteen backs-to-the-wall warriors from Egg Harbour. Because it was beginning to rain, a violent, gusting squall coming up from the south-west, freezing cold, sweeping sideways across the surface of the Sound.

Inside the *Toledo* no one even knew. The big LA Class submarine moved serenely through the depths: no swell, no chop, no wind, perfect temperature. Excellent soup and steaks for the SEALs, clean dry clothes, and a large selection of movies.

Out in the Zodiacs the rain was awful, pelting down on the rubber hulls as they made their way south. The SEALs, who were still wearing their wetsuits, were best equipped to cope with it, but Douglas Jarvis and his men were not so well insulated, huddled down inside their waterproof smocks, wearing hoods and Gore-Tex trousers. It was a wet and cold ride through seas which grew rougher by the mile as they approached the open waters of the South Atlantic.

★

Meanwhile, back in Egg Harbour, Ben Carey and his wife were wondering what had happened to Ernesto and Carlos – 'such nice young gentlemen'.

Eventually, shortly after 11.30 p.m., Ben decided to go out and take a look. He had seen the beams of their flashlights along the beach but they ought to have been back by now, especially in this weather. So while Mrs Carey went to bed, Ben made his way down to the beach, using his stout walking stick to help him along the shingle.

Of course he found nothing, certainly not Ernesto and Carlos. As he walked back to the house, he decided to make radio contact with the Goose Green emergency number, which the authorities had been transmitting all day on the Falkland Islands Broadcasting Service.

'Hello, this is Ben Carey over at Egg Harbour . . . had a couple of your boys in here this evening . . .'

'Yes, sir. Please go on.'

'Well, around ten o'clock one of 'em, nice young man called Ernesto, thought he saw a light out on the beach. So he and his colleague Carlos went out to investigate. I saw their lights along the water, but I haven't seen either of 'em since. And that was an hour and a half ago. I just took a walk along there, but I found nothing. The place was deserted. And now it's rainin' pretty hard, and I was just beginning to wonder if they was OK.'

'Mr Carey, thank you for your call. I think we'd like to send a helicopter up there and make a few checks. Could you listen for us, and maybe give us a flashlight guide down onto the jetty?'

'Oh, sure. Be glad to. How long?'

'No more than fifteen minutes.'

'I'll be out there.'

Ben poured himself a cup of cocoa, put another log on the fire, and sat down comfortably to wait. Nine minutes later he heard the steady beat of a low-flying helicopter.

He grabbed a big golfing umbrella and his flashlight, and headed out into the belting rain, closing the door behind him. He aimed the flashlight up and began turning it on and off.

Ben could see the lights of the aircraft up there and he saw it bank around and come into land, following the position of his light. It touched down on the wide blacktop along the jetty and he saw the pilot motion his thanks through the windshield.

What he saw next, however, surprised him. The helicopter's load doors burst open and one by one Argentine front-line troops, dressed in waterproof combat gear, came swarming out, sub-machine guns at the ready. There must have been twenty of them.

The commanding officer shouted, 'Which way, Ben?' in English. Ben pointed out along the beach and the entire group headed down onto the shingle and began running along the shoreline. The CO walked across and asked him again what time the two young troopers had left the house and Ben confirmed that it had been at ten o'clock.

He went back inside and sat by the fire until the CO knocked and came in. 'No sign of 'em, Mr Carey. We're quite worried. But there's not much we can do until it gets light.

'Just to check: you saw nothing else out there, or heard anything?'

'Not really, but I did see lights on the beach. And come to think of it, I thought I heard a very dull crackling sound at one point, kind of like a firework, but not so sharp. The walls in here are very thick.'

'Could it have been gunfire? Machine-gun fire?'

'Well, I don't really know what that sounds like. But anyway, there was not much of it. Just lasted a few seconds. Never thought any more about it.'

'OK. Thanks very much, Mr Carey. And good night.'

With that he was gone, and Ben heard the chopper clattering back up into the sky. What he did not hear was the Argentine CO opening up the line to HQ Mount Pleasant: *'Bravo Four Six, we have an emergency in Egg Harbour . . . two of our men missing after reported gunfire . . . possible SAS bandits now on the run in this area . . . suggest broadcast warning to islanders, and prepare for first-light search . . . weather conditions right now very bad, and these men are clearly dangerous. Lt. Colonel Ruiz, CO, Goose Green.'*

Weather conditions might have been bad in the helicopter, but they were a lot worse in the Zodiacs. For mile after mile Ed Segal and Ron Wallace drove the boats forward, their backs braced against the driving rain and cold. They made their sweep around Great Island, and set sail for the last twenty miles, now head-on into the wind and against the tide, a buffeting combination.

By 0100 they were running down into the wide waters surging in from the Atlantic. Wide and deep that was. They were driving into the wind and sea, using the kind of power which would normally hold them at fourteen or fifteen knots. Here it just kept them moving at ten knots over the seabed.

At 0140 Rick checked the GPS and ordered a two–degree course change at five knots only, to bring them onto the precise position of the RV – two and a half miles west of the kelp-strewn Elephant Cays at 52.11 south, 59.54 west.

Ten minutes later the numbers on the little hand-held GPS correlated. 'OK, guys, we got it. Any moment now the submarine should make contact, but I don't want to transmit anything above the surface of the water . . . I'm just gonna keep watching this thing – make sure the tidal drift doesn't drag us off our numbers.'

And there they sat, in the lashing rain, the pitch dark, the chill gusting wind off the South Atlantic. There were sixteen of them in the two inflatables, the bodies of Ernesto and Carlos having been heaved over the side a mile off Ruggles Island more than an hour ago.

The eight Americans, even Dallas, wanted nothing more than to get away from the freezing cold, soaking wet Zodiacs. Douglas Jarvis and his boys were as happy as any eight men could be to be finally off the hell-hole of East Falkland where they had been marooned for nearly three weeks.

Fifteen minutes later Commander Hunter ordered a 200-yard turn to the north. 'We're getting dragged off,' he said. But as the helmsmen made the course adjustment there was a sudden, massive roll on the surface of the water, as the 7,000-ton, 362-foot-long jet-black shape of the USS *Toledo* came shouldering out of the deep, not forty yards from the Zodiacs.

It was as if a full-sized destroyer had suddenly materialised from nowhere. Nuclear-powered, on a single driveshaft thicker than a telegraph pole, the submarine broke cover at an angle, its massive propeller thrashing below the surface. Then it seemed to lunge forward, making a mighty *s-w-i-s-h-i-n-g* sound in the long swells before coming to rest, its deck casing only eight feet above the waterline.

Captain Jarvis only just had time to mutter 'Jesus Christ!' before the bulkhead door at the base of the sail opened wide, and the submarine's deck crew emerged carrying boarding nets, rope ladders, and harnesses: '*OK, you guys! Make it real sharp now . . . get the hell out of those rowing boats . . . harnesses on, four at a time . . .*'

Dallas, Douglas, Ron and Peter were first aboard the Los Angeles Class ship, being half hauled and half climbing out of the Zodiacs which were now moored tight alongside. The boarding operation took less than fifteen minutes and Commander Hunter then took out his combat knife and slashed four great gashes into each of the rubberised hulls on the port side.

He leaned out and cast off the second boat before stepping onto the rope ladder, no harness, and hauling himself up onto the casing with a shout of *'Cast her away!'*

With one of the Zodiacs already sinking, the other began to ship water at a fast rate. Rick hadn't even made it inside the sail, with its door clipped shut behind him, and clambered down the companionway before both boats were on their way to the bottom in thirty-five fathoms, gone without a trace.

It was an expensive way to run a navy, but not as expensive as hanging around on the surface for half an hour trying to drag the heavy boats inboard and possibly being picked up on Argentine radar. Submarines like the *Toledo* cost a minimum $500 million apiece.

Nineteen minutes after she had broken the surface, USS *Toledo* made her turn to the south with all the Special Forces safely on board. *'Down periscope . . . and bow down ten . . . 500 . . . make your speed twenty . . . steer course one-three-five . . .'*

Captain Hugh Fraser had one thing in common with Douglas Jarvis. He wanted to get away from the Falkland Islands, or whatever the hell they were now called, as fast and as silently as possible.

1200 Thursday 28 April
The White House

Admiral Arnold Morgan had seen a few angry men in his time. But rarely had he sat in the Oval Office in the presence of a leading US industrialist who was, quite literally, fit to be tied.

'Mr President, I just cannot understand how this goddamned banana republic can ransack a massive US oil and gas field, march my men out at gunpoint and not raise as much as a squeak from the world's so-called superpower: not a threat, not even a goddamned postcard. Nothing.

'And you want me to go back and tell my shareholders, the Americans who actually own Exxon Mobil, that not only have we just been robbed of two *billlion* dollars but the President of the United States of America is not prepared to raise one goddamned finger to help us get it back.'

'Steady, Clint,' said Arnold, a fellow Texan. 'This is not quite as simple as it seems. We *are* doing something; we've got guys out there risking their lives to get this thing resolved in our favour. Two days ago we sent a communiqué to Buenos Aires, direct from the President, suggesting we all meet, right here in Washington DC, and come to terms as laid down by us.'

'What kind of terms?'

'The kind that will give you back both those big oil and gas fields along Choiseul Sound, and the one in South Georgia.'

'But we don't have any leverage down there, admiral,' replied the president of Exxon Mobil. 'No warships, no big guns, no goddamned muscle. *That's* the only language these guys understand. Jesus, we could raise an army from Texas shareholders who'd go down there and do *something*. We just can't sit here losing millions of dollars a day, not to mention our entire investment in cash, time, expertise, and plain ole Texas know-how. God damn it, President George Dubya would not have put up with it.'

Now President Bedford stepped into the conversation. 'Clint,' he said, 'I have decided to take you into our confidence. You have too big a stake in this to be kept on the outside.'

Clint nodded. Vigorously. 'Sure do, Mr President. Sure do.'

'Well, are you sworn to secrecy? Because there is no one outside this room and the US Navy Special Forces who knows what's going on. You will tell no one – not your wife, your children, your neighbours, your best friends, your fellow directors, not even your dogs. Because this is about as highly classified as it gets. So tell me, are you sworn to lifelong secrecy, so help you God?'

Arnold thought those last few words, delivered by the most powerful man in the world, had a resonant, damn nearly *holy* ring to them. He liked that.

'As my old grand-daddy used to say,' replied Clint: '*To the grave, guys, I'll take this one to the grave. Swear to God.*'

'OK,' replied Paul Bedford. 'Just so long as you remember: one word of this ever leaks out, the Secret Service will come looking for you, because you're the only person outside the military who could have leaked it. Right here, I'm talking treason against the United States of America. It's that serious. No one must ever know.'

'Like I said, Mr President. To the grave.'

'Right, I'll tell you what's going on. In the past few days, our Special Forces have obliterated an entire Argentine airbase at the north end of the Falklands, taken out all fifteen fighter-bombers on the ground, and blown sky-high probably the biggest storehouse of bombs and missiles in South America.

'A second team of US Special Forces has hit the Argentine naval base at Mare Harbour on the Atlantic side of East Falkland and wiped out the entire *Malvinas* defensive fleet – two destroyers and two guided-missile frigates.

'Basically, Clint, we're gonna go on kicking the shit out of Argentina until they come around to our way of thinking. I probably do not need to inform you this entire strategy was created by Admiral Morgan here.'

'That's good. Now you're talking my kind of language. Takes a Texan, right?'

Arnold chuckled, as did President Bedford, who continued: 'Our suggestions to the Argentine president have bordered on blackmail, intimating, somewhat elusively, that we may be in a position to have this wanton destruction of their naval and military capability stopped. But our last communiqué was very . . . well . . . arched – though I imagine the Mafia have a more graphic way of expressing it. And I should tell you that if the Argentines have not come to heel within the next twelve hours, we'll hit 'em again. And we'll keep on hitting 'em until they see sense.'

'Jeez, this is beautiful,' said Clint, beaming. 'Really beautiful. And I'd like you both to accept my apologies for my presumption in assuming nothing was happening.'

'It's happening, all right,' said the admiral. 'We're just waiting for a communiqué from Buenos Aires, confirming the Argentines agree to our solutions. And, as the President explained, one of the critical points of the agreement is the return of all the oil and gas on both islands to Exxon Mobil.'

'Gentlemen, you can't say fairer than that,' said the oil chief. 'And I'm real grateful to you both. And I wanna thank those brave guys down there for all that they're doing on our behalf. By the way, you said Special Forces – did y'all mean those Navy Sea Lions?'

Paul Bedford smiled. 'They're SEALs, Clint. SEALs. And not even I would dare to tell you whether they're involved.'

'Will there be any announcement of the next mission, I mean after it's completed?'

'Not a word, Clint. Ever. Like you, we go to our graves with our knowledge.'

'Well, gentlemen, this has been a very informative and uplifting discussion. You confidences are safe with me, and I must wish you both good afternoon.'

Clint stood up and nodded politely to them both. 'Mr President, Admiral Morgan, it's been my pleasure.' And with that the chief executive of Exxon left the Oval Office, cheerfully whistling that lone star classic, *Get Your Biscuits in the Oven, and Your Buns in the Bed*, originally performed by Kinky Friedman's Texas Jewboys.

'What the hell's that song he was whistling, Arnie?' asked the President.

'I couldn't tell you that,' replied the admiral. 'But that was one happy oil-driller when he walked out of here.'

'Probably feels he's won the state lottery after being two billion down,' said the President. 'Anyway, on behalf of Big Clint, what's our next plan in the South Atlantic?'

'Well, we got twenty Special Forces on their way into Punta Arenas, and Bergstrom is in favour of an attack on Rio Grande, Argentina's most southerly airbase. In the past eighteen months they've taken delivery of a squadron of brand new Dassault-Breguet Super Étendard F5 fighter-bombers from France.

'According to the National Security Agency surveillance pictures, they're all parked at Rio Grande, twelve of them. Those things can deliver an air-to-surface laser-guided missile with a nuclear warhead. They're lethal and could be launched from that new carrier they just ordered from France. Well, according to Ryan Holland they just ordered it. I'd say those Super-Es would be the Argentine military's pride and joy.'

'You want to send the guys in again?'

'Only if I can be absolutely sure no one's likely to be caught – and so long as Chile remains onside to help us.'

'OK, Arnie, you're calling the shots on this one. Even if those shots are ultimately in my name . . .'

2200 Thursday 28 April
South Atlantic 52.19S, 67.35W

The USS *Toledo* came smoothly out of the deep to make her rendezvous with the 3,000-ton Chilean Navy transport auxillary *Aquiles*. They were sixty miles north of Rio Grande, twenty-five miles east of the Atlantic entrance to the Magellan Strait.

All twenty-eight SEALs and SAS gathered up their kit and left the submarine for the almost empty light grey troopship sent by the President of Chile himself.

Before them was a 130-mile journey into the twenty-mile-wide entrance to the channel and then on down the long left-hand sweep of the Strait to Punta Arenas, the great Chilean seaport which sat at the foot of the Andes.

Once the *Aquiles* passed the headland of Point Dungeness, three miles off their starboard beam, the rest of the shoreline, on either side of the seaway, was Chilean. They expected to dock in Punta Arenas at 0700 on Friday, 29 April.

It was a relaxed, uneventful journey, conducted almost entirely in the dark, the Chilean CO following the buoyed ten-fathom channel for 100 miles. The SEALs and the SAS team had dined the previous evening on board *Toledo* – bowls of excellent minestrone soup and steaks.

But the spread laid out before them in the dining room of the *Aquiles* brought joy to their hearts: the CO had gone all out for the *Americanos* – *curanto*, a hearty stew of fish, shellfish, chicken, pork, beef and potato, accompanied by both *chapalele* and *milcao,* delicious Chilean potato breads. Douglas Jarvis and the other sheep-stealers had found their heaven on a twenty-three-year-old former hospital ship with German diesel engines.

They slept for six hours and prepared to leave shortly after 0630. They were showered and shaved, with freshly laundered clothes, and were carrying further clean stuff in their bergens. It had been a long time since Captain Jarvis and his men had felt this good. And when they finally docked in the Chilean Navy's Punta Arenas base, about an hour later, on a cold crisp morning, there was a spring in the step of the SAS men for the first time for two weeks.

Commander Hunter's men felt good as well. And so did their leader, until he saw with some dread a familiar figure standing at the bottom of the gangway. Standing in front of a long black Chilean Navy staff car was the unmistakable head of SPECWARCOM, Admiral John Bergstrom.

Good grief! thought Rick. *There's only one goddamned reason on this Earth he could be here. Where the hell does he want us to go now?*

A voice right behind him muttered, 'Holy shit, that's Bergstrom.' Dallas MacPherson was thinking precisely the same thoughts as his leader.

'Morning, Rick, and very well done,' said the admiral, holding out his right hand. 'Everything went according to plan?'

'Most of it,' replied the SEAL leader, smiling. 'You'll have received the signal that Captain Jarvis is safe. He had a few difficult moments, but he's right behind me, if you would like to meet him?'

'I'd like to meet him very much.'

Bergstrom didn't move from his spot, though, and Rick smiled again. 'I can tell you did not come all the way down here just for that.'

'Well, perhaps you and Captain Jarvis, and your deputy, Lt. Commander MacPherson, would like to have breakfast with me for a very highly classified chat.'

'Admiral, I would very much like to do that. But first I need to know what's happening to my guys.'

'Rick, everyone's flying out of here this afternoon – Chilean Navy aircraft to Santiago. It's about 1,300 miles from here, 'bout three and a half hours. A United States Navy aircraft is already waiting there, and everyone flies directly back to San Diego North Island.'

'Everyone?'

'*Nearly* everyone.'

'Jesus,' said Commander Hunter. And just then Douglas Jarvis walked down the gangway and joined the two Americans.

'Dougy, this is Admiral Bergstrom, the man who masterminded your escape. Admiral, this is Captain Douglas Jarvis, Diana's kid brother, my brother-in-law and a very, very fine Special Forces officer. Got his guys out alive, all of 'em.'

Admiral Bergstrom offered his hand. 'I'm very privileged to meet you, captain,' he said.

They shook hands, and Douglas Jarvis replied, 'I want to thank you. I didn't do much. The US Special Forces got us out, and if they hadn't arrived when they did we might not have made it.'

'Very British,' said the admiral, smiling. 'But right now I'm talking to the guy who went into the Falkland Islands, operated undercover and took out an entire Argentine garrison with all its weapons, including guided missiles. Then he kept his guys alive for almost two weeks more, behind enemy lines, on an occupied island, in very bad weather, with half the armed forces of Argentina conducting a manhunt by air and land. Correct me if I'm wrong.'

Captain Jarvis grinned. 'Well, you're on the right lines, sir. But I'm not much of a hero, just stumbling around, doing my best.'

By now the underwater SEAL boss, Lt. Commander Chuck

Stafford, was leading all twenty-five of the assembled Special Forces, in company with a Chilean Navy captain, to a long low building 200 yards from the jetty where they could sleep and relax before the flight.

Commander Hunter, Doug Jarvis and Dallas MacPherson, climbed into the staff car with the admiral and were driven to the officers' mess about a half-mile away. Inside, they were escorted to a private room that looked like something between a US situation room and an ops room.

It was without windows, painted bright white, with a large computer display screen on the wall, plus a line of consoles and keyboards. More importantly, for the moment at least, there was a group of silver covered dishes on the long central table, which contained bacon, fried and scrambled eggs, sausages, mushrooms, and toast. Two navy orderlies were already placing large glasses of orange juice at the four set places, and filling the coffee cups.

The Special Forces commanders helped themselves to breakfast and sat down at the four places. Before Dallas had time to attack even one of the three sausages on his plate, Admiral Bergstrom said, 'Gentlemen, we have little time, and I would like you to know what precisely you have been doing. In the broadest terms, the US government has decided to conduct a series of highly destructive raids on Argentina's most expensive military hardware – warships and fighter aircraft.

'Simultaneously, the President is demanding that Argentina sit down and negotiate a peace settlement with Great Britain, which will include the restoration of two billion dollars' worth of oil and gas to Exxon Mobil and BP.

'Failure to comply with this will be a deal-breaker. And that may cause the United States to take military action against Argentina. However no one thinks that's going to happen. Indeed, the President's close friend Admiral Arnold Morgan is suggesting the attacks on Pebble Island and Mare Harbour may already have brought them into line.

'However, if that proves not to have been enough we intend to launch a further assault on their most prized military possessions. And that, according to Admiral Morgan, will surely do it, because Buenos Aires does not wish to end up in combat against the USA.'

Finally, Bergstrom came to the point. 'Gentlemen,' he said, 'I have been asked to discuss with you the possibility of your undertaking this operation. The good news is that it should be swift, requiring only a very small team of eight men, operating in great secret, direct action.'

'And the bad news?' asked Lt. Commander MacPherson, an edge of resignation to his voice.

'Er . . . it's going to take place on the Argentine mainland,' replied John Bergstrom.

'Oh,' said Commander Hunter. 'Interesting. Do they know we're coming?'

'Of course not.'

'Just checking.'

'Well . . . again, to come to the point, the object of the attack is the airbase at Rio Grande – close quarters, if you understand me.'

'Rio Grande?' exclaimed Rick. 'That's the place down on the island of Tierra del Fuego, I believe. A full-sized military airbase – home of the Mirage jets, the Skyhawks and the Super Étendards?'

'Yes. That's the spot.'

'Well, admiral, for the moment let me assume you have a way of getting men in there. But, rather more importantly, have you thought of a way out?'

'Not really. We'll bring them in by helicopter overland from Punta Arenas. And we had rather assumed – after they had done their business, of course – that they would walk out to a safe point and we'd pick them up somewhere. Probably with another helicopter.'

'I see,' said Rick. But he did not look as if he saw. Not even one little glimpse. He sipped his coffee and rubbed his chin before saying quietly, 'And what would happen, admiral, if the men should have to fight their way out, and found themselves on the run, pursued by, as it were, very irritated Argentines? How then would they fare?'

The admiral looked a bit uncomfortable. 'Ricky,' he said, 'I know this is difficult. And we're not yet sure if it's needed – the Argentines might cave in beforehand. But we need to be ready, so let's go over and have a look at the chart and see what you think after that. I'm not asking the chaps to blow the whole fucking airfield up, merely to take out a dozen aircraft – time-delayed bombs, of course – then vanish. Our great specialty, correct?'

'Well, yes, sir. It is. But this is a big airbase and it's pretty tricky to walk into the lions' den when there are too many lions on the loose.'

'I was rather hoping most of the lions would be asleep when the guys arrived.'

331

'Yes. But if they woke up and the guys were caught they'd be tortured. And worse.'

'We know that. That's why we're giving it a lot of thought.'

The men finished their breakfast thoughtfully, and then walked to the chart table which showed the great triangular island of Tierra del Fuego, dissected by the wide desolate waters of the Magellan Strait right at the foot of South America. Almost through the centre on the eastern side of the terrain ran the dead straight north-south line of the Chile-Argentina border. 'Hostile to the right, friendly to the left, correct?' said Commander Hunter.

'Correct,' replied the admiral. 'Now, up here – right on the coast – is the port of Rio Grande, situated at the mouth of the river, forty-two miles south-east of the Bay of San Sebastian. That's this big inlet, twenty miles across.'

Then he pointed to a cross he had drawn eight miles inland from the airfield and thirty-five miles from the Chilean border. 'That's the drop-off point, and from there it'd be a pretty straight, easy walk in at night.'

'And what would you want the guys to do? Once they're in?'

'We essentially want them to take out the twelve Super Étendard strike fighters, and then get the hell out of there.'

'How?'

'Initially it's a walk, through very lonely country. But the guys will carry a satellite communication system. As soon as we receive the signal, right here in Punta Arenas, a Chilean helicopter will fly in and pick them up.'

The admiral smiled briefly. Then his face clouded as the SEAL leader asked: 'What's your timing on this?'

The hesitation was obvious. John Bergstrom stood up, turned away, and said quietly, 'If we get the OK from the president, it would have to be tonight.'

'*TONIGHT!*' Rick Hunter nearly jumped out of his chair. 'Tonight? A team of eight, ready to go, into almost uncharted land in the teeth of the Argentine enemy, on a mission that could get everyone killed? Christ! Are you serious?'

'I am, Rick,' replied the admiral. 'Because right here on this base, right now, I have some of the best covert Special Forces in the world, experienced veterans, experts in the black arts of SPECWARCOM, men who have done it before. And I'm not likely to have this much expertise, not this close to our objective, ever again.'

'Well,' said Commander Hunter, 'I guess we may as well give it some thought. By the way, any idea who might lead the mission – as if I didn't know?'

'I was rather hoping you would.'

Rick gulped, not for the first time in this war. And then he said, without emotion, 'Yes, sir. Do I get to pick my own team?'

'Of course.'

'Well, I'd like to take Dallas MacPherson as my number two, and I would select Chief Petty Officers Mike Hook and Bob Bland, because one's an expert with a machine gun and a radio, and one's an expert at breaking and entering. I guess I'm looking for volunteers for the final four spots. And I'd be happy with the two Petty Officers 1st Class who came with me to Pebble Island, that's Don Smith and Brian Harrison.

'The final two would need to be explosives guys, trained men who know how to set a timed charge and place a tailored charge right into the guts of an aircraft engine. I'd like Stafford's 2I/C if possible.'

At which point there was a minor interruption. 'Admiral, I should like to volunteer my services, if I may?' said Captain Douglas Jarvis. 'I owe my life to you both – and if, God forbid, anything happened to Rick, I don't think I could face going home without him. I want to come on this mission.'

He spoke from the heart. It would have been shocking to turn up at Blue Grass Field to be met by Diana whose husband had been lost trying to save him. But there was another impulse inside the soldier's soul of Douglas Jarvis. Like his brother-in-law, he could hear the sound of distant bugles and, as in the long-ago Sandhurst Cadets Boxing Championships, he was ready to come out fighting.

'Thanks, kid,' said Rick Hunter. 'I appreciate that, but you're not even a trained SEAL.'

'Well, I'm a trained British sea lion. And they're pretty good in a tight spot.'

'But you're not in the United States Navy. And I'm damn sure you have to be for this kind of work.'

'Well, maybe Admiral Bergstrom could second me, just for a couple of weeks?'

'I could most certainly make out a case for a decorated British SAS officer to become a United States Navy SEAL on a short-term commission. But, Douglas, you'd have to take a very searching examination . . .'

'I would?'

'Sure you would. We don't take just anyone.'

'Neither do we, sir.'

Admiral Bergstrom, a man with the most flexible command in all the US Navy, grinned. 'I know you've trained with our personnel before, at Hereford. But I must ask you, how are you at those rare skills just outlined by Commander Hunter? Like setting timers on specially tailored explosive charges?'

'Expert, sir.'

'Excellent, captain. You're in. Rank of lieutenant commander, like Dallas. Two-week commission.'

'Thank you, sir. I'm honoured.'

'And does he pass *your* selection board, Commander Hunter?' asked the admiral.

'He does, sir. Though I'm not completely certain what his sister, who also happens to be my wife, would say if she heard that.'

'Well, I'm afraid the lovely Diana is *not* going to hear that. As from this moment, gentlemen, you are a part of one of the most highly classified covert Special Forces missions the US Navy has ever mounted. No one leaves here today, not until we get the go-ahead from Washington and the helicopter is ready for the flight in tonight. Cellphones are banned. There will be no further communication with the outside world.'

Admiral Bergstrom stood up and walked to the sideboard to collect the coffee pot. And before he turned back to face the others, he added, 'By the way, gentlemen, failure would be unthinkable.'

CHAPTER THIRTEEN

There had been no diplomatic communiqué from Buenos Aires the previous evening. And nothing had arrived this morning, either. Paul Bedford stared hard at his friend Arnold Morgan.

'Do we wait longer?' he asked.

'Absolutely not,' replied Admiral Morgan. 'When someone's going to give up a fight, they give it up quick, before something else happens. These guys are rolling the dice one more time, hoping we're bluffing.'

'And, of course, we're not.'

'No, sir. We're not.' The admiral picked up the interior telephone and instructed the President's secretary, 'OK, send that e-mail right away, direct to the Chilean Naval Base at Punta Arenas, address I gave you. Attention Admiral Bergstrom.'

The e-mail read: *Goodbye French flock. Proceed this day.* Admiral Bergstrom was still sipping his coffee, talking to his three senior assault commanders, when it arrived. 'Gentlemen,' he said, 'we have clearance. We're going in tonight.'

Back in the White House, the President looked quizzical. 'Arnie,' he said, 'what do we do if the Argentines still don't react, even after this next attack?'

'We get serious,' replied the admiral.

'Meaning?'

'We take out the entire Rio Grande airbase and everything on it.

And if anyone finds out it was us, we come clean and say that Argentina's armed forces seized the Falkland Islands, including our oilfields, in an act of international piracy.

'After repeated attempts to negotiate a fair settlement, we were driven to remove their air-warfare capability from this planet because it happens to represent a threat to the fair-trading nations of the world.

'And in this we shall be joined by the governments of Great Britain and Chile – and anyone else we decide to press-gang into assisting us with our case.'

'And how, Arnie, do you propose we conduct this mass assault on Rio Grande – nuke it?'

'Oh, I don't think it will come to that. Think about 1976, when Israel's elite commandos stormed another nation's main airport and took it. Remember how they smashed their way into Entebbe in Uganda, completely overpowered a big force of guards, blew up ten MIG fighters, rescued 100 Israeli hostages, and took off back to Tel Aviv. Not bad, right?'

'No, not at all bad,' agreed the President.

'They came in by air. In four darned great Hercules C-130 transports. Landed in the dark, taxied right up close to the airport buildings, and the next thing Idi Amin's men knew, the Israeli commandos were on them, gunning down the terrorists and anyone else who got in the way. Twenty Ugandan soldiers were shot down in their tracks because they were not ready. Frankly, I doubt the Argentines would be much sharper.'

'You mean you actually have a vision of one of our big transporters coming in to land at night in Rio Grande and taxiing over to the main building where eighty of our guys exit the aircraft, rush out and open fire, blowing up the building, getting rid of the Argentine guards, and then destroying all the aircraft?'

'Subject to adequate reconnaissance, yes. I think it would work well. Very well.'

'And from where does this mythical US military transporter take off?'

'Oh, I think our very good friends in Chile might help there, eh? Our aircraft would, naturally, be redecorated, a nice shade of light blue and white.'

'And what do you think are the odds of it coming to that kind of a crunch?' asked the President.

'About 100 to one against,' replied the admiral. 'If the guys remove all twelve of those brand new Super-Es tonight, we'll have the Argentine government on the phone tomorrow morning asking for terms.'

1700 Friday 29 April
Punta Arenas Naval Base, Chile

Rick Hunter's team was huddled in the embarkation area, their faces already blackened in readiness for the insertion into Rio Grande. Each of them carried a personal weapon, the light, compact and terminally deadly CAR-15 assault rifle, which was close to perfect for work behind enemy lines. The CAR rapid-fired an extremely high-velocity .223-calibre cartridge, which was sufficiently light for each man to carry six thirty-round magazines.

The SEALs' rucksacks were carefully packed with standard combat gear, insect repellent, water, purification tablets, 'power' food bars, a little regular food, wire-cutters, battle dressings, knife, medical kit. Already stowed into the helicopter was the C-4 explosive with detcord and timers, one M-60 E3 machine gun, ammunition, two patrol radios, the PRC319 rescue communicator, which could send encrypted short-burst satellite transmissions – in particular the one from Rick which would probably read 'Get us the hell *outta* here!' There were also two hand-held GPS systems, and a dozen hand grenades.

Standing with Rick were Lt. Commanders Dallas MacPherson and Douglas Jarvis, Chief Petty Officers Mike Hook and Bob Bland, the beefy combat SEAL who would carry the machine gun most of the way. There were the two Petty Officers 1st Class, Don Smith and Brian Harrison, and the new man, twenty-six-year-old explosives wizard, Lieutenant R. K. Banfield from Clarksdale, Mississippi or, as the young SEAL put it, 'from raht down there by that *big* ole river.'

By late afternoon conditions were beginning to deteriorate. There were reports of claggy conditions over the Argentine coast, but the pilots were confident in the ability of the high-tech instruments in their HH-60H Sikorsky Seahawk, one of two purchased from the US during the past year.

By 1800 they were ready. In a rising wind, with rain sweeping across the airfield, the SEAL team jogged out towards the helicopter, ducking instinctively below the great whirring blades and clambering on board, weighed down by their heavy packs, but ready to carry out the mission.

It was dark now and they took off, clattering straight up to their cruising speed of 120 knots and heading south-east over the Magellan Strait. Rick Hunter sat up in his small private cabin, poring over the chart, wishing they had a better map and wondering what the terrain would be like between the airfield and the Chilean border, both west and south of Rio Grande.

Like everyone in the SEAL planning team, he regarded the getaway as infinitely more dangerous than getting in. That should be simple. *But if we should get caught, and have to fight our way out, that's not going to be so simple . . . I just wish I could tell what this terrain is going to be like.*

Doug Jarvis, one of the best night navigators who had ever worked at Stirling Lines, had brought up an interesting point. 'Let's say, for argument's sake, sir, that we get caught and we have to take out a few Argies. I know Coronado thinks we should immediately make our way west, following the river and making a beeline for the Chilean border. But I'm not too sure about that.'

'Why not? It's the fastest way to friendly territory,' said Rick.

'Exactly. And if I was an Argentine officer in charge of the pursuit, that's the way I'd go, sir. Right along the river with helicopters, looking for the filthy intruders trying to get into Chile the fastest way they could.'

Rick stared at the chart. 'What would you do, Dallas?'

'I'm with Dougy, sir. I'd go south, straight for those hills and the border at the Beagle Channel. No doubt in my mind. That's the way the Argies won't go, sir. They'll try to hunt us down along the short route, along the Rio Grande River.'

Rick allowed his gaze to wander down the chart, noting the several rivers which rose from the mountains south of Rio Grande. He stared at the high peaks that ran all the way down to the Beagle Channel, trying to hold a mental picture of the very last segment of land on this Earth before the icy wastes of Antarctica.

'It'd be a walk of almost eighty miles, south to the Beagle Channel. And it would be over a range of mountains, some of 'em 10,000 feet tall.'

'I know,' replied Douglas. 'But where would you rather be, sir – fighting your way through the mountains to safety, with a chance of rescue at any moment . . . or dead on the banks of the Rio Grande?'

'I'll take the mountains.'

'Good thinking, Ricky baby. Let's hope we don't have to do it, though.'

The one-hour flight passed swiftly as they made their way down the Magellan Strait and then turned east up Inutil Bay, seeing their first land fifteen miles south of Lake Emma, still in Chile. Less than a half-hour later, they crossed the border into Argentine airspace, thirty-four miles east-north-east of Rio Grande.

Twenty minutes later they flew into a fog bank that was drifting in off the South Atlantic. They began to lose height and almost immediately ran into another, and then another.

'These conditions are a damned nuisance,' the pilot called back. 'We keep flying in and out of the fog, and I can only just make out the coastline – those lights up there are San Sebastian.'

The pilot's observer was following his chart, and right behind them Rick and Doug were following theirs.

'Here we go, sir, here. We're looking for the river.'

'Got it,' said Rick. 'Then we go over another couple of small rivers, then this lake . . . then land here. 53.48S, 67.50W, eight miles due west of the airbase.'

'Fifteen minutes, sir . . .'

The team began to muscle up, zipping up their padded weatherproof Gore-Tex jackets, checking their waterproof boots, pulling on gloves, as the helicopter slowed down to eighty knots, the pilot trying to cut out the noise as they flew in over the cold deserted landscape below. All of them wore heavy-duty thick woollen hats, and all of them could feel the helicopter swaying in the gusting breeze as they came on down towards the Rio Grande River. This made their final gulps of hot cocoa from the specially provided flasks slightly awkward, but somehow they managed.

'GPS showing 53.47S, longitude correct.'

'TWO MINUTES.'

'There it is, sir. Dead ahead. Break left – not too close in case it's marshy . . . longitude correct, 53.48 right now, sir.'

'COMING IN.'

The chopper swayed to a halt, hovered and then touched down softly, the rotors now beating quietly but the engine still making a deafening racket in the night air.

The observer climbed out first, then Rick Hunter jumped down with Dallas and Doug right behind him. Then came Mike Hook,

Smith, Harrison, Lt. Banfield and CPO Bland who manhandled the machine gun and the communications system.

The observer jumped back on board and slammed the door tight. All eight of Rick Hunter's team watched as the helicopter took off, keeping low as it edged its way west towards the frontier.

The wind which was backing south gusted hard over the rough damp ground. It whipped away the sounds of the retreating helicopter, leaving Rick's men alone in the silence of the South American wilderness. The dark was all-consuming as more cloud, drifting in from the South Atlantic, brought down a wet night mist and blotted out the stars.

Rick and Doug took a long careful look at their compass and set off on course zero-nine-zero. In the absence of a path, or a track of any kind, the rest just stayed on-bearing and followed the firm stride of their leader out in front, going with the gradient, sometimes clambering over ridges, sometimes sliding easily down thickly grassed slopes, but always pressing forward.

Every fifteen minutes they all paused and strained their ears for any sound – perhaps a car, maybe even an aircraft – but for a long time there was nothing. Only the wind, which was now south-easterly.

Mike Hook heard it first, a dull rumble in the clouds to the north. *'Sir! I think it's an aircraft . . . coming in. Can't see it yet.'*

'Great,' snapped Rick. 'It'll give us a fix. Right now, everyone hit the deck . . .'

The eight men went down, secure in their heavy camouflage clothing, facing due east, peeping up over the grass, watching for the aircraft. They could hear it way behind them – and then, suddenly, it was on them, howling across the flat plain, right above, possibly only a couple of hundred feet, its landing wheels extended for touchdown.

They watched its lights all the way, even catching the slight bounce as it landed right ahead of them, less than a mile away.

'OK, guys,' said Rick. 'A few decisions have been made for us right here – the first one being that we don't wanna be stuck directly under the flight path of every incoming jet. If we're caught, we'll have to fight and kill, and if they subsequently catch us . . . well, don't wanna think about that, right?'

Without further talk they made their way left, to a point about a mile and a half off the outer perimeter of the airfield. They had some cover, and a fair view, between two huge rocks, of the take-offs and landings. They would also have a chance to observe the guard patrols. So far as they could see, there were no guard posts out here in this most remote part of the field, which, according to Dallas, was 'good to totally fucking excellent'.

And so they sat out the night, watching through their field glasses, sleeping in turns, one man always at the machine gun. They started their little Primus stove, found some fresh water in a stream, and boiled up some powdered vegetable soup which they ate with bread and cheese. They did not dare to try any more complicated cooking.

The next evening at 1930, with night now casting a pitch-black darkness over the airbase, they stowed their camp, leaving Don Smith to get their gear into rapid-exit mode and then maintain guard with the radio on in case of an emergency. Rick's seven-man team moved off in light rain at 1945 towards the Rio Grande base, home of the Super Étendard aircraft.

Rick and Doug had taken the view that the two checkpoint gates, one out on the right and one next to the main buildings, would be heavily guarded. But they did not know the extent of the wire which surrounded some of the field.

Rick led them forward, walking through the high grass into the teeth of the freezing wind. It didn't penetrate their jackets, nor their waterproof camouflage trousers. In many ways the wind was their friend tonight as their enemy was upwind of them. The SEALs would hear everything as they approached the field.

Rick ordered them to hit the deck again, but this time with their rifles in their hands. They crawled through the thick ground cover, making the final 200-yard approach on their bellies, in the 'canoeing' action that Doug had been taught at Sandhurst, out on Barossa Common, thirteen years ago.

When they reached the outer border of the base they ran into a heavy-duty wire fence. They could not tell how far it stretched in any direction. 'No sense hanging around to find out, either,' said Commander Hunter. 'Wire-cutters, Bob – let's go straight through. Then we'll take some kind of a mark inside, and this hole right here will be our way back to the rendezvous point: hit the hole and head due north on the compass for one mile and a half. That way we can't miss if we get separated.'

Bob Bland made short work of the fence, cutting a hole two feet high by four feet long, virtually unnoticeable in the grass unless you were looking. Rick made a note of the GPS position at the hole and radioed it back to Don Smith. One minute later the team was inside the perimeter fence, hurrying over to the main runway on which they had seen aircraft coming and going all day. Once there, they turned left down the blacktop, and went in search of the Super Es. According to Coronado, they were 400 yards down the main runway to the right.

They had travelled almost 300 yards when they came to the first group of aircraft, out on the left, nearest the buildings. They counted eight of them, all identical: A4 Skyhawks, the single-seater American-built low-altitude bomber, identifiable by its high curved top fuselage. And by the heavy clips for the 1,000lb bombs it could carry under its wings.

'These are not the ones,' said Dallas, who had spent much of the afternoon studying aircraft shapes.

In the darkness they moved on down the runway to the next group – twelve sleek black strike-fighter aircraft, a slight tilt to the nose-cone, the tail fins set slightly higher than the aft fuselage.

Jesus, guys, this is it.' Rick Hunter stared at the dark shadows of the supersonic French-built Dassault-Breguet Super Étendards. 'This is the bastard we're after.'

Dallas and R. K. Banfield immediately moved in to check the location of the hatches which covered the engines. They were simple to find, and even simpler to open. Within two minutes, the SEALs had their C-4 explosive ready to cut and shape like modelling clay, with two men assisting Dallas and two more helping R. K.

The two young officers placed the charges and inserted the fuse which would detonate the explosive. They then attached the detcord and ran it out to a position on the ground midway between four aircraft. Rick Hunter was waiting there to splice the four lengths of detcord into one 'pigtail' which he screwed into the timer, which he set for four hours. All four aircraft engines and much of their fuselages would be obliterated at precisely the same moment.

The entire four-aircraft project took the greater part of one hour, each three-man team sabotaging two aircraft. Then they repeated the operation twice more, ensuring that, barring a miracle, not one of Argentina's twelve brand new Super-Es would ever leave the ground again.

Only once did the SEALs need to hit the dirt, when a big Hercules C-130 came in and the lights at the end of the runway lit up half the field. The rest of the time they worked more or less undisturbed, although they did notice a guard patrol traversing the entire field in a couple of jeeps at irregular intervals, once at 2030 and again at 2115. Rick thought they were going too fast to notice anything.

By 2300 they had completed their task. A pale moon now cast light on the secondary blacktop strip that ran north–south at the far western end of the airfield against the ocean. They could see it was a parking area for helicopters, five of them, in plain view now the night was less dark.

This operation, thought Rick, has been a whole lot less trouble than it might have been. Swiftly, he led his six team-mates back up the main runway, walking fast, anxious to get out through the fence, back to their base camp, and out of there as fast as possible.

Up ahead they could see the great dark shapes of the piles of wooden telegraph poles that supported the wide gantry of runway landing lights, the ones they had seen light up only once during this entire evening, over two hours ago. Far away to the right they could see the lights of two vehicles speeding along the southern perimeter, though from this range they could not tell whether they were inside or outside the fence.

Either way, it scarcely mattered. If the security guards were driving right around the base, the SEAL team would just lie prone in the dark grass 200 yards from the outer track, until the jeeps had passed. No problem.

But one minute later, with the jeeps now only a half-mile away, there *was* a problem. With a sudden devastating flash of voltage, the runway landing lights came on. They caught the SEALs full in their fluorescent glare, lighting them up like small black figures on a milk-white background. Rick froze. He could not tell whether the distant guards had seen them. If they had been seen, with the fence still one hundred yards away, they were finished.

Rick had only one choice.

'RUN! RUN, GUYS, FOR FUCK'S SAKE RUN! STRAIGHT FOR THE FENCE. I'LL SEE YOU THERE . . .'

Dallas, Douglas and R. K. needed no second instruction. They set off like Olympic sprinters, with the other four right behind them, Bob Bland running while carrying the M-60 machine gun. The two Argentine jeeps were now bearing down, probably 600 yards away, as the SEALs hurtled through the high grass, led by Dallas and Dougy, still in the full glare of the runway lights.

They could see the hole through the wire now, but the ground

343

was very rough and each one of them stumbled and fell at some point, fighting their way back upright, racing, falling, getting up again, charging on, trying to escape the lights, desperation adding speed to their strides. Then they were lining up to get through the hole. Doug Jarvis realised with mounting horror that the CO was no longer with them. 'RICK . . . RICKY!' he yelled. 'Answer me. Where are you?' But there was only the revving of the jeeps' engines to be heard, and no sign of the commander.

Rick had allowed himself to fall behind a bit. He was back in the grass, lying face down, the light on his back, but still, he guessed, hard to see. If the jeeps kept going, fine. He would wait till they had passed, wait till the aircraft had landed, wait till the lights were out, and then make his way back to the rendezvous point.

But if the guards in those jeeps had spotted them they would slow down and make for the fence, with their radios and lights and instant ability to summon helicopters, maybe even dogs. In a race across country, Rick's team would have hardly any start on them. Rick knew he might very easily be looking at the last hour of his own and his men's lives. He needed to stay still and then move in from the rear, assault rifle blazing, if the guys were caught.

But now he could see the jeeps coming on, fast, 200 yards away. *Jesus Christ! Are they slowing? Fuck me. Yes, they are. They're stopping. Oh shit. They're getting out. At least three of them are headed for the fence.*

Rick lay still, making his preparations, squirming his way towards one of the big wooden pylons supporting the gantry. He felt the pin of his first grenade between his fingers, pulled it out and ran forward. He saw the soldier in the rear jeep turn towards him and raise his rifle. Just then, though, Rick hurled the grenade and dived sideways back into the grass, the soldier's bullets ripping into the ground two feet to his right. The grenade sailed high, landed in the back of the jeep and exploded, lifting the vehicle into the air, killing four men and blowing the second jeep forward onto its nose.

Rick came to his feet again and threw a second grenade, which hit the underside of the upturned jeep and blew it to smithereens. Rick came running in behind the blast.

The three Argentines at the fence had turned around, staring at the destruction, uncertain what had happened, half-blinded by the massive lights and stunned by the proximity of the explosion. Not one of them had even seen Rick Hunter, and for a split second they just stood there, their mouths open, bathed in a light that was brighter than the flames.

Then they ran back towards their burning vehicle. As they did so the SEAL leader stepped out from behind it. Rick's CAR-15 fired three lightning bursts and all three Argentine guards fell instantly in front of the fence.

Without a second glance, Rick bolted for the fence, diving underneath, picking himself up and running straight into the arms of Doug Jarvis, who had come back for him. 'Christ, Ricky, I thought you'd bought it . . .'

'No. Not me, Dougy. The only thing I bought was about thirty minutes for us to get the hell out of here. Come on, back to base – before we all get killed.'

0120 Sunday 1 May
Air Traffic Control, Rio Grande Base

Acting Sub-Lieutenant Juan Alvarez, his eyes glued to the screen, was watching for the second Hercules C-130 of the night to make its approach from the north. He had been talking to the pilot, calling out height and distance, when Rick Hunter wiped out the entire mobile guard patrol. Juan saw nothing.

His only other colleague in the control tower was twenty-one-year-old Jesús de Cuelo, who had been trying to read a book despite the noise of Juan's jargon-laden dialogue with the Hercules, and had been about to tell Juan to keep it down when the jeeps were blown up.

Jesús thought he had seen a bright flash down at the end of the runway, and he stood up to see what was happening. However, at that moment the Hercules came in, thundering out of the sky, its landing wheels hitting the blacktop with their usual heavy impact. Both men watched it taxiing in and it was not until the huge aircraft came to a halt that Jesús took another look down the runway.

'You see something way down there, near the big lights?'

'No. Where? What kind of thing . . .?'

'Sudden bright light – almost like an explosion . . . I think I can still see something. Turn out the runway lights – there's nothing else coming in till tomorrow, hah?'

Juan hit the big switch, plunging the distant part of the airfield back into darkness, and there, quite clearly now, were two flickering lights, almost a mile away.

'What the hell's that?' Juan asked.

'Can't tell . . . maybe a plane crash. Ha ha ha.'

345

Juan frowned. 'No. Can't be that. We'd have seen it.'

'Just joking,' Jesús said quickly. 'But it has to be something. Can you see the guards' jeep? We could get 'em on the radio – tell 'em to go have a look.'

'Wait a minute – I'll get 'em . . .'

Two minutes went by. 'That's weird. No answer . . . I'll try the guardroom.'

'Fat chance. They're all asleep.'

'Well, I'll have to wake 'em up, hah?'

That took a while. It was five minutes before the duty sergeant came to the telephone and listened to Juan Alvarez reporting that he thought he could see two small fires at the end of the runway, that he could get no reply from the patrol, and would one of the 100 lazy pigs in the guardroom kindly get down there and find out what the hell was going on, or else he'd call the airbase commandant.

The guard knew better than to argue with the air traffic control night chief who wore on his sleeve, he knew, the tiny gold crossed anchors and thick single stripe of a junior officer.

'Right away, sir,' he growled. But he took his time and it took about ten more minutes before he and his three colleagues were in a jeep and ready to go. Five minutes later they were staring at the burned-out wrecks of the two patrol jeeps and the charred remains of their colleagues who'd been inside the vehicles.

The area around them was pitch black, save for the single jeep's headlights and the dying embers of the fires, so they called in to the tower for Lt. Alvarez to switch on the runway lights.

When they finally came on the first thing the four men saw were the three guards, lying face upwards in the grass where they'd been slammed backwards by the impact of Rick Hunter's bullets.

'Jesús,' muttered one of the security men. And he was not referring to young de Cuelo. He crossed himself and said, 'We better get some brass out here. These men have been shot.'

Twenty minutes later the area around the still-smouldering ambushed jeeps was occupied by fifteen people, one of them Commander Marcel Carbaza, the camp commandant, and two of them doctors. Also present was the head of base security, Lieutenant Commander Ricardo Testa.

'No doubt, sir. All three men were shot, I'd say from bursts of expertly delivered fire. The bullets were less than 6mm calibre, and they all hit in the central chest area . . .'

346

'Hmm.' The camp commandant was thoughtful. 'Obviously military?'

'Oh, I'd say so, definitely.'

'Well, gentlemen. If that's the case we should perhaps stand by and be prepared for the entire airbase to go up. This looks like Pebble Island all over again. Special Forces, eh?'

Two men laughed. Nervously.

'But if it doesn't go up, then I must ask myself many questions. How did they get here? What were they doing here, shooting guards and vanishing? Or are they still here?'

And then his tone hardened. 'Lt. Commander Testa. I want this camp searched from end to end. Every building. Every aircraft. For signs of a Special Forces raid. Meanwhile get the helicopters in the sky, eh? If they're on the run, they're making for the Chilean border. Heading west, down the river. Take dogs if you have to. Then we catch 'em. Make 'em talk, hah? Clear up a few mysteries. *NOW GET MOVING!*'

Dutifully, the guards on the big Argentine airbase moved into action. Not what might be described as urgent action – at least, the SEALs would not have regarded it as such. But it was activity. They turned on every light on the base, runway, field, service area, fuelling area, and inside the buildings. Then they began the two-hour-long process of searching every yard of the place.

Patrols circled the airfield and drove up and down the runways before at 0025 the order was issued to begin a ground search on foot. Columns of men moved across the airfield and among the parked aircraft. Roughly at the time when the charges placed with such unerring precision by SEAL explosives experts MacPherson and Banfield blew all twelve Étendards to pieces. The shuddering simultaneous explosions shook the outfield of the airbase, especially the area in which four of the engines had blasted upwards and crashed to the ground – courtesy of Dallas, who was apt to be a bit heavy on the gas pedal when placing C-4 explosive.

Lt. Commmander Testa, who had been gazing out at the airfield from the control tower, almost had a heart attack. He knew a career-threatening explosion when he saw one, and he roared somewhat hysterically into the airbase tannoy system: *'ACTION STATIONS! ACTION STATIONS! WE ARE UNDER ATTACK – REPEAT, UNDER ATTACK! AIR SEARCH PATROLS GO!! ACTION STATIONS! ACTION STATIONS!'*

Rick Hunter and his men had a start, so far, of one hour and twenty minutes, which was not much of a match for a pursuing helicopter. But they had used the time well and the rising moon caught them jogging steadily across flat country, more than seven miles south of the base. Don Smith and Bob Bland were carrying the machine gun between them and Mike Hook was lugging the communications system. Thankfully, their heavy loads of explosive and detonation gear were a lot lighter now.

Their years of training made the going easy for the SEALs and their feet beat out a relentless rhythm on the soft ground of the grassland, their breath coming effortlessly. They knew that ahead of them the ground would begin to rise, up into the mountains, but that way lay cover, shelter and a chance to get the satellite system into action and call in rescue. Out here on the bleak coastal plain, with little tree cover, there was nothing for it but to run south, literally heading for the hills, away from the Argentine pursuit teams that could not be far behind.

Now, in the far distance, they could hear the muffled beat of helicopter rotors, the unmistakable clatter of those big blades echoing through the night. Doug Jarvis thought the aircraft would probably be the French-built Pumas he had seen on the north-south runway. Patrol aircraft like those were never heavily gunned but they could carry pintle-mounted light machine guns, which Rick Hunter thought was not a reason for overwhelming joy.

Strangely, the noise of the helicopters was growing fainter, disappearing away to the north-west, and Dallas confirmed what Captain Jarvis had thought in the first place. 'They went down the river, sir. Straight for the border.'

'Dallas, you'll probably end up an admiral, with that fast brain of yours,' said Rick, his breath coming fast and steady.

'Very likely, sir. Very likely. I was hoping to mention that to the President soon as we get back.'

'*If* we get back,' muttered CPO Hook, jogging along at an easy stride right next to Rick.

'We'll be all right,' said Dougy, panting only slightly. 'Remember, they've got a thirty-five-mile stretch of land to check out all the way to the border and they don't have a damn thing to go on. They don't know if we're in a vehicle. Whether we've been rescued, whether we had a helicopter. They don't even know if we're a force of two, six or twenty. My guess is we won't see those helicopters for several hours, not till they get sick of the river route into Chile. Then they might run a check to the north, and to the south. But it won't be yet. Mark my words.'

Acting Lt. Commander Jarvis was correct, as it turned out. The Argentine search troops thundered up and down their stretch of the river throughout the morning, all the way to Chile's eastern border and back. And it was not until 1500 – when Commander Hunter and his men had been running and jogging for fourteen hours and were on the verge of exhaustion – that Commander Marcel Carbaza's men finally switched their search pattern. First, briefly, to the north. Then to the south.

By now the SEAL team had covered a truly phenomenal thirty-eight miles. They were still moving steadily forward into the long snow-capped mountain range which guarded the northern approaches to the Beagle Channel. This was the five-mile-wide waterway that flowed ultimately into the South Atlantic, dividing Argentina and Chile in the extreme south. The final seaward fragments of windswept mountainous land, which includes Cape Horn, belonged to Chile.

The total distance from Rio Grande to the shores of the Beagle Channel was eighty miles, and the SEAL team was just about halfway there when they spotted the helicopters, battering their way up the foothills of the mountains, searching not only with high-powered naval binoculars but also with heat-seeking infra-red scanners. None of the Argentine searchers believed that an infiltrating assault team could possibly have got this far, but they were under orders to cover a fifty-mile radius, covering every yard of the ground.

Rick thought his best chance was to deploy among the rocks and lie low, under the lee, away from the scopes and gunsights of the helicopters. They were moving through a bowl-shaped valley, which they had reached through a rocky pass covered by snow. They hustled down the slope and turned along a side ravine staying low, listening for the chopper clattering through the pass.

It took half an hour, and when the chopper did show up it made enough din to start an avalanche, roaring above them and heading south, its search sensors sticking out in front. It missed them completely. The trouble was a second helicopter was coming the other way, and its search sensors, seeking body heat, could hardly miss them. And nor did they. The aircraft hesitated right over their lair, hovering and then edging away, looking for a landing spot right in the middle of the bowl, not 300 yards from them.

'Stay still, but get that machine gun ready,' snapped Rick. 'Dallas, Doug, Mike – come with me. We'll try and divert them.'

The four soldiers set off, running up through the rocks along the western edge of the valley. They were still able to see the big Puma, now on the ground, its blades whirring. But what they saw next was very bad news indeed. Three heavily armed soldiers had disembarked, and they were hanging onto three big black-and-brown Dobermann pinschers that were straining at their leashes. Rick could see their hideous pointed ears from where he stood. He did not have to imagine their salivating mouths.

'Fuck it,' he muttered. 'Let's keep going.'

But then he heard the dogs bark and realised they were loose, running on ahead of their handlers and searching for the scent. Rick, Doug, Dallas and Mike Hook climbed higher, but they could not make it high enough. The first dog raced around the corner of the rocks, its long powerful paws skidding, its breath coming in short eager bursts, a low growl of anticipation sounding in its throat as it spotted the SEAL commander. The Dobermann instantly adjusted its course to head for the higher ground and charged straight at him, barking now, fast as a racing greyhound, teeth bared, ready to tear Rick Hunter apart.

The SEAL chief, off balance, trying to hang on to a rock face, tried desperately to draw his pistol, struggling to get a bullet away in any direction.

If only to slow the raging beast down.

At the last moment Captain Doug Jarvis blew it away with his CAR-15, the bullets smashing into its head. And as he did so, the other two came charging up the stony slope, and Dougy felt obliged to treat all dogs equally. 'Fucking things,' he muttered. 'Anyway, I always preferred Labradors.'

However, the assault-rifle bursts which had wiped out the dog pack had attracted everyone to their position. The three Argentine troopers were racing after the dogs, sub-machine guns held.

Back in the ravine Don Smith had heard the gunfire but could not make out who was alive and who wasn't. Still, he could see the pursuing Argentines and he opened up with a withering burst from the big M-60 machine gun, cutting all three of them down.

Dallas never missed a beat. He could see the chopper still revved

350

up on the ground with just the pilot remaining inside. He ran towards it from the blind side, right on the pilot's seven o'clock . . . 200 yards . . . 150 yards . . . 100 yards . . . he still kept running . . . only eighty feet now . . . '*First base!*' he yelled.

He hurled his grenade underarm, hard, low and straight – a real 'frozen rope' – clean through the open door. He heard it smack into the instrument panel, breaking glass. A split second later it exploded with a massive roar that echoed around the valley, the explosion obliterating both helicopter and pilot. 'I shoulda played for the Braves,' he muttered. 'This stuff is getting fucking crazy.'

Where was the first helicopter? Commander Hunter had no idea, but he thought it might be making another search-line out to the right.

'Anyway,' he told his men, 'if our luck holds, the damned thing will return to base, and they might not work out the other one's – er – crashed, at least, not for an hour or so. We better put a few miles between us and this burning wreck, then we'll stop and eat and get the communications fired up. I don't think the Argies will conduct a rescue operation until it's light.'

So they pushed on, weary now, taking turns carrying the machine gun and the satellite comms system through the valley, then climbing again, up through the snowy passes. For leadership at these heights Rick handed over to the unerring instincts of the mountain man, the SAS's Captain Jarvis, who could follow the contours of the slopes and peaks, picking his way through the lower gaps, trying to limit their climbing and staying east where the escarpments were less formidable, going for the Atlantic end of the giant Lake Fagnano.

By 1930 the GPS was telling them they had covered fifty-four miles in eighteen hours, a superhuman feat of endurance and stamina through this kind of terrain. They seemed to be enjoying two real slices of luck. One, it had been an unusually mild autumn with less snow than there might have been. Two, the Argies seemed to have gone home for the night.

Rick Hunter's tired band of warriors found a dry spot under the lee of a rocky hill, unpacked their rucksacks, lit the Primus, and fired up the communications system. Mike Hook had sent their message away in a fast satellite 'burst' while they were waiting for Commander Hunter on the airfield, and now he was recording a new one.

This would give their current GPS position – 54.30S, 67.25W –

and an up-to-date situation report: *Have come under attack from Argie helos: anticipate further action first light. Heading Beagle Channel as per last signal. Staying east Mount Cornu. Rescue 54.51S, 67.20W, app 1100. Our course 180.*

CPO Hook projected the signal into space, praying it would reach Coronado off the satellite. Which it did, and the ops room there immediately signalled the ops room at the Chilean naval base at Puerto Williams, right on the south shore of the Beagle Channel, eleven miles from the rescue point. Parked at the base was one F/A 18F Boeing Super Hornet strike bomber, armed with its AIM-9 'can't-miss' guided missiles and powerful 20mm Vulcan cannon, ready for take-off at a moment's notice.

The pilot, Lieutenant Commander Alan Ross, wore the sinister patch of the VFA-151 Vigilantes, a red-eyed skull with a dagger in its teeth. He had been at Puerto Williams for just a few hours, having flown off a diverted US aircraft carrier in the Pacific, and arrived via refuelling stops at Santiago and Punta Arenas.

That Hornet 18F was all that stood between the SEAL team and certain death. Because even Coronado graduates could not fight an entire country's national defence system – not if that country was determined to hunt them down on its own territory.

In fact, Commander Rick Hunter himself was worried that he and his team were still on Argentine soil.

In weary silence, they cooked the last of their food: baked beans, ham, three steaks sealed in foil. They finished the bread with the rest of the cheese, drew straws for first watch and rested for five hours. Later they would head south once more, through the light shallow snow.

Sleep came easily to the exhausted men, and the watchkeepers found it hard to stay awake. But the danger up here was minimal, and they were all rested when CPO Bland summoned them back to duty. He had already made coffee, and with some reluctance the others crawled out of their sleeping bags and began to pack and pull on their boots. Dallas found a couple of packs of ginger cookies that he had been hoarding and they shared these before picking up the machine gun and the radio and setting off, with Dallas out in the lead. Still munching cheerfully.

They had five hours of marching through the darkness ahead of them, though much of it was surprisingly easy going because the ground began to slope downwards as the mountain began its long dip to the Beagle Channel. The first fifteen miles went by before they could see the dawn breaking, way out to the left. With each passing minute, the men began to feel the tension of impending attack.

'There are two possibilities for us. The Argies either believe they lost us and the Puma simply crashed into the mountain. Or they have found out that it did not in fact crash, and that we probably hit it.' Commander Hunter had been blunt.

At this point Lt. Banfield lapsed into deep Mississippi. 'In the first case, our worries are ovah and we're just gonna be walking in t-a-a-a-ll cotton. In the latter case, them boys gonna come *lookin'*.'

Dallas MacPherson and Doug Jarvis chuckled, even though they knew their situation wasn't remotely funny. They pulled down their hats and kept going. No one said another word as they made their way across the freezing territory at the end of the western world.

Two miles further on the mountain seemed to come to an end. In front of them was a long downhill slope, still thickly covered with grass and with a few copses scattered around it. There was a broad expanse of woodland at the bottom. Beyond that, out by the horizon, maybe seven miles from where they stood, was the shiny ribbon of the Beagle Channel.

'Well, this bit should be pretty easy,' said Brian Harrison.

But the commander stared down the hill, frowning. 'Not too easy if they decide to come after us in the next hour while we're walking over that exposed ground. What time is it?'

'0930, sir.'

'OK, let's get another message off, Mike, before we get going. Give 'em our GPS position, and tell them that we may come under immediate attack. And that if we do we will fire in a short SOS burst to the satellite, and then use our little TACBE – that tactical beam – to try and guide help in. If there is any.'

'OK, sir. I'll prepare the SOS so we can wing it off in seconds.'

'Good boy. Let's hope we don't have to.'

Three minutes later the SEAL team was on its way, walking through enemy territory and carrying the big machine gun and the comms system. The wind was getting up a little, bitterly cold, as they made fast progress down the hill, but it came out of the wrong direction this time, obscuring the sounds from the mountains. The sounds of two Argentine military helicopters which suddenly appeared, flying high and slow, above the peaks, plainly searching.

The SEAL team had travelled almost three miles downwards and roughly 400 yards separated them from the long stretch of beech wood ahead when they finally heard one of the choppers swoop in low, maybe 1,000 yards behind them. There was no point hitting the ground, not here. Their only chance was to run for the woods.

Rick's voice rang out. *'GO, BOYS, GO! RUN FOR YOUR LIVES. TAKE THE MACHINE GUN AND THE RADIO BUT RUN – FOR FUCK'S SAKE RUN . . .'*

They charged towards the wood, racing over the sloping ground. Out in front they could see the leading helicopter making a wide circle over the trees and then banking hard in a tight starboard turn, coming back in behind them.

The Puma swooped low, and now it was on them, raking the ground with its mounted machine gun, the bullets slamming into the soft ground, making lines in the grass. The second burst seemed only yards away as the SEALs pounded over the ground, and suddenly there was a terrible cry from Lt. Commander Dallas MacPherson. The most dreaded cry in the Navy SEAL's vocabulary. The team leader was hit.

'JESUS CHRIST – SUNRAY'S DOWN! STOP! . . . OH JESUS . . . SWEET JESUS – THE CO'S DOWN.'

Dallas ran back. He could see Rick clearly now, face down on the ground, blood pouring across his camouflage trousers. He couldn't tell if the boss had been hit in the stomach or the leg – all he could see was a lot of blood.

He looked up to see where the helicopter was, couldn't immediately locate it and yelled to Mike Hook to get to the wood, send the SOS message and open up the TACBE. He grabbed the machine gun from Don Smith and yelled, *'RUN!'*

Out on the horizon they could see the Argentine helicopters, flying together now, making a wide circle. They were plainly on their way back. Dallas banged a new ammunition belt into the machine gun, cranked the tripod down and swung around, lying in the grass to adjust the gun's sights for the approach of the choppers. Dallas was well trained, and he was ready to face the enemy.

Crouching next to Dallas, Doug Jarvis tried to lift Rick to check the injury. But within one minute the Argie helicopters were on them again, streaking in low over the grass, both of them firing now. Douglas flung himself over Rick Hunter to take the impact of any bullets himself.

Dallas hammered back at the Argies with the M-60 machine gun, firing every one of the two hundred 7.62mm bullets in the belt straight at the nearest cockpit. And as they overflew the embattled SEALs in the grass, Dallas rolled over, swivelling the gun with him. Somehow he kept on firing, scarcely realising he had already smashed the entire windshield of the lead helicopter with his sustained fire from the SEALs' most trusted weapon.

The pilot, unable to see through the crazed plexiglas and flying too low, fireballed into the ground. Dallas leaped to his feet, horrified to see the blood streaming out of an arm of Douglas Jarvis's jacket as he crouched over their team leader.

Dallas roared in fury as a thousand memories flooded through him, memories of how he and the CO had fought together before. He stood upright, trembling with rage, shaking his right fist, tears streaming down his face as he screamed at the retreating helicopter: *'YOU BASTARDS! YOU BASTARDS! . . . WELL, COME AND GET US, COME AND FUCKING GET US!'*

Which, unfortunately, was precisely what they were doing. The surviving Argentine helicopter, with its deadly machine gun, swung around for yet another attack. Worse yet, there was a new helicopter lifting up over the mountaintop. It joined the first one and they flew together some five miles east of the SEALs.

Captain Jarvis was hit, but not badly – his right arm was pouring blood but it had only been lacerated by a piece of shrapnel. He climbed to his feet and temporarily left the CO on the ground. They were totally exposed, facing the incoming helicopters which seemed to be taking their time, hovering above the snowy foothills. All too quickly, though, they made up their minds, and started in again towards the stricken Rick Hunter and his men.

Rick had just opened his eyes when Dallas spotted another aircraft, plainly a fighter-bomber, in the sky, bearing down at high speed from the western range out by Mount Olivia. 'Jesus,' he said, breathing hard. 'Now we're in real trouble. They got half the fucking air force here.'

And this one was not hesitating. It was travelling like a bat out of hell, racing low along the foothills of the mountains.

'JESUS CHRIST!' yelled Douglas. 'I think they're going to bomb us . . .'

'HIT THE DECK NOW!' shouted Dallas. *'HEADS DOWN, FOR CHRIST'S SAKE, HEADS DOWN!'*

The SEALs peered up through the grass, gazing in astonishment as the Hornet 18F came powering in at 500 knots and fired its first AIM-9 missile.

They saw an unmistakable winged-dart shape, glinting in the morning light, racing in at just below supersonic speed low over the mountain and then slamming into the newly arrived helicopter, blowing it in half. Two sudden fireballs plunged towards the ground.

'IT'S OURS,' bawled Mike Hook. 'THE FUCKER'S OURS!'

It was, and Lt. Commander Alan Ross from Springfield, Massachusetts had his finger right next to the missile button.

Douglas helped Rick to a sitting position. Then Douglas and Dallas stood to watch the split-second bright fire in the sky which signalled that a second missile was on its way, lasering over the foothills, a fiery trail behind it.

They couldn't see Lt. Commander Ross's fist clench in triumph as he banked the US Navy strike-fighter hard to the south-east. But they saw the missile streaking over the grassland, swerving at the last second before smashing into the first helicopter with such thumping force it spun the aircraft over before detonating like a thunderbolt, high over those lonely pastures.

'YOU LITTLE DARLING!' bellowed Lt. Banfield. 'YOU TIGHT-ASSED, FRENCH-FRIED LITTLE DARLING!!'

Now Brian Harrison came charging out from the wood to help. Half-running, half-walking, they manhandled Rick Hunter into the safety of the trees. In the distance they could see the Hornet slow down, somewhere out over the Beagle Channel.

But the only thing that mattered now to the SEAL team was the amount of blood their leader was losing and the obvious pain he was in. With the three Argentine helicopters all destroyed they probably had a half-hour to get organised.

They wrapped two field dressings around Douglas Jarvis's arm for now – stitches would have to wait. Doug himself took charge of Rick Hunter, lowering him onto a sleeping bag and covering him with another one, trying to stop the violent trembling which had already set in.

He and Brian Harrison cut away Rick's trouser leg to discover the extent of the wound, and to Doug's great relief he saw that the commander had been hit in his right thigh, not in his stomach. The bullet was probably still in there. It had missed the main artery, but the wound was bleeding heavily. Douglas stripped off his jacket and shirt, ripping up the shirt to make a tourniquet. He then injected morphine into Rick's arm and dressed the gaping wound as well as he could with a combination of field dressings and the rest of his shirt.

They had to get help fast. Mike recorded a new satellite message, giving the precise GPS at the point where they would reach the Beagle Channel. Staring at their chart, using his small ruler, Doug called it. '54.52N 67.22W. Tell 'em we'll be there in two hours, and we'll have the TACBE turned on.'

Dallas MacPherson knew they would either be there at that time – or they would no longer be alive. It depended on whether the Argentines realised there had been a minor battle out here, and that the foreign assault group they were seeking was still on the loose, heading for the Beagle Channel.

He thought they had a couple of hours maximum to get the two wounded men to the meeting point. Dallas assumed a loose command, ordering Mike Hook to fire off the satellite message immediately, and went to help Bob Bland cut two fairly straight beech branches with which to construct a makeshift stretcher. A couple of sleeping bags were fixed between the poles.

They rested the stretcher on the grass and lowered Rick onto it. Douglas was concerned to see the mission's CO was drifting in and out of consciousness. They had to get him some medical help, antibiotics and so forth. It was also imperative to remove the bullet.

They hoisted him up, Dallas and Brian holding the front poles, Doug, using his good arm, and Don Smith gripping the rear ones. The mighty Bob Bland carried the heavy machine gun, the ammunition belts draped around his neck. Lt. Banfield carried the main satellite transmitter. Mike Hook somehow hefted its other parts. They set off through the wood, walking slowly, carrying their heavy burden through the trees, then out into the light. No beat of Argentine helicopter blades sounded.

They rested after a mile, placing the commander on the ground. They tried to give him some water but he seemed unaware of what was going on around him. His head kept flopping back, and Doug was worried that the morphine had somehow had a bad effect.

They could see the Beagle Channel out in front now, though, and the rest of the walk was downhill. Rick's eyes were open but it was obvious that some kind of delirium was setting in. He was murmuring something none of them could make out.

'Come on, guys, keep going. I'm afraid we're losing him. If that poison gets into his system we'll lose him . . .' Doug's voice was urgent.

They all knew the clock was ticking for Rick. It was 1105 and they could not expect any rescuer, whoever it might be, to hang around in this hostile Argentine territory for long. Doug said, 'Gimme one of the ammunition belts round my neck – that's about all I can manage.'

They reached the waterway's bank and stumbled down the steep slope towards the water. Mike was aiming the TACBE everywhere along the shore. But there was a light mist over the water and they could not see more than about fifty yards. And they waited for five long minutes, then five more. At last Mike Hook heard it: the unmistakable growl of big engines crawling along the shoreline.

Two minutes later they saw it as well: a grey 450-ton fast-attack naval patrol craft, flying a national flag from its mast – red and white horizontal halves, with a white star on black in the top left-hand corner.

'It's Chilean,' said Dallas.

The men on the craft had seen them and the helmsman held her on the engine in the fast current. The SEAL team waved and they could see a big rubber inflatable being launched. On board was a young Chilean officer. 'No speak yet. Just hurry. Get injured men in right now. I come back for last two.'

Five minutes later everyone was on board the Israel-built gunboat *Chipana,* speeding across the Beagle Channel towards Chilean waters and the navy base at Puerto William on Chile's own south side.

The young officer smiled and they all shook hands quickly. Sub-Lieutenant Gustavo Frioli reassured the SEAL team: 'Doctor waiting. We get messages.'

They made it just in time. The naval doctor, Commander Cesar Delpino, had trained at Houston Medical Center and he recognised a dire emergency when he saw one, immediately administering a powerful dose of antibiotics and placing Rick on an IVD.

By the following morning, Tuesday 3 May, Rick's condition had stabilised. The poison in his system was now under control. He was still feverish, and Commander Delpino thought they should wait another twenty-four hours before removing the two machine-gun bullets that were embedded in his thigh.

Rick asked him if he would perform the operation himself. But the Chilean doctor told him no, someone else had arrived.

'A top Chilean specialist, I hope,' said Commander Hunter, grinning feebly.

'No. Your surgeon will be American, from the American submarine. It's right out there, beyond those buildings, alongside.'

'What submarine?' Rick tried to clear his head.

'A US Navy LA Class nuclear boat, maybe 7,000 tons. It's called the *Toledo*, I believe. I hear the plan is for her to wait here for a few days and then take you all home. The long way around, but a safe way. Out of shallow enemy waters, not on the surface.'

'How about the doctor?'

Commander Delpino laughed. 'I don't know about him.'

The following morning Lt. Commander James Scott met Rick Hunter for the first time, in the operating room. They shook hands briefly and the US Navy surgeon said, 'This isn't going to take long. You've been in good hands. No infection. We're leaving for home this afternoon.'

'Thanks, doc,' said Rick.

When he awoke, Dallas MacPherson and Douglas Jarvis were standing by his bed. 'Well done, sir,' said the Lt. Commander from South Carolina. 'We all wanna thank you.' And, in obvious admiration, he offered his hand to the SEAL team leader. Dallas himself would never comprehend the majestic embrace of that compliment.

And Rick Hunter's war was over.

0930 Thursday 5 May
Casa Rosada, Buenos Aires

The military communication from the commandant of the Rio Grande airbase had been decoded and presented in hard copy by Admiral Oscar Moreno to the president of the Republic of Argentina.

It read: *Rio Grande, Wednesday 4 May. Attack on this base on the night of 1 May and the subsequent air and ground pursuit of the heavily-armed intruders, has resulted in the total loss of twelve Super Étendard fighter-bombers, two military patrol jeeps, eleven guards, four Puma attack helicopters, and twelve aircrew. The identity of the enemy remains unknown. None have been killed, wounded or detained. Lt. Commander Ricardo Testa, head of airbase security, is currently under arrest, awaiting court martial.*

The president of Argentina could hardly believe his eyes. Yet his mind flashed back to the veiled threats contained in the communiqué from the White House which had arrived the previous week: the one to which he had not replied.

He turned to his Defence Minister, Admiral Horacio Aguardo, and then to Admiral Moreno and General Eduardo Kampf. 'Gentlemen,' he said, 'either directly or indirectly we are being sucked into a war with the United States of America – and, by any means, we have to stop it.'

All three of them nodded in agreement. 'Further defiance from us,' said Admiral Moreno grudgingly, 'may very well mean the Pentagon will come out into the open and slam the entire Rio Grande base, not to mention Rio Gallegos and maybe even Mount Pleasant.' He sighed, seeing his triumph going up in smoke. 'There appears to be nothing we can do about it.'

'We scarcely have a leg to stand on,' agreed Admiral Aguardo. 'The USA will plead its case to the United Nations, explaining that Argentina committed an act of international piracy, smashed the Royal Navy fleet in international waters, and stole a legal British colony, plus two billion dollars' worth of US oil and gas.'

'I think we are in accord, gentlemen,' said the president. 'I shall accept the American terms for the future of the *Islas Malvinas*. I have no choice.'

Again, all three men wearily nodded their assent.

0900 Thursday 5 May
The Oval Office

Admiral Morgan liked what he saw. He liked it very much. President Paul Bedford was just smiling and shaking his head. The communiqué from the president of Argentina was perfect:

'My apologies for the delay in replying to your previous dispatches. I trust you will understand that my government has been preoccupied in re-establishing normal working and living conditions among the good citizens of the Islas Malvinas.

'Now, in the interests of peace and trade, we are prepared to accept your terms and suggestions for a lasting treaty, and a punctilious handover of the islands from Great Britain to the Republic of Argentina over a two-year period.

'We do require international acceptance of the Islas Malvinas becoming a sovereign territory of Argentina by the year 2013, and we call upon both Great Britain and the USA to ensure this is understood by the Security Council of the United Nations.

'We regret the unfortunate events which led to the expulsion of the innocent personnel of both Exxon Mobil and British Petroleum from the legally owned oil and gas fields on the islands. And we agree to their immediate restoration – under fair royalty considerations for the Republic of Argentina.

'I will be joined by my senior envoys and advisers in Washington next week, beginning 9 May, and look forward to a cordial meeting with you in order to bring these matters to a mutually agreeable conclusion.'

'Thank you, admiral,' said President Bedford.

'My pleasure,' replied Arnold Morgan.

Monday 16 May
Eastern Pacific Ocean

The Nimitz Class aircraft carrier USS *Ronald Reagan* steamed steadily north, 1,000 miles off the coast of Peru. The eight-man Navy SEAL team had been on board for almost a week and would remain so until they docked in San Diego, 2,640 miles and five days hence.

Commander Hunter was still recuperating from his thigh wound, and was undergoing daily therapy in one of the ship's gyms. The Navy surgeon had decided to insert ten stitches into the gash on Captain Jarvis's upper arm.

The two of them were watching a satellite broadcast of the evening news before dinner when the anchorman announced that terms had been agreed for the peaceful transition of power over the Falkland Islands from Great Britain to Argentina. He added that executives of Exxon Mobil and British Petroleum had been present at the talks in the White House and that the two oil giants were returning to the oil and gas fields in both South Georgia and East Falkland.

There was a film clip of the men arriving at Mare Harbour in an Exxon Mobil tanker, and a further clip of Exxon's president, Clint McCluskey, saying what a privilege it had been to work with the President of the USA and reach a 'one hundred per cent oilman's deal'.

'You think we had something to do with all that, Rick?' asked Captain Jarvis.

'Wouldn't be surprised, kid. Not at all,' said Commander Hunter, smiling knowingly.

Saturday 21 May
Speed 7. Depth 400.
Course three-six-zero

Captain Gregor Vanislav was tiptoeing slowly north up the Atlantic. They'd been running for five weeks now, and *Viper 157* was 8,000 miles north of the Falkland Islands, 8,000 miles north of the sunken war-grave that had once been HMS *Ark Royal*.

He had been wary all the way, sliding quietly through the deep waters, slowing and listening for the sounds of a US or British attack submarine, staying clear of the land, following the line of the North Atlantic Ridge.

And now he was beyond the Ridge, 450 miles west of southern Ireland, headed for the shallower waters of the Rockall Rise, and then, 600 miles further to the north-east, into the GIUK Gap.

Here, moving stealthily in deep waters west of County Kerry, Captain Vanislav was entering the most dangerous stretch of his long journey.

It was right here, many weeks ago, that *Viper* had first been detected but then lost. If Gregor Vanislav could negotiate the next 800 miles safely he would have a trouble-free run home to Murmansk. But if he was picked up on the grid of SOSUS wires on the seabed he could expect the navies of the US and UK to come looking.

The Russian submarine commander assumed that by now someone, somewhere, knew that *Ark Royal* had been sunk by torpedoes and not by bombs delivered by the Argentine air force. The key to the safety of his ship and his crew was stealth: slow, quiet running.

And the further north he went, the less suspicion there would be. Any Russian ship had the right to run through these international waters. Indeed, they *had* to run through here, since it was the only way the Russian navy had to reach the rest of the world.

'Just get through the Gap,' Gregor Vanislav muttered to himself. 'That's all. And then we're safe.'

Six days later, Friday 27 May
Lexington, Kentucky

The US Army's latest Bell Super Cobra helicopter came clattering out of the sky above the long lawn alongside the main house at

Hunter Valley Farm. It had travelled eighty miles from Fort Campbell Military Base on the Tennessee border, and it was carrying just two passengers.

Diana Hunter had been worried almost senseless for the past five weeks, because the rigid secrecy surrounding highly classified Special Forces operations had made it impossible for her to discover anything, not even whether her husband and brother were dead or alive.

She watched the Cobra land with her heart missing every other beat, half expecting to see Admiral John Bergstrom emerge personally to break the worst possible news to her. But the first person to disembark was the unmistakable Captain Douglas Jarvis, lean, athletic, hatless, wearing a short-sleeved US Navy white shirt.

She saw him raise his left arm to assist the second passenger down the steps, and she watched the tall figure of her husband step carefully down onto the grass, betraying only the slightest limp. Then she wrenched open the french doors, raced down the wide stone steps and ran across the grass, hurling herself into the arms of Commander Hunter, tears streaming down her face.

She could manage no words except *'Thank God, thank God!'*, over and over. Until finally she turned to her beloved little brother, who was standing there grinning, a picture of health, his profession betrayed only by the bandage still covering his upper right arm.

Helplessly she shook her head, and asked lamely, 'Are you both injured? Were you in the most terrible danger?'

'Nah,' replied Rick Hunter. 'But I guess we had our moments.'

EPILOGUE

Saturday 28 May 2011
North Atlantic 62.40N, 11.20W
Speed 7. Depth 400. Course 53.00

Viper 157 ran slowly north-east up through the GIUK Gap, heading steadily for Mother Russia. At times Captain Gregor Vanislav cut the speed even more, to only five knots, which was just sufficient to make it to the surface on emergency propulsion, without wallowing, should the nuclear system fail. He was a very sound submarine CO.

They were west of the Faeroe Isles now – just east of the central dividing line between the UK and Iceland – heading into the Norwegian Sea. And Captain Vanislav was positive he'd been careful enough and remained undetected. He was wrong. The US listening stations on the east coast of Greenland and the one on the south-east coast of Iceland had both detected a transient contact moving slowly north-east.

Each had connected the tiny 'paint' on the screen to a submarine, and in Iceland they had sufficient data to list it: *'Russian nuclear, probably Akula Class. Nothing else correlates on friendly or Russian nets.'* The clincher came from the British, from the ultra-secret surveillance station near Machrihanish on Scotland's western Atlantic coast.

The sonar operators there, positioned considerably nearer than their American colleagues, had picked up *Viper* two days ago, and identified it immediately: *a Russian nuclear boat, running deep, slowly, almost certainly an Akula Class, series II.*

They immediately had the submarine positioned in a wide 100-mile square, but over the next forty-eight hours, by process of elimination and two further detections, they now had the submarine in a ten-mile square. The SOSUS system was on red alert for her predicted position the next time she crossed the undersea wire.

In the blackest of all possible Black Ops, two US hunter-killer submarines, fifty miles apart, guided by the satellites, were patrolling the northern reaches of the GIUK, closing in as the *Viper* moved unsuspectingly forward.

1800 Saturday 28 May
On board USS Cheyenne
North Atlantic

'*Stand by one.*'
  '*Last bearing check.*'
  '*SHOOT!*'
  '*Weapon under guidance, sir.*'
  '*Arm the weapon.*'
  '*Weapon armed, sir.*'
  Two minutes . . . '*Weapon 2,000 yards from target.*'
  '*Sonar . . . switch to active . . . single ping.*'
  '*Aye, sir.*'

1804 Saturday 28 May
On board Viper 157

'*Captain – Sonar . . . one active transmission . . . loud . . . bearing Green 135 . . . United States SSN for certain . . . close . . . really close.*'
  Captain Vanislav reacted instantly: attack, not defence. '*Stand by Tube Number Two . . . set targets bearing Green 135 . . . Range 3,000 metres . . . Depth 100 . . . shoot as soon as you're ready.*'
  '*Hard right . . . steer zero-three-five . . . shut off for counter-attack . . . full ahead . . . ten up . . . 200 metres.*'
  '*CAPTAIN – SONAR . . . TORPEDO ACTIVE TRANS-MISSION! . . . POSSIBLY IN CONTACT . . . RIGHT AHEAD INTERVAL 900 METRES!*'
  Captain Vanislav was going for the classic – but reckless – standard Russian defence of driving flat-out into the direct path of an incoming torpedo. But, too late, he shouted his last command –

'DECOYS!' – just as the big wire-guided Gould Mk 48 American torpedo slammed into the bow of his ship just for'ard of the fin.

The underwater missile blasted a massive hole in the submarine's pressure hull, and the thunderous force of the ocean smashed through the bulkheads as if they were made of cardboard. Captain Vanislav died instantly, along with his entire crew – much as the crew of the *Ark Royal* had done six weeks earlier.

Viper 157 went down in 750 fathoms of ocean, just a few miles short of the Norwegian Basin where the North Atlantic shelves down to a colossal depth of 12,000 feet, more than two miles.

Four weeks later: 0900 Saturday 25 June
Chevy Chase, Maryland

Admiral Arnold Morgan smiled a thin smile as he scanned the front page of the *New York Times*. The single-column story at the top left-hand side announced the resignation of the Prime Minister of Great Britain.

Arnold quietly rejoiced in the demise of any left-wing leader of a Western country. And anyway, that particular PM would never have survived the catastrophe of the Falkland Islands defeat.

What caught his eye far more sharply, though, was a front-page cross-reference to a story on page three, concerning the loss of a Russian nuclear submarine.

It was an agency story, credited to Tass, Moscow. The headline over two columns described the sub as 'missing, believed lost'.

The admiral read it carefully: *The Russian Navy's 9,000-ton nuclear-powered Akula Class submarine* Viper, *hull number K-157, has been lost in the North Atlantic.*

Naval officials believe that it sank in the Norwegian Basin north-east of the Faeroe Isles where the water is more than two miles deep. Both the search area and the depth are so vast no rescue operation is planned.

According to Russian Navy sources, Viper *missed first one, then a second satellite call-sign. Every effort was made to make contact, but the submarine was patrolling hundreds of miles offshore.*

When it missed its third call-sign, Viper *had been missing for possibly three days and the search area, given a ten-knot average speed, would have been 360,000 square miles. There has been no further contact between the submarine and its base, and Russian naval authorities now accept the submarine has sunk with all hands.*

A spokesman for the Russian Navy's Commander-in-Chief, Admiral

Vitaly Rankov, said last night: 'Sadly, we have no information as to what caused the accident, and at this stage we are presuming a nuclear-reactor failure, possibly at great depth. We may never know the answers.'

Admiral Morgan betrayed no emotion. He set the paper aside just as Kathy came in bearing coffee and toast.

'Did you read about that Russian submarine?' she said. 'I saw it on CNN just now.'

'I sure did,' Arnold Morgan replied. 'Took 'em long enough to admit they'd lost her.'

'You're always so critical of the Russians,' his wife said, smiling. 'Poor Admiral Rankov, he's such a jolly man . . . and anyway, you don't know when she sank, any more than they do.'

'Don't I?' grunted the admiral, darkly.